A COLLECTED QUARTET

The Continuing Chronicles of Sherlock Holmes

C. Thorne

ISBN: 9798308823469
Imprint: Independently published

Cover and interior design: L. Thorne
Library of Congress Control Number: 2018675309
Printed in the United States of America

To my brother and his family, and their new life, out in the countryside!

The Continuing Chronicles of Sherlock Holmes

The Case Of The Kaiser's Assassin

C. Thorne

THE CASE OF THE KAISER'S ASSASSIN

Sometimes even now I wake up in a haze of fright after dreaming about that night and the vivid fears that had been upon me in that singular span of hours, as it seemed the fate of western Europe rested in my friend's hands, lest an assassin's strike fell the leader of a powerful nation, and plunge the entire continent into the kiln of the greatest war mankind would ever see, for when all dwelt atop a keg of powder, as we did four years ago when the events of this case took place during an especially tense time in foreign relations, one knew that our fragile peace might be set ablaze by the merest spark. And Holmes and I were told that someone apparently wished for exactly that to occur.

Yes, I shudder to think of it even now.

It had been a momentous spring that seemed to contain a bit of everything, from a visit with my extended family in Scotland, to a lovely dinner my wife Mary and I enjoyed together at Floquet's, all capped off by she and I witnessing the Trooping of the Colour together, that grand and august parade of the Household Cavalry that traditionally marked the Queen's birthday. It was an event Mary had never attended, though I had been to several in the past. Yet I think looking back that nothing else offered in that verdant and rainy season matched the sheer number of fascinating cases it was my privilege to be part of alongside my dear friend Sherlock Holmes, and as I made clear above, none of those cases held close to the same importance as the one that finds itself revealed under my pen tonight.

It began on a rainy morning when for several days I had been staying at my former lodgings at Baker Street, paying a visit there as Mary enjoyed a week's holiday in Cornwall with two of her own friends. I had nothing of significance on my schedule for the day and had been quite enjoying the reminiscences Holmes and I were undertaking, recalling the time we'd apprehended a thief atop a church steeple, or the occasion we'd tracked a train robber across the country from Yorkshire to Glastonbury, and how oddly that adventure had turned out.

It was not an infrequent event that some telegram came to the door to interrupt matters, yet that morning it was a small note that reached Holmes, brought up not in the hands of Mrs. Hudson, but by a uniformed naval officer, whom the good landlady led up into the parlour.

"This gentleman comes bearing a note for you, Mr. Holmes," Mrs. Hudson told him tiredly, with a slightly peeved tone in her words, "and says his orders are to place it in your hands and no others."

"Did he now?" Holmes replied sardonically, as he rose and faced the officer, a lieutenant, I noted from his uniform.

Holmes regarded the man and said:

"Sir, I perceive, of course, that you are a career officer in the Royal Navy, that you originally hail from near

Southampton, and that you are at present untroubled by the knowledge of what lies within the envelope you bear, for though your curiosity is greatly stirred by the matter, your sense of duty prevents you from disobeying the order you were given, and peering at it yourself. Which is most honourable of you, if I may deem it so."

The man's countenance stayed dutifully blank in the face of the compliment, and he simply replied:

"It is not my place, sir, to speculate on the contents of the note I deliver, only to see it brought to you and no other."

Holmes extended a hand and said:

"Then allow me to present the means to fulfill your quest."

The naval lieutenant passed the stark white envelope to Holmes and then stepped back to the wall to his rear, though added stolidly:

"I was told to wait for you."

Holmes turned away from the man and strode to the window where he glanced at the envelope before tearing open the seal and unfolding its contents, which turned out to be a single piece of paper, though as to what was written on it, I could not see from where I stood. I did discern that my friend's eyes rapidly passed across the note before he crumpled it and thrust it into his deep pocket, then turned and said, as if issuing an announcement:

"Ah, this is acceptable to me, and I shall accompany you as requested to the location this demi-missive specifies."

The officer bowed formally to Holmes, nodded more curtly toward me, and then turned on his heels to vanish back through the outer door and down the stairs. I rose and hurried to the window to see him enter a carriage, which I gathered was kept waiting for us.

"Holmes," I said, "may I be privy to the nature of this note, or is it one of those matters destined to remain shrouded in professional secrecy?"

"Watson," said my friend, as he set a match to his pipe,

and then to the paper which he took out from his pocket before casting all into the fireplace, "I, myself, am permitted to know nothing more of the matter thus far than are you yourself, only that I was 'commanded' to appear directly at the office of a certain governmental official, at no less august a locale than White Hall."

"'Commanded,' you Holmes?" I said with a whistle. "If he thinks to order you he does not know you very well."

"Oh," Holmes replied, "the matter was couched in the polite language of a formal request, but under its flowery lines I recognized it for what it was, a cry for help from within Her Majesty's government, and therefore a summons I intend to honour, whatever the writer's erring expectation that he might *command* me."

"I see," I said with a chuckle, "well then I wish you an exciting and productive visit."

"Watson," my friend said with a click on his tongue, "if I were to ask you to accompany me I think it might serve to show the gentlemen of White Hall that I am no one's servant save perhaps the Queen's."

"Well I am flattered," I said, "but will that be altogether allowed...."

"*Allowed?* Watson, do you imagine I would allow myself to be dictated to by the government, or that I would answer this call and exclude you? My friend, as you were here to witness the case's beginnings, I should feel deprived of my own left arm were I to proceed in this matter without you. As he did not specifically restrict it, I think I may safely clutch at the liberty I extend to you. I am, after all, my own man in this world, a consultant guided by my conscience, not the employee of any other."

"Well said, Holmes!" I cheered. "So you term this a 'case' and think it will turn out to become one, and not prove to be merely a brief consultation on some matter or other?"

"I suspect, Watson, it shall reveal some deep and vexing matter of grave seriousness is afoot, as it so often is in the upper echelons of government, however rarely the public ever comes to learn of such recurring crises."

"Oh dear," I muttered, "then I suppose it best we not keep that naval officer in his carriage waiting."

"He has nothing better to do," said Holmes, "so I think I shall first finish my smoke."

However Holmes did not take long to finish his pipe, and the entirety of the morning to that point rapidly gained the tone of an afterthought, as we prepared for our trip to White Hall, that famed nerve-center of our globe-spanning empire. When we emerged out into the cloudy May morning, I followed after Holmes as he hopped into the carriage across from the naval lieutenant who had conveyed the superior's message, and saw that the detective had folded his hands before him in an absent manner, which I knew was less an indication of tranquility than a sign of intense internal speculation.

"Mr. Holmes," the lieutenant said with a frown upon seeing me, "do you mean to be accompanied today by this gentleman?"

"I do," my friend said, and nothing more.

The officer showed concern at this confirmation and seemed about to speak, but in the end only nodded once in a somewhat indecisive manner before tapping the ceiling, sending the carriage jolting forward, as our three-mile trip across the city began.

We arrived at White Hall two minutes after the chimes at Westminster signaled the ninth hour, and were immediately met at the sidewalk by an obvious clerk, who stepped toward the unnamed lieutenant, lifting two fingers to him, and with a slight furrowing of his brow the clerk nodded in return.

The two men, that being the officer who had brought us, and this clerk, who had clearly spent the last hour of the morning awaiting us, led us past a quartet of red-uniformed guards with tall bearskin hats, who stood clutching rifles just outside the door, and took us beyond a long desk at which several officious-looking clerks sat amid piles of documents and paperwork. Next they proceeded a few feet ahead of us up a wide stairway that split into two directions at a landing which sat at the foot of a massive stained glass window depicting a patriotic and martial scene. After taking us up the left-hand steps, we were next led down a lengthy hallway, and finally the men halted before well-polished double doors of a bright reddish hue which had been lacquered to a nearly reflective sheen above the wood's natural and complex grain.

"The gentleman who sent me to summon you awaits you within, Mr. Holmes," the lieutenant stated.

"Splendid," said Holmes, "for I look forward to him explaining why my morning has been so unexpectedly interrupted."

The lieutenant frowned coldly at my friend's characterization of matters, and seeing this, Holmes looked sternly at him and added:

"Oh, and my dear lieutenant, you truly must let go of the girl with whom you keep clandestine meetings, for such assignations are fraught with peril and rarely end well for men in the *delicate* branch of services, such as yourself. Think, now, could she truly find you as attractive as she claims?"

At this the lieutenant's jaw dropped, but before he could demonstrate any further reaction, Holmes opened the doors himself, unannounced, and strode beyond, even as the lieutenant regained enough poise to snap stiffly to attention and offer a sharp salute to five men whom I saw waiting at a vast rectangular table, each of whom rose as Holmes, followed by me, entered the room. Behind me the lieutenant then stepped back into the hallway and set the doors closed behind him, having been given something to think about, I felt sure, though how Holmes should know of that delicate matter I could not begin to guess.

In that instant I took in the room, which was military in its Spartan bearing, adorned only by busts of those national heroes Nelson and Wellington, elevated on pedestals in the corners, and by maps hanging mounted on the terra-cotta coloured walls. I did not know the men at the table but sensed instantly that they were highly-placed individuals, one wearing the uniform of a naval Commodore, another that of an army Brigadier of the Lifeguards, while the other three wore the finely-tailored suits of highly-placed bureaucrats who held elevated places within government service. The last man, he who sat the table's head, was bearded and bespectacled, and was considerably older than the others, in his sixties I imagined, judging from his chalk-white hair, and upon seeing me, his face lost some of its blankness and he demanded:

"This is none other than your friend and professional companion Dr. John Watson, I presume, Mr. Holmes?"

"You are well-informed, for it is he, Lord Crosby," Holmes answered, seeming to personally know the man, "and I trust you will have no objection to my friend's presence today?"

I saw the Brigadier frown and sensed he was about to speak up with just such an objection, when the man Holmes had called Lord Crosby said with an aura of finality:

"The doctor's presence today will be acceptable, so long as you are willing to vouch for him."

"Your Lordship, I name John Watson as both deeply patriotic, and wholly trustworthy," Holmes confirmed.

"Very well then," said Lord Crosby, "gentlemen, one and all, please, be seated."

Holmes and I did so, taking seats at the near side of the table, across from four of the men, with Lord Crosby to our right at the table's head.

"Firstly, Mr. Holmes, you have my thanks, and the thanks of all of us inside this room, Brigadier Billings-Russell, Commodore Spencer, and Misters Bryant and Dillingham, for coming to White Hall upon such scant notice. The decision to ask for you was one with little preamble, and arose only after our consultation this morning, and a 4-1 vote in favour of sending our note. Matters, you see, have developed rather rapidly."

"You are welcome, Lord Crosby," Holmes answered, rather arrogantly, I thought, in his acknowledgment that he was indeed granting something of a courtesy with his presence. "I take it this summons concerns a grave matter indeed."

He caught something on Crosby's face and said:

"Ah, permit me to alter my words... Rather this consultation concerns something of a grave *crisis*."

"It does," Lord Crosby agreed. "And *crisis* is the proper term, as I fear the German Kaiser is in danger of being assassinated, tonight, and here in London."

My heart jolted at these words, for I grasped the gravity of his statement, and well understood the magnitude of the consequences should that stubborn and harsh-natured grandson of our queen fall to violence upon our shores. It would in all likelihood usher our nation into immediate war with the rising power that Germany had become in so short a period of time.

For himself, Holmes leaned back in his chair and steepled his fingers before saying:

"I must know all."

Lord Crosby sighed and said:

"Yes, you see the nature of things, and why we are reaching out to you and your admittedly singular gifts, for I fear some warmongering madman, unknown to us, is toying with the Kaiser, and this unknown figure has for each of the past two nights during this, the Kaiser's visit to England, where he has come to pay a call on his grandmother and practice his bullying variety of states-craft, let it be known that he, this presumed assassin has the ability to get perilously close to that formidable man, and has twice now, without detection, snatched away some item possessed by the Kaiser, and it has in each case only been after the fact that the thefts have even been noticed."

How would such a feat of sleight of hand even be possible? I found myself wondering.

"What were the purloined items?" Holmes inquired.

"Two nights ago, at the reception at Marlborough House, where he was guest of the Prince of Wales, His Imperial Majesty noticed a platinum cigarette case had been taken by someone straight from the pocket of his suit coat. Concerning this, an issue was raised by the Kaiser's private secretary, Count Joachim Von Dienheim, though beyond his own blustering complaints on his temperamental master's behalf, little else was made of the matter, and there was not a good deal that we could do, puzzling though the situation was."

"Did the Germans regard it at that time as a threatening scenario?" Holmes asked.

"To be honest, sir, though Count Von Dienheim conveyed the Kaiser's ire, he privately confided his belief that it is likely his master somehow mislaid the item, and under the circumstances, we were inclined to agree."

"Until the second theft," stated Holmes.

"Indeed," said Lord Crosby, "and here things became more serious and less easily dismissed, for the Kaiser remained adamant that the cigarette case had somehow been taken from his imperial person, and insisted his security be tightened, which it was, both among the German secret service which travels everywhere with the Kaiser, and among our own operatives from Scotland Yard, who mill in plainclothes throughout private gatherings of royalty such as this—"

"The capability of those men is well known to me," Holmes interjected.

"Yes," said Crosby, "but even so, last night there was a second episode of theft from the Kaiser's person, even under so many watchful eyes, and with the Kaiser himself somewhat restlessly on guard. In this instance there was no possibility that the item had been mislaid, for it was in fact no less than a ring which rested upon His Imperial Majesty Kaiser Wilhelm II's finger, a gold band seen by many throughout the early portion of the evening, an heirloom of the Prussian royal house dubbed *der Ring des Kreuzfahrer.*"

"'The Ring of the Crusader'," Holmes said by way of translation.

"Yes," Crosby confirmed. "It was of some five centuries in age, and favoured by the Kaiser for its significance to his nation's lengthy history of crusading into the Baltic region, and beyond into Russia."

Holmes pressed his steepled fingers more tightly together as he said:

"And at what event did this more recent theft take place?"

"It was last evening between nine-thirty and eleven-thirty, at a reception at the London residence of Sir Francis Alabaster, the third Duke of Frye, who is married to a paternal cousin of the Kaiser, the former Lady Katarzina Von Breuberg. I say 'between' those hours, as no one, including the Kaiser, is quite sure when the theft transpired, we can only say that it was very near 11:30 when His Imperial Majesty noted the loss."

"He did not feel the item being taken from his finger?" I asked.

"Incredibly enough, it seems he did not," confirmed Crosby.

"That is almost unbelievable," I commented.

"Yes, Doctor Watson, it seems we are dealing with a person of almost preternatural skill at carrying out feats of theft undetected, even under the close supervision of so many, and thus it fans the flames of our concern, for we fear an assassin possessing finesse such as that would be all-but unstoppable."

"And what was the Kaiser's reaction to this second episode?" asked Holmes.

"Anger," Commodore Spencer answered, "outrage, an explosion of temper. I was present to witness all of them, and have no wish to witness these displays a second time."

"These responses on the Kaiser's part," said Holmes, "all seemed genuine enough to you?"

There was a gasp from the Commodore, who thundered:

"Surely you do not suspect that the Kaiser would..."

"I suspect nothing," said Holmes, telling them what he so often said to me, "I merely seek facts, and so I repeat my question, and bid you answer it."

Hastily re-taking control of the discussion, Lord Crosby said:

"As the Commodore and a number of others who were present with me could attest, the utter explosion on the part of the visiting sovereign left no one questioning the veracity of the Kaiser's sense of moral outrage, which outweighed all other thoughts he may have felt of possible danger. He was infuriated that anyone might seek to pickpocket him, deeming himself 'the most powerful man in the world.'"

The Commodore spoke up:

"Mr. Holmes, His Imperial Majesty Kaiser Wilhelm stated to me with the most aggrieved expression, 'I am an enemy to be feared.' He bade us we would do well to remember that."

To my surprise, and I am sure that of all others in the room, Holmes chuckled at this description, and said with a snort:

"Did he now? I can well imagine the scene."

Looking back to Lord Crosby, he summarized:

"These events you describe tell of acts of theft, which, however understandably annoying and criminally wrong, are not in themselves indications of the level of danger to the Kaiser's person that you told of a moment ago. Why then has a leap been made toward assigning menace and an understated threat of war to these actions?"

Here I saw looks pass among the five men at the table, until Lord Crosby finally said:

"Again, I speak of the need for supreme confidence here, but in truth the situation in Germany is not as unified, or genial, as the Kaiser and his government might wish to present. It has long been the case that certain resentments roil there, particularly among the Bavarians, who felt in the 1870s, and feel now, that it is Munich which should be the nation's capital rather than what they see as the stern backwater of Berlin. There is resentment among Bavarians that they find themselves ruled by the more martial Prussians, whom they regard as an unsophisticated people compared to themselves."

"Having been to both Berlin and Munich, I am inclined to agree," Holmes noted. "But there are other reasons as well?"

"In Germany today," Brigadier Billings-Russell took up the narrative, "many political philosophies clash, with the anarchist movement being particularly strong at present in Germany's industrialized cities, with some adherents to that crazed philosophy having taken oaths in blood to strike the Kaiser down, as always these contingents seek to destroy royal figures, with the Russian Czar likewise ranking high on their list of targets. Furthermore there are simply various disorganized mad men and vying entities with grudges, so that the Kaiser lives under a state of greater threat than does our own sovereign, or her heir, the Prince of Wales. Thus were the Germans quick to see considerable menace in these two actions, either as warnings or as an arrogant show of some would-be killer's capacity to move in close proximity to the Kaiser, as has been demonstrated."

I felt a definite chill at these words, and in considering the scenarios just revealed to us, deemed the matter utterly grave indeed, so I spoke up:

"Why does the Kaiser not simply cancel wherever he intends to be tonight, and return to the safety of Germany?"

Lord Crosby greeted my question with the impatient disdain of a schoolmaster confronted by a curious pupil he'd rather remain silent during class, but Holmes spoke up to add:

"Yes, well done, Watson, that was to be my next inquiry. An answer, if you please, Lord Crosby?"

Crosby swallowed back what I think may have been his

request that I remain silent during this meeting, and instead replied:

"That would of course be the most sensible solution to the whole of things, and frankly the most welcome to us, for if an assassin is to attempt some strike against one of the crowned heads of Europe, better by far it be in his homeland than here, where it then becomes our own problem, and one of almost incalculable severity, as you can imagine. Yet the fact is for all his overt rage over these episodes of theft, the Kaiser is a most stubborn man, deeply concerned with the image of stern Prussian courage for which his countrymen are so deservedly known, and it has been conveyed to us that His Imperial Majesty would see his retreat from the schedule already in place during this visit as an act of cowardice anathema to his sensibilities. He will not entertain the idea of a single deviation from his prepared agenda, and declares he would rather die a brave man than slink away as would a coward."

"I thought as much," said Holmes. "And where is the Kaiser at this moment?"

"Visiting the Queen at Buckingham Palace," said Crosby. "And tonight he attends..." The man's words faltered with dread and drew a deep breath.

"The performance of works by the Italian maestro Giacomo Puccini, by the London Opera," Holmes said.

"Correct," said Crosby. "You guessed?"

"I keep abreast of the functions within the city and noted that is the one most likely to draw a royal visitor. Puccini is something of a rising figure within modern music."

"Then you can imagine the logistical nightmare such a venue presents to us. In the opera house are a hundred points of concealment from which an assassin might strike. Of anyplace the Kaiser has thus far been, it ranks the most perilous."

"Yes, you hint at a strike from a distance," Holmes said, "as with a rifle, perhaps, and yet has not this unknown master of nimble-fingered theft shown to all that it is his preference to work at close range, within literally arm's length of the Kaiser?"

"Yes," agreed one of the clerks, Dillingham, speaking up at last, "but the Germans see these incidents as having been arrogant threats, boasts of prowess, if you will, a toying with the Kaiser and us all, and we are inclined to agree. The actual strike could come in any manner, from any source. A sharpshooter concealed among the rafters of the upper-gallery, or even a bomb planted in advance within the opera house, and rigged with a timing device, set to explode only after His Imperial Majesty is in place, and the performance has begun. It is, quite literally, a bodyguard's nightmare."

"Are you a bodyguard, sir?" I asked Dillingham.

"A tactical planner," he replied.

"I think you have little reason to fear such an outcome, sir," said Holmes, "as I would say to you all, for I do not see those means of action suggested by the stalker's behaviour."

"Can you be certain, though?" demanded Lord Crosby.

"Your Lordship," Holmes told the man, "do consider, this is a clever person who deeply values the thrill of a masterful chase, as demonstrated by his conduct thus far. It is only a most expert pickpocket who could carry out what we know this man has done. To remove a cigarette case from a royal pocket, to steal away a treasured heirloom from an emperor's very finger? *A genius* I would label this man. In fact the competence behind such skills is perhaps equal to my own talents. So unlikely is it that such a crime as the purloining of an item from the royal presence would even be attempted once, let alone twice, that I confess earlier my thoughts went out to the possibility that the Kaiser was simply...if you pardon my candor...fabricating the occurrence of each theft, for his own entertainment. I still cannot entirely rule this out, though an emperor who would play such a high stakes game would be a fool, indeed, and whatever his other faults may be, I do not sense that our queen's most formidable grandson is, in fact, a fool."

No sooner had the word left Holmes' lips than the double doors thrust open and a short dark-haired man in a striking suit of a conservative cut favoured by the Germans entered the room, with two subordinates behind him, each clearly, even to my eyes, plain-clothes policemen of some variety.

Rudely the man strode across the room, as the two plain-clothes guards took up positions on either side of the door, and fell into a chair at the foot of the table.

I noted that from the outer hallway the naval lieutenant was glaring at the intruders with volcanic outrage, but otherwise did nothing.

When the newly-arrived man spoke, it was in well-drilled English, but with a Teutonic accent so thick I knew at once these were emissaries from the Kaiser's entourage.

Turning toward Holmes, the man said:

"I am glad, sir, to hear you do not think our sovereign Kaiser a fool, or I should have to challenge you to sabers on my embassy grounds were the time more convenient."

Holmes smirked, and replied:

"On your embassy grounds would provide you with a more than considerable advantage, I should say."

"Then I suggest you do not give me offense," the short German man thundered. He looked across the table toward its head and said:

"Lord Crosby, you have conspired to hold this meeting without inviting a representative from our nation, even though the matter is of deepest concern to us! You must apologize this instant for that insult!"

"This is an internal matter, herr *Oberst* Von Mecklenburg," Crosby replied evenly, "and therefore it is no more of a slight to you and yours than it is to us when you fail to inform us that an internal security meeting is underway among you and your countrymen."

"How did you know this meeting was taking place at all?" asked the clerk named Dillingham.

The German, Von Mecklenburg, I took it was his name,

an *Oberst* the equivalent in rank to a full colonel in our own armed forces, was clearly delighted by the question, and said:

"Ah, very good, let the fact of my own arrival stand as a practical demonstration that all things which occur here in your White Hall are known to we Germans, and you can conceal nothing of importance from us and our confidential network."

It was a revelation that both angered me and also cast a frightful pall over my heart, for if it were true that Germany's infiltration of our nation was as keen as the man hinted, I could foresee nothing good arising from it where my country was concerned. When I was a boy what was dubbed Germany had been a disorganized patchwork of petty states, but within a generation had become a rival even for the British Empire, a meteoric rise surely unseen anywhere in history, and a frightening one.

"You did not even have the regard for my appointed dignity to rise upon my entrance, I note," Von Mecklenburg said, adding complaint to his menace. "That shall be remembered, I assure you."

Such a nasty personality, I thought, and so quick to take offense.

The man's eyes raked Holmes once again and fell even more disdainfully onto me.

"I know the identities of this pair," he said, fashioning a haughty smile of self-flattery, "one Holmes and Watson, I believe they are named, and mark it a sign of the inept fumbling of the British government that it would consult an amateur and his lackey and seek to bring them into this most concerning crisis behind the back of the German faction, we who are here on your soil as guests of your sovereign queen, Victoria, mother of our dowager empress? Is it some insult on your part to seek to remedy so serious a threat to the Kaiser's life by bringing in this pretender? This....'consulting detective'?"

Holmes said nothing, merely gazed emotionlessly at the

German, giving no sign of how he might have regarded the man's insulting words. Lord Crosby however, leaned outward toward the intruder, and said:

"Baron Von Mecklenburg, if we failed to rise at your entrance, perhaps it was because it was so abrupt and unheralded that we were given little chance. If we bring what you dub 'an amateur' into this matter, perhaps it is your own much-boasted of capability to spy on us you should consider, for I assure you Mr. Holmes whom you claim is known to you, comes to us with a long and distinguished record of achieving feats deemed impossible by other men."

"I remain unimpressed," the German taunted.

"Even so, my good fellow," said Crosby, whom I thought was holding his own in an admirably unruffled fashion before the hotheaded intruder, "in the final reckoning, I must state that the internal affairs of the British government, and how it chooses to proceed within its sovereign territory, is no business of the German nation, or its *uninvited* representatives."

Von Mecklenburg's face grew dark and he doubtless had some angry retort to offer, but Holmes cut him off by saying:

"Look at your hands, herr Von Mecklenburg, is it your wish to see them stained with royal blood?"

"What?" the German demanded.

"If it is your wish that you emperor survive to see tomorrow, might I suggest, you undertake an exercise which I grasp you have little practiced in the past, *and close your mouth.*"

There was a wave of shock inside the room at Holmes' bluntness, and indeed the short-statured German, Von Mecklenburg, appeared to be about to spring from his seat and loose his rage in a physical manner, when Holmes said simply:

"You are, I perceive, among the men most responsible for Kaiser Wilhelm's personal safety, and yet as you have twice failed to prevent these episodes of intrusion into your Kaiser's person, and forestall the theft of objects personally possessed by him. I suggest His Imperial Majesty's life may hinge on the outcome of what happens now in this room, and would therefore advise you to think of that man's blood spilling warmly into your own hands, as it may within hours devoid my assistance in this, our common cause. Thus I counsel you, herr *Obserst*, listen."

Incredibly, the arrogant German did close his half-open mouth and relaxed back into his chair, though his eyes still burned with a fiery dislike of my friend.

"We thank you, herr Von Mecklenburg," Lord Crosby said, attempting a more diplomatic stance than the direct candor of my friend, "and do invite you to attend the remainder of this meeting, as our distinguished guest. Mr. Holmes, you were saying...?"

Holmes focused his eyes onto the tabletop, as if trying to peer through it to the floor itself, and said:

"Here is how things shall go.... Lord Crosby, firstly I commend your wisdom in reaching out to me, for I suspect this matter would otherwise have stood unresolved, if not unresolvable. To our German *friend* present, I would suggest that as this is the final public event on his master's calendar, any attempt on his life that may be planned for his time on English soil would occur tonight, and he and all among his fellow Germans who wish to safeguard their Kaiser would do well to heed what I say now, and follow my instructions to the letter."

"I am listening," Von Mecklenburg said with a resentful tone.

"Pray do go on, Mr. Holmes," the Brigadier said softly.

I felt pride at my friend's audacity in the face of others who held so much worldly power, and leaned close to the table to hear what Holmes would say next.

"Lord Crosby, herr Von Mecklenburg, I shall also be in attendance at the London Opera tonight, or more specifically at the reception after the performance, in the grand ballroom below the north tower, as I feel strongly it would be there that any danger should present itself rather than during the opera itself."

"How do you know this?" Von Mecklenburg demanded.

Holmes held up a commanding finger, and without looking at the man said:

"I shall be in disguise, a fact which must be kept hidden from as many as possible, from all not presently within this room would be best, as must the very fact of my involvement in this case, for I fear if not apprehended tonight, our foe should learn of my presence, and flee and bide his time for some future opportunity abroad. My friend and colleague, Dr. Watson, will accompany me in a capacity I shall not reveal inside this room, however trustworthy I do judge each of you as individuals to be. I must be given nothing less than fullest cooperation as I carry out my methods and must endure no questioning whatsoever of how I shall proceed. All each of you must do is leave word with the relevant persons that one 'Major Philipi Caruthers' shall be attending tonight, and that he shall be admitted into the affair that shall unfold after the Puccini performance. Do all here understand these instructions, and agree to abide by my terms?"

"And if we do not?" Von Mecklenburg asked.

"Then," said Holmes flatly, "I will not help you, and matters shall unfold as they will...tragically if your inept past record against our masterful opponent suggests anything."

"Mr. Holmes, as for we British, you have our agreement in our entirety," said Lord Crosby gravely, and the other British gentlemen seated around him nodded and spoke out as well.

However, Von Mecklenburg growled:

"I am not satisfied with this arrangement. We have augmented the usual honour guard around His Imperial Majesty, creating a living shield about him far exceeding anything matching the norm for such occasions. His security is by far the finest in all the world."

"Not fine enough it seems," Holmes taunted.

Von Mecklenburg ignored this and said:

"All we require is that the British should maintain the usual control of the crowd within the setting and outside upon the street, and the rest can confidently be left to us."

"Oh, that is ideal," Holmes laughed, "considering how successful the German delegation has been thus far in its protection of the Kaiser."

Von Mecklenburg exploded and shouted:

"Have I not told you the guard around His Imperial Majesty has been heightened since last night? You, a chaser after house-burglars feel competent to dictate to we who are professionals what course we should take in the protection of our sovereign? Who do you think you are?"

Holmes stayed calm in the face of these charges, but asked:

"Perhaps the question should not be who it is I *think* I am, but rather who it is I know *you* are."

"What do you mean by this?" Von Mecklenburg cried confused and annoyed.

"In fact," said Holmes, "I am one who sees much about you, including matters which you would wish to conceal. *I know you via yourself*, herr Von Mecklenburg. I see that you are dressed by a left-handed manservant, that you were a sprinter in your school days, that you have recently had a broken engagement, much to your distress and personal shame, and furthermore, if I spoke of 'Baden-Baden' would that incite a memory you'd prefer not be spoken aloud?"

Confusion and a flash of guilt decorated Von Mecklenburg's face. He glanced nervously toward the two guards by the door and then demanded:

"Have we met before tonight? Am I somehow known to you?"

"Well," Holmes told him, "you claim to know of *me*, do you not, so is it not fair I should come to familiarize myself with you in return? No, herr *Obserst*, we have never met before this day, I had no knowledge of your existence until you entered this room."

"Then how is it you know of the things which you declare, and of the matter, at which you hint concerning..." His voice dropped. "...*Baden-Baden*?"

The German was truly in a state of deep upset, and Holmes smiled in triumph, having so easily undermined the other man's self-confidence and gotten the better of him in a handful of seconds. He said almost carelessly:

"Your left-handed servant is revealed in the tilt of the knot in your shoes and the slight angle of your buttons. Being so elevated a man as you are, I intuit you would not put your own hands to something so menial as cladding yourself. The matter of my knowing you ran sprints as a school boy, well it is rare for a Prussian academy not to demand of its students that they take part in rigorous athletic pursuits, so that when I perceive a lingering over-development of your calf muscles, it tells me you often ran sprints a decade ago when you were in school. The quality of this muscular development clearly displays itself when one knows the traces to seek, as opposed to the differing result of, say, much marching, as might be the case in a military man, or in the case of a peasant, whose legs would carry him in excesses of walking, and show more of a build-up of muscles higher up, in the thigh."

"I was top runner at my academy, where I competed against boys from the nearby *Volksschule*, but my engagement, sir, how was this ascertained, if as you claim I am unknown to you? For my part, I think it quite disproves your claim of my being a stranger before I entered this room!"

"It does not do to call Sherlock Holmes a liar, sir," I offered to the German.

"Save when he happens to be one!" the man answered.

"It is unusual," spoke Holmes, "for a German of your class and station by the time he reaches nearly thirty, not to possess a wife, which I see from several signs you do not. The most obvious of these being your lack of a wedding band."

The German hastily placed his right hand over his left. "But a broken engagement?" he challenged.

"In Germany it is the custom for the affianced couple to exchange rings of engagements, I believe, which are, in Prussia, far more slender than the typical wedding band. I see upon your finger the signs that such a band was worn in the recent past for at least four months, but is neither worn now, nor does it stand replaced by a wedding ring. It is most elementary then to state that this shows you have previously been engaged, and yet the arrangement fell through. From your reaction, and the subconscious covering of your left hand with your right upon my mentioning the fact—see, now you defiantly uncover it—I perceived your wish to hide that hand away, as if concealing unpleasant memories. From that I hesitate little to go so far as to say the breaking off of the engagement was neither on your part, nor was the lady's action welcomed by you. She found some personal fault in you, I gather?"

Von Mecklenburg stared venomously as he said through clenched teeth:

"I will not dignify that insult with an answer, but for what reason did you mention Baden-Baden?"

"Come now, sir," Holmes chuckled pleasantly, "I cannot think you truly wish me to speak of that matter amid present company?"

Von Mecklenburg blinked several times, rapidly, and charged:

"This matter could not be known to you. You are the devil."

He stood from his chair and announced:

"Lord Crosby, I will see that on our part your agents encounter no impediments to the plan your man Holmes, here, has detailed. If he is able to contribute to His Imperial Majesty's safety while at the event tonight, he shall have the thanks of Germany."

Looking back to Holmes, though, he said:

"As for me, however, I do not like you, sir, and find you *ein Angeber.*"

"You find me a 'show-off'?" chuckled Holmes. "Well, what can I say to that charge, when my unfortunate sense of professional vanity is a thing only too well-known?"

With a leer of profound distaste, Von Mecklenburg told him quietly in reply:

"I predict that it shall one day be your undoing."

He clicked his heels and marched from the room at so rapid a clip that the guards barely had time to open the door as he passed through, then set off on his trail at double-time.

"You see," said Holmes merrily as he removed his pipe from his pocket and proceeded to light it, asking no one's permission to do so, "our German visitor remains something of a sprinter even now as he runs away from a superior opponent."

There were several chuckles at this, but were soon cut short, as Holmes almost sedately exhaled a cloud of smoke and said to Lord Crosby:

"Incidentally, Von Mecklenburg's boast of his nation's total penetration into the inner workings of British government was, I feel confident in saying, something of a pointed exaggeration."

"That is good to know, but it still leaves the question of how he knew of this secret meeting," said Brigadier Billings-Russell, troubled.

"Ah, in that respect," said Holmes, nodding to one man across the table, the only one of the five who had not uttered a word throughout the entirety of the meeting, "I should focus on Bryant there, as I believe he may prove the Germans' source of information about this meeting, and sadly, I suspect a great many other previous matters as well."

There was an electrical pulse in the air after his words of accusation, several gasps, and Crosby said:

"That is a very serious statement, Mr. Holmes, and while I value your views and respect the contributions you have made to the nation in the course of your career, Mr. Bryant has spent a dozen years in White Hall and his service has often merited commendation! Bryant, what have you to say to this charge?"

Bryant sat as if paralyzed, then opened his mouth to speak, and closed it, and I thought even I could read guilt in the man's rapidly flushing face.

"It is true?" demanded the Commodore, turning his muscular bulk toward the man to his right.

Bryant swallowed and said nothing, which surprised me, as I would have expected the man to protest strongly against such a dreadful suspicion, whether he spoke truthfully or was lying.

"Yes," said Holmes, "I noted that when herr Von Mecklenburg made his boast about his nation's knowledge of matters our nation would rather see held secret, all eyes were on him, save those of Bryant there, who was most steadfastly gazing away. And when Von Mecklenburg finished his boast, his eyes locked for the merest instant on those of Bryant, which I found most telling then, and combined with Bryant's reaction, most damning now."

With that, Holmes took to his heel and departed the room with a cry of:

"Do see that my time at the reception tonight is not troubled in any way, gentlemen!"

*****

And so we left the corridors of White Hall, the morning not yet quite transformed to shadowless noon, and my friend seemed in excellent spirits, as he often was before his involvement in some pressing and intricate case. Though the lieutenant who had ridden with us to the meeting caught up with us to offer a return to Baker Street in the same fine carriage, Holmes declined and said he fancied a little stroll, then to me a moment later, once the man was out of earshot, he asked if I would care to join him in a light luncheon somewhere near-about.

"A little chop-house I know of up near Charing Cross would satisfy my palate nicely today."

Though I was glad my often finicky friend had found an appetite, my own thoughts were not on food, and walking beside him toward Charing Cross, I demanded:

"Holmes, I must know, what was that about 'Baden-Baden' the famous continental resort town, and why did mention of the place discomfit Von Mecklenburg so utterly, as I saw it did?"

Holmes cried out a true barking laugh of delight and said:

"Ah, that surprise bit of revelation was a thing of delight and beauty, was it not?"

"It certainly cowed him," I agreed, "but to what did it refer?"

"To him? Nothing. To his younger brother, Helmut, however...well, that is a sordid tale, for this morning I recollected a bit of information provided to me some years ago by one of my continental sources, concerning a well-connected young German from Berlin, who shared the same surname as the boor who intruded into our meeting, and who was noteworthy for having proclivities of a socially frowned-upon sort, however common such things may be under the concealment of shadows. Baden-Baden is, it seems, notorious as a place where men who so indulge go to sate their attractions to certain undertakings. There was a scandal concerning this younger brother which was narrowly averted, and apparently much money was paid by representatives of the Von Mecklenburg family to conceal this Helmut's activities at a spa, baited there as he was by blackmailers who prey upon the men who visit for unadvertised purposes. Our own Von Mecklenburg fears little more than for this story to leak out into the world, destroying his brother and tarnishing his family honour to the point his own career would suffer, for the Kaiser would certainly not wish a man with such a relation to serve him in so cogent a capacity."

I grasped his meaning, unpleasant though it was to contemplate, but said:

"It hardly seems fair that a man should be held accountable for his brother's misdeeds."

"Ah, but that is the way of the Germans, Watson, who do not see things in the same light as you, but believe a family is like unto a chain, with one weak link undoing all of a bloodline."

He said no more about that sordid matter, nor did I ask, but went with him into the chop-house, where the restaurateur, a dapper man round as an apple around his middle, greeted my friend with genuine ebullience, showing him to his finest table, and offering the best bottle of wine in his cellar, and Holmes and I were soon to set upon a very fine luncheon indeed, gifted to us by a man who gushed praises in remembrance of the unnamed but apparently significant favour Holmes had once done him, which the restaurateur declared he would never be able to re-pay should he live a dozen lifetimes.

"What else are my powers for, if not to see an innocent man liberated of accusations that properly belong to another?" Holmes modestly told the fellow, though I saw the man's gratitude pleased him, so that if my friend were a cat, I imagined he would have been comfortably purring at the liberality of the praise.

I was also reminded there, as I had been on a hundred occasions before, that I knew but a tiny portion of Sherlock Holmes' activities, and that his life was woven in and out of a thousand shadows, and was filled with more stories than either I or the outer world would ever be privileged to know.

*****

At Baker Street, Holmes spent nearly an hour reading several volumes he dug from a haphazard stack on the bowing bookshelf at the parlour's corner, then, seeming satisfied, retreated to his room, mumbling to himself, where I heard him sift through the stock of costumes he kept in a wardrobe there, outfits for surely every occasion life might possibly ever demand.

When he emerged, he was still himself—if indeed the "self" I always associated with him could be called the "real and only" Sherlock Holmes, and then he plunked down into his favourite chair and refreshed his pipe.

"Watson," he said in a happy tone, "I think a most interesting hunt shall be afoot tonight."

"Do you indeed?" I inquired.

"Oh, yes, most restoring and fortifying, for all indications are that I shall face off against a relative master at his grim art."

"Well you've hardly lacked cases of late, were none of those sufficient to stir this 'fortifying restoration' of which you speak?"

"Indeed, my dear friend, but they were as small satisfying meals in comparison, and this, Watson, is a veritable banquet for the mind, an employment of all my senses and skills.'

With a cry surely heard in the street beyond, he bellowed:

"I tell you, I am filled with life at this moment!"

"In a way, Holmes," I admitted, "it troubles me to hear you speak of this so lightly, when it strikes me as a grave matter. Should this assassin reach the Kaiser, well, it may ignite the charge of the political powder keg we read so much about these days."

"Oh, yes," he agreed, "which is part of why the challenge of this case is such an adventure, and I look forward to it as most men might the revitalizing effects of a holiday in the country, such as that your missus is indulging in at present."

"A holiday in the country?" I repeated incredulously. "But are you not troubled in the least by the consequences of a failure on your part?"

"Tell me Watson, which thrills a man more, a penny bet

over cards on a street corner, or when he gambles a thousand pounds in some Monte Carlo casino?"

"I see..."

"Yes, Watson, for the lives of a hundred thousand do ride on my skills tonight, and I am only too keenly aware of the precipice above which I operate. Rather than daunt me, it motivates me to supreme sharpness, and the thrill is little less than delicious."

Holmes remained in this state of inner excitation, and chatted most amicably with Mrs. Hudson when she appeared at four-thirty with a pot of tea, and beef pasties, even going so far as to invite her to partake along with us, and pouring her a cup at his own hand. She had known the detective for many years and recognized the sparkle that all-but shone from his Minerva-gray eyes, and while she said nothing, she gazed toward me with muted concern, and I read a silent plea that I'd do my best to look out for him, which of course I always would.

When she had gone back below stairs, I inquired:

"Holmes, the hour swiftly approaches, and you have not yet told me what is to be my part in tonight's events. You mentioned back at White Hall that mine would be a rôle you would not disclose there, but what is it I shall be expected to do?"

"You shall be exclusively involved in one of several undertakings I have long noted you carry out with much natural talent, Watson, your skills as a writer."

"A *writer*, Holmes?" I burst out. "Tonight? There?"

"I would ask you to play the part of one Mr. Byron Wentworth, who has been commissioned by, let us say a 'Viscount Lyons,' who incidentally does not exist, to interview guests and make notes of tonight's events for a reminiscence of the reception the Viscount intends to see published. I need you to mill most freely, mingling and pulling some subtle attention to yourself, and in this I think you shall draw the eye while finding volunteers in plentitude who will cheerfully bend your ear, and thus keep eyes off me, and attract a small portion of the attendees to you, and clear of my own path."

"Er, all right," I agreed, thinking the whole business slightly odd, though I supposed I could see some merit in the idea.

"Watson, though your name shall be different tonight, simply *be yourself*, and all shall be most well, I assure you."

"And what will be your own rôle, Holmes?" I asked.

"Ah," my friend brayed a laugh, "'Sherlock Holmes' shall not be in attendance any more than shall Dr. John Watson, but rather an old fellow, veteran of the Crimea, Major Philipi Caruthers, long retired from his military career but with many friends among those in high places, who humour the old fellow by seeing him admitted now and again to events such as these, owing to his long and fruitful service to Queen and Country. He is eccentric, possibly on the road to the madness of senility, but likable enough, and all this should see him left free to mingle about at liberty, neither drawing undue attention nor being perceived as someone one might wish to overtly engage, for those who do speak to him will soon note he is a tiresome fellow, best avoided. I think this is the wisest approach to keep me in view of the Kaiser at all times."

"You are fully satisfied, then, that an attempt on the Kaiser's life shall come to pass tonight?" I asked.

"Frankly, Watson, I have not decided that the chain of supposed logic presented by either our British friends or the continental faction is the correct interpretation of the facts, but I cannot rule out that possibility, but what energizes me is that I *am* certain our friend the pickpocket shall be among us, and I will challenge him."

"Why else might someone be demonstrating an ability to enter so closely into the Kaiser's presence, if not as at least some frightful warning?"

"Yes, and to steal from him with such expertise that I confess I am all-but envious of that talent..."

Holmes paused in mid-words to stare into space, and I imagined he was placing himself in such scenarios as had come to pass the previous two nights, and wondering if his own profound skills as a pickpocket would have passed muster, as did those of his unnamed foe, for my friend, I knew, hated to be bested in anything.

He sighed and said:

"Matters are always that much sweeter when one faces an adversary with admirable talents."

"But the Kaiser is, at least insofar as we may know, in genuine danger tonight?" I pressed, interrupting his reverie.

"He, Watson, like all the crowned heads of Europe, dwells in considerable danger in this perilous age, debased as it is compared to more sedate decades that came earlier in the century. If his life is not sought by the droves of benighted anarchists who loiter in the cities like lice on back-alley rodents, there are always scores of other would-be murderers to cast hazard onto his path, not to mention random lunatics and grudge-holders present at any time. Thus the facts hint at a direct peril which lies present in the reception tonight, and as yet this foe is faceless and his motives cannot be known. The apparent ease with which this factor moves in and out of the royal presence is the most troubling facet of it all. Given the sheer number of those the Kaiser has greeted at each social engagement this week, it could be any of a thousand or more who were presented to him, or who milled nearby."

"By the sound of it, it is among the most daunting problems of your career."

"Oh, yes, for here I must not only face the unknown, a challenge long familiar to me, but operate on another man's field of choosing. I am going in half-blind and hamstrung before an enemy who knows his plan in advance, and moves with a confidence little-seen in my own experience of the villainous classes."

"Holmes, could this stalker be a German? Have you considered this?"

"I have, Watson, and find it less than likely."

"Why is that? I can see a scenario in which someone

within the German fatherland wishes for war for the gains he might hope it brings him or his nation, and he could be willing to sacrifice his own sovereign to attain it."

"That is true, Watson, but if there is such logic in those audacious goals, why should this assassin not strike at once while on British soil? Why make the matter into a game, and prolong it across multiple nights of perilously toying with his target, and revealing his existence? No, I see here some boastful pleasure in the undertaking, much like a cat that toys with a mouse."

The high and mighty German Kaiser made into someone's mouse, I thought. "Then this truly is a bold and talented foe," I stated.

"Watson," Holmes told me, "this is a true and unrivaled master.

*****

The remainder of the afternoon passed quietly, and in fact Holmes surprised me by going into his room for an hour's nap, something I had not expected given the high state of his nerves and his overall excitement regarding what lay ahead.

For my part I took a stroll around the block and read a newspaper on a park bench amid the late-afternoon sunlight, before coming back to find my friend actively transforming himself into someone new and quite convincing, applying makeup and false teeth, and donning a moth-eaten but once-elegant suit, then presenting himself before me, back vaguely bent and withered by the passing of surely eighty years, as Major Phillipi Caruthers, retired, formerly of Her Majesty's 28th North Gloucestershire Foot, which served with such distinction at the Crimea well over thirty years before.

"Pleased to make your acquaintance, Mr. Byron Wentworth," the old wreck of a soldier cackled at me. "I hear it is to the reception at the opera house you are going tonight, just as I am. Say, have I told you of the time my regiment took a Russian flag at Alma? Eh? Well it is quite a tale, and if you insist upon hearing it, I suppose I can allow a few minutes to tell you...."

"Holmes," I laughed, "it is perfect, you are completely lost in this brash impersonation!"

"I thank you, Watson, and only break character now to bid you dress yourself for tonight. Go for elegance, but remember, you are a lesser order of being among those who shall have little qualm in regarding themselves as your betters, however much they may enjoy the time they condescend to spend talking to you. Tarry not overly long with anyone you interview, and keep stirring about the room, for anything might come to pass tonight, and my eyes shall rarely be upon you."

I took his instructions and put on my best suit and found a clean notepad among the shelves in the parlour, and set my mind to the rôle that would be mine throughout the perilous night ahead. I shaved and combed my hair in a differing style, one perhaps more commonly seen among men a few years younger than my earliest middle-years, and regarded myself in the mirror, hoping I would pass muster.

"My good Mr. Wentworth," Holmes said with amusement when he saw me emerge from my old room, "I think you shall effortlessly dazzle the hearts of the dowagers tonight!"

There is always a restless sensation that accompanies any lengthy wait but with so much at stake it felt like each passing second on the clock dragged by, and I was almost uncontainably anxious to be off. Holmes, however, while doubtless eager to begin his activities at the reception, maintained a cool head, and smoked with an almost preternatural aura of placidity that contrasted his earlier exuberance, as he allowed sufficient time to pass before he stood at last and almost calmly announced:

"All right, Mr. Byron Wentworth—as you must remember to always think of yourself tonight—I would judge sufficient time has elapsed, and we may make use of the cab I have standing at the wait outside."

"I am surprised," I stated," that the government made no offer of conveyance tonight."

"The offer was tendered, Watson, but think of the impression on certain eyes if a half-barmy old army major and a documentarian were to arrive on-scene in a government-provided carriage."

"Ah, well, yes."

With a last fortifying smile before he slid entirely into the character he would be playing for the remainder of the evening, Holmes said to me:

"To the field of battle we now go, my good man!"

We left Baker Street in silence and took up our places within the waiting hansom, driven by a towering, stooped Cockney fellow by the name of Tim, whom I'd encountered before, and who seemed loyally faithful to Holmes relating to some past incident neither had ever volunteered to describe to me, reminding me of the gratitude of the restaurateur from earlier in the day.

"Well 'allo, Mr. 'olmes!' Tim called with such vivid enthusiasm I wondered not for the first time if he was just perhaps a bit touched, "Almost didn't recognize you, I didn't, not in that get-up, lookin' like an old timer, but I'd know the Doc there 'most anyplace, even wiff 'is 'air combed all funny, so I figgered on it being you comin' along after!"

This was all stated with a certain simple pride that was child-like in its unaffected delight.

"Right you are then, my good Tim, it is, indeed, I. You recall your instructions, I trust?"

"Ol' Fleet Admiral and me," Tim said nodding to a sharply-groomed but decidedly ordinary-looking black horse at the hansom's fore, "are to takes you to the hopera 'ouse off the Court and let you hoff near the western entrance, by the big reception wing 'round the side."

"Indeed, Tim, that should be ideal," Holmes confirmed, "and as we are ready, I bid you, my good fellow, let us all be off!"

These instructions Tim followed to the letter, and with a rattle we began our trip across town as the light in the west lowered, and a vast orange glow took over the horizon there, vivid in the smoke that always filled London's skies.

Tim and Holmes chatted with a friendly banter that was quite unlike my friend's typically serious and even taciturn outlook, and I wondered again which of the many aspects of the man was most reflective of his inner nature, but knowing him as I did, I had to hold faith that I saw the truest display of who he was at heart when I caught him at his most analytical. Still, as I had often seen in the past, Holmes could display an almost merry and benignant personality when dealing with those he judged humble and true to themselves, such as the urchins who composed his "Baker Street Irregulars," or any of dozens of various street people and working class sorts like Tim. It was all a bounteous conundrum to mull over as we rolled on toward our destination, though ponder it I did, mainly to keep my nervous mind off what lay ahead.

"If you halt just about here, that should be fine, Tim," Holmes told the Cockney at our journey's end, and the man obliged by obediently pulling up to the curb and bringing his beloved nag Fleet Admiral to a stop.

"Right then, sir," Tim called back to him.

I hopped down but turned to marvel at the skill with which Holmes portrayed the slower movements of an elderly man as he rose stiffly and slowly lowered his way from the hansom to the curb, using his hands to steady himself. It was a perfect impression, and I smiled at its virtuosity, thinking to myself what an actor was the great Sherlock Holmes!

"Go on then, Mr. Wentworth, I know you have duties to perform," he told me in a voice suddenly aged by forty years or more, and with a wave of a knotted-looking old hand, liver-spotted and claw-like, he gestured to the gates. "Don't forget to give them the right name, Mr. Wentworth!"

He then emitted a laugh which evolved into a wheezing cough.

It was with some reluctance that I turned from the disguised Holmes, for there was a certain trepidation in me as I set off alone without lending direct support to my friend, and went to the entrance, where several City of London policemen stood, and to the well-dressed man at the entrance said:

"Hello, I am Mr. Byron Wentworth, acting in a private capacity for Viscount Lyons, and I believe my name was left here for admittance tonight?"

The constable-sergeant, a balding man of portly dimensions, gave me a look that was neither welcoming nor disdainful, and after running his sausage-like finger down a hand-written list, curtly intoned:

"I have you right here, Mr. Wentworth, pray, be admitted."

One of the policemen stepped aside, and a likely-looking lad of about twelve, dressed as an usher, lifted a velvet-covered rope, and I was just striding past him and making my way to the hall's doorway, when behind me I heard the cry of an old man, his voice loud with his presumably failing hearing.

"I am, sirs, Major Philipi Caruthers," cried the aged fellow, "formerly of Her Majesty's 28th North Gloucestershire Foot, at your service, constables! Have a look, do have a look, don't gape now, and you'll find my old commander's son, Brigadier Billings-Russell, has me down on his guest list tonight! Do you see it, sirs? Don't keep me waiting now, for at my age time mustn't be wasted, and it doesn't even do to buy unripe fruit one might never live to eat!"

The old man let loose a laugh matching the one from the carriage, and this too broke apart amid emphysemic coughs.

"A moment if you please, Major Caruthers," the constable-sergeant was telling him as I walked onward, and I could only image the odd look the putative old soldier was receiving, perhaps a humouring merriment, perhaps something less, but I did not linger to hear the conversation unfold as I made my way into the building stepping down a bright red carpet that lay unrolled underfoot.

As I passed from the darkness outside into the hall's brilliant lights, and the sounds of a chamber orchestra grew ever louder around me, I saw a veritable rainbow of ball gowns, worn by newlywed beauties and worldly dowagers alike, with more than a few fresh-faced debutantes from the Season mixed in, making the most of their brief time in the limelight at this prestigious state visit from a German sovereign who seemed to appear so often in our newspapers. And of course there were gentlemen with each of the ladies, tall and short, old and otherwise, and always young bucks prowling about, their swift-moving eyes taking in the women around them, and I noted that amid all of this milled uniformed guards from two nations, proving there was, as Von Mecklenburg had promised, a decidedly heightened level of security.

Letting my eyes pass by the lovely ice sculpture of a family of swans which adorned a nearby table laden with delicacies, I recalled my purpose, and set about doing as Holmes had instructed, and began to engage willing attendees in conversation concerning their experiences tonight at the opera and their impressions of this somewhat historic reception. I soon found that it was not always the ladies who proved the freest of tongue, and once or twice over the next hour, as my eyes sought out—and sometimes found—Holmes in his old officer disguise, it was I who had to break off from the long-winded commentary of several overly-helpful men.

Though the room was vast and airy and the air not at all stale, there was a certain almost oppressive aura in it all, with the waves of perfume and colognes, the scent of so many cigarettes smoked in discreet corners, the sounds of half a thousand voices chatting away, and the constant swirl of attendees passing all about me, to and from the dance floor and the buffet line. All this, of course, added to the rows of fine sorts who clung like ivy by the walls, talking to one another about their yachts and where their sons were serving overseas, or the politics of the moment.

For a simple doctor such as myself, not acclimated to

society on such a scale, it was almost too much, though I pressed on, determined to serve the function my friend had so trustingly laid out for me, so on I went, milling about, often seeing no more than a handful of yards beyond myself, always hearing voices lifting all around me, the crowds thicker in some places than others, til I gave up taking dictation of what was said by those who deigned to speak to me, and simply fell into *pretending* to jot it all down, which I felt certain was fine according to Holmes' instructions, as of course there was in reality no "Viscount Lyons" paying me to assemble his book.

Thus an hour passed in this fashion and half of another, and I found it all quite draining, and wondered how, so separated from Holmes as to have lost sight of him, I was contributing any good toward our common mission, so I stuck the pencil I'd been using to take notes behind my ear and set off to see if I could espy the great detective in the midst of this churning sea of party-goers.

It was not an easy task, and I found the crowd only thickened the farther I traveled from the outer walls and toward the heart of things, and sensed that the nearer I drew to the Kaiser, that great uniformed presence scowling upon a throne-like dais, the more intense it would all become, as indeed it did, so that by the time I was perhaps fifty feet from where His Imperial Majesty sat surrounded by both his retinue and a line of those whom he was to receive, I was all but hemmed-in by others, and had little room to move.

Then I heard a voice I recognized, high-pitched and antique, and knew I was close to my friend. I swiveled my head til I saw him standing half-stooped extremely close to a lady of late middle years with graying auburn hair and a fine plum-coloured dress of a very formal and costly appearance. The lady was clearly annoyed at Holmes' distracting presence, but bore her tribulation with fortitude, believing herself addressed by one whose service to the nation had apparently been august in some long-ago era about which she knew very little.

I wondered what the significance of this particular woman was that had her meriting Holmes' attention, but then caught on that he was merely manufacturing the chatter and using her for cover as he stood stooping at her right, cackling at his own little jokes while the lady waited, unwilling to move away, because from her position she, like Holmes, enjoyed an unobstructed view of the Kaiser in his seat.

I grabbed a cup of punch off a tray held by a passing waiter in bright red livery, and let its iced coolness combat the warmth which had begun to build inside me within this packed place. Despite my better judgment frowning silently upon such thoughts, I felt a great impetus to wish whatever was to occur tonight would simply happen, for this pretense, along with all else there in the grand ballroom, had grown wearisome.

It was precisely then that I saw a man moving sideways through the crowd, partway between where I stood, and the Kaiser's position, and something about this individual snagged my notice. I judged his age to be about thirty, his hair was of an ash-brown hue, and he was of about middling height, thus otherwise unremarkable, and yet...

I tried to see him through the methods Holmes had often tried—with some modest success—to instill in me, and was rewarded when I realized his hair had been newly-cut, and while he was wearing attire appropriate for the event, somehow I knew the suit was new, perhaps rented, and he was clearly uncomfortable within it, for it was not his usual mode of dress. This, I saw, was no figure of the upper-classes, but one as much ill at ease here as I was myself. Once I noted this about him, a number of alarm bells began to go off inside my brain, and I fastened my eyes unshakably upon him, for my instincts were shouting that he was simply *wrong*.

He was alone, I saw, no accompanying lady near him, and I watched as his eyes constantly traveled rapidly across the crowd, reminding me of a hunter scanning the bushes. I also noted that with every pass of his eyes, his gaze invariably ended fixed back upon the Kaiser, toward whom he was slowly but steadily approaching in as unobtrusively stealthy and indirect a manner as possible.

I gazed out, and saw to my shock that Holmes, still engaged in regaling the lady with his fabricated stories, did not see this man, and I felt my heartbeat increase, for I was certain this person was not part of the society among whom he so pointedly walked, even as he made every effort to blend into the surroundings.

I experienced a rush of enormous energy in me, and felt my muscles stir as this man drew ever closer to the Kaiser, now no more than twenty feet from him and still closing in, and I was on the verge of crying out for Holmes and lunging ahead, when in a moment of sheer grounding humility, I spied the fellow stop next to one of the uniformed guards, lean forward, and speak quietly with him, and watched the guard nod in agreement, a familiarity between them, and I realized the stealthy man I had been tracking was one of the platoon of agents from Scotland Yard working at the reception in plain clothes.

The energy drained from me til I felt a weakness that fell from my chest to my knees, as relief washed out from my every cell and fiber. "Oh, dear me," I muttered to myself, "that level of nervousness will never do, John." I even chuckled a little, so great was my relief.

I noticed a lady to my left had been watching me, and as our gazes met she raised an eyebrow as an unspoken comment on my odd behaviour, so I smiled back and nodded to her, before hastily moving off, feeling sheepish.

A further half-hour was to slowly pass, and though at some point the lady who had been enduring Holmes' chatter finally gave up her post, likely driven to sheer aggravation by the old officer's unending monologues, another woman took her place, this one a matronly looking sort in a bottle green dress of a type I tended to wince to see, for I knew the dyeing process typically involved arsenic, and as a doctor I was only too aware of the dangers inherent in its use in the world of fashion.

Finally the clock struck ten, and I saw something of a look of deep relief come onto the glowering face of the Kaiser, and I sensed that by some agreement his duty in being present to be gazed at while he endured those who'd merited places in the receiving line which for much of the night had passed before him, was done. The man rose to his feet, his great, overlapping collection of unearned war medals clanking against his barrel chest, as he swayed ever so faintly while his body readjusted after having sat for so long, and as several German plain-clothes guards closed around him, the procession with him at its heart began to move forward.

Had we truly made it safely through the night, or was the crisis to come now, I wondered, as a burning sense of anticipation pummeled at me.

I looked over at Holmes, whose eyes had lost their pretense of aged softness, and now radiated a hard intensity, as at his full height he himself moved toward the Kaiser and his entourage, weaving in and out of those around him, necessity taking precedence over politeness.

This, I sensed, was some supreme moment of importance, the time of maximum danger, and a tremble passed through me as I thought the whole future of Europe might swing on these next few moments!

It was at a maddeningly slow pace that the little group pushed through the great crowd, striking me as a flaw that no hallways had been kept cleared for the exit of the imperial party, but the Kaiser was all but surrounded by smiling, staring, bowing members of the upper classes, and at far less than even a strolling pace, he progressed through this immense gathering of people, some within merest inches of him, while his guards and retainers were swayed to his right and left, as gaps opened and closed near the royal presence, leaving me to think with a thunderclap of panic:

Why he has no real protection at all!

Through all this Holmes managed to weave across the crowd and keep time with the royal progress, something of a miracle, as for my part I found my efforts to stay with the procession a formidable challenge. Still, a minute passed this way, and then a second, as the slow-moving Kaiser radiated a mixture of sternness and boredom, and his guards sent their eyes back and forth while scanning the crowd no more than an arm's length from the royal person. Logistically and tactically, it was all a nightmare.

And then something happened.

What it was I was not at first certain but I saw a quick flash of movement from Holmes, and was startled to see that no one else seemed to be reacting to this, for the crowd continued to stare with almost awestruck fascination at the Kaiser, who went on walking toward the far side of the room, his back to me now, even as Holmes stayed rooted to one spot, allowing the entourage to move beyond him, no longer trailing it step for step. With difficulty I reached him, even as he began walking back toward the opposite end of the room from where the Kaiser was making his maddeningly slow exit, all eyes but our own still seemingly turned upon him.

And it was to my further surprise to see Holmes was not alone, but held a middle-aged woman by the arm, not overtly or with any oppressive force, but almost formally, as he appeared to be whispering into her ear while guiding her away from the crowd and toward a clearing in the vast chamber. She was clearly unsteady on her feet, and I fear she may have fallen were it not for my friend's clinging doggedly to her.

I saw the woman was certainly English, well-dressed, and her face was confused, as if waking from a dream. For a moment forgetting my other purpose in being there that night, I felt my medical instincts take over, and hurried toward her.

"Come along, Lady Markland-Howard," Holmes was saying in a gentle voice, "I am with you, and all is well. And look, here is my friend, Doctor Watson, a fine physician. Do be at ease."

I saw he was also discreetly but firmly in the process of pulling loose his disguise, and save for the old moth-nibbled uniform, was looking very much like himself again.

"Holmes," I cried softly as I caught up with him, "what is going on? The Kaiser...ought you not to be with him?"

Looking toward me with an expression of triumph and...something else I could not unravel, he guided the lady to a chair at the room's farthest end, then said:

"The Kaiser is in no danger, Watson, or at least no more danger than he ever faces, and the presumed peril which threatened him tonight, the one I was retained to diffuse, is over."

Confused, I gazed about us, and saw the Kaiser was now very nearly out of the hall and heading outside, where his immense and utterly pompous carriage awaited, with its team of black stallions, and its excess of bright gilding, impressing perhaps only himself. As for the lady, she was blinking rapidly from her place on a chair, and only now seemed to re-enter some sense of focus, as she uttered:

"Dear me, sir, had I fainted?"

Holmes said:

"Watson, if you'd be so kind, do fetch Lady Markland-Howard a cup of punch?"

I made my way to the buffet table and did so, then hurried back and handed it to the woman, who took it and sipped eagerly, as if very thirsty.

"In a moment you will feel better, Madam," Holmes told her, as a tiny smile danced at his lips.

"Thank you, sir," the lady told him. "I...find I can remember nothing of the last few moments. Dear me..."

"What is the last thing you recall?" Holmes inquired of her.

"Well...I was looking toward the German Kaiser, and I noted how...."

"Yes?" Holmes pressed.

"I was thinking how the medals above his heart gleamed, one in particular sparkled with a deep red enamel inlay, so very...*pretty*."

Holmes smiled more fully now and said:

"Yes, pretty indeed. Just the thing to catch the eye, was it not?"

"Oh, yes, yes," the lady, still not entirely recovered agree.

"Mildred!" I heard a man call, and turned to see a mustachioed gentlemen of approximately the lady's years rushing over toward us, confusion and worry vying on his face. "I have been looking for you! Have you had another... That is to say, is all well?"

"Lord Bransworth Markland-Howard, I presume," said Holmes, straightening and facing the man with a tone I could not read.

"I am he," said the gentlemen, who did not stop walking but pushed on til he had come to his wife. "Mildred, are you 'well'?" he again demanded.

"Yes," the lady replied, "I... Well I must have grown light-headed, I honestly can't say, for I remember only that I was led here by this gentlemen in the...in the old uniform..."

Holmes' attire puzzled her for an instant and was, once freed from the context of being fitted onto an apparent old soldier of quite eccentric aspect.

"Oh, you had me worried, my dear," said Lord Markland-Howard, who patted his wife's hand and said to Holmes:

"My thanks, sir, for your attendance upon my wife. We became separated as the Imperial procession passed by us, and knowing that she at times suffers from...spells, I became concerned."

"From *spells*, yes," Holmes said, and there was a faint chuckle in this throat, there for merely a second. I saw that some profound understanding was his, but I was still entirely in the dark.

"I...I shall take her home now," said Lord Markland-Howard, flustered himself, and clearly still upset, despite his obvious aura of relief.

"Yes," said Holmes, "well, then I shall leave you to the lady, and bid you both the finest of evenings."

He bowed to the woman and walked away from her and the gentlemen, not stopping til he had reached a corner a number of yards distant, with me hurrying behind after making my own bow to the couple at the heart of this miniscule drama.

"Holmes?" I called, absolutely puzzled, but aware a scene of some mysterious significance had just been enacted before my eyes.

Here my friend bent backward, hands on his hips, and let loose a genuine laugh that lasted a number of seconds, and drew the notice of several others who were standing nearby.

"Oh, my dear Watson," he said to me, "life is truly a farce, so by that humbling acknowledgement let us go home."

"But the Kaiser, and the matter of his safety that brought us here, Holmes. Surely things do not stand resolved?"

"Ah, but they do," the detective stated, and he began to advance rather more easily now out through the thinning crowd, and toward a little-used exit. He had reached perhaps the two-thirds mark of his rather hasty departure, when none other than the figure of Lord Crosby, whom we'd met that morning at White Hall intercepted him.

"Mr. Holmes," the man said, as if in disbelief, "are you going?"

"I am, sir," my friend told him, "for as you see, the Kaiser has left the reception basking in perfect safety. My work tonight, indeed all of our labours, are finished."

Crosby stood puzzled, clearly wishing to say something but just as obviously not knowing what that should be. Finally he quizzed:

"So...there was no attempt on the imperial life tonight?"

"None whatsoever," said Holmes, who throughout this interview had continued to make his way toward the exit, causing Lord Crosby to practically trot to keep up with my friend's notoriously swift stride.

"Then…we have foiled the plot?"

Here Holmes did pause, and with a look of amusement in his eye said:

"The clandestine action which would have been taken against the Kaiser was foiled, yes."

"How?" Crosby demanded. "Where is the assailant? I must know more!"

"Lord Crosby, I invite you to call on me at Baker Street, as this is only a fitting courtesy, seeing that on our last encounter I came in reply to your own summons. If you care to visit my lodgings at some point this week, tomorrow, alas, being out of the question, as I am previously engaged—"

Crosby's mouth fell open in dismay.

"—I will detail you on the relevant facts concerning this most remarkable little adventure."

At those words, Holmes took to his heel and strode rapidly away, leaving Crosby standing gaping and ruffled to stare after my friend, with me hurrying onward to catch up with him.

The night air outside struck me like a refreshing country breeze in comparison to the crowded surroundings inside, and Holmes was already waving down a cab when I reached him. He hopped up into the conveyance, as did I, and within half a minute of departing from the gala reception, we were already on our way back to Baker Street.

"Holmes," I cried, able to stand the suspense of ignorance no longer, "*what* has gone on tonight?"

"Oh, Watson, my dear simple fellow," he said as he lit his pipe and seemed amused to the core of his being, "what is life but, as the bard claimed, a comedy of errors?"

"Errors? A comedy? But the assassin tonight set us all on the brink of war!"

For the second time in a quarter-hour he brayed with laughter that went on for many seconds til it reached its end.

"There *was* no assassin, Watson, and never was any state

of elevated danger to the Kaiser in his time here, despite all this sound and fury from two very concerned governments, with my own haughty sentiments tossed into the mix. I did learn something tonight, Watson, ah, indeed I did."

"I do not understand, "I said, "the intrusions of this individual onto the Kaiser's person, the snatching of his personal effects...."

Holmes laughed harder still, giving me a rare display of the mirth that I suppose did lie somewhere inside his typically serious exterior. I had never seen him so giddy.

"Dear me, Watson, can't you guess? We have had it wrong from the start. Though there was a dazzling skill in all this that still leaves me mystified as to how it could ever have been acquired by its practitioner, a skill incidentally which to you alone I will admit exceeds even my own in the art of the pick-pocket, the demonstrations of audacious expertise which have occurred over the last two nights contained no malicious intent, but were rather a manifestation of a psychological illness dubbed *kleptomania*."

"Kleptomania?" I burst out. "I have heard of that. It is—"

"An irresistible urge to steal that which belongs to another party, particularly if the object is shiny and bright, in which case the compulsion to acquire this item can become no less than overwhelming."

"'It sparkled'" I suddenly recalled Lady Markland-Howard telling Holmes, and my mouth descended in shock.

"It was the lady, Holmes?" I demanded.

"The lady, Watson," my friend agreed pleasantly, "no criminal mastermind from the continent stalking royalty with malign intent, but rather a minor noblewoman caught up in *ennui*, who has somehow, probably subconsciously, mastered the fine art of stealing without detection. It was she who, following a similar reception line on each of the past two nights, saw some irresistibly 'shiny' object on the Kaiser's person and displaying a talent somehow acquired amid her years spent in quiet comfort on a country estate, discreetly helped herself to the Kaiser's effects, as she intended to do tonight while lost in her stuporous attraction. I spied her actions, and intervened, recognizing the affliction for what it was. Thus I took her arm as you saw and gently led her away from the path of danger. She was, I assure you, quite helplessly lost to her compulsion and well beyond any morality, or even the guidance of her own nature."

"It is remarkable," I said, awed.

"And really rather amusing at that, as so much energy and excitement have been expended all over one noblewoman's irresistible habit of taking things which fascinate a hidden portion of her inactive mind."

It was all almost beyond belief, so much worry for such a peculiar and ultimately non-threatening series of unintentional crimes.

"Will you truly reveal this to Lord Crosby, and betray the woman?" I asked.

"When Lord Crosby comes to Baker Street, hat in hand, I shall tell him all he needs to know, sparing only those details which would prove an embarrassment to Lady Markland-Howard and her husband. Furthermore, intend to reach out privately to Lord Markland-Howard, through you, Watson, and inform him that the lady's condition and actions are known, and the items she has purloined must be returned to the Kaiser through certain discreet channels which I shall myself provide."

"I shall be the one to approach Lord Markland-Howard?"

"I can think of no one better, Watson, for your bedside manner is as gentle and firm as any doctor could wish for, while my own nature has, you are aware, at times been dubbed 'cold.' I think you will find the mission a simple one, as Lord Markland-Howard was, I noted, fully aware of his wife's 'spells' and the implications of them, and I think he has made a practice, being an honest man, of returning the stolen objects whenever possible, though I am not certain he is as yet aware of what his wife has done in accomplishing the near impossible by pickpocketing an emperor."

"Dear me," I said. "Yes, I shall go tomorrow, if that is well with you, and do what I can. Hopefully the lady can receive some manner of treatment, for I have read of the emerging field of psychiatry and the good that is being done in addressing various disorders of the mind."

"You do so, my dear Watson, with my fullest trust."

And so I went the following day, meeting with that shamefaced and compliant gentleman, who was quite grateful for my suggestions regarding the lady's future treatment, and who agreed at once to allow me to take the Kaiser's stolen effects back with me so that Holmes could see them properly returned to that great glowering potentate who so unnerved most of Europe.

Soon after Holmes had his meeting with Lord Crosby, who was grateful to him not only for his identification of the facts regarding the Case of the Kaiser's Assassin, but in his having during his brief time at White Hall, pointed out the traitor Bryant, who duly confessed to his rôle in providing sensitive intelligence to the Germans in return for financial remuneration, and was shortly to face a battery of charges in the Old Bailey.

"This Bryant's downfall came because he wed a much-younger wife with expensive tastes," Holmes told me. "A perilous combination."

"So he fell into the Germans' pockets out of desperation and greed?" I noted. "Not from any real loyalty to their cause?"

"Indeed," said Sherlock Holmes.

He and I had one last dinner together at Baker Street, and then on the morrow I went home again to greet my wife upon her return from her holiday amid the moors and coves of Cornwall, Mary looking quite sun-kissed and revitalized by her time outside the fogs of London, and however much I may have relished my visit to Baker Street, my once—and future—home, and the adventures those sojourns always brought, I found there was a deeper peace in being back in my domestic life, the evening paper in my hand, a low blaze in the fireplace before us, and my dearest Mary beside me, filling me in on all which had transpired in her time away, as she knitted me a scarf in preparation for my professional calls on the windy winter streets in months that yet lay ahead.

It is a scarf I still wear, and greatly treasure.

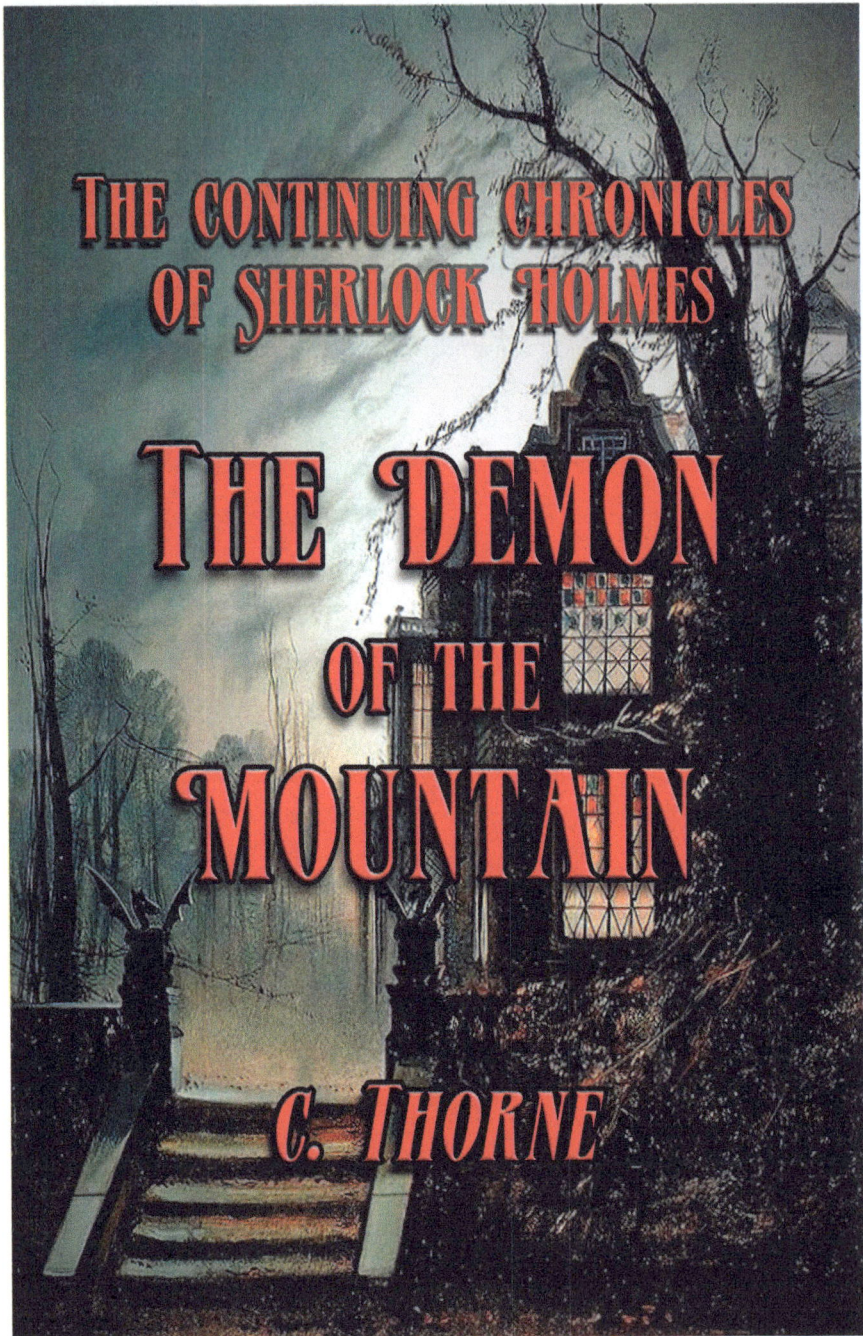

THE DEMON OF
THE MOUNTAIN

*N*ote: *As I complete my penning of this narrative on this blustery night, I grow conscious of the fact that it should likely be placed into that particular file I keep elsewhere, which contains accounts of cases that it is probably best no one read during the lifetimes of those who participated in them. In most instances when I have consigned these various adventures to that solitary archive, it has been because they concern personages of public renown, even royalty, but here the matter is different, for I make this determination based strictly upon the actions of Sherlock Holmes within this now long-ago mystery.*

I think once a reader, whenever this person may live, reaches the end of this story, there will be little question as to why I hold this view, or to what I am referring. As for what the decision Sherlock Holmes made at the resolution of "The

Demon of the Mountain" says of him and his innermost sense of what constitutes justice, well, I shall only say that I struggled for no small time to resolve my sentiments before coming to the realization that Holmes is unlike other men in either his abilities, or his outlook. I never heard him waver regarding his decision that fateful night, for I never again heard him refer to the matter in any capacity. But then he has always been a man who lives almost entirely in the present moment, and his life has always been a busy one.

Thus for now I think it best this tale remains unpublished, and leave it for readers in an age yet unborn, with the ardent hope that their judgment upon my dearest friend be a not entirely unfavourable one.

—Dr. John H. Watson
Harley Street, London
11 April 1895

******

It was particularly warm that September afternoon, and the breeze was stirring nicely in the leaves of every tree, leaving me to think, *ah, this is loveliness itself*. I had finished my cases a little early and affected my return to Baker Street, looking forward to a relaxing dinner and perhaps a stroll through Regent's Park to enjoy this clement stretch of weather, when I emerged upstairs into the parlour of the lodgings I shared with my friend Mr. Sherlock Holmes, only to hear him call:

"Ah, Watson! I am glad you have arrived as early as you did, for I am about to host a client."

"Oh, yes?" I inquired, if not greatly interested, then certainly not entirely devoid of curiosity.

"Yes," Holmes said, "a gentleman whom I believe is known to you, one Captain Douglas Morrison, retired from Her Majesty's 66th Berkshires?"

"Captain Morrison, of my own old regiment, is coming

here to Baker Street?" I exclaimed, as my attention focused on this unexpected news. Though I was pleased by Holmes' announcement, I was also more than a little taken aback.

"He is, in fact, due at any moment," my friend confirmed.

"Oh, my," I stated as I laid my medical bag down onto a chair. "I have not set eyes on that most admirable man since that infamous day on which he... Well I had heard of his return from the dead, as it were, having been declared missing and presumed lost during the Afghan campaign over four years ago. His story is little short of a miracle."

"Is that so?" asked Holmes, displaying interest. "I have heard the merest note of a tale of great heroism associated with one of that name, but as the matter did not concern a crime, the details fell largely outside of my focus."

Yes, I knew how he was in that respect, for while the grandest news story of the day could pass outside his notice, the merest petty crime on the other side of the city would soon become most intimately known to him down to its smallest detail. I was just about to share with him the remarkable facts of Captain Morrison's case history, when Holmes stopped me by suddenly calling:

"Nevermind, Watson, perhaps I may hear this story from the man himself, as I perceive he has just arrived."

It was true, for the noise of a departing hansom filled the air outside, and was soon succeeded by a polite rap at the door, followed by the sound of Mrs. Hudson greeting the visitor, whom she preceded to lead up the stairs and present before us in the flesh.

My first glimpse of the man was not what I had expected, and I felt my hands clench as I fortified myself against showing the reaction I felt within, for though as a former army surgeon I had long trained myself to mute my response to shocking sights of a medical nature, I admit that seeing my once-handsome comrade in arms, whom I'd known for a year during the campaign, looking as he did after his captivity among the enemy, did send a wave of shock rolling through me like thunder, for he was much changed, and not merely externally, but even down to the haunted gaze that came from his world-weary eyes. Where once had been the jaunty pride of a career officer from a privileged family, I now beheld a much thinner man, who leaned upon a tightly-clutched cane. I would have taken his age to be a decade beyond where I knew it to be, for he was my own contemporary. All of this bespoke only too clearly of the hardships he had endured in the hands of his captives in the lawless frontier of Afghanistan, and I cursed the brutality of those who had doled-out the afflictions this fine man had endured for the sake of his country.

Yet with the greatest of effort I stayed any betraying trace of this in my mannerisms or words, and stepped forward to greet this hero, who had known pains no man should be called upon to experience, even in the hazardous performance of a soldier's duties.

"Morrison!" I cried heartily, as I stepped forward and extended my hand.

He took it, and smiled wanly before replying:

"Regimental Surgeon Watson, my excellent fellow, good it is to see you once more, back in our homeland."

"And you, my most courageous friend," I replied.

Half-turning to where the continent's most celebrated detective stood, I said:

"Captain Morrison, may I present my esteemed friend and colleague, Mr. Sherlock Holmes, upon whom I am given to understand you have come to call."

Holmes stepped forward with an almost feline gracefulness and a certain humility rare to him, for something he had seen in Morrison had clearly had a profound effect upon his outlook, and I noted his mien was markedly different than it had been but a moment before. Showing great deference to the client, Holmes even deigned to hold out his own hand, a practice I knew he particularly disliked.

"Captain Morrison," he intoned gravely as he shook the soldier's hand, "it is a privilege to make your acquaintance, and I do thank you for calling upon me here at Baker Street. Whatever it is that brings you, sir, you may trust I shall do my utmost on your behalf. Now please, do have a seat and make yourself comfortable. Will you have a cigar?"

"I thank you, Mr. Holmes," Morrison replied, reaching into the box of finest Havanas Holmes held out to him.

I showed him to a chair and offered him refreshment in the form of tea, which the Captain took with neither milk nor sugar, then assumed my own place across from him.

There was always, I had long noted, a certain sense of inadequacy when one's own military service was measured against that of a person such as Captain Douglas Morrison, and I found I could only be washed-over with shame that I had ever for the slightest moment believed I deserved to feel any measure of pride in my own achievements while in uniform, when beside one such as this man, my own record was but a trifling thing. Yet I knew I would not have traded places with him and endured all that he had been through in the "Hell-lands" of Afghanistan.

"Captain Morrison," Holmes began at last, "I perceive you are thoroughly troubled by some recent and dare I say grave matter. I see from the weariness of your eyes that it has cost you sleep in recent nights, and that your fears are not confined to yourself alone, but to another person whom I note you not only esteem and value, but...love. I also note that you are a man who dwells with physical pain as his ever-present companion, and I have no doubt Dr. Watson has medicaments that might alleviate some of your discomfort while you are here."

Holmes' eyes turned to me, and I said:

"Yes, should you wish to avail yourself of them, I can provide you with tablets that may give some relief..."

"No," said Morrison, "though I thank you both. I have grown accustomed to my pains, and regard them as a badge, for they were incurred via the service I owed my Queen and country. I wish to keep a clear head, also, as I tell you of the state of my life in these most disturbing, recent days."

Holmes nodded, his concentration absolute, and for my part I withdrew my notebook and removed the pencil from inside, ready to take the notes that constitute the majority of those cases I have recorded over the years.

"May I say straight off that you were correct in all you said, Mr. Holmes," Morrison began, "my nights of late have been sleepless, though in light of events it is ironic, as you shall soon hear, that last night I slept better than I have for several days."

He paused and shook his head as if clearing away a great quantity of clashing thoughts, and announced:

"I suppose I should start some four years in the past, in the Bandar Valley, of the Makawa Mountains, within that frightful devil's parlour that is Afghanistan."

He swallowed and added:

"The worst nation in the entire world."

"Well described," I said, thinking back to the horrors I lived through in that forsaken and ever-quarrelsome land, and of the scar I still carried from the Jezail bullet that had wounded me there.

"As you will recall, Dr. Watson, we were hard-pressed that summer by resistance from the Ghazi irregulars, as well as the feudal tribesmen from the hills," Morrison said, "those ambush fighters of the ever-changing warlords who align with no one, and had taken many losses."

"Yes," I said, remembering the long hours, day and night, seeing to the wounded in my surgeons' tent amid swarms of flies and the hot, choking wind of the south-Asian plains.

"Yet," Morrison continued, "for about a fortnight we had enjoyed some success, and had overrun the encampment of a fierce tribal leader there, one Halim Abdul-Ali, and succeeded in killing the man, bloodied sword in his hand, and scattering his minions, terrible fiends one and all. This was an achievement of such triumph that Colonel Parsons, whom you recall was commanding the regiment at that time, gathered we officers into his tent the following morning, and unrolled his maps of the terrain, and said he was encouraged by the reports from our native-born scouts, before he declared that the precise location of the remainder of this Halim's men was known to us, and that by circling through the mountains, we might come upon them from behind, and destroy the lot once and for all, thus bringing peace to the area for many miles around.

"'Gentlemen,' said the Colonel, and I can still hear his great deep Yorkshire voice ringing out in that broiling-hot tent, 'this is an opportunity the likes of which has not thus far come along in this campaign. It is our chance to see the entire region for twenty miles in any direction pacified and brought into our hands.'"

I reflected that I knew of this meeting, though I had not attended it, and remembered the excitement that was in the air that day, for despite having a hard march ahead, followed by a battle in which it was expected the foe would fight to the last with all the ferocity of cornered rats, the knowledge that months of campaigning might lead in this way to victory was fortifying to the men's war-weary hearts.

"Still, there were objections," Morrison recounted, "particularly from some of the Afghans who marched with us, both as regulars in a native company, and the scouts who served us for pay. Generally honourable men, those, they seemed aghast with horror at the Colonel's idea of taking to the rugged mountains as he planned, and one and all and as a man they decried the strategy, telling us Halim's bandits had chosen the foothills there for the very reason that they were so remote and dangerous. But there was also more. 'The Demon of the Mountain dwells there' these men said, their eyes wide with fear."

I had not heard that name in nearly half a decade, and frowned in remembrance at how it could send even the bravest among our native scouts trembling with fright.

"'What of this *demon of the mountain*?' the Colonel

demanded with a scoff. 'What of such talk?'

"The Colonel stared down every officer before him and called them out by name, asking, 'Barton-Baker, do you fear this Demon? How about you Russell? Or you, Martin, or you Pryce-Kearns?' Under the Colonel's harsh gaze, one and all the men fell ashamed of their own reticence, and vowed their readiness to go into the places the Colonel had marked out on his map, leaving only the native Afghan scouts to tremble at the idea of venturing into this notorious wilderness, where even Halim Abdul-Ali had feared to tread."

"What was it concerning this legend that so frightened them, Captain?" Holmes asked.

"The worry," Morrison answered, "was not so much of the Demon, as of his vicious minions who dwelled beyond even the measure of whatever civilizing effects the long-ago coming of Mohammedanism has given to the Afghans, leaving the Demon's followers much feared as fighters."

"I see," said Holmes, "but, again, if I may bid you so, do tell me of this alleged 'Demon'."

And so Morrison told him of how a terrible spirit was said to reside somewhere among the lonely crests of the Makawa Mountains, a demigod claimed to be old when the world was newly-formed, a demon never dispelled by the coming of Islam to Afghanistan a millennia ago, and this entity's booming voice was heard amid the thunder of the peaks, and was worshipped by a tribe so primitive they were seldom seen, but greatly feared for all their invisibility, emerging only on occasion to strike by night, killing men, stealing away women and livestock, and leaving behind terrible mutilations among those who had crossed their path, living and dead alike. They were said to speak a language known only to themselves, a tongue older than Babel, and to hold no fear of any sort, for their devotion to their terrible lord, whom they worshipped at a great mountaintop shrine, was absolute.

Morrison's revelation left the room silent for a moment,

before Holmes inquired:

"And did the sense of resolution the Colonel imparted to his officers last?"

"No," Morrison admitted. "There in the commander's great sprawling pavilion, under the Colonel's taunting ridicule of the notion that British officers of the modern age could ever be daunted by a folk-legend among a backward people, some of us had even begun to laugh, but later, seeing the stark terror on the faces of our Afghan troops, whom we knew to be brave men, most of us were left wary once again. We had all listened to our scouts' stories around campfires, telling of the savage followers of the terrible Demon up on his mountaintop, and I confess looking on the expressions of undisguised dread on those dark faces, some of our resolution did fade. Upon seeing this, the Colonel grew angry, and told us to make ready for the march, which we did, however mindful we were that a difficult journey and a tough fight was coming. However...we had but slim conception of the horror that awaited us mere hours ahead."

While Morrison paused and his eyes hinted at the reflections within his mind, I drew a deep breath and waited, knowing something of what was coming in the narrative, though whether Holmes had any intonation I could not say.

Finally Morrison continued:

"We set off at a steady march and made good time, though somehow the farther we went into the mountains, up into those parts where no trails existed, the more we all became infected with gloom, and the more tense we felt by the hour. We were to strike at an enemy via a region he dared not travel through, and more than one of us had begun to contemplate *why* it was these otherwise fearless raiders of the late Halim Abdul-Ali shunned this ground. Why were the disciples of the Demon of the Mountain so feared that even Afghan raiders avoided them? I could see the farther we trekked, the more stark and sere and unwholesome became the land around us, and with a jolt I realized at one point that no birds sang there, nor was there even the flitting of the tiny swift lizards one saw everywhere in Afghanistan. They, too, it seemed, shunned this place, which was as soundless and desolate as Gehenna itself."

I nodded, tension filling me. As surgeon I had been required back in camp that fateful day, seeing to the many men who'd been wounded in our recent skirmishes with Halim Abdul-Ali's soldiers, but only this need had kept me from the horror that my comrades of the 66th would soon know.

And instant later, Morrison said:

"It was when we came to a deep ravine that we halted, and talk went up and down the lines, for we wondered if the Colonel should choose to march around the ravine, adding miles to our trek, or go directly through it in search of the opposite side, where it surely emptied out into some valley beyond. I do believe every man's instincts were shouting at him that it was unwise for us to step within this dark ravine, for the walls were steep, and the narrow passage was layered in shadows, even in the withering heat of daylight. When word came down that we were indeed to plunge within and shorten our journey, my own spirits plummeted, for I tell you, a soldier's mind is sharpened by facing death so regularly, and my own sense was that this ravine was a place of not merely peril, but..."

He halted and with a trace of apology at the word he would choose, said:

"*Evil.*"

"Evil," I repeated, and I did not mock him, but rather felt a definite quickening of my heartbeat.

"The senses are often to be trusted," Holmes remarked, nodding. "Kindly tell me more."

"It was the most profound sensation I had ever felt," Morrison admitted, "of being in the presence of a place that lacked all goodness, all mercy, all kindness, or which even knew of such things, even as ideas, and rude concepts. It was as if we hovered before the very mouth of Hades itself."

Holmes showed no reaction whatsoever, but listened with a honed keenness before he prodded very gently:

"But you did enter this place?"

His face locked in remembrance of what must surely have been the worst moment of his life to that point, Morrison said:

"We were mid-way through this dim ravine, able to proceed only in single-file, barely room enough to advance at all, barely enough space for us to breathe, when the attack came from above, and broke loose with a fury such as I cannot begin to describe."

And so we come to it, I thought, *the bloody ambush that had been the talk in camp for weeks after, and which had cost Colonel Parsons his career.*

"From all sides they fired on us, and not merely with the screeching hail of bullets, but also the downward plunge of thrown boulders, and even the firing of flint arrows, each tipped in poison, as we'd soon learn as men fell and turned red in the face as they writhed and screamed in their death-cries that they were burning from flames within them. The merest scratch from those arrows meant a death too terrible to further describe, and many were there who died in that tormenting fashion."

"Terrible," I commented, and truly meant the word. I then decided to spare him further talk of this battle, in which one-fifth of the regiment was lost in a few minutes time, so thus instead prodded him to advance in his narrative.

"And yet you, Captain," I reminded him, "I know of your conduct. Yours was among the bravest acts I have ever heard reported in the annals of the British army."

Morrison seemed to be rendered to an awkward state by my remark, for like all true heroes, he was modest before his own achievements, and said meekly:

"I thank you, sir, but I did no more than my duty."

You did far more than that, I reflected.

He then said:

"We took our stand for many minutes, even as so many of us went down under the fire of these unseen assailants, their bodies blocking our path, and I knew we were all to die there, every officer and man of us, to become a cautionary tale whispered in infamy, and I saw, the Colonel meant to let us do just that, preferring we fall with 'the bravery of Englishmen' rather than retreat, and something in me rebelled against the idea of being killed where I stood like a lamb in the abattoir, and so..."

He appeared about to hurry past his own act of courage, so I supplied it for him.

"*And so*, Captain Morrison, you inspired every man of the regiment who was there to see it, when you pulled out your sabre and charged alone up that ravine, clawing and lifting yourself upward in the face of withering fire, arrows falling against the rocks around you, none seeming to touch you, and you charged on even as a bullet struck the blade in your hand, and sent the sword flying from it, and to the awe of every onlooker, you surged up that steepest of hillsides into what looked to be certain death."

Uneasy at my description but unable to honestly deny it, Morrison confirmed:

"That was my action that day, yes."

"You are an admirable fellow," commented Holmes, "and though it may be inadequate, you have my thanks for your courageous service to the empire."

The rest Morrison told quickly, how he somehow reached the crest of the ravine alive, though his hands and knees were much torn by the sharpness of the stones, and there he saw all around him a hundred or more swarthy and squat men of a sort he had never glimpsed in all his life, looking in some ways more animal than human, their faces misshapen and their brows thick and broad, their arms long and strong, their chests broad as barrels, even as their legs were bandied and bowed and their postures stooped, and he and these creatures stared for a moment at one another, before several of them ran howling in flight from him, clearly fear-stricken, though they outnumbered him. This fired Morrison's resolve, and, still believing himself to be in his final moments of life, he charged after them, firing his service revolver and killing six of them in one long burst in which each well-placed shot found its mark.

There, even in the heat of battle, he was left awed not only by his own achievement, but by the fact the tribesmen there—if men they entirely were and not some proto-beasts lost to primordial history—were not striking him down, but either fleeing him or staring aghast in awe as they surrounded him in a vast pulsating circle of suntanned flesh and clothing made of hides and furs.

It was then that many of them began to chant a name:

"'*Arun-Kor*'," Morrison repeated it. "They called me '*Arun-Kor*', and some fell down before me with their warped and elongated faces in the dirt, as if worshiping me, even as about ten of them ran forward, eyes bright with emotions, and I thought then, out of bullets as I was, that my life was about to end, and how I wished I'd kept hold of my saber! They say when you are about to die, your thoughts flash back across the life you've lived, and to my surprise my thoughts went not to the higher call of duty or reached outward in that final second toward God Almighty, but to the little Dorset school yard of my youngest days, and it comforted me to think that though I would be dying there in the dust of that hideous place, the nation which surrounded that school would go on, and in some tiny way my death would serve it."

For a moment I think emotion nearly overwhelmed the Captain, but with an herculean effort, he mastered himself and regained the dispassionate calm with which he'd told his account.

"But obviously you did not fall," said Holmes when the Captain did not speak after a moment.

"No," Morrison agreed, "I did not, did I? Rather I was wrestled down by a dozen hands and carried off by at least as many, and I understood with dread that my fate was not to be a clean death in battle, but doubtless some terrible and prolonged torture, and I struggled with all my might to be free so that I could die resisting them, but they held me all the same, being terribly strong for their size, which was but a little greater than most of our women at home. I knew nothing of the regiment in the ravine, but somehow I noted the firing behind me, down below, had stopped, and I wondered if by my action perhaps my comrades in arms had been saved and were even undertaking the purposeful retreat which would save their lives. That would be something, after all, and a man might die with some peace knowing he had served others in this way."

"Which was exactly what did happen," I said, having heard of the matter a score of times in my surgeon's tent back at camp. "Somehow the bravery of your charge, Captain Morrison, which every Englishman who saw it took to have resulted in your death, seemed to frighten off the natives on the hill above, and spared all the officers and men of the 66th who were in the ravine a cruel fate."

Morrison nodded. "These four years I have always been so very glad."

I told him:

"The Colonel sent back scouts before nightfall to seek you, alive or dead, but you were not to be found, and the tracks of your captors seemed to vanish higher in the mountains, among apparently un-scalable heights, so that to the regret of all concerned, you were presumed killed and your body desecrated, unable to be brought back for decent Christian burial. A thousand toasts were drunk to you that night."

"At times in the days that followed," said Morrison, "I ardently wished I *had* been killed there, for though I was not tortured to death, as I thought I would be, mine was a strange hybrid state of captive and....well, gentlemen, forgive the term, but *living idol* to these people. They put me in a cage and cried out '*Arun-Kor! Arun-Kor!*' and I tell you there was worship in that word, as they brought me trinkets and offered me what I felt certain was the best of their foodstuffs, and even tried to set some of their women before me, and hideous and squat and ugly they were, worse than the men to see. And one and all they seemed to fall prostrate before me and sing chanted prayers *to* me, and yet I dwelled in a cage for two years there among them, tormented by the winds, the rains, and the snowfalls of winter, cold and wishing for death at times, though determined above all to one day escape and know freedom and England once more."

"Which to your credit, you have," Holmes stated, as he crushed his dying cigar in the ash-tray.

"What accounted for their strange behavior toward you?" I demanded. "Why were you kept alive in such a state?"

"I, too, wondered that many a time," said Morrison, "but it seemed the answer lay in the fact that there was a myth among their people concerning a hero who would come from the low country outside their mountainous homeland, whose courage would grant him immunity to the strike of a foe, and it would be a blessing to their own warriors to keep this great hero among them."

"Great Heavens," I breathed, "they thought you were a character from their legends?"

"Yes," said Morrison. "Yet still more terrible was their one god, the Demon of the Mountain, of whom we'd heard the campfire tales whispered by our native scouts. They worshipped this entity with all the frenzy which the heathen heart was capable, some, in their old age, even severing their own left hands—for all the men seemed to be left-handed, though I know not why—and laying them before the towering image of the idol as a sacrifice in flesh."

I winced at the idea.

"Each month, when the moon was at its darkest," said Morrison, "I would be taken from my cage and led up before the statue of this dreadful deity, and shoved to my knees before it, as if they were showing me to the idol, and at first I assumed I was to be given unto it as a sacrifice, yet clearly I was not."

"Can you describe this thing to us?" asked Holmes.

"The idol was immense," Morrison testified, "twenty feet or more, carved from stone, and inlaid with precious gems of an uncut dullness for all their size and doubtless value in the markets of the civilized world. Its skin was of an ivory tone, not at all dusky as was their own, and its features were of a man, yet...inhuman, twisted and cruel, its teeth pointed and curving, its eyes.... Oh, gentlemen, I do even here in the heart of London tremble to think on those eyes, which seemed to follow one even though I saw they were unmoving, and merely composed of some glittering black stone. One of its legs was bent at the knee, as if it were about to kick outward with great force, and in its vast hand...were a number of human skulls, actual relics of lives that once were."

There Captain Morrison shook himself, as if dispelling the hold of an abiding horror.

"They possessed such a statue, primitive as they were?" I demanded.

"Oh, yes, Dr. Watson," Captain Morrison told me, "which was one of the mysteries of that strange mountaintop world they inhabited, and long did I reflect on this during the months in which I endured my captivity, which led me to conclude that the idol was a thing of unimaginable antiquity, predating the time of the mountain tribe, crafted long before this age by some advanced culture which once dwelled in that land before recorded history."

I pondered the notion, and found it a confusing one, for all that I knew there was evidence to suggest the reality of such proto-scientific theories.

"The past," said Sherlock Holmes, "is a place of many shadows, and I think it probable entire epochs passed and were lost, now unknown to us, just as others may one day appear in our wake, once our era has ended."

"So I have come to think as well," Morrison agreed. "And thus in this cruel manner was I kept caged and alternately honoured and tormented those nearly two years. Some days children poked me with sticks as I lay in my shallow sleep, yet other days those same children knelt before me, crying out praise, their coal-black eyes filled with frank adoration. And there is more, for....difficult as this is to confess, and doubtless mad it may sound....at times in my cage, it was as if I could hear the guttural and frightful voice of the Demon as it reverberated in the air around us, speaking in its most ancient of languages, and I know I was not alone in hearing this, for when this sound came, the tribesmen there would universally fall prostrate to the ground, and tremble."

"You heard this?" I asked.

"I did," Morrison said. "By my honour, I did. A thousand times I have been seated in church in my boyhood in Dorset, and listened for the voice of God, yet heard nothing, but there on that mountainside amid savages and their demon...I heard words issuing from the chasm of some terrible *beyond*."

Silence had its instant as this startling admission was weighed in our minds. Finally Holmes inquired:

"And now tell me, sir, how did you affect your escape from the savages who held you captive?"

"Through a miracle," Morrison answered primly, "for so shall I always dub it. The leader of the village suddenly died one night, choking and clawing at the ground around him as he faded, and there came a quarrel between two strong men in the population, one called Orhok, the other Krim, and factions arose so that two great forces assembled, and began to clash with one another amid animal-like cries and frenzied battles, sometimes fighting with stone-edged clubs and obsidian blades, at other times with tooth and claw alone, and it was in the midst of one such contest that I used a shard of flint I had managed to acquire when I was dragged before the idol, and thus concealed it for months, awaiting my chance to either escape with it, or end my life entirely."

The admission, though understandable, seemed to me an especially sad one.

"I took the opportunity while the fiends were occupied in their warfare to cut through the ropes which bound my wooden cage, and slipped away, and though I was weak, I ran as swiftly as my legs would bear, down the mountain, dropping over precipices when no trail was at-hand, and through the night I hurried forward, though my atrophied bodied pained me, and I had little strength, and into the next day I still pushed on, ignoring the agony my journey cast upon me, certain I would hear them behind me at any moment, showing no mercy this time, until at last I came to a swift-flowing river, boiling with foaming waves crashing against the jutting rocks. I remembered this river from when I was carried up the mountain some two years previous, and being unable to walk another step, into its frigid waters I plunged without hesitation, though I knew the dangers of it, and let the current carry me on, aware it would lead downward toward some populated place in the low country under the mountains, though whether I would find friend or foe there I knew not."

"And as it happened luck was with you in that respect?" I asked him.

"Oh, yes, a lesser miracle, for I was washed breathless and half-dead from exhaustion against a bank where a little hamlet of clay-sided houses stood at the foothills of the mountain, and there I was seen by some women who were out washing clothing, and they called to the men, who pulled me from the river and laid me against the sun-warmed stones, and fed me hot broth and unleavened flat bread, for hospitality is a grave law in those parts, and as God willed it, I had come to one of the villages that was allied with us, and a runner was sent to inform the British outpost a league off that one of their own had been found alive."

Morrison smiled for the first and only time in the entirety of his visit to Baker Street.

"Before day's end a squadron of cavalry in bright red uniforms came riding out to the place, the Union Jack at their head, and never was I so relieved to see my countrymen as I was then, I can tell you, though I was scarcely recognizable as a civilized man, for my hair and beard were long, and even after my time of being washed by the waters, I was filthy from my two years in that nightmarish cage. But through my bruised lips I called out my name and rank and noted the regiment I served in, and in the most incredible moment imaginable, the men dismounted and saluted me, for even in my state I was still an officer in Her Majesty's army, after all, and the absolutely wonderful unreality of that instant made me laugh almost with madness as they lifted me up and carried me to a litter, and pressed a canteen to my mouth.

"'Welcome home, Captain,' a lance corporal with a thick Ulster accent, said to me.

"And thus was I taken back to the encampment, where I recovered under the ministrations of a camp surgeon, called Major Prescott Weymoth, and in due time was discharged from my regiment, and sent home, where I have been these two years, gradually recovering my health and strength, and trying rather vainly to regain some semblance of the man I once was, long ago."

Amidst the strong emotion his story had sent rising in me, I said to him:

"Captain Morrison, you, sir, are much more than the man you were, for by your action in charging up the ravine that day and saving your comrades in the regiment, and by what you have endured, and by the tremendous vigour demonstrated by your escape from bondage, you are in fact probably the most profound hero of which I have ever heard."

I rose and grasped his hand and vigorously shook it, overcome with admiration, and even Holmes, who seldom admitted that anyone was his superior, stared at the man with an expression of deepest respect.

"Captain Morrison," he said at last, "your account is the most remarkable ever imparted to me, and it is I who would be honoured to be of service in some way, great or small, to a man whose devotion to our nation has risen far above any demands of mere duty. You have but to name how it is that I may help you, sir, and with all that lies within me, I shall!"

It was a rare display of emotion from my friend, and I inwardly marveled that even he was touched by what the scarred and weather-beaten man before us had endured, and achieved.

"I thank you," Captain Morrison said, "and by your leave I will now tell why it is I have come."

"Please," said Holmes, with an open-handed gesture.

"To put it simply, Mr. Holmes, Dr. Watson, the tribesmen who worshipped the Demon of the Mountain have somehow followed me here...and found me."

"What?" I cried. "Surely that is— But by your description they are the merest primitives!"

"I know," Morrison confessed, "and yet circumstances show this to be the ghastly truth."

"You make this claim because you have seen the tribesmen here in England, with your own eyes?" Holmes asked, leaning forward in his chair, his tone undefinable.

"I admit I have not," said the Captain, "and yet the evidence all but bellows that this is the case, and that they threaten not only my life, but the life of the woman I have come to love, and to whom I shall be married next spring. Miss Martha Cooper, she is called, and she is the kindest creature in the world, who loves me despite my disfigurements, and the ways my many traumas have diminished me from what once I was. I could endure their coming for me, Mr. Holmes, and my sanity might even survive hearing once more their horrid cries of 'Arun-Kor! Arun-Kor!' but I cannot bear to think of them harming her because of me, not that innocent girl who has never wronged anyone in her life!"

"Be calm, my friend," I said to him in my most soothing manner, "all will be well."

He nodded with his head lowered and finally mastered his emotions, then reached into his pocket and drew out some object, which it took me a moment to recognize as a small length of red-dyed leather with a buckle at the end. A collar for a small dog.

"This belonged to Martha's poor little terrier, King Rufus, she dubbed him, as inoffensive and friendly a beast as dwelled anywhere in England. He'd stand on his hind legs for her and take treats gently from her fingertips, and yet…she found him, gentlemen, three nights back, twisted and broken as if by strong hands, and left lying on the lawn of her father's house in the village of Sutton, in Surrey."

The news was abhorrent, and I stared at the collar and thought of the agonizes its one-time occupant must have borne, the poor creature.

Holmes held out a hand and was given the collar, which he stared at for a long moment, turning the thing over in his hands before handing it back without comment to Morrison.

"There is more…so much more," said Morrison. "There is also this."

From the same pocket he pulled a strange section of rope, about two feet in length with several complex knots tied into it, and bound up in the knot-work were a number of foul-looking items. I intuited that there was clearly some talismanic purpose in this unwholesome artifact.

"It is a murderer's weapon," said Morrison, "used for strangulation. This was left on my own windowsill in the night, and I recognized it at once, for I saw enough of these during my captivity. It is termed a *bakluve*, and it is a ritual cord of strangulation, which the Demon of the Mountain's warriors fashion, braiding into it small objects of superstitious significance, which are said to give it mystical power when it is used to silently kill during their many raids on the villages below the mountains."

"Where they seize livestock and women," I remembered.

He bowed his head and added:

"And even children, which they consume alive."

I fell back in my chair and was aghast to think of the idea of cannibalism upon living children! It was simply the most abhorrent concept I had ever heard.

The cord was given over to Holmes, who held it in his cupped hands and peered at it with the most absolute attention. I saw that in its entirety the weapon consisted of a length of braided twine, each strand flimsy enough in itself, but which was given strength by being drawn together with others of like kind, and tied in among the cords were a number of teeth, and feathers, and other crude things, all ghastly to look at, and doubtless agonizing as a means of killing.

"You say that this was left upon your windowsill?" demanded Holmes. "When did this occur?"

"Last night," Morrison answered, "sometime between when I turned in just after ten, and this morning when I awoke about six, yet I heard nothing."

"I have noted from signs upon your person that you dwell in a house, just outside the city?"

"Yes, in the village of Dwayne, a little north of London."

"There is, I detect from your shoes, a small lawn around this place?"

"Yes," Morrison confirmed. "And I looked for footprints but saw none. It has been so dry lately, you know."

"Infernally so," I agreed.

"Perhaps I may fare better in seeking clues at the site of the occurrence," Holmes remarked. "Tell me of the layout of the house, and of your room."

"It is a cottage, really, for as I am as yet unwed and live alone, I require but a very modest place, quite small. I... I think as a result of my long captivity in so tiny a space I have somehow developed a feeling of being ill-at-ease in a large dwelling-place, though I think this may pass with time. So at present I possess but a sitting room, a meager kitchen, and my one bedroom, scarcely larger than the bed which occupies it."

"It is a single story, then, I presume?" inquired Holmes.

"Yes, and I sleep on the north side."

"So you sleep, then, near the window?"

"Directly beside it," Morrison admitted, "with the bed

against that outer wall."

I saw Captain Morrison was fully aware, as was I and certainly Holmes, of the implications of this layout in light of the fact the assassin's cord had been left on the outer window sill.

"So," the detective stated the sobering truth, "you are left with the knowledge that in placing this hideous object on your windowsill, the enemy was but inches from you, doubtless looking in on you as you lay helpless and sleeping."

"He could have struck me at any time last night," said Morrison. "It makes my heart tremble to think on that."

"Of course it does," I agreed, with sympathy.

"Captain Morrison, may I retain possession of this object?" Holmes asked.

"Please do keep it," Morrison said avidly. "for I wish never to look upon it again."

Holmes turned and placed it on the table to his left, out of his client's sight, and asked:

"Your intended, Miss Martha Cooper, tell me of her current whereabouts."

"She is in her father's house in Surrey, the house where she was born and has never lived anyplace else. It is a large home, with several servants, both her parents are there, and she has three brothers, slightly younger, who are as yet in residence and have not left to take up university, or their careers. I....believe she is safe enough, to whatever extent one can be safe from these savages who have somehow crossed the very planet to seek their revenge."

The idea that such primitives had done the thing he claimed and come so far continued to mystify me.

"One hopes," said Holmes, "the lady is safe enough with so many others in residence with her, yet I think I can go one better and shall have a word with one of my contacts in the police, to see if they may provide a constable to watch over the young lady's house while I bring this troubling case to as swift a conclusion as I am able. By your leave, Captain, I would make the same offer to you, and have a constable sent up to be on-hand, and thereby augment your own protection."

"It is the least that can be done, considering all the nation owes you, Captain Morrison," I added.

The man hesitated, reluctant to accept this offer of protection, but at last he nodded and said:

"Very well. And for the consideration, I do thank you."

Holmes placed his hands together, almost in the mode of one at prayer, and seemed pleased with the man's answer. "It shall be seen to within the hour," he said, then sprang to his feet and scribbled out a hasty note, which without another word he ran downstairs for Mrs. Hudson to send off per his instructions.

Returning back to the parlour by coming up the steps two at a time, such was the level of his energy, he said:

"I would like to visit your residence, Captain Morrison, and examine its grounds and the windowsill in question, if I may. I note that a train is leaving Euston Station in forty-three minutes, and with haste we can all be upon it."

"I welcome your visit," said Morrison, "for I don't doubt that you can learn more there than I was able to with my less-trained eyes."

"The sharp eyes of Mr. Holmes miss nothing," I assured the Captain. "You have placed your trust in the very best hands in all of the British Empire."

*****

As we rode the train the short distance up to the village of Dwayne, and from there walked on to Captain Morrison's house, I found myself recalling every memory I retained of my interactions with him in Afghanistan, before his capture, and though there were not many memories to sift through, I found the sole theme was that I had found him in those days to be something of an arrogant young man, puffed up with a peacock-like sense of self, cocky and jaunty, as infantry officers from a privileged background so often were. I found it difficult to reconcile those memories with the humble individual who now strode beside me, replying in a soft tone to Holmes' inquiries concerning the house and its vicinity. Morrison had paid a heavy price for his transformation, but I saw in him at present not only a hero to be admired, but a man transformed from one in whom casual haughtiness had resided, to a figure who had passed through fires which had melted away all that was base, so that I admired not only the soldier he had been, but the man he was now.

These musings soon fell away as we completed our ten-minute walk, and were shortly at a small stone cottage, which for the past few months the Captain had called home.

"And so we come," he said as we stepped out onto the grass surrounding the house, "to my residence, such as it is."

I recalled what Morrison had said about feeling more placid within a smaller space, and noted this must have been why he chose the dwelling, as more spacious accommodations would have been within his means. It struck something of a note of pity in me to think of a war hero living in so small a domicile, though I tried not to betray these thoughts through gesture or expression, lest they seem to be pity.

Holmes looked around him at the setting, with its numerous trees and bucolic stillness, a place where the houses each sat fifty yards and more apart, and I saw him frown, displeased, before he said:

"Man is a herd animal, and there is always danger in such relative isolation."

"Surely I am safer here than in crowded London," Morrison said.

Holmes replied with a sobering observation:

"On the contrary, sir, for these country villages draw the eye of far too many of a villainous sort, and amid the tranquility of the nighttime, they are able to move with altogether too much ease."

Holmes bid Morrison and I to wait by the walkway, and

stooping low to the ground, Swiss-made magnifying lens in hand, he began to methodically make his way across the grass, carrying out a careful examination of the earth below him. He advanced at a pace of mere feet per minute, so that the Captain and I were left alone together, watching Holmes make his way around toward the side of the house, where the bedroom window sat. As I did not observe him slowing or peering with particular closeness at any spot of ground, I supposed Holmes had not found anything of interest so far.

"Will there be anything for him to see, do you suppose?" Morrison asked me.

"I do not know," I admitted, "though if there is anything to be learned, we can rely on Sherlock Holmes not to miss it."

"I wonder what I was dreaming?" Morrison said.

"I beg your pardon?"

"Sorry," he said, as if only then realizing he'd said this aloud. "I was just thinking of last night and the intrusion which saw the cord left on my windowsill, and was wondering what I was dreaming about when the Demon's assassin stood there staring in at me, so vulnerable before his malice."

"Oh," I replied, "it's perhaps best not to dwell on such matters. You are alive, and shall stay so, and that is what's important, sir."

"I doubt the dream was of anything good," Morrison continued, despite my advice, "for I don't sleep peacefully anymore, not since coming back, or during any of those many months I was held up on the mountain. In my slumbering visions I relive it all night after night, and sometimes..." He took a deep breath and confided, "Sometimes I see it as it could have been, had they caught me as I made my escape. There would have been no mercy, you see?"

"But they didn't catch you," I reminded him, "which is greatly to your credit."

"No, only to God's," he answered, "for it is to Him I give thanks for my absconding."

A thought suddenly went through my brain, that left me

wondering if it was just possible the Captain's escape been the result of some diabolical plan among his foes on the mountain. I could not imagine to what purpose this may have been, nor could I fathom how it was these fiendish beasts among men had trailed him so far and come to be in England themselves, but once the idea had found its birth, it stayed with me like an itch in my thoughts, and I knew I should bring it up to Holmes at the first reasonable chance to do so, feeling in my heart that surely my perspicacious friend had already conceived the same theory well before me.

"May I tell you something?" Morrison asked me, as we waited. "One soldier to another?"

"Certainly," I replied.

"That first hour on the mountaintop, as I fought vainly, outnumbered a hundred to one, and saw them coming for me, I wished then that I had saved a bullet for myself."

I did not like to hear such a thing admitted, for all that I understood it, and as much as I knew that I should not have been immune to such a wish had I been in Morrison's place. So I told him:

"That is understandable, and no cause for shame."

"But what if I told you, Dr. Watson, that even amid all the adulation with which I have been greeted following my veritable return from the dead, I sometimes still wish I had? And that I find myself thinking that way even now?"

I turned to him and in my best bedside voice declared:

"Captain Morrison...Douglas, such thoughts should be resisted. If it is a miracle of the divine, as you say, that you returned home, then surely there was meaning in that, and God has a plan for you in His fashion. I should not be quick to cast aside the gift of a future which has been laid before you. Not when you have so much yet to come, including your marriage, and the joy that your children will one day bring."

"So I tell myself," the soldier confessed, "and yet..."

"Yes?" I asked, concerned.

With a burst of passion, he declared:

"This I vow, Dr. Watson, if it becomes clear that this foe seeks his revenge upon me, yet threatens my dear Martha in the process, I will do the honourable thing and lay down my life so that she might be spared the malice that should be focused upon me alone, when she is entirely innocent of any wrongdoing whatsoever."

I saw the thread of honour in that reasoning, but still cried out:

"I think this lady, if she loves you with the fullness of her heart, as you clearly love her, would tell you she would choose to face this danger rather than lose you, Captain, and in undertaking the act you just confided in me, however nobly intended that self-sacrifice may be, you should tear away her heart so that she should never recover. I have seen far too many times in my medical practice how loss can be a fatal condition, and it should little surprise me if this lady were to soon fade away and be lost herself, without you."

I saw my words had the desired effect upon the Captain, for he fell silent and contemplated what I had said. I added:

"Captain, have you found any other you may talk to concerning all that has transpired these last years?"

"Not particularly," he admitted. "People have been so busy lauding me for my service, and before that in pinning medals to my chest, that there has been little room left for anything else."

"Have you tried to speak of this with your intended?"

"Oh, no, I could not tell Martha of the thoughts I endure, not really, not without bringing my burden to her, for such is her love for me that I know its weight might crush her."

"I think you may find what you have described is a common enough circumstance in the lives of many soldiers who return from combat," I told him, "and I would wish you to know that you could always come and talk with me at any time. While I cannot match your experiences, of course, I do know something of the effects of war on the human spirit. So please, Captain Morrison, if at any time, be it night or day, I can be of service to you when a moment of darkness arises, you have only to summon me, and I shall do all that I can for you, even if but by listening."

My words seemed to touch him, for he turned aside for an instant before composing himself and saying:

"I thank you, Doctor, and may take you up on your offer."

No more needed to be said, for soldiers did not require undue shows of sympathy, nor did they seek them, but I saw Morrison valued what I had offered him, and it was a commitment I intended to honour should he reach out to me in any difficult hour. The wounds of the mind, the heart, the spirit, could, I knew, be as crippling as any to the body, but were seldom treated, and I felt the nation owed its military men better than to pin onto them a medal, and then turn its back.

It was about a minute after this that Holmes emerged on the opposite side of the house from which his investigation had begun, and though his face was unreadable, he did not leave us long in suspense.

"The ground is unfavourable for leaving behind many traces that show one's passing, yet still I found something."

"What was it?" I demanded, momentarily brightened by the news until he next spoke.

"That whoever came to be before the window did so barefooted, wearing no shoes."

Morrison started almost violently and cried:

"Shoes were unknown among the tribesmen of the mountain! Their feet were hard as leather. Oh, it is as I knew it was, they have come! They have found me!"

He tore the hat from his head and wrung it in his hands, bending it quite past easy repair, and I took hold of his arm and counseled in as gentle and firm a tone as I could manage:

"Captain, remember your dignity."

My words seemed to pull him away from where he teetered above an inner pit.

Holmes studied Morrison and said:

"Captain, do not be disheartened by my discovery, for

the knowable is always a better thing to face, as it is the unknown which presents the greatest danger. In fact what I have seen eliminates several possibilities, and allows us greater knowledge of our foe. By now my telegram to my friend in the police should have arrived, and I am certain he is even now seeing to the constables I asked to be provided to protect you, and your fiancée. Furthermore, you have *me* acting on your behalf, and that is the most powerful facet of this matter. You are my client, sir, and I place your welfare above even my own. I will not only see you guarded, but work tirelessly toward putting an end to this malice once and for all, for you above all men deserve to proceed in peace into the life you shall make in days ahead. No one has the right to take that from you, nor *shall* they while I am acting for you."

Holmes' words were inspiring, and I felt like raising a cheer, and Morrison, too, found great comfort in them, and a small smile played out on his lips before he cried out:

"You give me hope, sir!"

It was a simple enough statement, but one which veritably overflowed with poignant gratitude.

*****

As Holmes had said there was little else to be learned at the cottage, indeed beyond examining the lock on the front door and declaring it had never been picked, he said he had no need to even go inside, and we were shortly back at the depot, dining upon sandwiches bought there from a woman with a cart, while we awaited the next train back to Euston Station.

We three reached Baker Street just as the sun was setting, and soon after Chief Inspector Horace Gregory of the Metropolitan Police appeared in the company of four constables, each sent as a pair composed of one older man, experienced and wise in the job, and one younger, buoyed by the energies of youth. I recognized at once the wisdom in such an arrangement.

Holmes greeted Gregory and thanked him, to which the Chief Inspector gruffly but respectfully replied:

"Goodness knows you've helped us enough, Mr. Holmes, and more than a little good it feels to be able to begin to pay against our account. Selected these four men, myself, I did. Anderson and Thompkins here I figure to send out to the country to see to the lady and her family and stand guard there, and I've sent off a telegram letting the family know they're coming. I trust they'll be no objections from them. As for this pair, Adams and Lowery, they're to be with you, sir."

The Chief Inspector said this last part, nodding respectfully toward Morrison, for he, like most of the well-informed public of London, knew of the Captain and his improbable return home from Afghanistan, and it was with some deference and not a little admiration he looked toward the soldier.

"That should be a splendid arrangement, Gregory," Holmes commented. "The constables come armed with revolvers, as I asked?"

"Every one of them," Gregory confirmed, "and good stout billy-knockers, too, Of course describing as you did the foe they might be facing, I'd have given the order for revolvers even had you not mentioned it."

"Of course," Holmes said, deferring to the other man's perspicacity.

The detective turned to his client and said:

"Captain Morrison, I think there is little more I need ask of you tonight. Be assured that my work in this matter is just beginning, and that I shall be labouring toward its resolution even as the moon makes it journey overhead. Thus I bid you, return home with these two fine policemen, and take whatever slumber you are able, for your safety is greatly heightened now compared to last night. We shall speak further tomorrow."

"All shall be well," I told him.

Morrison nodded and hesitated only a moment before saying:

"I thank you, Doctor, Chief Inspector, and most especially you, Mr. Holmes, for all that each of you is doing on my behalf, and I should say, on behalf of my Martha."

Holmes reached out and for the second time in a few hours, shook Morrison's hand, before the Captain shook my own and those of the others, and then turned to the men who were to be making the journey to Dwayne with him, and engaged them in conversation as together they exited the parlour and made their way down the stairs and toward the street, where a police carriage waited to convey them all to Euston Station, and on north.

Once all the others had gone, including Chief Inspector Gregory and the constables he was dispatching out to the town of Sutton, in Surrey to see after Morrison's fiancée and her family, I followed Holmes back to the farther end of our parlour and took a seat as he went to the table on which rested the strangulation cord, the *bakluve*, Morrison had named it.

My day among clients had left me tired even before our hasty journey outside of town and back, and I found myself stifling a yawn as I watched Holmes begin his examination of the artifact from across the ocean. I noted that he held it in his hand for long moments, unmoving, simply staring, though whether evaluating the object or simply thinking, I could not say, nor did I interrupt him. Nearly fifteen minutes passed this way, I growing sleepier by the moment, Holmes standing still as a statue in profound concentration, until finally he startled me by saying:

"Watson, I shall be at this all night, and I see you are tired, as well you should be, tending to fifteen-month-old twins with head colds, and a gouty old banker who I doubt is ever obsequious to you."

With a jolt I realized he had somehow identified two of my most trying cases of the day, and I cried:

"Why, Holmes, however did you know that I had seen those patients?"

"I peered into your casebook, of course," he answered.

"Oh, I see," I declared, coming back down from my momentary puzzlement. I did not precisely mind him looking into my casebook, as I might have any normal flat mate, but still asked:

"And why did you do that?"

"I needed to know if by some chance you had been near Piccadilly Circus today."

"Why should it matter if I had been near Piccadilly Circus?"

"Because if you had, it would have meant the disguise I donned before traveling there, myself, was a good one, for if you had seen my impersonation in passing and not noticed it was I who was acting the part of a street barker who, by his flamboyant charms, gathered so much attention among passersby, I should have taken it as the strongest of signs that my self-concealment was superb indeed."

"But given your usual attention to your surroundings, wouldn't you simply have seen me had I gone by you?"

"Normally I think it likely I would have noticed you, Watson, though I confess even my powers of observation have their limits, and I was kept quite busy in my undertaking, for people were buying my offerings as fast as I could hand them out, and aside from running a profitable little enterprise in that hour, I was carefully taking note of not one but four suspects who were at that moment nearby."

"Ah, I see. And may I ask why you were impersonating a street barker as opposed to any of a great many other sorts?"

"There are two excellent ways of remaining unseen in public, Watson. One is to be unobtrusive and deflect the eye, and the second is to be so luridly visible that it disarms suspicion and renders one as so much background noise, something from which most people wish to shield themselves, and thus do. It was the latter of these tactics I was employing when I was out in Piccadilly observing individuals who interest me for reasons connected to a case I have abandoned for the moment, given Captain Morrison's standing as a hero and his pressing needs, but to which I shall return when this is done, and thus rid London of a cadre of villains undeserving of their present liberty. I saw from your casebook that as you were far from Piccadilly, I did not fail to spot you, and felt somewhat better about things."

I suppose it was no odder an explanation than any of the scores of others Holmes had previously provided me over the years as he explained the undertakings that constituted the pursuit of his work, so I allowed the matter to rest, my head somewhat spinning from weariness.

"Watson, my friend," Holmes said, his voice taking on a gentle tone, "really, I bid you, do turn in for the night. You do me no service by staying up, and in fact, frankly, you serve as something of a distraction given the concentration I intend to undertake in the nocturnal hours."

"I confess going to bed does sound inviting, but you will come for me should there be anything I can do on Morrison's behalf in this case?"

"I shall awaken you at once."

I needed no further urging but took to my room, and within a moment was asleep in bed, not to stir until dawn.

What I will report, however, is that my slumber, for all its apparent depth, was not peaceful, for I dreamt of Afghanistan, and of many of the horrors I witnessed there, men slashed and shot, dying on my operating table, and the regiment on the march coming upon burned villages, and the bodies of those left scattered about like so much cordwood under the broiling sun, victims of those raiders who took special delight in striking against their countrymen who showed us any courtesy at all.

And of course I dreamt of what Morrison had told Holmes and myself, of his torments and tortures there on the mountaintop, so far from the world of civilized man, kept as half demigod and half prisoner by the followers of the Demon, his feet poked at with sticks pulled smoking from the fire-pits, yet also given the best food the savages could offer. In one dream I realized I was there with him, in the cage, and one of my eyes...it seemed to be missing, gouged out in some frenzy of violence on the natives' part, and Morrison was trying to tell me something...something I desperately needed to hear, and his voice, when it came, was barely the dry whisper of a dehydrated man, but I caught a few words, and these made me shudder.

"*There's no true escape from Afghanistan for any man, Watson,*" he said inside the dream, "*for it burrows into our souls.*"

Exactly then I felt a terrible sensation, and realized I was reliving the circumstances of my wounding, namely that instant of unreality as the Jezail bullet struck me, sending the breath from my body as if I'd been punched, while its burning heat seared my flesh and tore into me, sending pain blossoming, and in its grip I fell, crying out, certain I was to die, knowing I was to lie buried under the rocky soil of that hot, dusty land, so far from home. It seemed so real that it was like no dream I had ever known, but was like unto traveling back into myself on that fateful day, and reliving its agonies and my dismal fear...

When I sat up in bed as the first rays of light were breaking over the Thames estuary, I felt glad to be excused from such dreams, and swung my legs over the side and put on my slippers, before making my way out into the parlour, where I knew I would find Holmes, still at work on Captain Morrison's case.

"Ah, Watson," he called, "you stir at last. Come and look at this, for it is rather remarkable, and entirely telling."

I stepped through the parlour toward the open space Holmes dubbed his chemistry laboratory, wherein he had set up a number of burners, copper wiring, and glass test tubes suspended on racks above all manner of multi-coloured fluids and powdery compounds, and as I did I saw somewhat to my horrified surprise that the *bakluve* strangulation cord had been dissected in the night, and that Holmes had separated it down to its individual parts, and reduced many of these to ash or gritty powder.

"Why have you done this Holmes?" I demanded.

"I should think that obvious, Watson, to carry out experiments upon the item and its constituent parts. It is a curious thing, is it not, that this Afghan tribe, which Captain Morrison noted kept no livestock and knew nothing of agriculture, should use the teeth of a cow rather than the ferocious beasts one might suppose would be added into a weapon of war."

"The teeth of a cow?" I repeated.

"Yes, and if you would gaze at where I have sliced the teeth into thin fragments, you might note several are stained with various colours."

I did note that this was so, and that one of the fragments of enamel was now hued a pale pink, another a brighter orange, and two a vivid blue.

"How did the teeth come to acquire these colourations?" I asked.

"From my experiments, of course. I wished to know the late cow's point of origin, and was aware that the grasses native to various regions of our island react differently when exposed to select compounds. The pink and orange tell me little, but ah, the blue now, which as you see I tested twice for absolute accuracy, informs me that the acids I washed over the tooth fragment reacted as one might expect had the cow spent its life consuming flora common in the southeast of England, or more particularly Kent."

"You can detail where an animal lived, *from its teeth*?" I asked, amazed.

"Not merely an animal, Watson, but a man. Give me a skull, or even so much as a single tooth, and I can learn much indeed. I would know, for example, by a few hours' tests that you were raised amid the heather of Scotland."

"Remarkable," I stated.

"And now," he said, "for another detail I found most curious concerning the weapon of strangulation."

"Yes?"

"The cord is made of hemp."

"Of hemp?" I wrinkled my brow. "But, Holmes, virtually every rope in England is made of hemp, so why should this be remarkable?"

He smiled and said:

"Exactly."

"I am lost…"

"Think back, Watson, to the several years you spent in Afghanistan, and tell me of the ropes there."

It took me a moment, and then I exclaimed:

"Jute! The ropes in that part of the world are not fashioned from hemp, but from fibers of the jute plant!"

"Which grows plentifully in southern Asia, yes," Holmes agreed.

"So," I began, knitting together these clues and hoping I was getting the matter right, "we are left with a supposed Afghan weapon made of domestic hemp, and festooned not with the teeth of predatory animals common in the Makawa Mountains, but an ordinary English cow from Kent!"

"Bravo, Watson, you have it."

"Which tells us," I questioned him, "that Morrison is not truly being deviled by one of the followers of the Demon of the Mountain, but by someone in England, who is impersonating that rôle?"

"The evidence I uncovered here in my lab during the night certainly hints at this as a strong possibility," Holmes said proudly, but with the caution of circumspection.

"Then it is an amazing discovery!" I cried.

"I thank you, Watson."

I was quite impressed, and even pleased, until I considered the implications of my words, and so demanded:

"But who would do such a thing to a war hero such as Captain Douglas Morrison?"

Holmes stepped away from the laboratory and stared out through the window at the golden sunrise forming around us amid the foggy air of the city.

"It is only one possibility," he admitted, "but I mark it a strong one, and the discovering of the identity of this vile person is the next challenge in this case. My mind has already spun several threads which I intend to follow today."

"Well it is a most extraordinary show of progress in so short a time," I offered my friend.

"Thank you once more, Watson," he said. "Now, I think a little breakfast might do us both some good before we begin our campaign for justice."

Mrs. Hudson soon brought up a tray of grilled kidneys and soft-boiled eggs, with crumpets, and a pot of very dark tea, somehow intuiting that the stimulation of such a beverage would be welcome after Holmes' long night, and at our table, we tucked in, Holmes proving especially hungry after the use of so much brain-power.

"What now?" I asked around bites of the delicious fare. "Where will you start?"

"At the War Office, I think," he said.

"Really?" I asked.

"Well, yes, for thanks to Mycroft, as much as to my own efforts, I do have certain inroads there, though it is the unheralded clerks, rather than those administrators who rose through government sinecures, that are the true force within any civic office. It pays, Watson, to enjoy the good opinion of such men whenever one is able."

"And this visit to the War Office might tell you...what, exactly?"

"Perhaps nothing at all," he said primly.

"Or possibly a great deal?"

"It is a theory, and a starting point."

"You think then that it is possible Morrison has somehow made an enemy?"

Holmes shrugged and threw his napkin down onto the tray.

"Who can say, but when a military man of extraordinary

heroism finds himself the victim of someone's malice, who but another soldier might know such an intimate detail of the case as to be able to falsely construct a *bakluve* with such precision as to have fooled the Captain's eyes, as it should surely have fooled any man who did not possess the doggedness that I do."

It was a dismal hypothesis, for as a rule soldiers stuck together, and looked out for one another, for alone among all men they knew the tribulations of the battlefield, that unparalleled experience available nowhere else in life.

It was then that there was a ring at the bell, and a minute later Mrs. Hudson came up bearing a telegram, which she handed off to Holmes before she gathered up the breakfast dishes.

The great consulting detective read the telegram, then let it drop from his fingers onto the table with something like a look of satisfaction.

"It is from Chief Inspector Gregory, who reports that all four of his constables passed quiet nights at their posts guarding Morrison up in Dwayne, and his intended's family in Surrey, and that there has been nothing to report in that regard."

"Well that is splendid news," I said, relieved to hear this.

"Yes," he agreed. "So, we have our respective intentions for the morning, myself to the War Office, and you...let me guess, a rheumatic widow today, and a railroad man with an abscessed tooth?"

I chuckled. "Something like that, no doubt, for I do have several calls to make among patients after my regular surgery hours, and a doctor never knows what might turn up there."

Holmes rose to his feet and reached for his walking stick, hat, and Ulster, and declared:

"Then with those thoughts on the merits of variety as an adornment to the crown of life, let us depart to our individual labours!"

We went down to the foyer together, chatting lightly, and had just reached the doorway after calling our farewells to

Mrs. Hudson, I about to head up to Harley Street, Holmes off to Westminster, when I saw my friend freeze mid-stride, and so turned to look, eyes in the direction he stared, only to see a boy in a page's livery, clearly from the telegraph office, come running full-tilt toward us, crying out:

"Mr. Sherlock Holmes! Do wait, Mr. Holmes, it's just this minute come for you, and the boss said take it over straight away!"

Somehow I instinctively knew this second telegram held dark tidings, and watched with an increase in my pulse as Holmes took the paper from the boy and tossed him a coin, before turning from me. An instant later, from his expression alone, I apprehended it was indeed grim news.

Holmes turned back to me and let the telegram fall into my hand. It was again from Chief Inspector Gregory, and its report superseded his earlier one, for it read:

COME AT ONCE TO STATIONHOUSE.
ADAMS HALF-DEAD AFTER ATTACK MOMENTS AGO.

After the optimistic start to the morning, it was disturbing news to read that Adams, one of the younger constables assigned to guard Captain Morrison, had been violently attacked. Would he even remain alive when we arrived in Dwayne?

"Holmes...!" I cried, more in shock than from quite knowing what I intended to say.

But my friend was already beyond me, frantically waving down the nearest passing cab, and leaping into it with such swiftness I barely had time to climb up after him.

"To Bedford Square!" he shouted. "And the police station there!"

******

It took us half an hour to arrive, but we were both inside the stationhouse a moment later, Holmes pushing past secretaries and constables alike, seeking out Gregory, who was not in his office.

"Well if it ain't that Sherlock Holmes," hissed a voice off to our left.

I saw Holmes glance in the direction of these words, then with a sneer of dismissal he pressed on, but I let my eyes fall on the man who had spoken, a weather-beaten Cockney in a threadbare suit, stooped and unshaven, malodourous and clearly a person of no repute whatsoever, yet to me he said:

"That was Mr. Holmes what banged me up for a three-year stretch at Cold Harbour once, and now look at him, too good to stop and say hello to an old foe. I curse him and the day he was born!"

It was doubtless a sentiment common enough among scores of criminals who had crossed Holmes' path, and I pushed beyond the man, pursuing my friend, and forced myself to think no more on that wastrel and his malicious hatred of the detective I considered the finest of men.

After another moment Holmes located Chief Inspector Gregory, and demanded of him:

"What is the situation regarding young Constable Adams?"

Gregory's face was more angry than grave, and he roared:

"Attacked from behind this morning, not twenty minutes after sending me the telegram bearing the news I passed on to you, that the night around Captain Morrison's house was uneventful. In the morning light Adams was less guarded, I suppose, a mistake for any copper to ever feel at ease when on duty, as you know, and next thing he heard a rustling in the bushes behind him, and a cord was around his neck, drawn tight, and though Adams struggled, he was soon seeing black specks before his eyes and knew he was losing consciousness."

"What saved him?" I demanded.

"Constable Lowery did!" Gregory declared. "The older

man saw the struggle and ran forward, billy-knocker in hand, and the assailant fled from him so fast he was soon lost in the underbrush of the woods there, and thus far neither Lowery nor the local boys from the stationhouse near Dwayne have found our fellow."

"But this Adams is alive?" I asked, my thoughts focused on this question.

"The village doctor who saw to him says he'll live, but the poor lad's voice may be ruined. Another thirty seconds and he'd been past all helping, so it's much he owes to Lowery."

I was relived at the news, but Holmes showed no reaction, only asked:

"And this assailant who nearly took Constable Adams' life, what of his appearance?"

Gregory straightened and squared his shoulders and admitted:

"Short as a woman but strong, bow-legged, swarthy-tan, like no man Lowery had ever seen before."

I felt my heart freeze and saw Holmes' expression falter and fall like his theory of the morning.

"It is one of the followers," I breathed, *"the minions of the Demon of the Mountain!"*

*****

Within the hour Holmes and I were on a northbound train out of Euston Station, heading to the village of Dwayne in order to be with Captain Morrison in light of this latest horror, and I paused only to notify my office via telegram that I was canceling my surgery hours for the day. Holmes said little on the brief journey, but sat in a state of contemplation, displeased with this most recent event, and thoroughly annoyed with himself, for while he made a practice of following the threads of evidence wherever they lead, I knew he detested it when one of his carefully-formulated theories was cast asunder, particularly in so confusing a way.

When we arrived just after 10.30, Holmes hurried on ahead of me, his pace always swifter than my own, and reached the cottage Morrison leased for his residence. I was but two minutes after him, hot on his heels, but found myself stopped by one of the local constables on duty there.

"All right, sir, and what business have you here, if I may ask?" the man demanded of me.

His mustache was brushy, and was just finding its first threads of white in among the dark brown he'd known all his lifetime, and for an instant no words of explanation for my presence leapt to my lips, but Holmes came to my rescue when he stepped forward from amid several members of the police who had gathered on-scene and announced:

"He is with me, Constable, and I thank you for your watchful prudence."

"Right then, Mr. Holmes!"

This Constable did not strike me as a bad fellow, certainly, his interruption of my progress had nothing of a personal nature to it, and he stepped aside and told me:

"On in you go then, sir."

At Holmes' side, I saw Morrison was within his cottage, still speaking to several policemen, one of whom was clearly a local detective, for only one in that profession would wear such an unfashionable brown suit.

Rather than approach Morrison, who was occupied in any case, I saw Holmes set out onto the lawn, and it seemed he instantly located the spot where the attack upon young Constable Adams had taken place.

"The ground," said Holmes, "is so much more conducive to the retention of footprints than it was upon my visit yesterday."

"Yes, I'm certain the morning dew was still on the grass when the assault happened," I agreed.

"Precisely," Holmes confirmed, before dropping down on one knee and for the next several minutes examining the lawn most avidly, during which time he did not speak, but all at once he shot to his feet, cast back his head and roared out a mighty shout of:

"Ha!"

"Holmes, what is it?" I demanded, noting that his cry had caught the attention of every constable around us, who stared at him with frank wonder.

"The events," he told me, "are clearly imprinted upon the ground for me to read, and occurred in a way that fits every particular of the account both Adams and Lowery provided to Chief Inspector Gregory."

"Yes?" I asked.

"But, Watson, I see something beautiful in the dirt."

"Beautiful? What could that be?"

"Do you remember when Captain Morrison told us shoes, or indeed footwear of any kind, were unknown among the disciples of this so-called Demon of the Mountain?"

"Oh, yes," I agreed, "your client was most adamant about that, and the tracks from yesterday showed no shoes either."

"Well, Watson, I invite you to come close, carefully now, and peer down at these small footprints right here, which, incidentally, tell me the assailant was as described, a diminutive man, about the size of a woman or growing boy, and tell me what you see."

I did so and after gazing for a moment made out the faint outline of where a bare foot had been pressed repeatedly into the soil.

"Holmes...I...note that as Morrison claimed was true of all such minions of this alleged Demon, the attacker was barefoot."

"Yes," said Holmes easily, waving a hand at my words, "but do you perceive the most important detail of all there, before your eyes, Watson?"

"If I have not mentioned it, then I think I do not."

"When a person goes without shoes his entire life," Holmes explained, "his toes grow in a manner which is decidedly and undeviatingly straight, but look there, Watson, see the gap in between the second toe and the largest? It is true our fellow was barefoot when he struck, but he has spent the majority of his life wearing sandals, which have driven apart those two toes, and have as a consequence brought about an indelible change in the structure of his foot. He did *not* spend his life barefoot!"

"So he was not one of the primitives of Afghanistan!" I echoed. "And your theory regarding some domestic enemy may yet be alive and well!"

"And further strengthened, Watson, by the fact that I can tell you from the position of the feet that Adams' attacker was right-handed, as are 9/10ths of mankind, despite Captain Morrison's account of most of the natives of the mountaintop —"

"Being left-handed!" I finished for him, excited, and glad to see his hypothesis restored in status.

"It simplifies matters immensely, Watson, even as it also complicates them, for now that I am back to being armed with a strong working knowledge, I must sift through a great many unknowns in order that I might come at the truth of things, and deliver my client from his undeserved torment."

With those words he marched past me into the tiny cottage, where Morrison sat in a pose of dejection, with the local detective and another constable standing nearby.

Ignoring these men, Holmes said to the retired soldier:

"Captain, I beg your forgiveness, you endured what should not have been, and too hasty was I last night to send you back here again, underestimating the peril you were to face."

Morrison looked at Holmes and me both and said nothing, then gave a slight, shallow nod of his head, clearly caught in the midst of a very private sense of agony.

"I am only glad the London constable, this Adams fellow, survived his ordeal," the local detective said, facing me rather than Holmes, speaking to fill the silence the would-be target of the morning attack seemed determined not to break.

He was a man of average proportions and height, this county detective, with a thick handlebar mustache and a wave in his hair that gave him a sort of handsomeness at odds with the baritone growl of his voice, and the decidedly unfashionable cut of his suit-coat. He held out his hand to me and said:

"As we have not had an introduction, sir, I am Inspector Stanhope Maddesley, of the Essex Police."

"Good to meet you, Inspector," I said. "I am Dr. John Watson, of London."

"And Scotland sometime before that, as I hear from your voice," he noted.

"True, indeed," I confirmed, "though away from my birth country these many years."

After introductions were out of the way, Maddesley explained to both Holmes and myself that he had called for a bloodhound to be brought to the scene of the attack on Adams, saying:

"We spare nothing when it comes to an assault on a fellow officer."

The dog, it was claimed, had trailed the scent of the short, dark man from the lawn and through the woods, til it lost him for a time at a small creek, but found the trail again on the far side, and then pursued it once more to a nearby railroad yard, where it was finally lost altogether.

"I figure the little villain leapt atop a moving train and was hustled off," Maddesley opined. "I sent telegrams to police stations down the line as well as to the railroad itself, hoping we might catch the brute still on the train, but nothing came of it. Little devil seems to have somehow given us the slip."

Holmes seemed to find significance in this last detail, for though he made no comment, I saw it rooted itself in his thoughts.

When he had gleaned all that was useful from the Inspector, Holmes, who clearly had scant patience for anything which kept him from the desired conversation with his client, said to Morrison:

"Captain, I come armed with a growing grasp on what is occurring in this most serious matter which surrounds you, and would offer you lodgings in a safe-house, where no harm might come to you."

Morrison looked up now and finally spoke, telling Holmes:

"Is that my fate then, to become a prisoner once again, returned to a cage that is somewhat larger than the one I sat in atop the mountain, but a cage all the same?"

"It is hardly a cage, sir, I assure you," said Holmes, "but accommodations fitting of a hero of the nation, as you are. You will be guarded, and your every need will be seen to by men who shall regard it a great honour to be of service to you."

Morrison closed his eyes and sat that way for so long I wondered if he was to reply at all.

I offered:

"Remember, Morrison, it will only be for a short while, just until Mr. Holmes sets this matter right and brings in this villain, then you shall be free of it once and for all."

Morrison spoke then, and as he did I felt my flesh break out in goose-pimples, and my hair almost seemed to want to stand on end, for it was a like a mirror of my horrible dream of that morning when the Captain looked directly at me and said:

"There is no escape from Afghanistan, Doctor, for it infects our very souls."

*****

"And Martha? What of her and her family?" Morrison had demanded, as we walked toward the train station in the village of Dwayne, several Essex constables among us.

"The police are tripling the guard on her house," Holmes had told him, "and even bringing in dogs specially trained to patrol a setting, and swiftly deal with unwanted intruders. She, too, will be quite safe."

"Then that much is well," Morrison answered.

This thought seemed to mollify him for the moment, as throughout the ride on the train, and during our time in the carriage which we took across London, he had sat stoically, saying little and betraying even less of what he might have been feeling, but I reflected that his gloomy words back in Dwayne probably described his sentiments with little subsequent alteration. He was a man of action, and to be set under the protection of others rankled his pride.

The safe-house to which Holmes conveyed Morrison was in the heart of the city, and was provided courtesy of a connection with Holmes' brother Mycroft, who was employed in some nebulous capacity deep within the government, and as the carriage in which we rode out from Euston Station conveyed us there, we halted for a moment before tall gates, which were soon separated to admit us within.

It was only as we came to that hidden fortress of a site that conversation began once more.

"What *is* this place?" Morrison asked, as our carriage came to a halt, and a serious-looking man in a nondescript dark suit began to stride toward us.

"It is, Captain," said Sherlock Holmes, "one of quite a number of clandestine outposts within London which Her Majesty's government maintains in case of any number of eventualities, such as civil unrest, or even foreign invasion."

"As if that could ever happen," I remarked, thinking of the power of our navy.

"It is a sanctuary of safety surpassing any castle in the land, and you are expected by a number of men who know of you and the magnitude of your service to the empire."

"I see," Morrison uttered, hesitantly.

"I have been inside on more than one occasion," Holmes told him, "and it is a wondrous facility, far larger than it may seem based on the brick building we witness before us, as in fact the installation continues far below ground into a network of hallways and rooms great and small, that contain facilities of all manner of description, including armouries and medical stations, and lodgings quite literally fit for royalty, as it is to this place, or another like it concealed elsewhere in the city, that in a moment of extreme emergency, the Queen and her family would be conveyed for safekeeping."

"And to think, I, a man from rural Dorsetshire, am held worthy to be admitted here," the Captain said with something close to awe.

"My friend," I told him, "you have most surely earned the right if anyone has."

I will not describe the events that passed in the next quarter-hour, for Holmes has cautioned me against telling too much of this place, which is meant to stand hidden in open sight, so I will merely say that Morrison was greeted therein like a hero by other military men, and that this elevated his spirits, so that when we made our goodbyes—and Holmes assured him once more than he would spend his every moment labouring to end the threat which stood against him —Morrison seemed almost cheerful as he disappeared within the fortified door, and went off to the lodgings prepared for him.

"Ah, Watson," Holmes said, "I feel a sense of duty partially fulfilled in knowing I have sent my client off to the one place where he may find himself utterly secure in every particular. Here he shall be free of all danger while I work on his behalf."

As the driver turned the carriage around in the cobbled courtyard of the facility, I asked Holmes:

"Are you satisfied progress is being made toward resolving this situation?"

"Oh, yes," Holmes answered without hesitation, "I feel I am on much solider footing than I was even this morning, for several facts are suggested to me in light of the recent developments."

"Really?" I stated. "For me I feel more puzzled than on top of things. Where I began yesterday evening hearing of a threat to a man which seemed a clear case of a foreign enemy stalking him across the planet itself, I was soon urged to trade that idea for deeper puzzlement after the coming to light of facts that suggested a certain ersatz nature to the murderous weapon left behind at the client's home."

"Yes," said Holmes, "that was so."

"And then," I continued, "things shifted once more to come around again to eyewitnesses actually *seeing* one of the tribesmen with their own eyes as he attempted to take a policeman's life! Add to that now being stranded on the rocks of bewilderment as you, Holmes, suggest to me that despite those eyewitnesses there is something false about even the swarthy little assassin himself, who certainly seemed real enough in his ability to scamper away and vanish from even the most thorough pursuit, as the minions of the Demon were skilled at doing back in Afghanistan."

"Not the most *thorough* pursuit, as you claim, Watson," Holmes said testily, "for that honour belongs to the progress I exert in tracking down the culprit. Any other investigation is, by its nature, at best second-rate."

"Holmes," I said, feeling myself want to grow annoyed at this splitting of hairs, "I acknowledge you have no equal in your profession, but come now, you know what I am saying. There are contradictions and false leads at every turn, yet you tell me you grow ever-closer to solving the case."

"And so I do, Watson, and so I do," Holmes said, smiling and then giving something like a low private chuckle.

"Well, tell me something then."

"I can tell you," Holmes said, as he began to smoke, "that where the matter seems clearest, it is at its most murky, and where it appears nebulous, it is there I find the strongest hints of truth."

"Holmes, you are too much, I ask you for clarification, and you mock me by—"

"The native assailant is but an *agent*, Watson," Holmes interrupted me to suddenly reveal.

"An agent?"

"Yes, of a more sinister master, whose desire for revenge is of an exceedingly personal nature. He wishes Captain Morrison not merely dead, but terrorized and ruined before his end comes."

"However do you come to that conclusion?"

"Elementary, Watson, when the facts are finally knitted together. I ask you to consider what is known, and what I have discovered. Firstly, the nature of the weapon left on the windowsill."

"It is of domestic construction, not Afghan," I agreed, "but might not one of the Demon's minions have come here and created his device from what he found on-hand?"

"Perhaps, though why he would do that when the *bakluve* could easily be carried within a pocket and conveyed from his homeland, I do not know, but I would think no true tribesman would wish to make a long journey without his favoured weapon on-hand, especially given that Morrison has described it as having a religious significance to every warrior in the tribe, almost like a crucifix, one imagines. No, it says much that such a thing should be made here in England."

"All right," I conceded, "but what else?"

"The footprint, Watson."

"It belonged to no shoeless mountain man, you say, but to one long accustomed to sandals."

"That is correct, and deeply telling. Then there is the matter of how a man born in the most remote mountain chain in the world would know how to find a foreign land across the planet, or have the money to buy passage on a ship, or even be capable of speaking in any of the civilized languages in order to give instructions to the ticket-sellers as to where he intended to go."

"I cannot even begin to imagine such a scenario," I concurred.

"And once in England, assuming this primitive somehow overcame all obstacles and reached the shores of this sceptered isle, how would he have located Morrison?"

"How indeed," I said.

"So, no, Watson, all these are not merely improbabilities, but insuperable barriers, which tell me the attacker is one who, though born in Afghanistan, I doubt not, comes from more advanced stock, and has been in England for some time. Yet I have named him but an agent, for he has someone directing his actions, and only one with a considerable grudge against Captain Morrison would formulate such a strategy, and employ an agent on his behalf to act violently as the facts show this dark-skinned fellow has."

There was a pause, and Holmes revealed:

"I think the man was sent to kill Captain Morrison last night, or at the very least to inflict the gravest suffering yet onto him."

"Dear me," I said, struck by the utter vastness of the scenario Holmes had laid out, "then we may be thankful the constables were there. But who is behind it all?"

"That, Watson, I do not yet know, for though my deductions have taken me this far, I am left with much work yet ahead."

"Then what is the next step?"

"In that regard I am returned to where I was this morning, and shall shortly go to the archives of the War Office, and follow some threads which I feel suggest themselves."

"Ah, yes, the course you were about to undertake before the second telegram."

"And you may still have enough of the afternoon to see a few of the patients you had been planning to visit."

"Then even after our train journey we are back to where we were hours ago," I reflected.

"No, Watson, we are much farther along than that," Holmes declared with passion in his voice, "for, as ever, my noose begins to tighten about its quarry!"

*****

As Holmes predicted, the afternoon was still lengthy enough to see me take up my medical bag and, stopping only for a light tea courtesy of our landlady, I was soon off to tend to my patients, spending my time treating a workman's infected thumbnail, prescribing drops for a newlywed lady with an ache in her inner ear, and delivering the good news that a progressive eye disease which had afflicted an elderly gentleman seemed to have slowed to the point he might simply pass the length of his lifespan without losing his sight, as had once been feared.

I was feeling rather pleased with life as I made my way back to Baker Street, with the warm wind tickling at my ears as it tried to dislodge my hat, and I stopped for a refreshing lemon shandy at the Cornish Cavalier public house off Porter Street, before I went home to see if Holmes would show up in time for dinner.

I opened the front door and stepped into the parlour, the sun almost hot against my back, my spirits jolly, when I heard Mrs. Hudson call out:

"Doctor Watson....?"

"Yes, Mrs. Hudson, it is I," was my answer, my attention only half-focused upon her.

"*Doctor Watson???*" she called again, more urgently this time.

Only then did I really hear the note of alarm in her voice, and then I saw a sight that filled me first with horror, and then an utter rage, for in the doorway to the kitchen Mrs. Hudson stood, her head bent slightly back from the pressure of the terrible blade that was being held to her throat by a grinning brown-skinned man who had wrapped himself behind her, barely taller than she, but with arms corded with well-developed muscles.

I felt the medical bag slip from my fingers and heard it strike the tile of the foyer floor, and inside me my heart raced. How I longed to rush forward and grapple with this hideous creature who would so abuse a woman, but I knew if I moved suddenly I was as good as sentencing Mrs. Hudson to death, and likely myself as well, for I was unarmed, and he had a knife that gleamed with sharpness. And so instead I stared into the man's eyes and my tongue felt thick, my limbs heavy, and I tell you with candour that I had never felt as helpless and filled with futility as I did at that instant, while time itself seemed to slow around me.

All I can say via description is that it was as if the sheer danger of the moment reached far back into my brain and plucked out the whole of my knowledge, such as it was, of the Pashto language I had picked up from my time in Afghanistan.

"Take me instead," I said slowly, hoping I was correctly conveying my intentions in this foreign tongue. "Take me and let this woman go."

For emphasis I touched my chest and nodded toward Mrs. Hudson.

I saw the man's head tilt, and thought that though I had perhaps gotten some of the language wrong, he understood my meaning. Instead of complying, however, he pressed the knife harder to Mrs. Hudson's throat, and though she bore the insult with great courage, neither crying out nor fainting away, I noted the depth of her fear when her eyes locked onto my own.

"I think you understand me," I continued in Pashto, "and I give you my sacred word that if you release her, I will step into her place, and pledge I will not resist you, or seek to escape. I will willingly be entirely your prisoner, with my very life left solely in your hands."

The little man took in my words, and I could see the thoughts turning in his head, even as he kept the cruel, curved blade, its edge glistening, poised to end Mrs. Hudson's life with the smallest motion.

"Yes," I told him, fully intending to honour the promise I was making, "myself for her. I will not trick you, I swear it on my family name."

There was a change in his eye, a wicked flash of cruelty, like a small ignition of fire, and I knew at that instant my offer had been rejected, that the fiend meant to kill Mrs. Hudson, and do it for the savage joy of the act itself. Then he would likely come at me an instant later and strike me down as well, I knew.

It was an instant in which I felt the cold presence of death itself in the air.

How this would have played out we shall never know, for moving swifter than my brain could comprehend, like a shadow suddenly given animation, I saw Sherlock Holmes appear in the kitchen behind the Afghan assassin, and leap forward and clamp both of his powerful hands on the arm which held the blade, giving it a ferocious outward jerk, sending the knife to the floor, and all but wrenching the assailant's arm from its socket. Holmes then threw the man to the ground, even as Mrs. Hudson lurched forward, grabbing at her throat.

I rushed to her and moved her behind me, stepping between her and the scene at the kitchen door.

"Are you all right?" I demanded, and looked toward her neck, relieved past description to see her skin remained undamaged.

"I am," she said primly and with fortitude.

"Thank God!"

Feeling a Scots bloodlust boiling in me such as I had only known twice in my life, and each of those occasions on a battlefield, I was quickly by Holmes' side, where he had pressed the assailant to the floor, and held him fast in a wrestler's grip, even as the man writhed like a snake and threw the whole of his weight upward, though Holmes' own strength was the greater in this contest.

"In my pocket, Watson," he called, grunting with exertion, for the little man was a deceptively powerful foe, "bring my shackles out and bind him!"

I needed no further urging, and in a handful of seconds

this was done.

Even as Holmes and I lifted up the would-be killer of a woman we both ardently admired, and set him into a stout kitchen chair, the Afghan snarled and bit at us, and kicked his feet, seeking to injure us, necessitating Holmes to shackle his ankles as well, and then with rope, fasten him onto the chair itself.

Watching from the doorway, Mrs. Hudson said nothing, and there was a steadiness in her that I found I could only marvel at, and admire.

"Mrs. Hudson," Holmes said at last, penitent and abashed, "I am so dreadfully sorry for this. It was…unforeseen, as I had no expectation that this man would come here, or seek to harm any who might be present. He is acting out the orders of one who controls him utterly."

"The Demon of the Mountain," I said ruefully.

Holmes' only response was to give me a look that held my eye for a moment.

"Enough of that!" Holmes said coldly to the Afghan, who was rocking in his seat, as if attempting to break it apart by this effort alone.

"How did you know he was here, Mr. Holmes?" Mrs. Hudson asked, sounding clear-headed though quite buffeted by the shocking indignity she had endured. "And how did you come to appear from behind just when you did?"

Turning to Mrs. Hudson, Sherlock Holmes explained:

"Through sheer providence, not through any planning of my own, for I was coming home from the War Office after what I confess was a not entirely productive afternoon spent examining old army records, and finding little return for my effort, when I noted the traffic on Baker Street was heavier than usual, so instead I came up the alleyway around side, and from that vantage point noted the window to the kitchen was ajar, something I knew to be odd, for you would never leave a window open to such a degree, Mrs. Hudson, if indeed you opened it at all."

"I would never," Mrs. Hudson agreed.

"Thus I went to it cautiously, to ascertain whether all was well, for house-breakers do strike even so respectable a neighbourhood as this one, of course, and arrived just as Dr. Watson was making his brave offer of self-sacrifice to the wretched devil, and saw only too clearly the truth of the situation. I pulled myself up and through the window as quietly as I was able, but in doing so I sacrificed swiftness for stealth, and crept across the floor, noting the deterioration of the situation, and perceiving that the man meant to do the worst sort of mischief."

"So he did intend to do murder then?" I asked.

"Oh, yes," said Holmes, peering almost apologetically toward Mrs. Hudson, "it was his mission handed down from his master."

Mrs. Hudson merely nodded at this news, never under any illusions about the man's intent.

"While I was unafraid of him," Holmes said finishing his narrative, "I was frightened I would not reach him in time to prevent bloodshed, or worse, that some sound rendered by my crossing of the kitchen might alert him to my presence, and compel him to act against you, Mrs. Hudson."

"Had he harmed you, Mrs. Hudson, I vow he'd never have seen another minute," I spoke out, "or I'd have died trying to make it so."

My blood was still boiling, so that took every ounce of the decency of my better nature to stay my hand, which still burned to reach out and strike the hideous person shackled to the chair.

"Quite right, Watson," Holmes said, seemingly reading my very thoughts, "it would be dishonourable, indeed, to beat a handcuffed man, deserving of scant consideration though he may be."

Showing she possessed the best strengths which lie in the hearts of Englishwomen, Mrs. Hudson walked past the prisoner, and put a kettle on to boil, and announced steadily:

"I'll have dinner for you gentlemen with only a slight delay, for it'll take more than this fellow to upend the timetables of *my* kitchen!"

Holmes turned to her and said:

"Mrs. Hudson, you are a dynamo, and an absolute marvel, but I must ask a favour. Pray, tonight do not be at home. Is there somewhere you might like to go? A new company of players has come to the Empire off Albany Street, and I hear they are quite good. Or perhaps it might be a felicitous evening to call upon a friend?"

Taking the hint, Mrs. Hudson laid aside her teakettle and removed her apron, before saying:

"I think I could find something to occupy me for a bit."

"Splendid," said Holmes, who offered some coins to her, which with only a momentary hesitation, Mrs. Hudson took, thanking him before stepping away through the same kitchen door where her life had hung in the balance but moments before.

When she was gone, Holmes bent at the waist and studied the Afghan intruder for a long minute, then smiled and stood once more.

"Yes," he said, "this one is from Kabul, not the northern mountains, where the Demon held its brutal sway. I see by many indications that this man knew life in the city from a young age onward. I think also he understands more English than he would like to let on, which is to be expected since he has been in England long enough to have lost something of the tanned overtones life in a torrid climate gives to a person. Is it as long as...three years?"

The man's only reply to Holmes' question was to deepen the leering grin that had resided so horribly on his face ever since he had given up his efforts to free himself, and instead sit docilely in his chair.

"Watson," Holmes called to me, "I have a favour to ask."

"Of course," I replied.

"I require you to go upstairs, and into my bedchamber,

where in a trunk with green felt on top you will come across a small stack of printed handbills. I need you to look through the collection until you espy one which reads 'Count Normo the Hungarian Strongman Coming to the Queen Anne Theater.' Take that outside and tack it to the wall below the first lamp-post, then hurry straight back."

I could not follow the logic of the request, but knew it doubtless had meaning in the complex mind of Sherlock Holmes, so I did as he asked, and completed my task by affixing the notice onto an empty spot on the wall I had been instructed to find, then strode rapidly back into our lodgings, even as the last of the sunlight dipped low in the west, and evening's shadows were falling over the city.

I found the scene in the kitchen much as I had left it, though with Holmes leaning against a counter, eating something as he read what appeared to be one of his monographs, even as the Afghan assassin sat unmoving in the chair, his eyes burning toward me as I made my way in. I somehow knew he had not yet spoken a word, and wondered how long Holmes intended to keep him there, and what his next course of action was to be.

"Watson," my friend remarked, "were you aware that wide variations exist in the sound of brass bells, even those of comparable size?"

"Er, no, no, I was not," I admitted, unsure why I was facing this question. "But I did as you said outside, and the handbill is now on public display."

"Excellent!" Holmes said, tossing his monograph on the subject of bells to the counter and smacking his hands together. "Do take a seat, Watson, out of kicking range of this one, I advise, and do have some of these excellent lemon biscuits I have discovered stored in Mrs. Hudson's cabinet here."

Though I didn't particularly want a biscuit, I nevertheless complied and took one, which was, even under the circumstances, absolutely delicious.

"Well, you have your man, so what now?" I inquired.

"This, Watson," he replied, and proceeded to do the one thing I would have absolutely least expected, when he produced a key from his pocket, and walked across to where the prisoner sat.

"Holmes, you mean to release him?"

"You," he said to the Afghan man, ignoring me and leaning low, "are, for all the vileness of your conduct, but a slave to the ambitions of another, and thus lacking free will, your actions have not been entirely of your own choosing. Where this other offered you nothing save captivity and cruelty…"

Holmes lifted the sleeve of the Afghan, and I saw bruises and scars on his brown arm, telling of fierce abuses the man had borne, much of it recent.

"….I give you something you have not enjoyed in a very long while. *A choice.*"

He reached to the man's legs, and unlocked the shackles there, an act which seemed to shock the prisoner as greatly as it did me. I expected the man to begin kicking, as he had earlier, but he made no motion.

"Yes, a real choice, I say," Holmes repeated, as he held the key before the chair, where it caught a spear of dying sunlight and seemed to gleam. "You can go to the East End, and dwell among those few of your own kind which are to be found there, and be free…."

He fit the key into the shackles on the man's hands, and turned it, before taking them from his wrists.

"Holmes!" I cried out. "What is this? The man nearly killed Mrs. Hudson, and meant to do the same to me! He has attacked others, including a policeman. He has killed Captain Morrison's fiancée's little dog!"

The detective ignored me, but continued to speak to the man.

"…you can find a ship, I dare say, and work for passage back to your home in Kabul. Or you can go wherever you like in this wide world."

The man was bound now by but the rope about his middle, which Holmes was untying as he gazed into his dark eyes.

"Or," Holmes declared, "you may return to slavery, and the master who beats you, and sends you to carry out the crimes for which he, himself, should be punished in his own stead, for it is he, I know, who is their author, and you but the tool he employs to see them carried out."

"But, Holmes," I protested, "this man is—"

Holmes held up a hand to silence me, and continued to stare at the Afghan, his face but inches distant, as with a last, slow movement, he unbound the rope, which fell to the floor.

I tensed, waiting for the foul intruder to spring, but he did not, though his eyes remained locked onto Holmes. He rose and, looking briefly at me, hurried to the same window by which he'd entered Baker Street, and in an instant had hoisted himself through it, dropping out into the dimness of twilight.

"Holmes, what have you done?" I demanded, stricken at this utterly inexcusable lapse in judgment. "Do you truly think you have done some good deed tonight in offering such a man freedom? Do you expect he will take it?"

Holmes looked at me with a semblance of cold delight, and said:

"No, Watson, I do not. I think he shall return straight to his master. And that is why we must hurry. Come, Watson, if you mean to join me at all!"

With that he was out the front door like a shot, bounding in the night, and, as usual, I trailed behind him.

"Why, but you've given him such a head start!" I called.

"Of course I have!" Holmes agreed.

"Surely you don't think we can catch him?" I demanded, as we ran down Blandford Street.

"Catch him?" said Holmes. "Certainly not, nor is that our aim. I offered him freedom, and if he has taken it, well, so be it, for a slave deserves liberty, but I am confident he will not act to seize the gift I have held out before him, and in fact, as you see, he has not."

"Then…"

"Watson, do you forget the handbill I asked you to post? And did you see it was about one of twenty, all varying each from another? It was a signal, Watson, a sort of raising of the colours on the battlefield, if you will, for it summons my army to action."

"Your army?"

"My Baker Street Irregulars were thereby mobilized by your own hand, and are now out in the city by the score, the best trackers in London, all those eyes and ears and small stealthy feet, so swiftly in pursuit. The man, whom I counted on to choose slavery over freedom and return straight to his master, is now seen and tracked and followed by a legion he would scarcely even notice, and thus he shall in but a little time lead us straight to the man we seek, the mastermind behind it all, he who hates Captain Morrison for reasons I confess I can but halfway suspect. But before the moon rises above us I think I shall know all!"

As if in answer to his claim, an urchin boy of no more than eleven, came running toward us.

"Mr. 'olmes, he's heading up off toward Weymouth Street now. Benny's following him at a distance, and soon he'll be trading off with Hungry Jimmy up near Cavendish! That fellow we're tracking for you is movin' just like a squirrel, climbing straight up over fences and into trees to drop down on the other side! But we haven't lost eyes on him yet, nor will we let you down!"

"Excellent, Samuel, exactly the news I sought to hear!" Holmes shouted back at the boy, before flipping him a coin, which the lad caught in mid-air, a look of delight on his face. He tugged his forelock and cried:

"Thank you, Mr. 'olmes!"

"You heard him, Watson, onward, toward Weymouth, and then to Cavendish!"

It was tiring, but I scarcely felt it in my excitement, as for over an hour we thus hurried along, met at various points by members of the Irregulars, who kept us posted with updates, all of which seemed to confirm two things, that the man we pursued was sure-footed and swift, and that he was heading in a generally south and eastward direction, perhaps toward the river itself.

Finally Holmes exclaimed:

"To Holborn, Watson, for that is surely where he is heading."

We found a cab to take us the last of the way, stopping at a prudent distance, so we could find more of the Irregulars, and go the last of it on foot. Time would indeed prove Holmes correct, for as we neared the interior of Holborn, Basil, a serious-faced boy in a shabby suit, who walked as proudly as a bishop, came running up, his eyes shining and his voice heavy with the sheer excitement of pursuit.

"We got him, Mr. 'olmes! He never knew we were on his heels because we kept trading off, all spread out, like, and there were so many of us watching he didn't see nothing. But we got him because he went in an upstairs window of that tall house there. The one with the black shudders and the double front doors!"

"Splendid, Basil!" Holmes told him, placing a well-earned coin in his hand. "You and the others have done most remarkably sound work today, and I'll soon be bringing you all together to mark a victory celebration with all the trimmings and none spared, in which we shall all elaborate the thrill of the chase, and the most excellent sensation that comes from a hard-won victory!"

The boy gave a throaty cry of glee, and ran off to share Holmes' promise with his friends, and seemed to melt away into the shadows with all the stealthy mastery of an alley-cat on the prowl.

"And that, Watson," Holmes said, "is one of the many reasons the police shall never match me, for they have nothing like the hundred sets of eyes that watch London on my behalf at all hours, unsuspected but as deft as eagles in the air. That is the power of my Baker Street Irregulars!"

Saying this, he moved on, keeping to the dark space of an alleyway, as he stooped behind some discarded crates and regarded the house into which our quarry, thinking himself surely safe from pursuit, had vanished. It was no hovel, but a well-appointed residence with an ivy-covered wall around its perimeter, and two looming gargoyles on either side of steps which led up to it in all its mid-century Gothic splendor. An eerie place, somehow, that suggested a pose toward the macabre, but not the abode of a poor man, to be sure, though how and why its owner should be mixed up in such a lurid business I could not think.

"What now, Holmes?" I asked in a low voice, as I stared up at a yellow glow that came through the mullioned windows.

"We confront the true foe of Captain Douglas Morrison."

"Shouldn't we summon the police, or obtain a magistrate's warrant?" I pressed.

Holmes actually turned to stare back at me before replying:

"Watson, as I am not employed by the police, nor do I proclaim it my custom to set my innermost compass according to rules laid down by other men, I have not the tiniest scruple concerning making my own entrance within that house in the next few moments."

"By breaking in?" I asked.

"By none other means," he confirmed, "for our foe deserves nothing else."

He studied me and offered:

"It is, of course, an illegal action on my part to break into another man's home, and should you care to absent yourself and preserve your good name, I shall not hold it against you in the slightest."

"Holmes," I said, "you know me better than that. I will

never fail to go wherever the case takes us, always by your side."

"You are a fine friend, my good fellow," he told me. "Now...." he studied the house, then the sky, where a dark cloud was on the verge of drifting across the moon above us. "Another moment, I think... Almost there....And... Now, Watson, with me!"

Keeping low to the ground, his profile rendered small in this way, he rushed across the lane and up the front stairs beside the twain gargoyles, and plunged into the shadows along the house's northeastern side, and I came to stand by him, no more than a few paces behind. He listened and waited, and seemed to hear no sound, nor did I. I expected him to see to the lock on the front door and enter that way, but instead he removed a tool from one of his pockets, and after a few seconds of quiet labour in the stillness, had a window open, just as the moon emerged from the cloud which had cloaked it. The entire matter had been but the work of half a minute.

Holmes peered into the room, and listened, then hopped up easily and dropped within, before extending a hand, and helping me do the same, my thoughts all filled with the hope that I had been even half as silent as he, my heart going rather fast with the thrill of what it was we were undertaking.

My companion moved with a masterful stealth across what looked to me to be a large retiring room, designed for relaxation, filled as it was with books and the marble busts of figures of renown, such as Byron, Wellington, Beethoven, the American, Poe, and several more, with half-dead, brown-leafed potted palms set next to overstuffed sofas and several straight-backed reading chairs, all arranged around a deep, broad fireplace which looked to have been left unused since the other side of the spring just passed.

Holmes paused with his hand resting on the closed keyboard of a grand piano, and listened. Around us at first I heard no sound whatsoever, and then, my ears having grown accustomed to the setting, I detected the faintest note of a conversation taking place somewhere beyond the door, across the house.

The detective lifted a finger to his lips to caution me to say nothing, then crept across the floor. He listened a long moment at the interior door, and opened it with meticulous care before stepping into an outer hall, which ran on either side of a grand, albeit somewhat neglected foyer, where a number of black trefoils sat inlaid upon ivory-colored marble underfoot. In decline the place may have been, but by any scale, it was a mansion into which the Afghan assassin had fled.

Holmes set off across the foyer til he came to a door beyond, from under which came the flickering glow of candlelight, which danced with a golden aura against the reflective stone of the floor. He motioned me to come forward, then nodded to the door, and withdrew a revolver from his coat, and a smaller pistol, rather like a derringer, which he handed to me. Next the detective held up three fingers, and I felt my heart jolt, reminded as I was of those invariably long seconds which swirled around a man just before the start of battle.

Three fingers....

I tensed, but told my muscles to relax.

Two fingers....

And still the voice came from within the room, a drone that sounded like some instruction being given by one displeased.

One finger....

I lifted my derringer, and—

Holmes burst through the door and dropped low into a crouch, covering the two figures within the semi-darkness, while I stepped in behind him and did the same.

There were two men visible in the candle-flame in this, the home's morning room, which along the outer wall contained a series of floor to ceiling windows aligned to face the rising sunlight each dawn. The first of the men I saw was the Afghan who but a little while before had held a curved blade to Mrs. Hudson's throat, and toward whom considerable anger still boiled in me, making me glare at where he stood in a pose of almost reverent attention, but the second figure was seated, and was, I saw, an Englishman, perhaps thirty-five, quite fine-featured on the hemisphere of his face which was set toward me, but when he looked over in surprise, I noted the far portion of his visage was ruined by scars, and his eye on that side was quite gone, as were his legs above the knee.

The Afghan sprang at Holmes, a knife in hand, but rather than fire at him, Holmes sidestepped the dark man's sweep and struck him a fierce blow to the temple with the butt of the revolver, sending him sprawling to the floor.

"Cover the Englishman, Watson," he said to me, as for the second time that day he clapped handcuffs onto the assassin, even as I pointed my own smaller weapon at the ruin of a man who sat staring back at me with an expression of low, cold anger slowing percolating through him.

"You hardly need to point that thing at me" the man spoke, his voice deep and somewhat mellifluous, for all that it contained a rattle deep within his throat, and as a doctor I sensed he had borne many wounds, even beyond those I could readily see.

"I think I shall be the judge of that," I said, as I kept the derringer aimed in his direction.

The man laughed, then let loose a wheezing cough and announced:

"Well, this is hardly sporting, two on one, or should I say two upon half a man, as you see I am."

Holmes returned to my side after securing the shackles onto the unconscious Afghan, and removing the knife from the floor beside him.

"Not as fine as the *Pashtuni* blade from earlier tonight," he declared evaluating the weapon. "That one I intend to use as a letter opener, and I think it shall be a fine souvenir of the time I bested a dark-hearted man, whose very soul had rotted way within his equally decaying house."

The man chuckled again, a wet sound in the darkness, before saying:

"I think I know your name, sir. Would it be Mr. Sherlock Holmes?"

"None other, Holmes answered. "And I think I may safely mark you as one Howard Morebaugh, late a Lieutenant of Her Majesty's 61st. Dunbar Rifles."

"It is good to know I have not been entirely forgotten in my present state," this man, Morebaugh commented, his ruined face showing much anger.

"No," Holmes told him, "quite copious records exist in the War Office to tell any curious researcher about your abbreviated, and somewhat chequered career in uniform. Whereas my client is every inch a true hero, you, sir, are fit only for expressions of ignominy, both as a soldier and now here in your civilian life, where you have plotted the end of a far better man than yourself!"

"Well," I stated, "for my part I am unfamiliar with this man. What is his history, Holmes?"

"It is a tale of disgraceful conduct, self-inflicted bad luck, and a heart twisted by ideas of revenge, which serve to sustain him."

"Now that is a lie!" this Morebaugh thundered, then descended back into his coughing.

"A lie you name it?" questioned Holmes. "I think it only too true, for never have I met a former army officer whose conduct toward a one-time comrade-in-arms comes close to being half as sordid and cruel as your own."

Holmes stepped forward and yanked a pistol from the man's jacket, causing Morebaugh to growl in annoyance.

"Planning to use that at the first opportunity, were you?" Holmes said with a victorious smile. "It'd take a far better man than you, villain that you are, to conceal a firearm from me."

Holmes then leaned back against the wall, looking rather pleased as he lit his pipe and said:

"Do steel yourself, Watson, for the tale which shall now

be unloaded like so much refuse off a scow shall test your fortitude."

Looking at Morebaugh, Holmes asked:

"I shall tell of your evil, sir, though do feel free to step into the narrative when you like, as there are still one or two very minor points I have not had sufficient information to tie together."

"I shall gladly offer my narrative," he said, "for it is a tale of injustice and grievous harm that came onto me because of another man's actions, and before I am through I think you may see your great hero, Captain Douglas Morrison, possesses feet of clay."

Could it be, I thought, *that this man truly had some legitimate grievance against an officer so universally hailed as a hero?*

I was determined to disbelieve this charge until it was proven to the fullest, though perhaps seeing with his remaining eye some flicker of this reaction on my face, the man shackled in the chair smiled in a foul manner and said:

"Oh, yes, for it was Morrison's actions which set me into the condition you see here."

"Yes, at an engagement by the Kunar River, on the twenty-first of November, 1879," Holmes said. "I read of this brutal skirmish, and saw that the official record in the War Office reflected no fault among the officers in command of the action. Your wounds that day, terrible though they proved to be, were not the result of ineptitude on my client's part, but simply what might be called bad luck."

"Bad luck?" the man cried, then coughed harshly. "Bad luck is when a bolt of lightning strikes one dead. I name it cowardice that saw Morrison send my men into the fray ahead of his own, with him at the rear, with the result being my ruination that you witness before you tonight."

"I understand your sentiment regarding the terrible wounds you bear," I told him, "but you sought your commission of your own free will, and such fates are among the manifold fortunes of war."

"You understand nothing!" the man cast back at me.

"The record also showed it was a Colonel Bryson Wade who commanded Her Majesty's forces that day," Holmes told this Morebaugh, "and far from being blamed for the outcome of the hostilities there, for his actions that day the Colonel was decorated, as was Captain Morrison, who was under him. As were a number of men who fought on that bloodstained morning. It was, I might add, for all its fury, a resounding British victory."

"I tell you, only a coward sends other men to fight in his place!" the crippled soldier said, teeth bared in rage.

"Perhaps," Holmes agreed, "but the scenario you describe that day was not a case of cowardice, for the order of battle came straight down from Colonel Wade, and Morrison was merely seeing his instructions carried out, and the place he assumed on the field of battle was the one directly assigned him by his commander. I further note that according to the records of the War Office, Captain Morrison most definitely did enter into the thick of battle, leading his own regiment forward under enemy fire, once your own company had faltered after their courageous charge, and that Morrison and his men faced considerable risk in so doing. There was no official judgment of misconduct or cowardice on the part of any who stood in command that morning... including you, who fell wounded among your comrades in the thick of the opening salvos."

"No!" Morebaugh shouted. "You lie about what occurred there!"

"You, sir," I spoke up, "seem to be confusing misfortune with wrongdoing. From what I am hearing, you doubtless did your duty in going forward in the assault, as ordered by your immediate superior, Captain Morrison, but when you were hit so violently, as I see you were..."

I took in his scarred face, his missing eye, his lost limbs, and felt regret that war could do such things to a man.

"Well," I finished, "the fault was not in he who gave the order, nor in he who saw it handed down, but in the enemy you faced. So why is it you have haboured such hatred for another soldier, who ultimately did you no wrong?"

"You look at me, and dare ask that question?" the man roared. "I was once a handsome fellow. Women adored me. I was temperamentally unfit for army life, and sought my commission only because it was so deeply expected of me in my family, where my oldest brother would inherit all, my next oldest went into the Church, and I was left with few alternatives but the army commission I was goaded into taking, against my better judgment. I was also but three weeks away from resigning my rank, and re-entering civilian life in an honourable fashion. *Three weeks*, I say to you, and I could have come home a hero, duty done! That coward Morrison, and that butcher Colonel Wade, they took that future away from me!"

"And as this Colonel Wade," said Holmes, "whom you denigrate so readily, died for his country not many weeks after the skirmish in which you were wounded, falling while he was in pursuit of bandits near their riverside encampment, he came to be beyond the reach of your cold desire for revenge. Thus it was that all of your malice came to be focused onto Captain Morrison alone."

"Yes," the man admitted.

"Then based on all that I have heard tonight," I said, "both that which was spoken by Holmes and by your own admission, I name you a disgrace to the uniform you once wore, and to the nation you once served."

"And to that," said Holmes, "I will also name you a villain, a blackguard, and a creature of cruelty for attacking a fellow officer who never wronged you in any manner, a far better man in every way than you, for I saw your service record, Morebaugh, and you were never a credit to the army, or the oath you swore. Twice reprimanded for dereliction, deemed untrustworthy by your first commander. Universally detested by the men who served under you. You are the worst that our nation produces, not just detestable, but loathsomely self-pitying."

"So you name me," said the man, "yet you are not the one in this chair. At first I was glad to hear of Morrison's death up on that mountain, above that accursed death-trap that was that ravine, happy he had joined that merciless Colonel in oblivion, but when I later read of his homecoming, and saw him dubbed a hero, and went on later to read that he was to be married and have all the things in life which his orders denied me...for what woman would ever look on me now and feel anything but horror? It was justice that I sought, for how could I allow him to have the happiness he took away from me?"

"I understand the motivations," I said, "however heartily I disagree with them, but why did you choose this strange method of vengeance?"

"Why?" Morebaugh threw back at me. "To torment the man before taking away all that was precious to him! To inflict fear by reminding him of the torments of his past, and lead him to believe the enemy he'd escaped had found him again. Finally, to take his life entirely, and I soon would have. That was my plan!"

"But the Afghan man who was acting as your agent, even your assassin... How came he to figure into this?" I demanded to know.

Holmes, who had been listening quietly the last few moments as he looked on and smoked, exhaled a thick gray cloud and said:

"I believe I can answer that. Do you know the Afghan custom of *merana-nang*?"

I paused, suddenly closer to understanding, for I did, indeed, know this term.

"It is," I declared, "the debt a man comes to owe when his life has been saved by another's actions. It is among the most sacred traditions of the Afghan people, rendering the one who was saved the absolute servant of the other."

"Correct," said Holmes, "and though a villain and a disgrace to his uniform this man Morebaugh may have been, he did once intervene to save the life of an Afghan man who was facing certain death in a landslide, and Morebaugh pulled him to safety. Thus the condition for the code of *merana-nang* was enacted, and in effect this Afghan—far more honourable than the monster he serves—became the slave of this scoundrel here tonight."

"And it was because of this honour the Afghan's actions have demonstrated that you spared his life tonight when it may have been far safer to simply shoot him as he charged at you," I said with deeper understanding.

"Yes," Holmes confirmed, "it was because he is a man of honour trapped by his sense of duty that I stayed my shot."

I shook my head and thought on it all, and much concerning the case suddenly felt changed.

Holmes continued:

"The Afghan, whose name I do not know, tended to Morebaugh while he was in army hospital, and at his master's command left behind all those that he loved in his native country, and came home to England with him, where he has cared for him ever since, tending day and night without compensation to the many needs of a crippled man. So deep is the bond of honour inherent in this code of *merana-nang*, that when Morebaugh sent this Afghan out to fashion the *bakluve* cord, and to kill the young lady's dog, and thus terrorize her family and Captain Morrison alike, he felt he had no choice but to obey, whatever his own feelings. He even affected tribal attire, as he was bid to do, shedding his sandals and going barefoot, as the followers of the Demon did. Thus owing to the nationality of the agent, Morrison was made to believe his enemies had returned, and his two-year long nightmare had come again."

"It is as cruel an action as I have ever heard of, Holmes," I said, disgusted to the marrow of my bones.

"Accurately stated, Watson," he agreed. "But now the

campaign of this heartless devil has been brought to its end, and liberation of a sort may be possible for this faithful Afghan here."

Holmes gestured to the man who was only just beginning to stir on the floor.

"His name is Hassan," said Morebaugh .

"Is it now?" said Holmes. "Then for all that he has done wrong in your service, I yet judge this Hassan a more admirable fellow than you, who traded honour itself for the sake of hollow vengeance."

"So, Holmes," I pressed, "your offer to this Hassan back at Baker Street was a genuine one? Had he not returned to his master, you would actually have let him take his freedom?"

"Oh, yes," Holmes answered, "though I held the odds of his so doing were slim indeed, because of his grasp of duty. And as you see, I guessed correctly."

"But had he not led you here to this house, what would you have done instead?"

"It would have meant a little more work on my part, extending the capture we have undertaken here by perhaps a day, but by the time I returned to Baker Street tonight, I had the name and history of this man, Morebaugh, within my possession, and had sufficiently pieced together the facts to know he was our villain. It was only his location which I was denied for a moment."

"Hassan led you back to me," Morebaugh rued.

"*Straight* to you," Holmes agreed.

"I told him to throw off any pursuers by varying his route, and taking all necessary subterfuge!"

"So he did," I said, speaking up on my friend's behalf, "but the man has never been born who can elude the pursuit of Sherlock Holmes."

"I'll whip him with horse-leather for his failure," Morebaugh vowed, "and lay his heathen flesh bare under my lash!"

"I do not think the opportunity to abuse this fellow

Hassan shall ever arise for you again," Holmes told him.

"Oh, yes, for now you'll summon the police, I suppose," Morebaugh sneered with contempt. "As if a prison cell could add in any way to my misery, or iron bars forestall me from inflicting my punishment on this little brown dog here, for I assure you, if I so ordered, he would lash his own back bloody, for that is the power of command I hold over him."

"You are ghastly!" I spat out.

"Oh, I shall give him the command, you'll see. He will do anything whatsoever I say, for it is the burden which binds his soul."

Holmes put away his pipe and walked toward Morebaugh with menacing slowness, his eyes flinty.

"Take you to the police you say?" he asked, then smiled almost evilly. "I have merely given you time tonight to confess all. In fact, sir, you have sent a man to hold a knife to the throat of my landlady, whom I esteem above all women save the queen to whom I owe honour, so do you imagine that I am a man who would allow such an offense to stand unanswered?"

For the first time that night I read fear in Morebaugh's single eye, though it was gone just as quickly, and he said arrogantly:

"I have nothing left to fear in this life, whatever you have in mind to do to me!"

"Is that so?" Holmes taunted.

"This is now a matter for the police, surely...?" I said nervously.

On the floor at Holmes' feet Hassan stirred, and the Afghan man sat up, though his hands bound.

Holmes said to him:

"Hassan, I could easily have killed you not once today, but twice. Would you say then that under the inviolable code of *merana-nang* your life belongs now to me?"

"It is so," Hassan said in a low tone, before bowing his head before my friend.

"Excellent," said Holmes, "then you are mine."

"Holmes!" I said with utmost disapproval. "You mean to take this man as a slave, when you have condemned this horrid disgrace of a soldier for the same practice?"

Holmes made no answer, but leaned low and unshackled the man's wrists, and pulled loose the cuffs off his hands.

"Rise," Holmes commanded, and Hassan instantly obeyed.

I gripped the derringer tightly but did not raise it for all that I expected this Hassan to leap violently at Holmes, yet I saw that he merely stood silently before the detective in a meek and servile pose.

"Watson," Holmes said to me, "you see before you a man who as surely lives by a code of chivalry as ever did Sir Galahad long before him."

Remarkable, I thought.

"Hassan," said Holmes, "doubtless you have endured much at this Morebaugh's, hands. His abuse of your self-imposed debt of honour was, I am sure, a daily exercise in cruelty, and you have borne it with a perseverance which would stand a credit to any man. I suspect, then, that as your bond to him is hereby severed, there is much for which you might wish to re-pay him?"

A flame appeared in Hassan's eyes as he looked at his former tormentor.

"You can but speak in jest, sir," Morebaugh choked out. "We are Englishmen you and I, and he a soul-less savage from a heathen land, counting for nothing. You can't truly mean to let him loose on me, Holmes …"

"Listen to me, Hassan" Holmes said in a quiet voice as full of righteous anger as I had ever heard.

At this command the brown-skinned man turned to face Holmes.

"I see the scars on your skin where he has beaten you, and I know that he has taken you far across the Earth, forcing you to leave behind all that you loved in your homeland, your wife, your children, that he has starved you, ridiculed you, struck you, even as you dutifully undertook all that he bid you to do, however much it may have appalled you to lash out against others, as you have done of late, much, I suspect, against your will. Thus, I shall now be going, but I leave him with you to redress as you see fit the many wrongs you have suffered at this callous monster's hands. So to you I say do as you will as a free man. I hereafter and for all time release you from your bonds of enslavement."

If Holmes' words shocked me, his next action was still more a surprise, for from his pocket he produced several bank-notes and told the man:

"And if you chose to do so, go home to Kabul, and be with your family once again. This is sufficient to see you aboard a ship for the voyage."

Hassan took the money almost reverentially, knowing what it meant to him, re-igniting, I did not doubt, a dream which had all-but died in his soul. He then seized Holmes' hand and kissed it, and bowed repeatedly.

A third surprise came when Holmes pulled out the knife which he'd seized from Hassan at the start of the melee, and set it back into its owner's hand. He nodded gravely toward it, and then with a turn so rapid his Ulster swirled after him, strode away into the foyer.

"Wait!" Morebaugh cried. "You cannot do this! I do not deserve such a fate."

"Ah, but I think you do," Holmes called behind him.

I stood rooted to the floor, unsure what action it was I should take, for though the soldier in the chair was a villain of the lowest sort, surely I should still save his wretched life, should I not?

To me Morebaugh beseeched:

"Dr. Watson, please, I beg of you, do not abandon me to this savage. Call the constables, take me to prison, but not this!"

From the foyer I heard my friend's voice, as he told me:

"Come, Watson, this is no longer our affair."

"You have a pistol in your hand," Morebaugh cried as he saw Hassan lift the blade. "Shoot him for God's sakes!"

Even as I stood trapped between my sense that Holmes had not followed a moral course in setting these events into motion, and yet feeling the Afghan *was* through some unwritten code of justice entitled to rise up against this loathsome Englishman who had abused his honour and enslaved him, the matter was abruptly decided, as Hassan slashed outward with a single stroke to the throat of the erstwhile puppet master in his chair.

A gasp left me, and a sense of finality arose, as the man who had sent an assassin to cut down Mrs. Hudson, died in her place.

With a last glance at the body before him, Hassan crossed the room and climbed out the window, and was almost instantly gone into the night. Where he went after that—home or otherwise—I was never to know.

My anger dissipated, and I felt limp, unsure if I had not made myself culpable this night in an act which may have cast me among the unrighteous.

I heard Holmes return to the room and found he was gazing steadily at me.

"Watson," he said evenly, "do not look so troubled. The world is a better place now without this deranged soul in it."

"You did it because of Mrs. Hudson," I charged. "Your taking vengeance for what was done to her outweighed your every other consideration."

"There were many aspects to consider in this matter," Holmes said, "but, yes, Watson, no man may trespass against those under my protection and believe he will escape unpunished."

As I still stood in the flickering candlelight before the body of the one-time soldier, lost in my thoughts on these last minutes, Holmes placed a hand against my shoulder and said:

"It is now time for us to depart."

As we walked back across the dark yard and into the road

beyond, Holmes, seeing how I remained troubled, told me:

"I did not sentence Lieutenant Morebaugh to death, Watson, nor should you imagine his blood lies on your hands. Rather we left the choice to a man whom he vilely abused, and that man chose to become his executioner. And for that choice, I feel only a gladness tonight."

"A gladness?" I demanded.

"Completely," he replied.

Holmes, I reflected from somewhere within my overwhelming shock, was simply not like other men.

******

The rest of the tale is easily told, for all
that I am uneasy in telling it.

Sherlock Holmes was able to return to the fortress within the heart of London, and give personal assurances to Captain Douglas Morrison that neither he nor his fiancée in Surrey would ever again be troubled by either the cultists of the Demon of the Mountain, who had not followed him to England after all, nor from the enemy who created the pretense that they had done so.

"Though it takes any obligation you might feel to me very far," Holmes said, "I solemnly ask you, Captain Morrison, to respect that in binging the case to its conclusion, and restoring peace and safety to your life, it was necessary for me to create certain obligations of honour that I cannot violate, only tell you upon my word that both you and the woman you intend to wed are now quite secure. My gift to you both is to undertake this case without fee, and to present you with all the tomorrows it shall now be yours to enjoy."

Morrison did take Holmes at his word, and asked nothing more, and thus we all parted with handshakes, as the case came to its end.

Of the fate of Hassan, the longsuffering prisoner of honour, I can say nothing, though with time I found that I could not in good conscience judge him for the vengeance he elected to take upon the fiend who enslaved and tormented him. It is my truest hope that he did indeed return home to be with his own loved ones, from whom he was so long parted.

THE CONTINUING CHRONICLES OF SHERLOCK HOLMES

THE YEW ALLEY GHOST

C. THORNE

THE YEW ALLEY GHOST

That danger often comes from unexpected sources is a truth which has been driven home to me upon many occasions in my life, both as a soldier, and later through my involvement in the work of my friend, Sherlock Holmes, but I think never was that lesson demonstrated with quite so startling an effect as when it came from a source which I would never have suspected of being capable of such drastic violence.

The morning began like any other, with Mrs. Hudson bringing up a lovely breakfast tray, along with a pot of excellent tea, as Holmes and I discussed the day that lay ahead, I, seeing one of several patients I had acquired in those early days of my practice, Holmes mentioning some chemistry experiments he intended to conduct for the purpose of isolating certain compounds in blood stains.

Seated across from me as he was, far from the window, engaged in our light talk, I believe even Holmes was surprised to hear the ringing of the front bell at so early an hour, and when Mrs. Hudson showed up a slight young woman of perhaps twenty years of age, quite meek of visage and soft-spoken, the breakfast dishes were hastily cleared away and with courtesy the putative client was shown to the comfortable chair Holmes reserved to offer visitors to 221B Baker Street.

I saw that Holmes' gaze was fixed curiously upon the woman, evaluative but in no way troubled, nor did I sense any danger when I took a seat opposite her and opened the pad on which it was my custom to take notes, yet in retrospect I see there were signs from the first that there was a great tension in the woman, which at the time I put down to the strains often present in guests to Baker Street, tormented as so many have been by the very issues which brought them in to consult with Holmes.

"I am Helena Nichols," the young woman said, her accent northern and sharp, with a tone of agitation in it. She paused, as if the name should mean something to us, which at the time it did not.

"And how may I be of service to you, Miss Nichols?" Holmes asked courteously enough.

"*Mrs.* Nichols," she insisted.

"Ah, Mrs. Nichols then," said Holmes indulgently, though, like I, I am sure he noted that there was no wedding band upon her finger. "Pray, what brings you to Baker Street this morning?"

As we waited for her reply, the woman hesitated, and I saw her chest rise and fall with the rapidity of her breathing, which as seconds ticked past became something close to hyperventilation, and I wonder now, did I even then begin to sense the element of peril in her presence?

"You are known to me, Mr. Sherlock Holmes," she said at last, a darkness in her tone. "Known to me from

your work, and the actions you have taken against others...
your intrusions, into their affairs....your *persecutions* of the
righteous!"

At this accusation I saw Holmes stir, and I set aside
the writing pad and was, myself, about to rise, for my every
instinct had begun to call out to me.

"You have," the woman keened with a savage hiss, "sent
my husband, Barty Nichols, to prison, and for that malice I
shall strike you down!"

With those words of promise, before even Holmes with
his almost preternatural speed could reach her, the woman's
hand dipped into her purse, and with a violent motion she
flung the contents of a jar toward my friend.

With his extended left arm, Holmes pushed me
downward, crying:

"Stay back, Watson!"

I did not heed him, yet even as I grasped her arm a
second too late to prevent her actions I saw a small black shape
travel through the air and arrest its flight against Holmes'
chest, where it fastened to him using tiny claws. With a burst
of horror I realized it was a jet black scorpion, about the length
of my middle finger, and its tail lashed downward, striking the
detective with a thorn-like stinger.

Seeing the hideous creature stab her target, the woman
cackled a gleeful cry and shouted:

"Sherlock Holmes is a dead man! Barty, I have avenged
you!"

Holmes swept the scorpion from him with his left hand,
and without hesitation smashed it underfoot with a violent
stomp that gave off a sound like the crushing of a desiccated
eggshell.

"Too late, fool!" Helena Nichols called, even as I grasped
her in my strongest hold. "The sting of the Kaiser scorpion
means *death*!"

Holmes' face showed nothing, neither anger nor fear nor
pain, but kept upon it an element of unreadable blankness,

even as he threw off his jacket and pulled open the front of his shirt, tearing the buttons asunder, and to my utter horror I saw a profoundly red welt the size of a dove's egg rising above a perfectly round hole in his flesh, where stinger had met his skin, and even as the foul woman keened with cruel laughter, I clung to her arm, and forced her down into the chair.

"Take heed, Watson," Holmes said, his words a grunt, for I knew he was already in considerable pain, "I perceive she is armed with a concealed dagger as well."

I took hold of her distant arm, so thin I felt the bones most prominently below the skin, and detected a blade strapped under her sleeve, so pulled that arm behind her as well and held it fast to the small of her back, aware even as I did so that my every instinct was to take care not to inflict pain upon a woman, so ingrained in me it was to conduct myself as a gentleman.

She had counted on that obsequiousness, and that is how she got to him, I thought ruefully, and tightened my hold on the writhing form below me.

I knew I needed to attend to Holmes, who, if the woman's claims of the creature being a Kaiser scorpion were true, bore a grave injury, but I could not get to him and yet restrain her at the same moment, so I shouted to Mrs. Hudson, whom I heard coming courageously up the stairs, summoned by the noises above.

"Pray, Mrs. Hudson," I cried, "do hurry and fetch a constable!"

She did so with much haste, and the knowledge that representatives of the law were coming caused the diminutive woman in my grip to fight still harder against me, her rage granting her a strength nearly paralleling my own as a man.

"He'll die!" she shouted up into my face, her teeth bared, all but spitting. "I know there is no antidote to the Kaiser scorpion's sting, for these last months I have worked for a chemist at university, who makes medicines from venoms. I have bided my time there, waiting for the deadliest of poisons to use against the cruel Sherlock Holmes, and when I saw the arrival of the Kaiser scorpion from German West Africa, and heard of its power, I knew I had found my means of revenge!"

I tried to recall of whom it was she spoke, and finally remembered a case from a year previous concerning a young clerk at a railroad company, Bartlett Nichols, who had sabotaged an engine there on behalf of a radical political movement, causing a collision which injured a dozen passengers, and closed a railway line into London for several days. Yet I also remembered that this man had had no wife, at least at the time of his conviction and the twelve year sentence it carried, despite this assailant's claims in the present that she was that person.

With admirable alacrity, Mrs. Hudson located a constable, and I heard the man's hobnailed boots stomping as he ran head-first up the stairs, and flung open the door.

"Mr. Holmes!" he declared with distress at seeing my friend's now-ashen countenance.

"Ah, Constable Murray," said Holmes with a small smile, his voice caught in a panting for breath which threatened to overcome him. "I am afraid you find me rather the worse for wear this morning."

"This woman is the assailant!" I told Murray. "Do restrain her while I see to Holmes!"

When Murray had taken hold of the so-called Mrs. Nichols—I still knew not the truth of her claim to be wed to the railroad saboteur—I rushed to my bedroom and snatched my medical bag off the floor.

"Dear Watson," said Holmes, now drooping into the chair behind him, his limbs trembling, "my condition is grave, as I feel the venom at work. She did not lie, I fear it was indeed that deadly tropical creature which assaulted me today."

He attempted a smile, then leaned back in the chair, and I saw with concern that even his lips were losing all colour.

Mrs. Hudson let loose a cry and shielded her face with her hands, overcome by the situation which had so suddenly unfolded upon us that morning, clearly afraid, as was I, that Holmes was beyond all help.

Mrs. Nichols, as she styled herself, cackled with delight to see her malice at work, and vowed:

"It is the hour of your death, Sherlock Holmes!"

Such an evil woman, I thought.

Out of the corner of my eye I espied to my surprise and, I uneasily confess somewhat to my satisfaction, Mrs. Hudson strike this Helena Nichols hard across the cheek with the flat of her hand.

"That's quite enough from you, villainess!" she cried heatedly, her face wearing an expression more stern than any I had ever glimpsed upon it.

It was a contest against death itself, I knew, yet I had a growing hope that I possessed a treatment worth attempting, for from my medical bag I drew a device I had kept on-hand in my time as an army surgeon in Afghanistan, where snakebites were not uncommon. It was a thin brass tube of some two inches in length, with a rubber bulb at the end, and by fitting this securely against the site of the sting, and depressing the bulb, it sometimes became possible to create a vacuum and draw out venom.

And so I attempted, crushing the bulb over and over in my fist, deflating and re-inflating it to create suction, wiping at the green-tinged fluid and thickened blood it drew forth. I kept this up for minutes unceasing, until with relief I cried:

"Holmes, I think it is working!"

My friend seemed to try to speak, then his mouth drooped and his face lost expression as he fell forward into a trembling faint, and Mrs. Hudson rushed to him and held him upright by the shoulders.

"Do keep at it, Doctor!" she cried.

And so I did for another five minutes, until my hand doubled into a cramp, and I wondered if I could possibly repeat the process even once more, yet just as I thought this, Holmes' eyes fluttered open, and he leaned back against the chair of his own volition.

"Watson..." he gasped, and Mrs. Hudson and I leaned forward to hear him, "I feel cool death, once near to hand, receding into the distance, and think you have saved my life today."

The Nichols woman, in the process of being shackled by a newly-arrived second constable, while a third divested her of the dagger she'd concealed against her forearm, let loose a thunderous howl of anguish, and called:

"No, he cannot live! My beloved must be avenged!"

The savage outcries of the mad-woman echoed throughout 221B Baker Street as she was half-carried by constables toward a waiting paddy-wagon, and even from the street below, where a crowd had begun to gather, I heard her howling in disappointment.

For her dark wish that a fine man be taken from the world, was not to be granted.

*****

The long hours of that first day were still dreadful at times, for Holmes' breathing progressed only amidst struggles, while his body thrashed in bed as the remaining trace of venom burned through his bloodstream, and the foulest of hallucinations overcame him to the point it was twice necessary for me to apply all my strength to hold him in place, lest he flee raving into the darkness. With piteous regularity, he cried out to people who were not present, his deceased sister most of all.

"Water!" he would call out during moments of clear-mindedness, and would gulp down great quantities, which would soon pour from him in violent sweats.

Yet it was a testimony to his sheer strength that I report he was to survive the sting of one of Africa's deadliest creatures, and by the second day I judged the crisis had passed. Such a relief it was to see Holmes, though still pale and in pain, resting peacefully, and as the day went on, his complexion surrendered some of its gray tones, replaced by a healthy flush.

On the morning of the third day, he was able to sit up and ask that some parsley broth and well-crusted toast be brought to him, which Mrs. Hudson saw-to with the greatest of delight.

After taking his first meal in nearly half a week, Holmes looked at the many telegrams and letters of well-wishes that had come for him, sent by grateful clients, and even by Inspector Lestrade of Scotland Yard, who had called at Baker Street as Holmes lay in a stupor that first night.

"I will take a personal interest in that woman's case, Doctor, you can rely on that," he declared solemnly with a stony firmness. "An amateur he may be, and altogether too interfering at times I could mention, but many of us at Scotland Yard have formed a fondness for Mr. Holmes. That radical who attempted to take him from us shall neither be granted bail nor see daylight again for many years after *I've* given evidence against her for attempted murder, believe you me!"

I told Holmes of Lestrade's words, and though he showed no reaction, I guessed that the promise surely held value to him.

"It was but one token of the esteem with which you are held by many," I continued, as I sat in a chair beside his bed, a spot I had rarely abandoned in the days since the crisis began.

"But not universally regarded, it seems," Holmes said weakly as he sipped from a glass of barley-water Mrs. Hudson had brought up to him.

"No," I agreed, "only by the good people of London. Among evil-doers, you are justifiably detested as few have ever been."

He gazed out at me for a moment, then said:

"Watson, you must be exhausted past all endurance. Pray, do take to your own room and sleep a while. I can see to myself."

"I shall soon," I promised, "but I will stay a little longer, for I cannot tell you how marvelous it is to see you clear-headed and sitting up again. We were all deeply worried..."

"That woman, Watson..." Holmes began, interrupting my further declarations of concern and relief, "what news of her from the time of my incapacitation?"

"As we heard from her own lips, she calls herself 'Mrs. Nichols'," I told him, "and claims to be the wife of that radical Bartlett Nichols, the railroad saboteur whose evil plots you foiled. He'd wanted to disrupt the railroads into the city to call attention to his dogma concerning the un-necessity of all institutions, social, religious, and political."

"Yes," Holmes said, still weak in his voice, "I remember him well, a clever plotter of mayhem, but too proud to hide his own rôle in the calamity he authored, and so he was easily bested. Though, Watson, I suspect you will find my assailant was no lawful wife to the man, whatever her claim."

"Exactly right," I agreed, unsure how he had deduced this there in his sick-bed. "Since taking over the case, himself, with great vigour I might add, Lestrade's investigations showed no marriage license between the woman and this Bartlett Nichols. Her claim is an anarchist's fantasy, part of her own rejection of the ceremony of marriage."

Holmes released a long sigh, and with bounteous self-reproach said:

"I failed to perceive the threat she posed, Watson. The fairer sex is often a source of peril, as I know full well, and yet I so docilely allowed this would-be Corday the very access to me from which she struck."

"You can hardly be blamed there Holmes," I said consolingly, "for I saw nothing in her to cause alarm, either, and—"

"Yes, Watson," Holmes sneered, "but I am hardly *you*, now, am I?"

It was the dismissive tone that heartened me, for however disdainful of my insights and intellect his response may have been, it showed he was fast-returning to himself, and so I smiled with relief at the slight, and said:

"No, my friend, you are unlike any other man in the whole of this world."

*****

Just as word had spread far and fast of Holmes' sordid brush with death, so the news of his recovery traveled rapidly as well, and though he was left weakened for some days after the attack, he bore his injury well, though his pride remained abashed over his failure to perceive the menace that had come before him in the form of a woman.

"I was as foolhardy as any rank amateur, Watson," he said more than once.

"I think you do quite well for yourself as a rule, Mr. Holmes," said Mrs. Hudson, who was upstairs in the sitting room with us, helping go through the letters that had come that morning.

"I thank you, Mrs. Hudson," Holmes said with the indulgent patience he seemed to demonstrate for her in greater quantities than was his habit toward anyone else on the planet.

When gathered into a stack, the letters bidding him a speedy recovery could have been set nearly a foot in height, with more brought in with each post. Despite his evincing scant emotion, or even approval, concerning these jotted well-wishes, I know the sentiment had to have pleased Holmes at least a little, for he looked over each note that either Mrs. Hudson or I handed to him, then mentioned with a word or two whom it was who had written.

"This card is from Mrs. Christensen, the Danish fishing heiress whose emerald I saw returned," he told us. "And this note is from Mr. Justice Fatherby, up in Nottingham, who hanged the murderer of the Bolton family on my expert evidence back in '78."

"A hanging? Well dear me," Mrs. Hudson said, placing a

hand over her heart.

"Before my time," I said, having no idea to what case he referred.

"A well-deserved fate, I assure you," Holmes said, clearly relishing the memory, "for poisoners are the most odious of murderers, and to kill six at the dinner table over a minor argument is particularly repellent."

"And, look, Doctor Watson," Mrs. Hudson said, "a cable from America, from the Providence, Rhode Island Police Department, wishing Mr. Holmes good health and long life."

"Ah, that is Commissioner H. Treadwell," commented Holmes, "who has cabled me for advice a time or two in recent years. A fellow of excellent wisdom, for seeking out my aid."

Almost with awe, Mrs. Hudson stated:

"Do you see, Mr. Holmes, even so far as that news of you has spread?"

I knew she enjoyed having one of the more renown men in the city as her tenant, and Holmes, however much he may have pretended otherwise, enjoyed this tangible proof of the diffusion of his well-deserved fame.

*****

It was a full week after the incident, and Holmes was nearly himself again, that there came to Baker Street a former client, one Colonel J. Basil Morley, retired from his long career with the 8th Surrey Rifles, whom Holmes had aided some seven months previous concerning a series of thefts from the armoury of the regimental headquarters. The Colonel had naturally wished to see the thefts stopped before his upcoming retirement, which was due in a matter of weeks, and Holmes had solved the mystery with alacrity, requiring but a few hours to see through to the heart of the matter and name the guilty party, a corporal who was selling munitions on the black market. The Colonel had been profusely grateful, and had proclaimed Holmes:

"The finest man I have met in these many a year!"

So it was that when the Colonel came up to Baker Street bearing a gift of expensive cigars, my friend took the time to sit with him in the parlour and enjoy a bit of conversation.

"Very glad am I, Mr. Holmes, to espy you looking so well," said Colonel Morley with his deep voice and tone of indisputable command. "Based on what was in the papers and spoken in the reports one hears swirling around even up in Suffolk, where I've retired now, I half-expected you'd be far worse off, for it was at death's very door that the reporters had you posed."

"My flame, as you see," said Holmes, "is rather difficult to extinguish."

At that the Colonel boomed out a hearty laugh.

"In truth he was not far from the Valley of the Shadow," I answered, smoking along on one of the excellent cigars myself. "It was a small miss, but a miss all the same."

"On fractions of inches do soldiers mark their lives," the Colonel declared soberly, "and count their blessings when in the path of fire the fickle dice of chance bounce their way."

A light of reflection rose in his eyes, as he perhaps recalled occasions from his own career when bullets had not missed their targets by those same proverbial inches.

"In that regard, I owe much indeed to Watson," Holmes told his guest.

"Then so do we all," the Colonel stated, lifting his cigar to me in a demi-salute.

"It was an old army doctor's trick," I said, "sucking out of the venom with a device."

"Ah, through the little rubberized bulb, yes," the Colonel remarked. "Fine work then, my good fellow. Seen it done a time or two myself off in the Himalayan Kush. So many vipers there among the rocks, you know. Our pickets were always getting stung along the ankles by those foul slithering beasts."

"The fault was mine in not perceiving the snake when it was before me that morning," Holmes stated, retaining that aura of frustration I had noted in him since the incident. "I should have known danger when it reared its ugly head."

But her head was not ugly, I reflected, *and that had been the problem.*

"Who can blame you there," claimed Morley, "for I ask you, what man since the start of time has ever understood what roils within the female heart? You took that girl for what she seemed, and a dozen times more likely it was that she came to you a damsel in distress. Don't let yourself feel too badly about it all."

I knew the Colonel's words were meant as commiseration, but I also grasped that however sincerely spoken, they rankled Holmes, as they suggested there was a feat of discernment which lay beyond even him, a failing to which my proud friend would never admit.

"Well," Holmes said with finality, "I do not intend that such a thing shall happen twice, for I have learned painfully and well from my ordeal, and will never again be tricked by any woman, however meek her approach."

The words were spoken with such vigour that I caught in them the tone of a vow.

"Then all shall be well with you," the Colonel told him, "for I doubt not your powers of discernment. Thus let me then progress to the second part of why I come today to London."

Holmes gave him a nod, and the old soldier shifted in his chair and said:

"I take it that under the advice of the good doctor here, Mr. Holmes, you are to rest a bit longer and regain your fullest strength, and so I should very much like to extend to you an invitation to come up to the country and be my guest at the family estate in westernmost Suffolk, and let the open skies and good clean air work their wonders on restoring your famously Herculean constitution."

I knew the invitation was unfurled with the noblest of motives, but I understood equally well my friend's detestation of the countryside, for he saw London as his natural element, and the source of his native strength. In that as in so many things he was the opposite of most men.

Thus I was unsurprised when in the most polite manner, Holmes declined the offer, which to his credit the Colonel took in good form.

"I'll tell you, though," the retired officer said near the end of his stay, "it has been a rather strange stretch of weeks up at the old place just lately."

"Oh," I asked, "and why is that?"

I could tell Holmes, for his part, was now listening more closely after his visitor's declaration, for all varieties of strange goings-on of were always of interest to him.

"Well," said Morley, "to be candid—and mind you, this has no bearing one way or the other on why I offered my invitation—it seems the old ghost out in our yew alley has been making a reappearance this summer."

"A ghost?" I asked, and I saw Holmes' attention stray, for he held all ideas concerning such matters with at best ill-concealed contempt.

"Yes," Morley chuckled, "if you can believe such a thing. As a boy growing up there I heard all about the ghost from our old servants, who frequently claimed to have seen it, though I don't mind telling you I never did, and still have not. Accounts of the thing, though, go back to the 1300s, at least, and now after lying dormant for many years, it seems for whatever reason the spectre is again putting in appearances, around twilight, now, out in our yew alley, just beyond the house itself."

"What is it that people say of these sightings?" I inquired.

"Same now as it was in my boyhood," Colonel Morley told me, "a glowing golden figure, like a person, only rounder about the edges and floating rather than walking. Quite menacing, according to those who have encountered it, not at all the friendly sort of ghost one hears about in delightful campfire stories. It has been seen for the past fortnight now by several on staff, and more to the point, has captured the imagination of my eleven-year-old grandson, Barry, who is staying with us until the school term at Collinsdale begins in September. It is his absolute obsession that he see the thing before summer ends, so in his charming little mania the boy sits out in the evenings and keeps his eyes peeled from a vantage point near the edge of the yew alley."

"Indeed?" I asked. "And has young Barry had any success in the matter?"

"Not to present he hasn't," the Colonel answered, "though I tell you, that is not from a lack of dogged determination."

"And what, specifically, is the legend concerning this phantom?" Holmes broke his silence to ask, though with a tone that suggested disdain rather than tremendous interest, as if he found all such ideas both tiresome and banal.

"Well," said Morley, "some say it is the ghost of a young nun from long ago, but others flip this claim onto its head, and in fact the way I grew up hearing it, it is the spirit of a man who lived on the property around the time of the Great Plague of the fourteenth century. They say he was a brute, somehow immune to the effects of the Black Death, and so he would rob the houses of the afflicted, and often the victims themselves as they lay dying, and in the lawless conditions of the catastrophe he grew wealthy, or did for a time, for it seems when the plague was waning, the surviving relatives of those from whom the man had thieved came and seized him, and shut him up inside a charnel house where the yew alley was planted some two centuries later, and there he was left until he perished from hunger."

"Such a ghastly tale!" I exclaimed.

"Rather an interesting one," Holmes said. Then with approval he added:

"It tells us of the prevailing morality of the time the story had its birth, for back then crime was met with stiffer punishment than today, as you see."

"Yes, well," said Morley, slightly ashamed, I think, to be confessing accounts of a phantom on his land, "the story is what the story is, and as I have said, I've never personally seen the thing, either as boy or man, and don't know what to think of this recent rash of reports of it being out there on any given night."

I'm sure Holmes could tell you his thoughts there, I mused.

"I'm certain if anyone can verify the existence of your resident spirit, it'll be your grandson, with the dogged efforts of boyhood," I said, offering my thoughts.

"He is unceasingly determined at that," the Colonel agreed, and I sensed he wished to dismiss the subject, so we did so.

In fact he stayed but a few minutes beyond the closing of this topic, and after once more wishing Holmes all the best in his recovery, took to the door, leaving behind the gift of the cigars, which I knew Holmes would put to good use.

"Fine fellow, him," I said once the Colonel had gone on his way and climbed into a cab out on Baker Street.

"Yes," Holmes agreed, "a most excellent former client."

"And dare I ask," I inquired, "what you make of his tale of a ghost seen on the grounds of his estate?"

"Absurdity, Watson," he told me, "for ghosts no more exist than does that great scaly monster in the waters of that loch up in your birth country."

"If you're predicating the spirit of the yew alley upon those terms, then I wouldn't be so sure it doesn't exist," I enjoined, defending our great national legend of the beast of Loch Ness, which every Scot took pride in championing when aspersions were cast upon the creature's existence...whether he truly believed in it or not.

"Eyewitness accounts are invariably faulty as a rule," Holmes told me, "and in the case of ghosts, more than a few tall tales are generally involved. Now, if you'd be so good as to fetch my Stradivarius for me, I think I shall try my hand at a little music for the first time since my inconveniencing by that sordid woman."

I went to his bedroom and returned with the requested case in hand, and was rewarded moments later by the ethereal sound of Bach's second violin concerto filing the cozy environs of Baker Street.

I felt a deep sense of peace that evening, and figured we'd see no more of Colonel Morley, amiable chap though the man was, and expected that in days ahead, as his strength returned, Holmes would find new mysteries to draw him away from Baker Street, but in at least part of that far-reaching assumption, I was to be proven humblingly incorrect.

*****

It was on the second morning following Colonel Morley's visit, and breakfast had just concluded, that a telegram was brought to the door of our Baker Street abode, soon to be conveyed upstairs by Mrs. Hudson.

"An urgent matter," Holmes noted, "judging by the alacrity with which she transports the cable to our door."

The mystery lasted no more than a quarter of a minute, for when Mrs. Hudson placed the paper in Holmes' hands, I saw my friend frown, as he informed me:

"This comes from Colonel Morley, late our guest. He writes that the grandson he mentioned in connection with the boy's ghost-hunting, has gone missing."

"What?" I cried, as a chill passed up my spine. "Does it tell anything else?"

"Not in his bed this morning, it seems, nor had the bed been slept in. Last seen yesterday evening when he claimed to be going upstairs for the night."

"This is dismal news, Holmes!" I cried out. "There are a score of ways for a boy of eleven to come to mischief in the country. Wells, ponds, perhaps even stumbling across an adder's nest in the woods."

"Not to mention *crime*," said Holmes. "Abduction for

ransom…or for fouler purposes than that, for there are those, as you know, who prey upon children."

"The worst sorts of villains!" I said.

He leapt to his feet, showing the old, familiar energy that always overtook him when confronting a mystery. Though that forcefulness of stride had been absent in the days since his brush with death, it was fortifying to see it return.

"To the country, then!" he cried. "When is the next train to Suffolk?"

I consulted the schedule and gave him my answer as he ran to the bedroom to prepare for his journey, and then raced to the laboratory at the far end of the room, where he took from a shelf the case with which he sometimes traveled when out seeing to his investigations. I knew it contained a chemistry set in miniature that he had used a number of times with great effect.

"Forty minutes until the train, Watson!" he called. "We have not a moment to spare!"

When I hesitated, he demanded:

"Well, you are at liberty to accompany me, I presume?"

"I was only waiting for the invitation!" I replied happily, for after spending much of the past week fearing that my friend's days of adventuring were done, it was marvelous to receive this summons.

We were out the door in a trice, calling farewells to Mrs. Hudson in the kitchen, and were sent swiftly across London in a hansom cab driven by a tiny slip of a man, who smoked a stunted pipe, and squinted against even the light of the morning sun as he hunched over the reins in his leathery hands. A peculiar fellow to be sure, but he got us to Liverpool Station in good time, and a few moments later saw us buying tickets to Ipswich, and our journey of some ninety-five minutes up to Westerfield Station, in the heart of that distant city, was underway.

I reflected that I had been to Ipswich twice before in my life, both times in my days as a soldier, and on one of those had stayed at the Great White Horse Hotel, which Mr. Dickens had made famous in *The Pickwick Papers*. There'd be no such luxury for us today, however, and no sooner had our train bustled to a stop than Holmes had leaped outside, chemistry case in hand, and raced to find the first available conveyance to take us eleven miles to the town of Cottersfield, near where the Morley estate lay.

As we jostled along, and the cobbles of Ipswich gave way to the dusty lanes of the countryside, I looked several times toward my companion to see how Holmes was faring after his illness and recuperation, and upon my third such glance, he said to me:

"Though your skills as a physician are first-rate, Watson, you may safely take a day off in that regard."

"I fear you must allow me my worries, Holmes, for we nearly lost you."

"I assure you I have not only recovered from the consequences of that lapse in my instincts of self-preservation upon that lugubrious morning, but am entirely invigorated by thoughts of the case which lies before me."

"Good to hear!" I said heartily.

"I am never tired when working," he added, "only when swept up in the receding tides of lethargy and boredom. Indeed, the more hours a case requires, the greater my energies grow."

Yes, I thought, *but when the case is done, you all-but collapse in exhaustion.* My friend, I thought, medically-speaking, invested far too much of himself in his undertakings.

About half an hour into our ride, nearly halfway to our destination, I happened to glance over, and in a field off the roadway sat a caravan of Irish gypsies, their handful of little wagons, each merrily painted, spread out in a fallow field, where the inhabitants seemed to be less encamped than merely stopping for a morning break in their endless travels.

"Odd, Holmes," I remarked. "I did not think we'd be likely

to encounter such a band up here this time of year."

"Well, they must always be somewhere, mustn't they?" he replied.

"I suppose so," I agreed, not letting his patronizing tone ruffle me.

"One finds them scattered across the countryside," he added, "and they are an odious lot as a rule, though I have had recourse to involve such as those in my investigations a time or two. For the right price they can be forthcoming with knowledge of a useful sort, and as strong-arm men for hire... well, one sometimes needs to turn to unorthodox means to achieve certain ends."

I did not know what to say to that, but as the caravan receded from my view and our coach rolled along far out in the quiet countryside of East Anglia, the Irish wanderers were soon out of my thoughts, replaced by the unavoidable question of whether it was just possible we might find Colonel Morley of the opinion that a ghost had played some rôle in his grandson's abrupt vanishing.

It was a silly thought, certainly, but still a thrill danced inside me when I remembered the tales I grew up hearing in Scotland, told me by an old neighbour woman from Fife, who claimed malevolent spirits sought out children in the dark hours of night, and that she herself had seen spirits many times. It was all nonsense, of course, the lurid imaginings of an old woman whose fanciful tales had delighted my brother and I in those days, yet I'd be lying if I failed to admit such deeply-instilled ideas vied against the logic of my better nature.

*****

It was a little before noon, and the warm summer sun was high overhead, when, despite him having been Holmes' client in the recent past, we arrived only for the first time at the estate of Colonel Morley. The grounds, I saw, were well-kept, with many mature trees above an immaculate and flourishing lawn, in the midst of which sat a sizable dun-brick manor house, and in front of that, somewhat out of usual custom, flew both the Union Jack, and the crimson and gold colours of his old regiment.

No doubt alerted to our coming by a sharp-eyed servant, we had only just drawn up before the house's great sandstone façade, an 18th century addition to a far older structure, I hazarded, when a rush of three figures came pressing through the doors. Colonel Morley led the way, but to the rear of him, a respectful few paces behind, was another, younger man, tall and with a distinct military bearing, the faintest traces of an incipient whitening at his temples, and to Morley's right was a woman of comparable age, whom I intuited must have been his wife. I noted that she was stout and graying, but from her expression of sober command guessed her to be an imperious sort who doubtless ran her household with the expected efficiency of the spouse of a career army officer.

"Mr. Holmes!" the Colonel cried, approaching us with haste. "Dr. Watson! I am so relieved you have come with such alacrity, sirs! You have my thanks, as matters here are utterly upended by young Barry's troubling disappearance!"

"Has the boy ever wandered off before, either here or at home, or at his school?" asked Holmes without undue preamble as he strode from the coach.

"Never!" Morley replied. "He is as fine and proper a lad as could be asked for, if at times rather too imaginative."

"He was happy to be spending his summer here?" Holmes demanded. "There was no one he unduly missed from home and with whom he might have set off to reconnect? Or anyone new in his life? A local friend perhaps?"

He was tossing these questions in a rapid-fire manner, but Morley took them in stride and answered:

"He showed every sign of enthusiastically embracing his time here, and just the other evening expressed his sorrow that the summer ever had to end, and he return to school."

A healthy enough sentiment for any boy, I thought.

"You have alerted the constabulary, I take it, and initiated a search on your own?" Holmes asked as he stopped at last in front of Colonel Morley and let his eyes pass over him and the others, pulling from their persons clues that would, I knew, have eluded the perception of even the most intelligent of ordinary men.

"Yes, all of that," Morley confirmed with an impatient agitation that he nonetheless held under a tight control.

"Tell me the steps taken, thus far, to locate your grandson," Holmes instructed him.

Morley began:

"Searches, as you said, have been made of all the places one might fear a boy could end up to his peril, and the constables are going around the countryside searching with our groom and groundsman in tow, along with some of the tenants, who are lending a hand in this worrisome hour."

"That is to the good," said Holmes shortly. "Then let us proceed indoors to—"

But here Colonel Morley burst out:

"Wait, Mr. Holmes, I must tell you, there is a new development just this last hour, and we don't know what to make of it, or what it signifies!"

Holmes set his case down on the ground beside him and, all attention now, demanded:

"New development? What is its nature?"

"Come, let me show you," insisted Morley. "It is quite peculiar!"

At this he hustled by us with impressive velocity for a man of increasing years, toward what I knew was the yew alley of which we'd been told, that scene so connected with the history of ghostly activity on the estate. We were at his heels and nearly there when he called:

"It is a *stain*, Mr. Holmes!"

"A stain?" Holmes demanded.

"Of some sort, yes, though highly unusual. Like nothing I have ever seen. It lies in the grass of the yew alley, precisely where the ghost has been seen. It showed up all at once this morning, a few yards from where Barry would spread his blanket and sit in wait for the spirit he was so determined to see."

Oh, surely this was not good, I thought.

"And you say this oddity was not there at any other time?" asked Holmes. "Nor even last night?"

"Never in the past, sir!"

It was Mrs. Morley, keeping pace with us from behind who answered this in her throaty tone of voice, breaking her weighty silence at last.

"I have never seen such a thing in all my days as this mark on the ground," she stressed, "and I know not what it signifies, but connected as it surely is to my grandson's being taken there among those spirit-haunted yews, it tells of *something,* one may be sure!"

Her grandson's *being taken,* I thought, noting her words. So that was the mindset there, was it? That the boy had not wandered off into misadventure, as his grandfather, the Colonel, seemed to hope, but been deliberately transported away by someone... or some*thing,* I noted, thinking of her reference to the "spirit-haunted yews."

I knew Holmes had noted her term as well, though he said nothing.

We came to rest at a spot perhaps a dozen yards into the long yew alley, where the bushes, ancient and gnarled with interwoven branches, grew tall, and I saw plainly the mysterious marking upon the ground. It was dark brown, nearly black, perhaps the color of coffee left long-brewing, and was spread out in the shape of...

Oh! I hated to think so but the connection was absolutely there to be made, for it was undeniably in the shape of a boy of young Barry's age, limbs askew in what leaped out in my mind as...terror.

"We have not touched the stain," Morley told Holmes, nor have we approached it any closer than two yards, let us say, for we held out hopes that you were coming in response to my telegram, and knew you'd wish to see it untrammeled and in its purest state."

"Ah," said Holmes, "then you did well."

He knelt just beyond the long marking on the ground and set about opening the case which contained the portable chemistry lab.

To my eyes the discolouration looked like nothing so much as a shadow permanently suspended in time, in defiance of the sun, with the suggestion of arms outstretched in what was either defense, or absolute surprise.

"Again," Holmes asked, "you are certain this stain was there neither last night nor at any time before it was noticed this morning?"

"Absolutely sure, sir," Mrs. Morley replied with a tone that left little room for argument. "We set out at first light to seek Barry, most of the household, I mean, and were this marking in the yew alley, then, we'd have seen it, yet we did not, nor did we until later in the morning, after many others had also passed near this spot."

"Yes, it was after my telegram had been sent," Colonel Morley added, "or I'd assuredly have mentioned it."

How very strange, I thought. *And how disturbing.*

Holmes drew exceedingly close to the stain, his face mere inches above its impenetrable darkness, before he removed from his case a flat wooden object, rather like a tongue depressor in my own medical practice, and used it to delicately touch the marking.

"It is dry," he noted aloud, then leaned low and carefully sniffed at it, before slowly raising up, and frowning. "And is not paint or any dye, nor is a burn mark, for the ground below is not charred by fire."

"It is not of this world," whispered Mrs. Morley under her breath, perhaps to herself.

Holmes frowned once again, whether in response to the woman's sentiment or for other reasons, then enunciating each syllable with care, stated:

"It is decidedly most peculiar..."

"It is clearly supernatural," Mrs. Morley said, now openly voicing her thoughts.

Holmes ignored this and from within his case removed a test tube and a scalpel, and a set of tweezers, and careful cut out a patch of the stain perhaps the size of a man's littlest finger. He dropped this into the test tube and sealed it, then stared a moment longer at the area before him, and I could read both contemplation and consternation in his eyes.

"What was your grandson's height and weight?" he demanded.

"I confess I do not know precisely," Mrs. Morley replied, "though he was an average-size boy, neither tall nor short, thin nor stout."

"That is fine," said Holmes. "The stain is not a precise match for a boy's figure, as you see, and there is, I do perceive, an overall foreshortening effect I find curious, but note that it does crudely approximate a suggestion of a human form. There is clearly a head, a torso, even limbs...which appear splayed, as if—"

He arrested his words, though I felt sure his thoughts were mirrors of my own in regards to what pose the shape suggested, and from where he knelt studied once more the darkening on the lawn, and appeared to sink into deep thought for a long silent moment before at last rising and announcing tersely:

"I require each of you to stand very still where you are and make no further intrusions into the yew alley. You were also wise not to touch the stain, and I advise you not to do so, now or in the future."

"Is it harmful?" Mrs. Morley asked.

"That, Madam, remains an unknown."

Holmes pulled a magnifying lens from his chemistry case, and assumed a pose and manner with which I was familiar from past cases, as he stooped low and peered intently at the ground all around him, proceeding at an exceedingly slow walk over the next quarter-hour, until he had covered the entirety of the alley, taking it in, then traveling around the entirety of the lawn in its vicinity, studying what looked to me each separate inch of the earth below. Finally he rose back to his full height and stood a moment staring into space itself, before he resumed his normal stride, and returned to us at last.

"What did you find, Mr. Holmes?" the Colonel demanded, unable to wait.

With a dissatisfied flatness in his tone, Holmes replied:

"I found nothing,"

"Nothing whatsoever?" Mrs. Morley pressed, as if unable to believe what she had heard.

"I saw neither traces left by the boy over the last day," Holmes clarified, "nor the tracks of anyone else whom I ascertained was not of the household. None of the tracks, so far as my methods allow me to say with certainty, were made overnight, based on the effect the morning dew would have in altering such imprints. There is no sign that any abduction at all took place within the yew alley. For our purposes, it lies as innocent as a lamb pasture."

While I was sifting out precisely what these findings indicated, Mrs. Morley, who was to my right threw up her hands and intoned:

"Then Barry has vanished into thin air! You see, gentlemen? It was the ghost! The ghost of that cruel man *has my grandchild!*"

I looked toward her, as did Holmes.

"You are a believer in supernatural phenomena, Madam?" I asked her, though it was clear that she was.

"A 'believer', no, Doctor Watson," she said with emotion, "rather a confirmed eyewitness, as I have seen the ghost on two occasions in my years of residence here. It is a glowing figure which hovers in the air itself, transmitting menace and anger, a cruel spirit in death, to be sure, as it was in life, robbing from the sick and dying as the man did, and meriting the punishment he received. I know the ghost to be real, and if, as you say, no human has taken my grandson, what possibility does that leave but his tragic encounter with the horrors of that which lies beyond?"

Beside her Colonel Morley appeared both embarrassed by his wife's words, and also moved by a desire to conceal the fact.

Holmes however, looked steadily at the woman and said:

"You misapprehend me, Madam, when I say there was no sign of any abduction within the alley, for this does not indicate that I attest to a supernatural authorship of the event, but rather that I am ruling it out."

"*Ruling it out?*" Mrs. Morley repeated. "How could that be so, when surely a man would have left behind traces of criminal actions?"

"For the simple reason," Holmes answered with forbearance, "that had the boy been taken in the alley, I should have seen the signs such an action would have left behind. Thus this can only mean that if an abduction has indeed occurred—"

"You can doubt that Barry has been taken?" Mrs. Morley demanded.

"I am not, shall we say," Holmes told her, "released from considering many possibilities, with hostile abduction being but one. As for the idea that the deed was perpetrated by the shade of a man centuries dead, if indeed such a person existed at all outside of local lore, that explanation I do not begin to entertain."

"Well I am not so closed-minded as you," Mrs. Morley said with a scoff. "For what evidence would a ghost leave when it snatched a living boy away into another realm? I suspect there would be none, just as you have discovered! So how does an absence of evidence rule out the supernatural, Mr. Holmes?"

"It is in the nature of a non-event to leave behind no evidence," said Holmes evenly. "And I rule it out, because the supernatural does not exist."

Mrs. Morley was stymied for a moment, as if unaccustomed to being challenged in this or any other regard, and Holmes went on, undeterred.

"To continue, I can now say that if there was an abduction, it occurred elsewhere, not in the yew alley itself. To this moment, that is what I have learned in the case."

"But the stain!" cried Mrs. Morley.

"I do not yet know what that signifies, but I have a theory, which I shall for the moment, keep to myself."

He turned, then, to his client and inquired:

"Colonel Morley, owing to our haste, I am lacking one introduction. Who is the second gentlemen in your retinue this morning?"

He spoke of the tall man standing to the couple's rear, who had emerged from the house at our arrival and gone to the yew alley with us, though he had said nothing to that point.

"I am sorry, Holmes," Morley spoke up to say, "the distress of these events has sent my manners flying. May I present my former aide-de-camp in the 8th Surrey Rifles, Lieutenant Terrence Peters, retired. He was away on leave at the time of your investigation into the armoury matter last spring, and presently works in the capacity of my assistant in the composition of my memoirs, for after three years serving under me, he knew my habits, sparing me having to break some new fellow into my stubborn ways."

"At your service, sir," said the Lieutenant, with a small bow to Holmes, before extending a hand toward me. "And you, Doctor, I could mark as a fellow army man, even had I not the advantage of foreknowledge."

I shook the proffered hand, finding nothing objectionable in the man, but Holmes glanced sternly toward Peters for an instant before asking:

"Where were you serving when you received the gunshot wound to your upper right arm?"

The Lieutenant gaped an instant, then demanded with surprise:

"Was the fact of my wounding previously known to you, sir?"

"Only by present observation," Holmes answered. "I perceive that you are, as is the case with most men, right-handed, yet there is a looseness to the fit of the sleeve of that arm, which with most men is usually present, however slightly, on the left side."

Here both the Colonel and Lieutenant Peters looked down at their sleeves for verification of the claim.

"Don't bother to seek out confirmation," Holmes said almost lazily, "it is only discernible to a uniquely trained eye, such as my own. I noted this fact about you, sir, and combined with my knowledge of your military career, it suggested that there is a degree of withering in your right arm, most likely as a result of a bullet wound while in uniform."

Peters' face took on an expression, somewhere between embarrassment and distaste, and though I said nothing, I thought it rather an uncharitable observation for Holmes to offer, singling out the man in this way, given that his affliction had been incurred in Her Majesty's service.

"It was near the Hindu Kush, under the Colonel some years ago," Lieutenant Peters finally confirmed. "I was shot by a bandit while on patrol near the Jhelum River. Sent my assailant to Hell with my other arm, however."

Visible only to me, who knew his mannerisms so well, I noted something in the man's words seemed distasteful to Holmes, though quickly I told Peters:

"I can sympathize, as I, too, was wounded during my time in Afghanistan."

"Then we are brothers via the shedding of our blood for Queen and Country," Peters offered with a friendly smile.

Holmes, however, was not done with the man, for he stated:

"I perceive your spouse, Lieutenant Peters, is frequently away, and that matters are strained in your home life."

Oh, surely that was too much, I thought as Peters,

offended, his theretofore pleasant expression slipping away, hotly cried:

"Now see here, sir!"

I little blamed him, and was wondering if Holmes entirely knew the rudeness of his last statement, when I caught the fact that he was giving the former officer a sharp stare of evaluation, as if seeking something in his unguarded reaction, though what this apparent exercise in deliberate provocation signified I could not guess, only grasped that for whatever reason, the taunt had not been accidental.

Whatever the motivation had been, Holmes turned back from Peters, as if finished with him and caring no more for him one way or the other, and said to Morley:

"Let us go now into the house, where I will speak with all of you, and perhaps others there on staff, if I require it, for I have many questions."

"Of course," Colonel Morley replied, hurriedly, before the glowering Peters could give voice to his outrage.

Glancing over his shoulder at his now red-faced assistant, Morley added:

"We shall *all* grant you our fullest cooperation, as this matter supersedes any other considerations."

"Quite right, sir," Peters said, though with a final scowl cast at Holmes before he stepped off ahead of the rest of us, clearly putting all possible distance between himself and the detective's future offenses.

"Actually," Holmes stated, "Lieutenant Peters need not be present from this point forward. I shall not need him in future, as he is, incidentally, fully uninvolved in the disappearance of the boy, and therefore of limited interest to me."

"I never doubted his innocence there," said Morley, "but still I suppose it is good to have the matter confirmed."

"No," Holmes went on to add, startling even me, "on a habitual basis the man is a boorish lout toward his wife, but not an abuser of young boys. A boy, after all, might strike the coward back."

Every face, including my own, turned rapidly toward him.

Those who committed violence toward women were never looked on fondly by Holmes, I knew, whatever his recent outlook following one of the 'gentler sex' nearly killing him, but I wondered what clues he had seen upon the lieutenant to mark the retired junior officer as such a man?

"I cannot think that claim is true, Mr. Holmes," said Mrs. Morley, "for I know the lieutenant's wife, Violet, and have never perceived her to show any signs of fearing her husband, or being harmed by him. Had I seen these, I assure you, I should have spoken to my husband."

"There are many varieties of harm one might inflict upon another," Holmes answered, "and ways a victimized woman may conceal her state. Were I you, madam, I might speak closely with the lady upon this subject when next you see her. It is not unknown for a woman to confide only to another woman. And you, Colonel, might be wise to dismiss Peters from your service, for I do not judge you to be the sort who'd wish to be associated with a wife-beater."

These words had the effect of ending all talk for a moment, as each party considered what Holmes had said. Finally Morley answered solemnly:

"I will look into your claim, as I do value your insights, Mr. Holmes."

"I am glad to hear it," Holmes commented. "In the meantime I would rather not be unnecessarily in your assistant's presence."

Though his eyes widened at those words, Morley drew himself back to the case at hand, and as we closed-in on the house announced:

"It is possible the Constable-Sergeant from town, who is overseeing the official search for Barry, may join us, as he is due to check in and deliver his report. He came by not long before your arrival and promised another update before midafternoon."

"That is fine," said Holmes with a deep indifference that still managed to make it sound as if the decision regarding the constable's presence rested with him alone. In his hand he was conveying the case in which rested the chemistry set, with his sample from the yew alley sealed within, and I was most curious to find what he would learn of it.

We went up to the house, above which on the lintel stood an old carving of an owl with outstretched claws, swooping in upon a snake, and I saw Peters, who had marched ahead of us a little distance, stood waiting within the entryway,

There the Colonel said uneasily to him:

"Er, Terrence, would you mind perhaps going to my study and in my absence sorting through my writings from last night?"

Lieutenant Peters appeared surprised by this request, and gazed from his employer toward Holmes, as if aware the motivation for the directive had originated with him.

"Certainly, Colonel," he replied after an instant. "I'll be on-hand should you require me."

With a final belligerent glance at Holmes, Peters set off into the house, and was quickly gone from sight.

"I still think you are wrong about him," Morley said with a sigh, as he guided us into a vast and well-appointed drawing room on the ground floor opposite the yew alley, not at all the severe setting I might have expected in the home of a military man.

Not replying to this sentiment, the great consulting detective merely absorbed his surroundings with a roving eye.

"You entertained in this room last week," Holmes stated. "A gathering of military wives, perhaps?"

"Why, yes," Mrs. Morley answered, gazing around her in puzzlement, and I likewise saw no possible sign that such an event had transpired.

"The meager quantity of dust atop the Japanese-style partition placed in the far end of the room has recently been disturbed," Holmes explained lightly, "thus I intuited it was made use of not long before."

Facile enough, I thought.

Mrs. Morley offered us refreshments and proposed to ring for the butler, and in truth I could have used a spot of tea to pick me up after our journey, but Holmes pointedly declined, and announced:

"With your cooperation, before I analyze the sample you saw me take from the stain in the alley, I shall continue my investigation by interviewing you, Colonel and Mrs. Morley."

"Of course, sir," Mrs. Morley answered.

"In the previous day," Holmes began, "did you notice anything whatsoever unusual either here in the house or upon the grounds?"

"It was an ordinary day," Morley answered, causing his wife to nod silently beside him.

"Were there visitors of any kind?"

"None," Mrs. Morley replied.

"How did each of you spend it?

The pair answered, telling of unremarkable activities, such as replies to letters, going over household accounts with the cook, and the cleaning and oiling of shotguns in their cases, as the Colonel insisted be done once a fortnight throughout the year, whether or not the guns had been fired. Yet Mrs. Morley reported an incident which in its own small way did draw itself outside the mundane.

"I went unexpectedly to town," she admitted, "out of aggravation, I confess, for my cat, Wellington, he is of a mischievous nature, and I had come in from a walk with Barry out along the tree line—he wished only to speak of his efforts to see the ghost, a wearisome conversation, I say somewhat guiltily now—and had taken off my bonnet and laid it upon a table in the drawing room and was having some tea after my stroll, when I looked down to see Wellington had captured the bonnet in his paws and quite torn through it with his teeth. He ran from my scolding, and so aggrieved was I at my loss that I summoned my companion, Mrs. Drummond, who goes everyplace with me, and one of the house-maids as well, in case we stopped by the market and there was carrying to be done. We went into Cottersfield to see the milliner, Mrs. Ferguson and her daughter, and be measured for a new bonnet, identical to the one I'd lost."

"And while in Cottersfield," asked Holmes, "were you conscious of anything out of the ordinary? Did you see anyone who stands out in your mind as unusual?"

"Quite the contrary," Mrs. Morley claimed. "It was as staid and uneventful a trip as could be imagined."

"And where," Holmes asked, "was the boy, Barry, during the day?"

"Here," the Colonel supplied, "outside playing through the morning, and with me when I dined at noon. As for the rest of the day...well, boys will roam and find their adventures, won't they? He was back in time for dinner, which was later than usual that night, and if he made no especial mention of his activities, neither did he betray signs of anything out of the ordinary."

"Of what did he speak at dinner?" asked Holmes.

"We have raised our children, and they theirs, to keep silent at table," Mrs. Morley said, with a slight touch of pride.

"After dinner, then?" the detective pressed.

"We retired to the parlour," Mrs. Morley revealed, "and there we congregated for a while, and of course, as you might guess, it was his plans to see the ghost under the yews that was the subject which dominated his mind."

"Was he allowed to go out and seek the spirit?" asked Holmes.

"We had no objection if he did so a reasonable hour, and near the house," Morley stated. "It was his time to waste, as it were. It was, or so I thought, a charming little pursuit, one he would look back on in his dotage in the next century as a pleasant memory of a long-ago summer spent with his grandparents."

There was poignancy in this statement, and even Holmes was silent a moment before he asked:

"So he was back inside at the aforementioned 'reasonable hour'?"

"By 8.45, yes, and sent up to bed," the boy's grandmother confirmed. "I tucked him in myself."

"I presume he was not checked on in the night?"

"Certainly not," the lady answered, "he is quite old enough to be beyond such things, though it was generally I who would go in and see him in the morning, and so energetic a child was he that I never had to rouse him, he was always up and at the waiting to begin the day. It was abnormal, I felt at once, not to find him in his room, and to discern that his bed had not been slept in."

"How did you determine that?" Holmes asked.

"The covers were still turned down as I had left them, and the pillows plumped. The bed had obviously not been occupied in the night. Even my untrained eyes could detect that."

"So his disappearance, whatever the cause, was between, let us say ten last night, and six this morning?"

"Yes," Mrs. Morley said simply.

"What were your own specific movements last night, Colonel Morley?" Holmes next asked.

"I worked with Peters dictating my recollections of a skirmish in the hill country of northern India back in '62," came the reply. "Peters stayed on and dined with my wife and Barry and me before setting off for his home in Cottersfield, then I sat up alone after dinner, answering correspondence from an old friend, Brigadier Herschel Scott, also now retired, and living in Cornwall. Finally I went up to my room near eleven, and was asleep, I'd judge, by half-past."

"You sleep separately from your wife?"

"Yes, as it happens," Morley replied.

If he felt the question intruded into the privacy of his marriage, he did not show it, which I had long-ago decided was the best manner in which to handle Holmes' personal and often odd, inquiries.

"And when did you last set eyes upon the boy?"

"Just before I went into my office alone last evening," said Morley, "to see to the correspondence I mentioned."

"Did you speak with him?"

"For a moment."

"And what was his disposition?"

"He was his usual self, I would say. Neither agitated nor downcast. He spoke with me about his intentions to stalk the ghost if it did not soon appear, and I told him a little story about one of my staff officers in India, who lost a leg attempting to stalk a particularly cunning tigress in tall grass. Barry expressed sympathy for the man, and said he would have more care than the fellow did should he ever hunt a tiger, himself, one day, as I hope he shall."

Despite the gravity of the circumstances, the Colonel gave a fond little chuckle, and added:

"Ah that lad..."

"And you, Mrs. Morley?" Holmes asked next. "After seeing the boy to bed, what time did you turn in?"

"I am in the custom of an early retirement, and was asleep before nine-thirty. I was among the first awake this morning, as I often am, and was about the house, as usual, just as the servants were first up seeing to the fires and taking on the rest of their duties. As I said I went up to rouse Barry, thinking he was sleeping oddly late, and I assumed it was because he had sneaked back outside behind my back to keep a watch for the ghost."

"Had you encouraged him to do so?" Holmes asked her.

"I had not," Mrs. Morley said firmly, "and intended to have a firm word with him if he had, though I did speak honestly with him and told him of the occasions I had seen the phantom, and I think these accounts did perhaps inspire some of his tenacity in that regard. I had seen the ghost, and he ardently wished to as well."

She added this with a defiantly raised eyebrow, as if daring Holmes to tell her again that the shade in the yew alley did not exist.

"You mentioned the staff were already about their duties upon your arising," he said. "Who are the persons in residence in your household?"

I supposed he posed this question to her rather than to the master of the place, for the reason that a woman might be expected to have a fuller knowledge of such matters, and indeed she answered at once.

"As for family," she began, "just Jonathan and myself, and of course Barry, who is visiting."

"And the others on-site?"

"The lieutenant, who is employed by my husband, does not reside here," she answered, "but there is Watkins, our groom, the groundsman, Clark, the cook, Mrs. Blithewaite, the scullery maid, who is a village child called Becky, the two house-maids, Ada and Ivy. There is also the butler, Hardy, and my ladies' maid, Mrs. Drummond, who alas, is indisposed, and has not left her room since last evening."

Now there was an aberration, I thought to myself.

Feeling the need to say more by way of clarification under the weight of Holmes' stare, she added:

"It is an unfortunate, recurring affliction, headaches that come upon her in several instances a year, and until their passing leave her nearly blinded by scintillating lights within her eyes. She is an excellent companion at all other times, and I do not hold the infirmity against her, for like a soldier she bears her suffering courageously and without complaint."

"A kinder attitude than many mistresses held toward their servants," I said.

"I am not illiberal by nature, Doctor," she replied.

I again wondered if this could possibly be a clue of some significance, the lady's companion being absent with a supposed condition coinciding with the boy's disappearance. I said nothing, however, and left it to Holmes to formulate his own perceptions. He said nothing of this, however, and simply asked:

"That is all who live here on the grounds?"

"That is the entirety of our household, yes," Mrs. Morley stated. "We have had no housekeeper here since the retirement of Mrs. Darrow some three years ago, as our family in residence had by then dwindled to just Jonathan and myself, our son and two daughters being grown and gone elsewhere. Also there is the matter of this place having stood empty of all save a minimal maintenance staff during the years we were in India, until our return in '73."

Holmes nodded and declared:

"That is sufficient for the moment, and I thank you. I now require a small room where I might conduct some experiments of a chemical nature. A place where it will not do damage if I require the lighting of a small flame, perhaps."

"I know of a place that should fulfill your requirements," said Mrs. Morley, who then rose and crossed the room to tug a velvet rope which dangled twelve feet from the ceiling, summoning the butler.

"In the meantime," Holmes said, turning to Colonel Morley, "I suggest the search efforts be kept up. As I cannot as of yet narrow matters down, this remains is the wisest course."

"It shall be," Morley said.

I saw upon his normally stoical features a certain dejection vying with the worry, and a vague consternation, for I think he had hoped that by some miracle Holmes would produce the missing boy within minutes of his arrival.

"Should the Constable-Sergeant you mentioned make an appearance to report on his attempts at progress," said Holmes, "do kindly inform me at once."

"Of course," said Morley.

It was then that the butler, Hardy, a lugubrious-looking stooped-shouldered specimen of the profession, cadaverously pale and dull about the eyes, came into the room and received his instructions to escort Holmes and myself to the far side of the dwelling.

"Very good, Madam," he intoned with a well-practiced bow, prior to showing us to a stone-sided mudroom off a side entrance.

Before he left us alone, Holmes stopped him a moment and asked:

"Tell me, Hardy, have you any thoughts upon the matter of the missing boy?"

"I am sure I do not, sir," Hardy answered without expression or emphasis.

Ah, I thought, *the stubbornness of all good butlers, who drain themselves of opinions and personality to show their dedication.*

"And what are your thoughts concerning accounts of the ghost here?" Holmes pressed him.

"I cannot speak with authority upon such phenomenon, myself, sir."

It was an odd turn of phrase, and indeed Holmes did not let it stand un-annotated.

"You *cannot*? Why is that?"

"I cannot speak of it, because I have not seen it, sir."

"But you have, of course, heard talk?"

"I have, sir."

"Moreso recently?"

"Yes, sir, particularly of late, for several on staff claim recent experiences of encountering the phantom."

This reflected what Morley had told us back at Baker Street two days previous.

"Was there any particular event which seemed to precede these sightings?" Holmes asked the man.

"Not that I am aware, sir."

"But the legend did pre-date these supposed manifestations of late?"

"It did, sir. I have heard tales of the yew alley being haunted since I first came into service here, well before the rash of claims made this present summer."

"Did these tales imparted to you in the past differ markedly from those ghostly intrusions reported in recent weeks?"

"Yes, sir, somewhat."

I was surprised to hear this and demanded:

"In what ways?"

"Well, sir," said Hardy, looking toward me with his blank eyes, "in most of the accounts I heard in the past, there was more than one ghost said to haunt the yew alley."

"How extraordinary!" I burst out.

"Tell me of them," Holmes instructed.

"There was said, sir, to be the ghost of a man, and the spirit of a lady. The former malevolent, the latter benign."

Somehow, though I could not think why, this revelation seemed unsettling.

"And do you hold that these tales have any merit in the world of reality?" Holmes asked him.

"As my mistress declares she has seen at least one of the ghosts herself, sir, it is not for me to contradict her."

A perfect reply for a loyal servant to offer, I thought, almost amused.

"And what did young Barry report of the matter?" Holmes asked with something of an air of finality to the question.

Hardy paused for the slightest instant, before he dutifully answered:

"That when he met the ghost, he hoped he could go away with it into the netherworld."

*****

"What are your thoughts thus far, Holmes?" I asked when the butler had departed, his last statement still ringing in my ears.

"That three elementary possibilities are supported by the facts, Watson: the child has absconded; the child has been taken; or the child has met with misfortune beyond his planning or control."

"Well, er, yes," I replied, "that is rather rudimentary, but I mean have you formed specific ideas, given the testimony and evidence?"

"None to speak of," he answered simply, looking away from me and beginning the work he had before him by opening the chemistry set.

"What was it that made you declare Lieutenant Peters to be...as you said he was?" I inquired, finding the idea of the brutalization of a woman so loathsome I could not openly speak of it.

"His knuckles bore signs of bruising," Holmes told me, "though I knew with his withered arm he was no avocational boxer, and gathered him to be a man who took his self-pitying frustrations out in other ways. Also the care demonstrated in his attire lacked a woman's touch, telling me he was deprived the attentions of a loving spouse. Furthermore there was, though I doubt you or the others noted it, a single scratch, nearly healed, upon his neck, just above his collar. It was made by the fingernails of a woman attempting to defend herself from an attack she should not have been obliged to endure. All this came together to paint an only-too telling portrait of that braggart's conduct in the domestic side of his life. Namely, he is one who beats his wife."

"I see," I said, feeling regret that I had shaken the hand of such a brute. "Fortunately you have planted the seeds of knowledge in Morley," I added, "and I shall take up my own interest in the welfare of this lady."

"As shall I," Holmes added, "when this case is done. Also I mentioned my knowledge of his wedded state to fluster him, as I find few men can manage both a concealment of guilt, and unexpected outrage at the same time, and I noted no hint that he was hiding undue worries where the boy's disappearance was concerned. Thus I knew he did not merit suspicion in that way at least. Now...on to my experiment. Let us see what the stain from the yew alley might tell us."

I fell silent and gazed on as Holmes turned to the portable chemistry set, and laid out certain items in preparation for the experiments he was clearly eager to undertake, for I could tell the stain in the yew alley had greatly roused his curiosity.

Carefully and precisely, he set a ceramic disk about the size of a tea platter down upon the shelving there, and un-stoppered the test tube which contained a sample of grass and soil from where the yew alley had borne a stain the colour of a moonless night sky, the entirety of it so suggestively shaped like a young boy. Using a scalpel, Holmes divided this into three parts, and then removed a trio of glass vials, two in liquid form, red and green, the third holding a grayish powder, a minute portion of which he skillfully combined with a small quantity of water, until it too attained a fluid state. Next I watched him take three separate droppers and drip a quantity of liquids onto the soil samples. In two cases there seemed no reaction, but in the third—upon which Holmes soon fixed the whole of his attention—a slight crackling was heard, followed by a boil of crystalline foam, reminding me of the effect of hydrogen peroxide poured onto a cut.

"Remarkable!" I exclaimed, though Holmes said nothing, merely looked on with total concentration, his eyes glued before him.

For half a minute the colourless bubbles continued to rise and expand before collapsing upon themselves, at which time Holmes withdrew a sample of the resultant liquid, steaming hot, and squirted it onto a petri dish, which he then heated still more over a low blue flame blazing upon a portable apparatus. This almost immediately began to simmer, then boil, and become thick, like molasses, so that what remained took on a tar-like quality, with a slight redness below its dark surface.

Holmes scooped away a little of the tarry material and spread it onto the tiny glass plate, which he slid in beneath a portable microscope he removed from inside the chemistry case. He placed his eye over the ocular and studied what he saw there.

"Fascinating, Watson," he said a minute later, almost with a sigh.

"What does it mean, Holmes?"

"It means, my dear Watson, that this is no ectoplasmic secretion from the darkness beyond the grave, but a rather moderately sophisticated compound made by someone who knows a little about the science of chemistry. Alas for this as-yet unknown person, I know a good deal more, and now understand how our supposed ghostly residue was formed."

"So it was a deliberate act?" I asked.

"Oh, yes, most definitely," he answered, sounding less focused and more contemplative, "which tells me a good deal more about this case than I could be sure of even half an hour ago, whatever my growing suspicions. Someone, you see, has plotted to throw off lesser investigators by making it seem as if a supernatural act transpired in the yew alley, when in the end, our 'ghostly shadow' came from a laboratory. I could create the same effect with half an hour's labour."

"A ruse, then," I exclaimed. "Someone has made use of the ghost as a smokescreen!"

"Indeed, and now we might cross two of the aforementioned possibilities off that little list I gave you, for I think it safe to proceed on the grounds that the boy has fallen victim to the dire crime of abduction."

"Even more frightening," I allowed.

"Astute, Watson, for there is nothing in any infernal realm darker than the human heart."

For a moment I was elated at his discovery, but then asked:

"But are we not now set back to square one in this matter? For knowing the cause is hardly the same as possessing the solution."

"Small steps, Watson, small steps."

He stood in thought for a moment, facing the windows that lay on the north end of the mud-room, while small summer breezes tossed the tops of the shrubbery beyond, and then a smile pierced his mouth, and a light seemed to spring up in his eyes.

"Of course," he said quietly. Then louder to me he repeated: "The perpetrator was delayed, and thus so was the effect of chemical formula."

"Holmes?"

Turning in my direction, he said:

"Though, you are correct, Watson, that the case is far from finished, matters now begin to unfold at a more rapid pace, for sometimes the falling of a single stone may lead to a great avalanche. It might interest you to know that the compound which was used to create the boy-size marking on the ground does not have an instant effect before the eyes of its user, but requires twelve hours to fully process once poured into place. However, once the chemical has begun its final reaction, the shape would manifest in mere minutes."

"What is the significance of that, Holmes?" I asked, puzzling through this information but not quite connecting it.

Holmes set about re-packing his chemistry equipment into the case, apparently having learned all he needed from the samples, then asked:

"What did the family say concerning the stain when first they set out on their search this morning?"

I recalled:

"That was not to be seen until mid-morning."

"And when was the boy discovered to be missing?"

"At first light."

"*Before* the stain had appeared. Tell me, Watson, do you think that timing was desired in our perpetrator's plan, or was it that party's intention that the stain should be seen by all immediately in the morning, thus adding to the appearance of the supernatural?"

"I see...yes," I said. "You've said the process required

twelve hours to fully set up, so the timing of the application in the yew alley was somehow bungled!"

"Precisely! For some reason the placing of the chemicals onto that spot was delayed by roughly three to four hours beyond when I suspect the abductor—or his accomplice— wished it to be in place so that it could be seen in the morning, shortly after the boy was discovered missing."

"Yet, as this person was delinquent in laying down the chemical, something beyond his control interfered with the time-table!"

"What domestic action do we know of from yesterday, Watson, which was unexpected and took perhaps, three or four hours to complete?"

Instantly my mind fastened upon it. "The unplanned trip into town!"

With a hard smile, wholly predatory, yet also well pleased, my friend turned rapidly on his heel, the case containing the chemistry set in-hand, and without waiting for me, strode out of the mud-room and back toward the chamber from which we'd come forty-five minutes before.

*****

Holmes entered the drawing room door, where Mrs. Morley sat with a woman of middle years, to whom she was conversing closely as we entered, the words—

"...is it any wonder, then, that he shall perhaps prove irretrievably beyond our reach now...."

—were leaving her lips, and it was with surprise and, did I imagine something approaching guilt, that she pulled her head back from its proximity to the other woman, and looked up, her lips forming a startled O.

"Mr. Holmes!" the Colonel's wife said, rather in the way of an exclamation.

She recovered herself and demanded:

"Have you news?"

"I have not."

Disappointment showed on her face.

"May I, then, present my companion and lady's maid, Mrs. Drummond, who, blessedly, has recovered from her headache and its effects, and now has joined me to lend what comfort she may in this time of worry."

I bowed my head toward the woman, who rose and curtsied to me, but Holmes entirely ignored this polite exchange, and instead demanded:

"Mrs. Morley, you have said you went into town yesterday afternoon."

"To order a new bonnet, yes."

"And what was the time?"

Lifting a finger, he added:

"Precisely now!"

"We left around three o'clock. Closer than that I cannot be."

"And the hour of your return?"

"Sometime just after seven."

"You have told us you were accompanied by your lady's maid here."

"Mrs. Drummond," I said, using her name by way of demonstrating politeness, for Holmes was speaking of the woman as if she were not among us.

"Yes, naturally," Mrs. Morley confirmed. "I rarely go anyplace without her."

"Is that so?"

Holmes took a sharp step forward and looked at Mrs. Drummond in such an intense manner that she shifted on the sofa, and I saw a blush begin at her jawline, and spread up the soft flesh of her cheeks, for though it was not tactile, the stare he gave her was a thing of utmost intrusion, almost improper for a gentleman's eyes to probe a woman in such a meticulous evaluation. I could only guess at what Holmes was searching out in her, though I knew he never gazed at anyone but that he learned much indeed.

"Hmmph," he snorted. "This fails to surprise me."

And just as suddenly as his eyes had locked upon the woman's person, his gaze shifted, and a light which had been veritably shining there appeared instead to dull to nothing, for all at once Mrs. Drummond seemed of no further interest to him.

Turning back to Mrs. Morley, he demanded:

"And which of the two house-maids in service here was the third member of your party on the trip into town?"

The question seemed to surprise the woman, perhaps unused to outsiders taking an interest in her staff, but after a pause she said:

"Ada, the younger of the two, and the more recent addition to our household servants."

"Have the butler bring her here at once," Holmes said sternly.

Clearly in the habit of delegating rather than doing for herself, Mrs. Morley nodded to her companion, Mrs. Drummond, who stood from the sofa and went to the far corner, where the braided velvet rope dangled just above the floor, golden tassels at its end. She gave it a delicate pull, then returned beside her mistress.

There was something almost electrical in the air, like the atmosphere before a storm. I could discern it and saw the two ladies could as well, for Holmes had brought it into the room with him. There seemed almost an anger about him, barely suppressed and ill-concealed, whereas it was more usual for him to remain coolly detached when in the midst of an investigation such as this. I felt myself wanting to worry about him, and wondered if it might not have been too soon for him to end his recuperation at Baker Street, and be expending himself in this way. If so, as his doctor I blamed myself, for there was even the faintest gleam of perspiration upon his well-formed brow.

I was about to ask to speak privately with him in the hallway, to inquire how he was feeling, when he began speaking once more.

"Tell me of this girl," he instructed Mrs. Morley, and there was something so forceful in his voice that I felt once more that he was not quite himself. "How long has she been with you? What is her character? And what has she said of herself in relation to the vanishing of your grandson?"

Yes, I was quite taken aback at the fierceness which roiled within my friend's questions, and saw Mrs. Morley likewise recognized the forcefulness in his inquiries, for without preamble she docilely answered:

"Ada has been in domestic service here for ten months, and I have not had cause to complain about the performance of her duties. She...."

I saw her eyes go out to Mrs. Drummond, her lady's maid, before she continued.

"The unvarnished truth is, Mr. Holmes, that we took the girl in through a charity programme that finds domestic positions for fallen women, from the streets of London. Off Sultan Street in Camberwell, in her case."

"I see," Holmes spoke up.

Not a good district at all, I thought. I knew of such social improvement programmes, and had read of their notable successes in delivering women from the streets of the East End slums, and thought on the whole it was a meritorious undertaking. Even Mr. Gladstone was known to travel out into the poorer districts of London in the company of his wife, and invite fallen women to return home with them, in order to see them conveyed to organizations which would offer them training and the hope of a better existence.

It was then that Hardy, the Butler, appeared.

"Madam rang?" he intoned expressionlessly.

"Fetch the house-maid Ada and bring her here," Mrs. Morley told him in a manner which reminded me of a general ordering a soldier to the front.

Hardy betrayed no sign of any thoughts on the matter, simply bowed and set off to fulfill his command.

Mrs. Morley shifted on the sofa and asked:

"Am I to take it that you suspect Ada of playing some rôle in the matter of Barry's disappearance, Mr. Holmes?"

Smiling coldly at her, Holmes said sarcastically:

"A rôle? I had thought, Madam, that you were satisfied that the boy's absence had a supernatural cause?"

"I believe in the existence of the yew alley ghost, Mr. Holmes," she told him, "but—"

"Then why do you inquire as to a culprit, if you are convinced your grandson was swept away by a phantom from the Middle Ages?" he replied curtly.

"I assume you had me summon the girl for a reason..." the lady pressed, awkwardly.

"And so I did," replied Holmes.

This was inexcusable, and I felt a disproving annoyance rise in me, though I said nothing. Not so her companion Mrs. Drummond, however, who burst out:

"Sir, you are most rude, and it is unbecoming of a gentleman to speak so to a lady as careworn as my mistress is at this difficult time. Have you no feelings?"

Staring back at her with such frigidness that the woman, even amid her righteous indignation, was the first to lower her eyes, Holmes said firmly:

"I only voice the lady's stated opinion, and echo it back to her."

Before anything further could be said, he turned on his heels and went to a window, before which he stood regarding a small stand of decorative trees at the perimeter of the lawn.

I went over beside him and said in a whisper:

"Why this discourtesy to your client's wife, and her companion? I do not understand, Holmes."

"Do you not," he replied disdainfully, in a slightly louder tone than I had employed, though whether within the hearing of the women I could not say. "I have recently been lead to death's very doorway by a woman because I deferred to her on the basis of what she was, Watson, and I shall not make that mistake twice. Not when spiders abound among that sex, and I suspect one of them is guilty of much in the matter at-hand."

"A woman has taken the boy?" I asked, startled.

"I did not express that sentiment," he corrected. "In truth we are in the midst of more than one act of crime, however much one may serve to overshadow the other."

"I doubt Mrs. Morley would harm her own grandchild, Holmes," I protested. "Yet you speak to her in a tone that lacks all mildness and courtesy, despite what she is enduring."

"Mildness and courtesy, you say? I have treated her with a directness warranted by the urgency of this matter. I saw no rudeness in that, and in future intend to converse with women without the nearly fatal deference shown the would-be assassin at Baker Street. How you speak to others I leave you to decide, but I tell you this for your own edification—Watson, once again a woman is to blame for a degree of the malice which has played out here. After reflection these past days, I begin to see how much evil in the world comes from the feminine half of the society, and often passes little suspected, and much excused."

I shook my head at this, and as a doctor knew I was seeing the effects of the wound Holmes had received that recent morning, not to his body, which had healed, but to his once towering self-confidence, which had clearly been shaken to the point that it had left this alteration in him. I only hoped this effect, and the exaggerated mistrust toward women that it revealed, would not prove lasting, yet the moods and reactions of my friend, I knew, were not like those of other men.

A few minutes passed with a web of silence spun about the room, until Hardy returned with the summoned house-maid, Ada, behind him.

My first thought at turning toward her was that this Ada was a strikingly pretty young woman, perhaps in her early twenties, and I felt some surprise at this, for I knew it was the usual custom of ladies of the house to select female servants of plain features and humble dispositions, but it seemed

Mrs. Morley owned sufficient confidence in herself—and her husband—to not make this a disqualifying factor.

"The house-maid Ada, Madam," Hardy said in a sepulchral tone.

"Madam?" the maid asked in her turn, dipping into a curtsey, her eyes averted with full propriety.

"Er, Ada, yes," Mrs. Morley said uneasily, "this is Mr. Sherlock Holmes, from London, here to investigate Barry's disappearance, and he has some questions he would like to put to you."

"Yes, Madam," the girl replied, evenly.

Ada raised her eyes to gaze full-on at Holmes, neither challenging him nor wilting away. If I'd expected Mrs. Morley's announcement to discommode the young woman, I saw that the words had no discernible effect on either her expression or the steadiness of her voice, and realized that she was possibly a person with some confidence about her, and this realization brought to mind how difficult survival must have been in the life she'd once led on the streets, and the effect it may have had on instilling self-reliance into her.

Holmes showed no sign that her steadfastness impressed him, and immediately launched onto Ada a question that caught me very much off guard:

"What did you tell the boy to lure him outside last night?"

Ada's eyes widened, but her face stayed much the same, save that she blinked twice before demanding:

"Sir?"

I caught the Cockney in her accent, out of place there in the fens of Suffolk, and saw that though she gave every sign of being puzzled by the inquiry, she lost none of the confidence she projected.

"Ah, are you to feign puzzlement then?" Holmes utterly sternly, as he advanced on the woman and began to circle her in predatory fashion, moving around her side, and then coming forward again until he stood very close to her, his piercing gray eyes locking on her own, of a delicate sky-blue.

"Your question of me, sir, I do not understand. I led no one out of the house last night or any other night, and if you are referring to young Master Barry, I will tell you I have never spoken to him upon any occasion here or elsewhere."

She said this with such a mingling of bewilderment and earnestness that I realized I very much wanted to believe her. With a start I recalled the words Holmes had just imparted to me about how easy it was to fail to suspect in a woman what one might be only too willing to believe of a man, and a wave of guilt washed over me.

Stay impartial, John, I told myself.

"Then I ask you, *Ada*," Holmes continued, "or whatever your name originally was before your supposed reclamation in the London charity-house, to think for a moment....of your neck."

"Sir?"

"Oh, yes, such a lovely little neck. I see it is slender and pale and doubtless an endowment of some pride to you, as it is a feature which has certainly drawn the admiring eyes of men often enough."

"My...my neck, sir?"

Ada appeared at a loss for words, and with a face as innocent as a lamb, she gazed almost helplessly toward her mistress, who likewise seemed swallowed-up by puzzlement. Beside her, though, the lady's maid, Mrs. Drummond, sat silently, though clearly, I saw, frowning her disproval of Ada, and I guessed what her own sentiments had been concerning a young woman from the reclamation project coming into employment in the Morley household.

"I mentioned your neck, Ada," said Holmes, "because I ask you to imagine how it shall feel when a hempen rope is fitted around that delicate bridge between head and body, and you drop through the floor to hang until you are lifeless."

There came a gasp from Mrs. Morley, and from Ada a momentary curdling of her once-placid face, and against this

Holmes threw out:

"For hang you shall, girl, spinning and kicking in the air, if this is a case of murder!"

The words were abrupt, and spoken with such force that I almost felt struck in the chest by the intrusion of so macabre a subject there in the sedate drawing room. Yet the exercise had its effect, for almost as if beyond her self-control, Ada burst out:

"Murder? No, he said he'd never hurt the boy!"

Her mouth flew open, realizing the confession which had slipped from her.

"And so swiftly as that we have an admission of guilt," declared Holmes, a look of blackest triumphant taking over his pale face, his eyes almost feline in their menace.

"Mrs. Morley sprang to her feet and cried:

"Jezebel! We took you into this house on charity and gave you a chance at self-redemption, and this is how our kindness is returned! What is it you know?"

I believe she would have advanced on the guilty maid had not I held out a restraining arm, and said:

"Pray, Mrs. Morley, do leave Mr. Holmes to his work."

After peering at me for an instant, the lady nodded and sat back onto the sofa, where Mrs. Drummond touched her arm and said:

"She is a viper, Madam!"

"Well now," Holmes said triumphantly but also in a quieter tone than he had used a moment before, "the truth leaps out as guilt confesses itself."

Ada now lost her look of self-mastery and her eyes flew about the room, realizing how in her lapse she had revealed herself, and was now trapped. She also looked chagrined to have been jolted so easily.

"It wasn't me, Madam," she declared, gazing toward the sofa, and I saw that like some stage actress, she was attempting to force tears into her eyes. "That man, he made me do it. I was so frightened by him, and I had no choice. I was scared, and that's the Gospel truth!"

"Tsk, and now you compound your crime with lies," Holmes said with mockery, still standing very close to the girl. "To abandon this charade and tell me everything is the only hope you possess, and quickly, for the hangman's rope is closing in around you."

Ada opened her mouth and seemed about to speak, then shut it, and when she next spoke, her voice was entirely different, no longer the façade of the meek country-house servant, but the brassy tones of a streetwise woman of the East End, as stubbornly she said:

"What can you do for me if I rabbit on him?"

"Come clean with me," Holmes said, his voice divided between sternness and indifference, "and when the hour comes I shall testify in front of the law that you have claimed yourself coerced beyond your capacity to resist."

"Not good enough," Ada said sourly. "It's barrels and eels, and I know it. See I'm given a deal and I'll talk straight away, here and now."

If I expected Holmes to throw her words back at her with a ferocious threat, I was surprised, for he became almost gentle when he said:

"It is well known that I have friends within the police and the courts as well, and I tell you I will speak to them about you, but you must show yourself worthy of my intervention."

I saw the swirl of deliberation in Ada's mind, but still she hesitated.

"I know," spoke Holmes, "a great deal more of what has transpired here than you might suspect I do."

"You don't know me at all," Ada boasted.

"Oh, but I do. I know that you are ambitious, and a far brighter girl than you want the world to know, as playing the rôle of the meek, contrite sort has served you more than once. It impressed the simple Christian folk of the reform society, after all, and got you out of London, where so many of your fellow *demimonde* of a less determined disposition remain behind. It brought you here to a fine country estate, where you were just biding your time until the next opportunity for self-advancement arose, and you thought you'd found it."

He paused and added:

"I know that you steal candies from your mistress' dish in the parlour at every chance, for look, there is a little smear of orange left behind on your left fingertip, even in the midst of this crisis, showing how recent your misconduct has been."

Ada's eyes dipped to her hands.

"I know that you have bullied the little scullery maid with whom you share an attic room here, so that she sleeps on the floor each night, no matter how cold the weather, so that you might occupy an entire bed by yourself. Oh, such a luxury for you!"

As if her fate had just been told by an oracle, Ada's eyes widened with wonder at how this shameful fact could possibly be known to Holmes.

"And I know your mother," he continued, "is still alive in the East End, and that the scarf you keep tucked inside your pocket is the one gift that pathetic soul ever gave you."

Here Ada's eyes both hardened and took on the first look of true hurt I'd seen in them.

"Don't you dare speak of my mother!" she seethed.

Holmes gave her a smile that had little of kindness in it, and promised:

"With or without you, Ada, I'll have him soon enough, and knowing this, a wise girl might begin to assist me, while still the chance remained, by turning on her benefactor....this would-be master of a daring crime. Your..."

Leaning closer still to the girl, he added at a whisper:

"....*lover*."

At that word, normally forbidden for a gentleman to utter in the presence of ladies, Mrs. Morley closed her eyes, though I could not discern whether it was in shame or anger that the woman she had taken into her house should so deeply betray her.

Yet heedless of the lady's reaction, Holmes pressed on.

"Far from being of benefit to you, Ada, the man I seek has set you down a dreadful path, and your involvement in the plot in which he has embroiled you as his accomplice out in the yew alley—oh yes, I know what it was you did there in crafting the stain—can only lead to your ruin. Even your death. If you do not aid me, I promise you I shall see that it goes as hard for you as I can make it, but if you tell me all that you know, so that I might put right the terrible wrong against an innocent boy and his family, I will do what I can for you."

"And what would that be?" Ada asked, her eyes going sharp once more.

"A much better deal than you'll have if I act against you," said Holmes, with a jaunty snarl. "So I give you one chance, and one only, to earn your reprieve, by telling all."

The pretty housemaid stood unmoving for just another moment, then nodded, and without asking Mrs. Morley's permission, pulled out a chair and fell back into it in a most unladylike pose.

"It is true, is it not," stated Holmes, "that the unexpected trip into town to see the milliner with Mrs. Morley, delayed you from the schedule laid down for you? It was your mission, I believe, to slip out in the late afternoon and pour the chemical he gave you in order to make the suggestive shape in the yew alley?"

"Yes," Ada confirmed ruefully. "He said it would need half a day to set up, so wanted me to pour the liquid there in the rough shape of a boy, so that it would be spotted at first light, when the party had just started off looking for the missing child."

"The idea being to suggest, amid the fertile climate of so much recent talk of the supernatural, that it was a ghost from local legend who had taken the boy?"

"Yes."

"A ghost," said Holmes, glancing toward Mrs. Morley, "that despite rumours has remained unseen upon the estate this past fortnight, save in the imaginations of those here. And all of that was set in motion by your own false claims to have crossed paths with the entity in the yew alley, was it not?"

"But I tell you, *I* have seen it!" Mrs. Morley cried out before the girl could answer.

"Lately?" Holmes demanded of her.

"No," the lady admitted.

"And when you did, was it perhaps on full-moon nights, after a rain-shower, when the yews leaves, noted for holding water long after a storm, would have shone suggestively in the moonlight?"

At this question, Mrs. Morley fell silent, clearly offended, and ignoring her in any case, Ada said:

"He told me to begin spreading the rumours of my encounter two weeks before the boy arrived for his summer holiday, and said others would fall in line and claim they'd seen it as well, a 'contagious hysteria of the imagination,' he termed it, if I merely got the ball rolling. And so it did! I made my claims, pretending to be all scared and mystified, and the second night took my room-mate, the scullery girl, little Betsy, out into the darkness with me, and played at seeing the ghost chasing after us, and so simple was Betsy I soon had her reduced to tears, convinced she'd seen it, too, and had even felt its cold touch against her back while we ran from it, though of course that was really me clutching at her in the dark, and there was never anything there at all!"

She gave a haughty laugh.

"The stories among the servants took off with a life of their own," she bragged, "and I admit I was rather proud of what I'd set in motion. Within a week half the staff were saying they'd seen the thing, bunch of fibbers. Mr. Hardy, that sheep-faced old butler, tried to hush us up, but it was far too big a story by then, and some of the claims they made, oh, you should have heard the inventions. All I could do to play along and keep a straight face!"

"Maybe they weren't all inventing, you foul girl!" Mrs.

Morley thundered from the sofa. "For many have seen the ghost going back five hundred years!"

Ada stared insolently at the woman, and again let loose a giggly sort of laugh. "So stupid," she said without a trace of shame.

"Whatever the truth of the ghost's reality," I offered, with I hoped a diplomatic nod toward Mrs. Morley, whose anger, I noted, was quickly blooming toward rage, "I think we can safely presume there never was a ghost apparating during the time young Barry was here on holiday, or even a thing legitimately mistaken to be one."

"Of course not, Watson," Holmes declared. "A tale of a ghostly encounter invariably tells us more about the claimant than it does the nature of any life that may follow this one. An interest in a swirling rumour of the preternatural can be forgiven in a boy of eleven, but for adults to have fallen for such nonsense is worthy only of castigation."

To Ada again, he stated:

"I presume you made opportunities to place yourself in the boy's path throughout the summer, and tell your nonsense concerning the phantom?"

"That was my mission," Ada said with a smile of pride, "and I done it well. Had him eating out of my hand, wanting my stories about the ghost told over and over, and it wasn't hard to prime him to be outdoors last night, when the man was ready to come for him, leaping out of the shadows like a jungle cat with knockout drops on a cloth, grabbing him from behind on the cobbles of the patio... Weren't no trouble at all to get to that boy. Over and done with in a second, and he was gone, easy as pie in the sunshine."

This causal admission of how she had betrayed the child and lured him outside into the clutches of a heartless plot made revulsion swirl inside me.

"And now," Holmes said, showing no reaction to her confession, "it is time to tell me the rest. Describe for me the appearance of this mastermind behind the abduction. How did he approach you, and what was it that he promised for your sordid cooperation?"

"That last bit's easy," Ada said proudly. "He *liked* me, you see. Men usually do, because I'm not old and fat and ugly like some I could name around here."

She cast a glance at Mrs. Morley, and Mrs. Drummond said:

"You are a fiend!"

Ada next revealed:

"He promised to keep me in finery when he had this house."

"That's absurdity," I voiced, less concerned with the girl's feelings after her unwarranted swipe at Mrs. Morley's appearance. "A landed man with even the merest pretentions of being a gentleman wouldn't take to consort a woman raised off the streets of London."

Ada laughed. "Oh, think me a mad little fool, do you? I'd never want to be wife to one such as him, no, but there are ways a girl can live right well off a man's feelings for her, better than a wife, even, and he promised to set me up in town, and keep in fine style, whatever else was going on back here at this house, once he owned it."

"Own this house?" Mrs. Morley burst out.

"Oh, yeah," Ada taunted. "Always has wanted it, ever since he was here as a little boy. His dad, you see, used to work on these grounds doing something, he never said what exactly it was, and he fell hard for this place, did my fella, so when he come back from America, where he went over as a boy, and soon his fortune made good 'n proper, it was all he wanted. Knew you'd never sell, though, not unless there was a good reason."

"Like the tragic memory of a grandson disappearing from the grounds," I said.

"Yeah," Ada agreed, "not to mention the tainted history of the place, a ghost being on-site? One that snatches away children, never to be seen no more? Who'd want to live here then?"

It was a diabolical plan, almost absurd, and yet in its daring it had threatened to succeed, and still might.

"And the schemer himself," said Holmes. "What was his name?"

"Said to call him Peter, but I knew, of course that weren't his real name, no more than mine's really Ada."

"And his appearance?"

"Good looking bloke, ain't he? Regular height, light brown hair what falls down over his forehead in the wind, eyes brown as a stag's, strong as an ox, and brave, so brave..."

It was the description of a smitten woman, I knew, despite whatever claims of disdain for the institution of wedlock Ada might have professed.

"Nevermind all that, you cunning little rodent, where, is my grandson?" Mrs. Morley demanded in a rage.

"That is the one thing I cannot tell you," said Ada, staring with hate-filled eyes at the woman who had provided honest employment for her, despite her chequered past, "for it is the one thing Pete never told me."

"It might interest you to know," Holmes began, "that your 'Pete' has left you behind, and has no intentions of ever seeing you again."

"Now there you lie," Ada laughed.

"Do I? I confess you know the man more intimately than I, but think, girl, what further use for you, has he? Would you return for a loose end in your scheme? You might consider yourself quite lucky he didn't invite you along in his act of absconding, and do away with you in some convenient hollow between here and town."

At this charge Ada showed a considerable diminution in her haughtiness, and fell silent in rueful thought.

"I've told you everything, just like you asked," she said after a moment. "Now you'll help me out, right?"

At this Holmes replied with but a cold smile, and it was at this precise second that there was the sound of the great front doors opening, and the noise of heavy footsteps in the entryway, making all our eyes turn there, as Colonel Morley trod inside with his military bearing, trailed by a country policeman in uniform.

"Ah, the Constable Sergeant of whom I have been told," Holmes remarked, turning away now from Ada, and seemingly putting her from his mind.

"Constable Sergeant Welkirk at your service, sir," the man said with a nod of his head. "You are known to me, even out here, with much admiration, Mr. Holmes."

"What news, gentlemen?" I called out.

"None, I am afraid," answered the Colonel.

"None indeed," Constable Sergeant Welkirk confirmed. "We have hunted high and low around the countryside for miles, and there is no trace of the boy."

"Then you will be cheered when I deliver the tidings that I have here before us one of the culprits in what I can confidently tell you, Colonel, was indeed the abduction of your grandson."

"What? Her? The house-maid?" Morley thundered. "What have you done with the boy?"

"She is of no further use, Colonel," Holmes interjected, and I will tell you all. In fact having wrung all the information from her that she has to give, your timing is excellent, for I was just about to inquire from your wife if there was a secure closet in the house where I might lock the villainess away until the police could take her, but as you are here, Constable Sergeant, I commend her to you."

Taking Sherlock Holmes at his word without asking questions, Welkirk crossed the room and slipped handcuffs around Ada's slender and truly lovely wrists.

"I think one of our cells in town might fit the bill a little better," he remarked.

"Wait," Ada barked at Holmes as the Sergeant walked her to the door, where another constable waited, "you promised you'd aid me!"

"Ah, yes, so I did," said Holmes. "Constable Sergeant, this woman claims she was coerced and compelled into acting on behalf of the abductor, with whom she had formed a romantic attachment. There, Ada, you see, I have spoken on your behalf, as I promised. Now address me nevermore."

As he turned from her, the girl was pulled from the room cursing Holmes' very name, and loathsome though I found her, I did feel my scruples somewhat disjointed at Holmes' lackluster efforts to further advocate for her, as he'd indicated he would. His words had been weak at best, evidence of deceit at worst. None of it was in keeping with the man I knew, and once more I reflected that the sickness that had overcome him following his narrow escape from death had left him changed in ways I marked as no improvement.

Holmes seemed not at all chagrined at his deceitfulness, however, as he told Morley of Ada's revelations, and asked the man:

"Think back, who in the past meets the description she has given? Here as a boy many years ago, let us say twenty or more, and of the appearance she gave?"

The Colonel's eyes took on a distant cast as he ran through the fields of memory, and then all at once burst out:

"Why it must surely be Tony Turner's son, Willie!"

"Tell me of him!" Holmes commanded.

"Turner was the engineer who saw to the dredging of the fetid pond one summer, '60 it was, and being a widower, he brought his son with him. I found him a likely boy, good-natured and quick to smile, but moody and spoiled and audacious, as well. I always thought the army would bring out the best in such a solid lad, and chip away the bad, though he was gone from here long before coming of age. Got into fisticuffs with my own boy, Evanston, and got the best of him, though Evanston was no weakling. I liked the Turner lad despite the flare-up, and often saw him walking in our woods, and once climbing the tall oak that used to stand at the property's edge, before the big storm in '73 felled it, a hundred feet up he went, and laughed down at us, sure-footed as a mountain goat, and fearless to his very heart."

"I remember him differently!" Mrs. Morley exclaimed. "A ruffian, that child, no good at all, and glad I was when the work was done on the pond, and he and his too-indulgent father were gone."

"It seems, Madam, that he has returned," Holmes told her, ironically.

Leaning out toward Holmes, but for some reason finding my own eyes, Mrs. Morley added fiercely:

"He bloodied my Evanston's mouth and blacked both his eyes! The wild gypsy-child, I used to call him."

"To think," said Morley, "these twenty-three years this house and the grounds has stayed so strongly in his mind, apparently every moment of his life. I heard that his father had gone off to America to do engineering work in the fortifications being built during that nation's internal war, and after that went on into the growing west, to Denver, I heard it was, and the boy went with him. It seems he has come back after somehow making his fortune off in that wild land, and still with his eye on this place..."

It was all strange, I thought, a man's determination to claim a place he'd been but once in his youth, but as a doctor I knew how compelling the force of obsession could be, and clearly this Turner must have set his mind on becoming master of the house, through whatever means were required, even so bizarre and criminal a plan. An unrestrained force, I judged him, and wondered how it must be to possess so fearlessly determined a heart, undeterred by laws or their consequences.

"Now you know his name, arrest him!" Mrs. Morley shouted.

"I am afraid it will not be so simple," said Holmes. "I doubt very greatly that the man calls himself by his father's surname any longer. He might go by any name, and be passing himself off as nearly anyone. Furthermore, he will soon learn that his scheme has failed, and slip away, most probably back to America, where one might hide til the end of time itself."

"And my grandson?" Morley asked.

"I do not think it is in the nature of a risk-taker such as this Turner to keep a stolen boy with him," Holmes stated. "Too dangerous, given the police are out in force searching for him. No, assuming he has scrupled at murder, and left young Barry alive…"

Mrs. Morley exhaled rapidly and loudly.

"As I believe he has," Holmes said, an eye on her, "for killing the boy would have been far simpler than abducting him, yet he spared him, demonstrating to me that Turner has that many principles at least. So I must now think, where would the boy be deposited, in safety, but kept out of the way? And in not too distant a place, at that, for time was a great factor in arranging all of this."

"There is a small cave near the creek," suggested Constable Sergeant Welkirk.

Holmes looked toward him, interested, until the policeman added:

"But we searched it thoroughly and found no sign of anyone having been inside for ages."

"Where else have you searched?" Holmes inquired.

"Every barn in this section of the county. Outbuildings, under the bridge over Bishopsgate Creek, haystacks, everywhere the mind could conceive of to look, my men and I did, as did the parties who have volunteered, and are still out now combing the countryside."

"Then it is likely Turner has somehow spirited the child away," said Holmes, whose eyes were deeply reflective of the churning seas of his mind, "most probably with the aid of a confederate."

"Another like Ada somewhere?" Morley suggested.

"You are sure that Lieutenant Peters played no rôle whatsoever?" I asked Holmes.

He told me:

"Peters is a coward who brutalizes his wife, not one to nebulously gamble on a long-term reward promised him from a child-abduction plot. He is a fruitless prospect, and upon his ignorance in this entire matter I would stake my professional reputation."

"Then we are at a standstill, even now after learning so much?" Colonel Morley asked, his voice mired in misery.

But I saw that Holmes was walking slowly away from him, toward the window, his head bowed, his mind churning, and I held my breath, for I sensed that he had fastened on to something of significance. And I was right, for an instant later he whirled back toward us all and, his eyes blazing like torches, exclaimed:

"'The wild gypsy-child'!"

He roared this so loudly that the ladies on the sofa flinched, and Morley demanded:

"What?"

Suddenly, though, a light went off in my own head, and I knew the reference.

"The Irish gypsy caravan we spied coming in from Ipswich!" I cried.

"Of course!" Holmes shouted. "So focused was I on arriving at the culprit, I gave little thought til now of the means by which he might have secreted the boy away, but as you say, Watson, it is the most likely connection. Irish gypsies are notorious thieves and confidence men, hated across the realm for their predatory ways, and even, I fear, their involvement in the abduction and sale of small children, for there is a sordid market for such, even here in England, let alone on the continent."

At mention of the sale of children—into ghastly fates, I did not doubt—I shuddered, and said:

"And to think, we may have rolled right by him this very morning!"

A great rush of activity then burst upon the house as Holmes unfurled his plan and the Constable Sergeant cooperatively accepted it as stated, mentioning only that without a warrant he could not enter the gypsy's wagons, to which Holmes promised to provide him with the legal grounds to do so, should he find the child to be present.

Upon hearing this, Welkirk sent one of his men into town on the double, to bring back three other constables, and their two fastest wagons.

In the meantime, Holmes retrieved his chemistry case off the floor, and as I trailed him into an empty side-room, he told me:

"In among my chemistry apparatus I keep effects by which I might transform myself via disguise."

"And this will benefit the infiltration of the gypsy caravan?" I asked.

"Immeasurably."

I watched as Sherlock Holmes vanished from the world, and in his place came a tramp, down on his luck, shabby in hat and heels, weary of eye, stooped of back, and four inches lesser in height than Holmes' towering six feet, a man whipped by life, and more than a little crazed around the edges. In short, perfect prey for the ruthless gypsies.

The transformation complete, Holmes returned to the room where Colonel and Mrs. Morley and the Constable Sergeant stood waiting, and told them all:

"In this guise shall I approach the caravan, while you, Watson, you, Colonel Morley and you, Constable Sergeant and your men, shall wait concealed in the woods, not to approach until I signal for you by raising my arms above my head. Then you must rush in, expecting resistance, I doubt not, and retrieve the boy, if I am correct about him being kept concealed within one of the wagons."

"Ah," said the Colonel, an old military man, "a pincer action! My personal favourite for overwhelming a foe!"

"Precisely," Holmes agreed, "but do remember, the assault must come only at my signal, for I will get farther in this disguise than would the police devoid a warrant which might require many hours to attain, and by engaging in conversation with the thuggish wanderers, and I shall learn what I may. If they have the boy, they will not be able to deceive me upon the subject, and he will soon be home again."

"Oh, sir, let that be so!" Mrs. Morley exclaimed, placing her hands above her heart. "And all of you, do be careful..."

*****

We were off no more than twenty minutes later, with such great alacrity did Constable Sergeant Welkirk assemble his fellows, and set off at a nearly break-neck pace back across the country road down which we'd come, and an hour saw us at the spot where we'd passed the caravan trespassing in some farmer's meadow, though I was little surprised to see it had since moved on.

"Now," said Holmes, "we come rapidly to the part wherein finesse shall play its rôle, for we must proceed to the point of spying the caravan ahead in the distance, but not draw so close as to be seen in return. Carefully now, and with greater slowness let us proceed!"

And so we did, progressing at a lessened pace, and it was another full-forty very long and weighty minutes before Holmes' sharp eyes became the first among us to sight our quarry, nearly half a mile distant atop a hill, where the gypsies appeared to be taking another break, spread out as they were on a tree-lined expanse, allowing their horses to graze, sitting together at several small foldable tables, each lined with teapots and light fare.

"Hold here, at this low point in the woods, Sergeant!" Holmes said urgently, his blood high, the thrill of his work upon him, however dangerous what he had planned might have been.

"It is the same band of vagrants?" the Colonel asked hotly, desirous of the battle ahead.

"It is, sir," Holmes told him. "And Fortuna is with us, for a thick wood surrounds the clearing upon the hilltop, ideal for concealment. Keep to the plan, all of you! I shall go forward on the road, giving the impression of being a wanderer, and shall approach the caravan with a story that will be of interest to those there."

"It sounds dangerous, Holmes," I said, knowing nothing else to add.

"It is, Watson," he confessed without qualification. "Now, creep close, all of you, but stay concealed, and should I raise my arms in the signal, sweep in like a storm and be ready, for when cornered Irish gypsies are known as fierce fighters. If I am right, we shall have the boy home with you before sunset, Colonel. To your places now, and stick to my plan with precision!"

"You heard the man," said Constable Sergeant Welkirk to his officers. "No deviation, now, and no mistakes. Have your truncheons at the ready, for a fight may be coming, and Heaven help the man who lets himself be spotted early by our quarry!"

And so as Holmes walked on apart from us, raising my worries for him, his stride unusual, as if weary or partly lame, his back bent, the rest of us stayed low and proceeded off-road into the woods, creeping up the near-side of the hill which was playing host to the gypsies. We were able to reach a spot behind where a large plane tree had fallen in the last year, and lined up there, within easy sight of the group, and in an unexpected plus, even within hearing, for the curve of the hillside acted as a natural amplifier of sound, like an amphitheater.

It took Holmes many minutes to follow the curve of the dusty country lane, moving as he was in a world-weary shuffle, a stick in his right hand, worn boots upon his feet. He paused at the roadway's crest, as if just seeing the caravan for the first time, and several among that group, an older woman with steel gray hair and burning black eyes, and two younger men, perhaps her sons, spotted him as well and paused, standing rigidly as they stared out at him.

A fission of fear went through me, thinking only now of the calamity should the gypsies, thinking themselves alone upon the fens, no witnesses, simply decide to try to rob Holmes rather than listen to him, yet I also thought surely that would provide the necessary legal grounds for Welkirk to rush the encampment, would it not?

Holmes gave the wanderers a broad wave with his left arm, and set off toward them at the same low-key and unhurried shuffle, giving the impression of a man in no haste to be anywhere, for being homeless, he had nowhere to go.

"Ahoy there!" he cried to the gypsies. "Might a weary traveler upon these same roads approach and be among you for a moment?"

I saw the wheels within the gray-haired woman's mind turn as she sized up this newcomer and measured him against her perpetual hopes that she might exploit him, as she made a practice of doing to all outsiders she encountered.

"And fer what purpose might that be?" she called back, her accent thickly that of Connaught, in the far west of her native island.

"If a man might set his hopes on sharing a cup of tea with you, he might find himself most glad indeed," said Holmes.

"We don't give away what we own, man," said the woman, "though we might sell you a cup, or make other arrangements."

"Fine, fine," said Holmes, whose advance had never slowed during the tentative conversation. He was now within the perimeter of the caravan, and a look of simple, slightly wary good-nature was set upon his dust-smudged face.

No one among the tribe spoke words of welcome, and the eyes of the nine within the group turned toward him, hard with suspicion.

As if unconscious of the group's reaction to him, Holmes walked up next to the woman and removed a ha'penny from his pocket and held it out.

"For a mug of tea, mayhaps, and a bite of bread and cheese, if you have it."

The woman looked a moment upon the ha'penny, and then took it from his fingers.

"Sit," she said, pointing to a three-legged stool. "Saoirse," she called to a young and somewhat cowed girl who had been standing back by the most distant of the brightly-painted wagons, gaping at the interactions, "fetch this one a cup and something to eat. Be hasty!"

The girl, Saoirse, surely no older than twelve, scrambled to carry out the instructions, and I could spy worry in the green-gray eyes of the girl, very thin, she was, and with her great mass of auburn hair, long-unwashed by the look of it, left tangled loose about her shoulders. I told myself it could have been a projection of my imagination, but something in my instincts as a physician told me that she was an oppressed soul, the lowest among those in the caravan, and that fright was her main lot in this world. She moved quickly, and in a number of seconds had the demanded items set on the tiny fold-up table before where Holmes stood.

I saw his eyes flash out to her, sweeping her from head to foot, and then go back to the food.

Though the bread looked stale and its grain coarsely-ground, Holmes plopped onto the three-legged stool and set about shoving the offering into his mouth, and gulping the tea to wetten it down his throat all the easier. He then pushed a mouldy rind of some questionable cheese in behind all this, and wiped his lips with the back of his arm. The unappealing meal, such as it was, vanished in an instant, and Holmes leaned back, as if staring at the sky itself in thanks.

"First food I've had since the night afore last," he claimed.

"Well, you've eaten, so now be on with you," said the matriarchal gray-haired woman, clearly the leader of the group, she being the only one to have uttered a word thus far.

"Hold now, hold a moment," said Holmes, humbly with less a tone of challenge than supplication. "Having paid a ha'penny in the matter, mightn't a weary old fellow sit just another few moments and enjoy the good fortune of his meeting with such fine people as yourselves?"

The woman stared back before saying:

"A moment."

As if incognizant of the suspicion and ill-hidden hostility arrayed around him, Holmes slumped upon the stool and appeared to sigh away a great weight on his shoulders.

"A cruel life it can be when a man lives upon the road," he said, his accent unrefined and rural, with perhaps a hint of the Midlands in it. "I thank you, missus for easing my way even this much."

"Where is it you're heading?" the gray-haired woman demanded, less conversationally than with some covert shrewdness to her question. Behind her stood two strong-looking and nearly grown boys, and I did not like her or them, and I did not like the situation in which Holmes had placed himself, a hundred yards off and alone.

"Where am I heading, missus?" he replied. "Wherever the road may take me. To Canterbury, mayhaps, or mayhaps in the opposite direction, to Liverpool. In fact..."

He leaned out and fixed the woman with his eye.

"....mayhaps it is providence itself that moves in my life today, for I have met your people before, and never once have I been done wrong by their advice when they've consulted the unseen oracles through the cards."

Now the woman's gaze changed, no less unfriendly, but perhaps with a purpose, sensing that the winds may have shifted and were blowing a chance to profit her way.

"I can tell you what awaits in either direction," she promised, "Canterbury or Liverpool, for I, myself, know much of the future, and the cards know all!"

"Bless you, bless you!" Holmes said, then coughed, as if his lungs had borne much to distress them in his wanderings. "You see," he said, as if confiding a secret, "I do not wander these roads of fair England without purpose, no, no, in fact..."

He looked around him carefully, as if making sure no one

else was there to hear him.

"I know of Danish gold," he told her, "a hoard of treasure, long-buried, for I saw it in a dream, and it was no regular dream, I vow, but so vivid that I left the life I had, and have taken to wandering these three years in search of it."

Now a great many heads turned his way, the eyes interested, curious, rapt with attention, for the Irish gypsies were well-known for being a superstitious lot, given to placing great store in dreams.

"What was it you saw?" the woman demanded.

"A battle!" Holmes replied. "From long ago, when tall dragon ships sailed the coasts, and terrible men in mail slew all they found, taking away what was never their own. A great jarl, as the Danes called their kings, buried his loot in a place, and in my slumbering state I stood beside him and watched him do so, and then that same day he was set-upon by soldiers of a Saxon king, and slain before he could return to his loot."

"And how will you find this treasure?" the woman asked, avarice in her voice.

"That is why I wander, searching," Holmes said, "for so burned into my mind is the memory of that spot, that when I see it, I will know!"

Whether the woman thought him mad and sought to exploit him, or was overcome with desire to know more, I could not say, for I sensed that she was in her own right something of a skilled actress. She said:

"I can tell you much, perhaps all, of what lies ahead for you, traveling man, but I do not read the cards without due recompense."

"Oh, bless you, good lady, and fear not," said Holmes, who took half a sovereign from his coat and held it gleaming in the sunlight. "I am a poor man, but this coin has traveled far with me, for I have saved it for the day it would serve its purpose and point me on the way to the fortune I seek as my own!"

Her hand a blur, the gypsy woman snatched the coin

from his fingers and just as rapidly set it down inside the neckline of the billowing white homespun blouse she wore.

"Sit then!" she intoned, pointing back at the folding table. "You have bought my attention for a little while, and caught the notice of the spirits which are always near a seer such as myself. I shall certainly tell you something of your future, though it may not be what you wish to hear."

"A future where I find my treasure, I pray!" Holmes said with the illusion of great hopefulness in his voice.

"We shall see," said the woman, "we shall see, but first tell me what you saw of this location, and how you will know this place."

"By a tall gray rock jutting below three mountains beyond it," said Holmes, and I knew he was describing a site in Cumberlandshire where I had gone with him that spring on a case.

The description meant nothing to the woman, and a small sneer of disappointment crossed her face.

"That is all? Perhaps you are a mad-man," she said, "or perhaps you, too, have something of the seer in you. The cards shall tell me which it is...."

I could almost have forgotten at that moment why we were there, so fascinating was the theatricality of the woman's taking of the cards from the hand of the downtrodden girl, Saoirse, who'd fetched them from the lead wagon, and her lifting them high above her head toward the sky, and my ears rang with the trilling syllables of whatever it was she cried out in that ancient language known as Gaelic:

"*Leis na h-uilebheistean agus leis na h-uile dhiathan, nochd dhomh dè a thig a-màireach!*"

She shuffled the deck and then laid the cards on the table as she commanded:

"Divide them into three."

The fact that Holmes did so made me wonder if he had not yet discerned the signs he sought of the boy's presence, and I watched as his long white hands cut the deck into three, and at the woman's instruction he tapped the top of the middle pile, which the woman then fanned out, reversing the cards there.

She placed the cards back into one stack, and one by one turned nine cards over and laid them out in the shape of a tall, uneven cross.

"Poor man," she said, frowning, "you have never known love, and never shall, though much else will you possess, for you will live many lifetimes before your death. In your past I see much loss, and much...."

She swallowed as her frown deepened and her eyes darkened.

"....deception."

As she hissed this word, several of the men near the wagons shifted and I saw their poses tighten, not liking her revelation.

"There is much animosity surrounding you," she went on as she turned over an additional card, "for you are a man with many foes who would seek to harm you, including a great adversary, unknown to you now, but who shall come for you in time."

Holmes said nothing, and showed no reaction which I could discern. His eyes were not taking in the caravan, as I expected, but were riveted on the woman. Surely, I thought, *he* could not truly be interested in her words?

"You have but three souls in this world you trust, though one of them less than the others. You are loved by a woman, not your mother, but maternal all the same... And your mind is never at rest, but churns like the sea in storm, never content, always hungry for more...like a gluttonous fire, consuming, seeking..."

"I seek the treasure, yes," said Holmes. "I will not rest until I find it."

The woman looked up from the cards and stared harshly at him in a way that reminded me of an expression I had often seen Holmes wear when he was evaluating another, seeking hidden signs of significance. I had the strongest sense that something had changed, that no longer was this an exercise in theater, that the woman, a shrewd old con and survivor of much in a hard life, had grasped some telling revelation she had not put to voice.

The tension around us all became very great.

There was a moment of silence broken only by the wind, and when Holmes next spoke, and he said in his own voice, not the wheezing humble imprecations of the tramp.

"And my future, Madam?" he asked with unaffected clarity.

"To die twice," she said.

Then so under her breath that I barely heard her, she whispered:

"But you will never truly fall."

All time stood still, and then:

"You should never have accepted the boy last night," Holmes said to the gypsy matriarch, then very rapidly he stood and thrust both his arms above his head.

The signal!

Moving as one, shouts issuing from their lungs, the force of constables surged out of the wood and swept into the field, Colonel Morley, seeming all at once far younger than his years with them, and I beside him.

Atop the hill, the men of the caravan leaped to action and rushed to meet us, violence erupting, just as Holmes had predicted.

Stepping around the gray-haired woman with her dark eyes—she was "Black" Irish, I judged—Holmes closed in on the tallest and strongest of the young men, and ducked the man's roundhouse swing, only to rise up fast as a cat, and strike him thrice with hard jabs to his stomach and ribcage, before sending him earthward with a last great blow to his temple. The man collapsed like a sack of sand, unconscious.

The battle was swift and not without bloodshed on our own side, for one of the constables was soon to be found rolling in agony, full-length on the ground, his nose and jaw broken by a flailing *shillelagh* made of knotted blackthorn.

I made to rush to him and offer medical aid, but a swift Irishman, reedy and powerful, was on me, grappling, an adept wrestler, and he soon had me onto my back, arms locked in a hold, while he raised his skull above my face, meaning to smash it down onto me like a hammer.... Only for my assailant to be thrown headfirst through the air, as Holmes, with his sinewy might, chucked him from me, and set upon him with a series of blows that quickly left the man out of commission.

"Are you injured, Watson?" he called, turning to lend me a hand.

"I am well enough," I answered, though in truth was very much shaken up.

I was just reaching to take Holmes' hand and rise, when I spotted a movement to his rear, and realized with horror that the gray-haired matriarch had pulled a dagger from up inside her blouse-sleeve and was plunging it downward at Holmes' unprotected back in a killing strike.

Yet just before the blade met its target, an earthen vase exploded into pieces over the gypsy woman's head, and she fell to the ground, limp as a rag doll, eyes white and rolling upward in their sockets.

The girl, Saoirse had come up behind the would-be murderess and stuck her down, her eyes going out to Holmes while her breath came in panting gasps audible from several feet away. Staring at us, she burst into tears and ran off on her bare feet, finally crawling under one of the brightly painted wagons, where she rolled into a ball, sobbing wretchedly.

After the fall of the matriarch, the battle against the Irish ended quickly, and the police had the entire band, save the girl Saoirse, in shackles.

"Do forestall clamping that one in chains," Holmes had said to Welkirk, as he drew near to the wagon under which the girl cowered, "for I think you will find she is not of this tribe, but its slave, and that her unfortunate story will prove not unlike that of Barry Morley himself."

"She was herself taken by this heinous group?" asked Colonel Morley, who approached us now, panting, winded, but with his soldiering spirits in high form from the skirmish.

Holmes looked toward the cowering girl with something like tenderness in his eyes, the first such look I had seen from him since the morning of the attack back at Baker Street, and nodded his head.

"They took me from my family's farm in Cornwall last year," the girl said, gazing up, frightened.

"Those devils," Morley intoned.

I looked at her more closely now, and saw bruises covering her arms, and it struck me that the treatment she had doubtless received her at the hands of these criminal wanderers, thieves and much worse that they were, was surely appalling.

"Yes, poor child," I finally said.

As I stared at the dagger gleaming upon the ground, I reflected that twice in recent days women had nearly succeeded in killing Holmes, and yet today one of the fairer sex had also saved him. I hoped he might see this, and lose some of the harsh sentiments toward women that had descended onto him since the initial incident, for I did not approve of the distrustful statements about women he had recently made. Therefore I was quite cheered by what he said next.

"You saved my life with your action, Saoirse," Holmes told the child. "And for that I thank you, and shall see you done right by, and returned to your family in Cornwall. Now you can further help me by saving me the trouble of a search and pointing out which wagon holds the boy who was brought to these people in the night."

"The red wagon," she said, sitting up and pointing.

The Constable Sergeant, his eye already showing the bruising it would soon evince, nodded and went to the wagon with Colonel Morley walking swiftly beside him, as I knelt beside the injured constable on the ground, and set about examining his broken nose.

"You did not know yourself which wagon it was?" I asked Holmes, once we were together a little distance from the others, and I was feeling at the unconscious man's face in order to set his jaw.

"Of course I did," Holmes stated, "for I knew it was the one the men guarded most closely. The one I saw each of their eyes repeatedly go to."

"And yet you asked the child, Saoirse," I pressed him.

"The girl has borne many abuses, Watson, and there is empowerment in contributing to the downfall of a foe. I allowed her to tell me so that she might feel less powerless, as surely she does to a healing degree after striking down the witch-woman who was clearly her most ardent tormentor."

It had been an act of kindness then, on Holmes part, and I approved deeply of his show of concern toward this girl to whom he owed much indeed.

A moment later a bellowing outcry of sheer joy split the country air, and showed Saoirse's words correct, for inside the wagon, bound hand and foot, a rag over his mouth, his eyes red and puffy from crying, young Barry Morley had lain the entire time.

His grandfather soon had him free of his bonds, and a soothing banter spilled from him as he patted the boy's cheek to revive him, saying:

"Barry, my boy, you are all right now, lad...come on... wake up a little more...that's it. Let's get you home to your grandmother, and your bed."

"Grandfather, is it you?" the child asked sleepily, dazed.

"It is, my boy, it is I come at last with the help of these fine men, and you are safe!"

"I finally saw the ghost last night," the boy mumbled, "just before that man grabbed me and put the cloth over my face...I saw her...the lady in the yew alley..."

"There's a lad," Colonel Morley said, paying his grandson's claims no heed. "It's all well now, boy, as you're with me among friends and the law, and we'll soon have you home right as rain."

"She glowed, Grandfather," the boy said as a false sleep once again overcame him, "she glowed so very beautifully in the dark...."

I left the constable, who despite his injuries was standing and doing his best to shrug off his pains, and knelt on the grass beside where Morley had laid the boy down upon his own overcoat. His pulse was slow but regular, and I was relieved to tell the Colonel he'd soon he feeling more steady.

"He's plainly delirious," said the Colonel. "Poor child had so wanted to see the family ghost that he'd let himself be misled by the venal and horrid housemaid, Ada, and even now in his dreams he speaks of what I suppose never truly was."

"Plainly," said Holmes, who stood a moment looking on, before walking over to offer the other child present, Saoirse, a drink of water, and speak with her in low, gentle tones, much as one might a skittish horse.

Half an hour later Barry Morley was awake and walking on his own power, and I looked closely into his eyes and asked him to follow my finger as I moved it about. I asked him several questions about himself and his treatment by the gypsies, one of which I whispered in his ear and felt relief when he answered in the negative, for no child in the world deserved an ordeal such as the one I feared may have been his, yet all too many endured just such vile assaults, I knew.

Two of the constables went off to bring up the police wagons, while the others stood guard on the gypsy band, whom Constable Sergeant Welkirk had ordered to sit upon the ground, pending transport back to the station.

Reviving slowly from her injury, her coal black eyes bleary and focused only on Holmes, at whom she glared with a viperous intensity, the gray-haired matriarch began to venomously chant what I took for some arcane incantation:

Gun òl uisgeachan na mara thu sìos! Na sluig an talamh do chnàmhan agus nach spìon e a-mach iad gu bràth! Gum b' fheàrr le do nàimhdean thu, fàgaidh na friogais thu, bidh do luchd-gràidh gad bhrath. An losgadh agus an losgadh thu, nàmhaid mo chridhe!

"It'll take more than rhymes to daunt me, woman," Holmes told her with a laugh, "for if being cursed could kill a man, I'd have been in my grave long years before this, done-in by far more menacing villains than you."

He turned away and paid her no more heed, as the constables lead her and all her kind, three women, the remainder men (for I had heard of immoral polygamy being the norm among this kind) to the prison-wagon, and the rest of us went into another, bound for the Morley estate.

We were back in town in good time, and after we left the station, Holmes detoured a moment, bidding us wait for him, as he led Saoirse to an inn there, the Four Keys, and paid for her to have a room.

"Lock the door and wait for me here," he said to her, "and I shall soon return to obtain details from you of where you previously lived. I'll see you sent back home by train at first morning light."

It was a second and more unexpected righting of past wrongs connected to the Morley case, and as the sun was lowering in the west, we were back at the family house, Welkirk, the Colonel and Barry, Holmes, and myself.

Hearing the wagon pulling up outside, Mrs. Morley and her companion rushed outdoors, and upon seeing her grandson looking safe and returned home again, the Colonel's wife let loose a great cry, and ran to sweep the lad up into her arms.

"Barry, my little soldier-man," she sang out, "I was so wretchedly worried for you! I'll never let go of you now, I think!"

She half carried and half led the boy indoors, speaking of a warm bath and a filling supper before bed. At the doorway she paused and turned and smiled warmly while expressing a brief but clearly heartfelt thanks to Sherlock Holmes.

"You are a worker of wonders," she said, before disappearing inside her home.

Though his emotions were more contained, the Colonel likewise let loose a long breath where he stood beside the wagon, and reached out to shake Holmes' hand, and my own.

"Mr. Holmes," the Colonel boomed, "this is not the first time I have sought your aid, and never have you left me disappointed! You are a true wonder-worker as my wife has said, sir, and any reward I might offer, in addition to your fee, you shall have!"

Though I may have questioned the timing of what he was about to say, I saw Holmes' eyes go past the Colonel to those of Lieutenant Peters, who now stepped out from the house to stare at the assembly outdoors.

"Do not dismiss that man from your service," Holmes said nodding to the lieutenant, "for the loss of income would see him relocated elsewhere in search of employment, and his much-troubled wife would lose the safeguards I hope might soon be in place for her. Rather monitor him as regards his marriage. Look out for Mrs. Peters, and should your assistant continue violence against her, summon Welkirk, who shall deal with him in short order. Will you not, Sergeant?"

Welkirk, who had known nothing of any allegations of wife-beating, nonetheless took on a stern visage and replied:

"Most definitely I shall, Mr. Holmes, for I do not countenance any man's cruelty toward a woman."

"I thought not, as I perceive you were raised by a widowed mother, unless I mistake the signs, and know you have sympathies for women in general."

"I do at that, sir," the Constable Sergeant agreed, fixing a hard, albeit well-blackened, eye upon Peters, though saying nothing further.

I was cheered by these words, as I had hoped I sensed a lessening of my friend's anger toward both women in general and himself in particular, the latter for having let down his guard that fateful morning.

Yet he was not done, for to Peters he said in a serious tone:

"You have heard what has been said before you tonight, Lieutenant, and know that I, too, shall be keeping an ear open, for I have many sources, as you might imagine, and should I hear that you have resumed the persecutions of your spouse, I shall most assuredly deal with you."

It was a short declaration, but one that so dripped menace that Peters merely swallowed hard, his face flushing, and after an instant, he took to his heel and marched back inside the house.

Mrs. Morley took Barry upstairs, to see a bath run for him after a light supper, and put him to bed, where she promised him she'd stay in his room with him through the night.

Just before he left the drawing room where we were all assembled, however, Barry turned back, and to Holmes he asked in a small trembling voice:

"I was sure I saw the ghost among the yew shrubs last night, but you say it was just pretty Ada tricking me, sir? There never really was a ghost at all?"

"There was not," Holmes told him firmly but by no means unkindly. "For ghosts are merely stories, misunderstandings, and most usually, lies."

Somehow, even more than the relief that also occupied the boy's eyes, disappointment filled them more deeply still as he turned back to the hallway, and his now-silent grandmother.

"You have certainly done well by us, Holmes,' said the Colonel. "More than I could have asked."

But there a minute smile played out on Holmes' lips: a smile of anticipation.

"I do thank you, Colonel," he said, "and have seen your matter to its conclusion with the return of the boy, and the revelation of the faithless servant in your home, but, ah, I think you overlook the fact that the entirety of my work is not done."

"The perpetrator, Turner," Morley agreed. "The scoundrel who caused all of this."

"Indeed," said Holmes. "He yet eludes my net, though not for much longer."

"Clearly he is an audacious and daring foe," the Colonel said. "And while I cannot imagine he shall ever trouble us again, and surely shall know this house will never be his for any price, he remains at large, as you say. However will you be able to find and apprehend him, Holmes?"

"That plan, Colonel," the detective said, his smile broader now, the look of the hunter I knew so well writ large upon him, "is already fully-formed, and even now my net slowly begins to close around him."

With those cryptic words, which revealed no more to me than they had to the Colonel, Holmes accepted a cheque for his services, and we set off toward town in the Colonel's own carriage, conveyed by his driver, Watkins.

And now I must add a detail concerning an incident which I have ever-after struggled to explain, for ere I tell the remainder of what unfolded in this far-reaching case, I pause, strictly in the interests of truth and full disclosure, however you might receive what I shall write next, for as we set off into the blackness of the country night, Holmes and I, amid the sound of crickets chirruping in the grass, I happened to turn and gaze over my shoulder for one last look at the house which my friend had restored to happiness, and for the merest instant, like the after-flash in the eyes that comes after seeing a strong light suddenly shining out in darkness, I saw a glowing form, human-sized, human-like, golden and bright, not menacing, no, but sad, lonely, weak, and trapped, there and gone again faster than the duration of a blink, so rapid from its beginning to its end that I told myself perhaps I had never seen anything at all, yet I knew despite the doubts of rationality, it had been there, whatever it was, female and forlorn, hovering in the shadows of a deserted yew alley.

*****

We returned to Cottersfield, to the Four Keys Inn, where Holmes had rented a room for the girl whom the gypsy matriarch had called Saoirse, and he asked me to go upstairs and check in on her, and have her come down and join us in a late supper, which I did, finding her timid, and worried about the eyes, and much pity did I feel for this child, stolen by people whose own lives embodied so much evil, and I tried not to think of the abuses she must have known ever since.

"You will be all right now," I promised her. "As my friend Mr. Holmes has said, we'll have you home again as swift as we can."

"Thank you, sir," she said simply, her little hands protectively folded together in front of her waist.

"You were very brave today," I told her, "and what you did there on that field this afternoon most likely saved Mr. Holmes' life."

She sat with us at table, and at first seemed reluctant to eat, but once she began, she ate heartily, and Holmes kept her plate filled, as he gently asked her questions about her family and the gypsies.

"Saoirse is the name your captives have set upon you," he said. "Tell me, what is it you are truly called?"

"My name is Rachel," said the girl. "Rachel Webber."

"Then that is what I shall call you," said Holmes, "and nevermore shall you ever hear that other name spoken."

And so young Rachel Webber told of being taken from her own bed in the night, through an open window on her family's farm, and carried off with a blade at her throat, and then turned into the servant of the tribe, with one of them, a tall red-haired fellow named Cathal, promising he'd have her for his wife in due time.

The girl trembled to recall this, and when she closed her eyes, I gave my head a little shake, telling Holmes he should ask her nothing further.

It was a horrid situation, and I wondered how many other bands of gypsies there were crisscrossing England, bringing such miseries onto the innocent.

"There is a nurse for hire in town," Holmes finally said at meal's end, "who enjoys an excellent reputation according to inquiries I have made, and I have sent for her. A kind woman, she will stay with you tonight, Rachel, and sit with you on the train to London, and from there upon a second train that shall take you to Cornwall, where she'll see you returned to your family."

"Thank you, sir," little Rachel said. Then a worried look came into her eyes, which had for a moment brimmed with happiness. "But, sir...what if they come back, and take me again."

Holmes looked steadily at the child and said:

"I ask you to trust me when I tell you, those villains shall not see freedom until long after you are a woman grown, and I find it likely they shall one and all be expelled from England after their time in prison is done."

"Good," was all the girl said, though fear was still in her, alongside great relief.

The nurse, a plump and soft-faced woman called Mrs. Dowsey, arrived shortly after, and once she had spoken to Holmes, went upstairs with the girl, and I felt a happy warmth, knowing my friend had done right by the child.

"Goodbye, Mr. Holmes, Doctor Watson," Rachel said just before she vanished from sight. "And thank you."

"Child," said Holmes, "it is I who owe you my own thanks."

Yet when she was gone, everything changed.

"Now, Watson," Holmes said, a seriousness upon him, the fire I'd seen earlier blazing again in his eyes, "ours shall not be the delight of warm bed tonight, for much lies ahead. Are you with me?"

Though I was tired, and could never match Holmes' seemingly unending vigour while upon a case, I replied:

"Of course."

"Splendid," he said, "for in the interior world of my being, I have been diligently at work on our next step, and know my course of action."

"What shall that be?"

"Clearly our man, Turner, or by whatever name he goes, has had to spend some not inconsiderable time locally while setting his snare for the Morley child. I considered that he was staying with the gypsies, but as you saw, I looked inside each wagon, and discerned no traces that he had ever been there. Which left the probability of accommodations in town."

"And this is the sole inn!" I said excitedly.

"Precisely! He has been here, I'd stake a pound against a shilling on that!"

He sprang from his chair and approached the landlord, a Mr. Prescott, who was behind the bar wiping out newly-washed glasses in preparation for closing down for the night. He was a wide-shouldered man with a heavy mustache, and a part down the middle of his well-oiled black hair, probably dyed, I judged, for he looked well past fifty. I imagined he was a man who had laboured long to reach the point of owning the establishment, for I saw in his build old muscles, still strong from days of strenuous work.

Holmes was on him with his questions, asking if a man meeting the description we had of this suspect Turner had stayed beneath his roof.

"Normally I don't discuss my guests, a matter of confidence and privacy, you see," said the landlord, "but from what I overheard said to that girl at table with you, I think in this case good should better be served if I would, for I think you are a man about the work of justice, are you not?"

"I seek to right a deep wrong against a child and his family," said Holmes, to which the landlord's eyebrows raised, "and to reel in the villain who brought about this injustice, and stop him from committing other offenses of like kind, for he is, I have deduced, a man of great energies, who enjoys his plottings and his misadventures rather as a drunkard enjoys gin. He is ambitious, and does not scruple at upending the lives of others for his own amusements."

"I can tell you, then," said Prescott, "that the only guest meeting that description we've had here at Four Keys called himself Longbrook. Not like to forget him, sort of a strong-natured, memorable fellow, I'd say. Good-looking, with a deal of flash to him, if you like. Touch of American in his words, somehow, but just a bit."

"Interesting…" Holmes muttered, his eyes alive with the electricity of rapid thought.

The landlord turned the registration book around to us and pointed out the man's signature, which Holmes leaned close to and peered at for a longer time than I might ever have guessed a mere scrawl merited.

"There is much to learn from another's handwriting, Watson," he voiced, as if intercepting my thoughts. "See how he strikes his t's with such force, yet loops the bottoms of the letter 'y' with sloppy disregard for making its ends connect? Vigor and impatience! And this confirms all I have heard of this man, for he is an energetic type, filled with bravado, yet also somewhat careless, and confident to the point of being recklessly headstrong. Women are likely to be fascinated with the attentions and flattery of this schemer, but also to soon grow angry with him, and feel themselves mislead and ill-used, as we have seen with the maid who so readily gave him up under the mildest pressure. Which for our cause is all excellent, for a cautious man is apt to be wiser than a gambler, and one who long-holds the affections of a woman is less likely to be betrayed by her, as this fellow was by his paramour back at the Morley house."

"He promised Ada much, but would ultimately have delivered nothing," I said. "A villain in full, in other words," I summed-up.

"Quite."

Without asking for the landlord's leave, Holmes quickly

and carefully tipped out a quantity of charcoal residue onto the space around the signature in the ledger, and nodded with satisfaction when several fingerprints showed up. These he soon lifted from the page using a strip of thinnest foil, which he dropped into a glass jar no larger than his thumb.

"His prints," he explained to Prescott, the landlord. "They will be unlike those of any other man in the entirety of the world, as are your own, or mine or Dr. Watson's here."

"Remarkable thing, that," Prescott said.

"From these," said Holmes, "I can now identify the fellow who stayed here, no matter what he may call himself, or by what disguise he should seek to conceal his appearance."

The landlord then offered:

"He stayed in room number four upstairs several times in recent weeks—"

"Always the same room?" Holmes interrupted to inquire.

"Yes, sir, always asked for it special, on account of the view out into the fields. In these parts on business, said he was, taking orders for roofing repairs on behalf of a company in Birmingham, and was back again this week, spending the last three nights here, but he left last evening with a jaunt in his step, I noted, and never returned. My daughter Molly, who acts as our maid here at Four Keys, knocked on the door to bring him up his breakfast tray, part of our service here, you see, and said his bed had not been slept in and all his possessions were gone."

"Indeed!"

The landlord shrugged. "Thought it odd, but none of my concern, I figured, how a guest conducts himself. He'd paid up to morning tomorrow in any case, so no loss on my part whether he was in the room or not, was how I figured it."

I nodded.

"Tell me, has Molly cleaned the room?" Holmes asked him, and I caught a hopefulness in his voice.

"Not as yet, since the man paid to tomorrow, as I said, and we don't intrude on a guest lest services are asked for particular, like."

"Mr. Prescott, I thank you, sir," said Holmes, "you have been of immense help to me in my cause. I bid you, though, might it be possible for me to see the chamber he previously occupied? This room four?"

Not waiting for a reply, Holmes set coins on the counter, paying for lodgings there, though I doubted he had any intention of spending the night within the Four Keys.

"I reckon no harm in that ambition," said the landlord, his bulging walrus mustache bouncing with the words. He did not touch the coins, though his eyes focused on them. "Just so you know, though, sir, I'd have said yes to the request without you needin' to pay for it."

"I know you should have," said Holmes, "and that is why I presented the money. A generous spirit is rare in this world, and deserves to be rewarded."

Only then did the landlord give him a grateful nod, and pocket the offering.

Key in hand a moment later, Holmes bounded up the stairs and soon had room four opened.

"Careful where you step, Watson," he told me, "in fact stay back near the door, lest you disturb something I might find to be a clue."

"What are you looking for?" I asked.

"His whereabouts," Holmes answered stonily.

I let loose a little laugh and jested:

"Holmes I do not think you will find him concealed in this chamber."

"Oh, there you may be more wrong than you know, Watson!"

What? I had been joking but could there truly be some hidden chamber?

I gazed about the room and as I could see the entire space, even under the bed, and found it empty, I thought Holmes was barking up the wrong tree, but stayed back in the doorway as he instructed while he stooped low and slowly made his way across the room, the lens he'd pulled from his overcoat in hand and pressed up by his eye, methodically taking in its every board, wall, ceiling, and corner of what looked to me a tidy and well-kept little room.

"Does he know you are on his heels, Holmes?" I asked. "If so, might he have left some trap concealed here, in wait for you?"

"Unlikely, though I am proceeding with such an eventuality in mind."

Had he grown more cautious after the incident at Baker Street? I wondered.

Holmes continued to take in his surroundings for another long moment, before he turned to a small table with a single wooden chair before it, and then he let loose such a throaty exclamation of sheer glee that I admit I stared bemused before the sound of it.

"Holmes?" I cried.

"This is marvelous!" he shouted, so rapt by some discovery I think he was completely heedless of others in nearby rooms hearing his yell of exultation. "Look, Watson, the ash tray! It is full!"

I did look over to see that several days of ashes lay within the unadorned tin dish, though how this merited the great detective's manic glee I could not understand.

"In such a well-attended establishment as this," he said delightedly, "I mark there is no possibility that the landlord would allow a new guest to find a dirty ash tray in his room, so these all must date to the time of our suspect's occupation!"

"Yes?" I asked, putting much confusion into the syllable.

"Ah, Watson, as you have never, despite my not infrequent encouragement, read the manuscript for my monograph *Upon the Distinction Between the Ashes of the Various Tobaccos* you fail to appreciate what a gold mine lies before my eyes."

He leaned toward the ashes, careful with his breath, I noted, lest he scatter them with each exhalation, and examined them first visually, then under a magnifying glass he still clutched, and finally, after removing a small microscope from within the portable chemistry case, in that manner as well, painstakingly brushing through the sample under the lens with a single toothpick.

"It is wonderful!" he cried. "More than I could have hoped for!"

"Yes?" I demanded.

He rose to his full height, suddenly transformed into the very image of beatific joy, like some saint upon a stained glass window.

"I'll have him, Watson," he smiled. "I shall definitely have him."

He thundered past me and galloped down the stairs toward the front door, case in hand, I at his heels, as ever the slower man of our pairing. Calling a farewell to the helpful landlord, he was almost instantly outside in the dark running toward the house of the man I knew to be the driver who had transported us to the Morley estate that morning.

As under the dark sky of night he knocked loudly and with rapidity at the man's door, I demanded of him:

"Well, are you going to tell me what it was you found in those ashes to merit such a display of manic exuberance?"

With a great smile beamed less at me than at the world entire, Holmes threw back his head and barked out a laugh:

"It seems during his years in America, our man Turner acquired a preference for a specific variety of tobacco, and now shuns our domestic varieties in favour of a broadleaf grown in the commonwealth of Kentucky! I saw none other below my lens, and a most useful clue that was."

"Because…" I said aloud as I worked this matter out, "not every tobacconist would sell imported Kentucky broadleaf?"

"But a few, in fact outside London," said Holmes, "and none hereabouts in the countryside of Suffolk. No, I think Turner is to be found in the nearest city large enough to provide him with the fulfillment of his acquired vice, and yet be sufficiently close that it is not a thing of overbearing inconvenience to make frequent journeys to this little town by Morley estate he covets, so that he might oversee the unfolding of the cruel plot he has set in motion!"

"Norwich!" I cried.

"None other!" confirmed Holmes.

At that moment the door to the house opened and the face of the town's drive for hire peered out.

"'Tis after dark, gentlemen," he said, frowning, but with a civil enough tone in his words. "I keep daylight hours."

"Even for triple the fare to the station in Ipswich?" Holmes inquired, and enticingly held a bank note out before the man.

The man stared at the money with almost a physical hunger in his eyes, and said:

"I'll get my coat, and fasten up the team."

Back went we across the same country roads that we'd twice hastened down that day, though in the blackness, lighted only by a single lantern hanging out before the wagon, nothing seemed familiar to my eyes at all. The branches of trees, perhaps almost majestic in the sunlight now seemed like clawed hands, bedecked by talons, reaching down for us in the dark. To the driver's credit, he earned his exorbitant fee, and had us in Ipswich just before the clock struck midnight, and, duly paid, was on his way home again without an excess of words.

Within a few minutes, Holmes and I were aboard the final train of the night from Ipswich to Norwich, one county over, the city lights flashing past, to be replaced by more unbroken rural darkness, the interior of the train dim as well, and silent of the usual conversation of daytime hours, the main noise the clacking of the wheels on the tracks below. I had to battle a sense of drowsiness that threatened to come upon me in such an environment.

"I do not think we will find any tobacco shops open before eight at the earliest," I said, "so why the haste tonight?"

"I doubt not that Turner is keeping an ear out for how his plan unfolds back in Cottersfield," Holmes claimed, "and though he may not yet have heard of the arrest of the Irish gypsies, or the return of young Barry Morley from the slavery that should have been his fate, he shall in short order, likely sometime on the morrow. After that, the world will be wide open to him, and he will flee elsewhere, probably back to America, his hopes dashed, his conspiracy foiled, and a new plot will take root to stimulate his mind and fulfill his ambitions, as I doubt not many others have before this. I think that is how he made his fortune, less by some lucky strike out in the broad spaces of America, but via his machinations at the expense of others."

"All with an eye to obtaining the estate he coveted as a boy?"

"Not entirely, though that would have fulfilled much in the heart of this confidence man and adventurer, for it would place him into a sphere of legitimacy in society's regard, and for all his audacity and daring, that is something he has heretofore lacked."

"So time is limited, then," I said, understanding.

"It is, and the moment I step out in Norwich, I shall be narrowing down the shoppes at which I shall inquire, and if luck be with me, Watson, I shall confront this doer of black deeds before the sun is far above the rooftops."

My friend's words would turn out to be a prophetic remark indeed...

*****

The train ride between the cities was not long in duration, being but a forty mile trip, though the late hour narrowed our options as to how to spend the intervening hours until dawn. I thought we were either to linger in Thorpe Station, or perhaps seek out a hôtel for a few hours slumber before the trials of the morning, but Holmes had an entirely different idea.

After obtaining a penny-directory of Norwich from a stand, he set off into the sleeping city which surrounded us in all directions, and announced:

"Come, Watson, tonight we walk!"

"With an eye to locating tobacconists?"

"Indubitably. Let us survey the area while we wait for the sun, for time is precious."

Armed with his guide and the map printed within, Holmes set off toward the city's main thoroughfare, and passed several tobacco shoppes, studying each a moment before discounting them via some qualifying equation carried out in his head.

"No," he muttered before one, "decidedly not prosperous enough to import tobacco from the subtropical fields of faraway Kentucky."

Before another he declared:

"A definite possibility, Watson, but the housing around it...I cannot see our man Turner residing hereabouts, however briefly he intends his stay in Norwich to be."

"Holmes, do you feel you know him so well that you can hypothesize as to where he might live?"

"I have formed a portrait, let us say, Watson, of his type, and can deduce with some acuity what such a man might undertake when about his existence, and what he would not."

"I see," I conceded as we walked on.

"Somehow I think you do not," Holmes said, challenging my statement. "Man is, by an almost invariable rule, a creature of habit, and is far less prone to originality in behavior than we might like to imagine. Give me a few germane facts about an individual, and I can reduce him to a member of a herd and tell you what he is likely to think, to do, to *be*. This Turner is not only no exception to this rule, but falls, I think, quite plainly into a very broad type, which for my purposes I dub 'the audacious criminal.' In perpetrating crime for the thrill of the act, he thus differs markedly from, say, one who commits wrongdoing out of some necessity, as would, let us say a starving man, or a penniless drunkard desirous of gin. In fact I would go so far as to note that all criminals, regardless of any other details which may be singular to them, invariably fall within seven categories, and once identified within one of these orders, proceeding against them becomes a more uniform matter."

"Fascinating," I admitted. "I had never thought of categorizing criminal behavior in such a way."

"Yes," Holmes mused in closing, "I really should compose a monograph on the subject one day, for I think it should aid police forces immeasurably."

We continued our progress through the sleeping city, coming to several shoppes of interest to Holmes. As we did so, I worried about being stopped on our perambulations and questioned by a suspicious constable, or perhaps encountering street thugs who surely prowled about at night no less here than in London, but Holmes proceeded with a buoyant and preoccupied confidence that I thought may well have dispelled all intrusions.

I followed along trying to hold myself up in a like manner, tired though I was by this time, and quite drooping with hunger: the penalty for accompanying a man who seemed to forget to rest or eat, or recall that anyone else had those needs. I had also learned almost from the start of our association, that though I was not lacking in vigour by the standards of most of my contemporaries, when upon a case, I could not match my friend's limitless energies.

After we had walked on for some not inconsiderable distance, Holmes paused to smoke, and remarked:

"I have marked two prosperous and entrepreneurial-minded establishments on this map, Pennyworth's, and Sutton's by name, as likely being worth a visit at first light, and as you see, in making our rounds tonight I have saved us several hours that would otherwise have been spent on the undertaking in the morning. I further noted another tobacconist, Howard's, on Price Avenue, that stands within the realms of possibility for supplying Turner with his uniquely-identifying preference."

"That is excellent," I said.

"Of course, and yet, Watson..." he began.

"Yes, Holmes, what is it?"

He thought a moment before finishing:

"And yet, my good Watson, my instincts, which I trust as a sailor does the sails above him, tell me I have not yet located our target."

"Have you anything upon which to base this?"

"I have not, and yet..."

Holmes once again removed the map from his pocket and studied it, for unlike London, wherein I knew he could call to mind the details of every alleyway from Seven Dials to Grosvenor Square, Norwich was not so precisely known to him.

"King Street is a possibility...yes," he muttered at last. "The area is one I could see Turner occupying, judging it worthy of his pretentions, for I'll wager he owns himself to be a man equally at home in the rough conditions of the American West, or among things of a finer nature now and again. And, ah, I now see there is listed a large and fine tobacconist there, one Spencer and Son, near some fine properties available for short-term lease. I cannot say why it is, Watson, but at times my instincts veritably sing out to me, and though I cannot always justify this testimony by any logic, I have profited much in the past by heeding its call."

"So to King Street then?" I asked him.

"At once!" he agreed.

Scenic even in the dark, parts of it quite Medieval, other sections modern and pricey, King Street sprawled silently around us, its cobbles wide and old, true cut stones instead of the cheap brick underfoot in much of London, and I found my tired jaws yawning just as the clock struck the last hour before dawn.

"Five o' clock," I muttered.

"The final hold of night," Holmes affirmed, and I noted that somehow he sounded even more vigorous than he'd been before we'd started our explorations of nocturnal Norwich.

We located the shoppe Holmes had remarked upon, and peered in through its great front windows to a display area decorated with elaborate pipes and smoking jackets and the accoutrements of its prosperous proprietor's trade. I also saw with leaping heart, for it seemed a significant detail, that there was a wooden statue of an American Indian in the lobby, right inside the door. It was as tall as a figure from life, dressed in carven buckskins, and with a vast headdress full of feathers above a stern visage and hard wooden eyes. *Chief Red Owl*, read the name carved by its moccasin-clad feet.

"Look, Holmes," I cried, "surely seeing the trappings of western America like that would appeal to Turner in some way, owing to his time spent there, for I have heard cigar stores there often display carvings of Indians in just such a manner!"

"*Yes*," Holmes drawled with keen satisfaction, "he comes here, Watson. I have no evidence to support my suspicions, but tell you all the same that my theory shall shortly be proven true."

"I do not doubt you," I said my flagging spirits bolstered above my bone-deep weariness.

"And look, Watson," Holmes added, "again fortune stands with us, for the owner is an early riser."

He pointed to a notice-board against the glass of the door, which gave the shoppe's opening time as seven rather than eight, or even the nine 'o clock hour that some London proprietors gave.

"How wonderful!" I said. "Time shall be with us!"

"A distinct advantage," Holmes called it.

And so it was, but the time for the owner's arrival seemed to extend out like days, until at last I spied a gentleman in gray tweed, sportily dressed, almost dapper, coming toward us down the way, a brass-topped ebony-wood walking stick in hand, which he tapped against King Street's great Medieval cobbles.

"Surely that's him," I said quietly.

"It is plain enough to the eye that he is a native of this city, married, for he, of course, wears a ring, is a near-constant smoker of cigarettes, for there is the tell-tale yellowing of the fingertips that practice produces, and look, he holds a half-smoked cigarette now. I further see he is a lifelong player of cricket, for I note the callus between his right thumb and forefinger, which long involvement in the sports leaves almost like a trademark. Furthermore he sleeps on the right side of a double bed directly below a broad window, which is often left open at night, though not, I think, due to his own preference, but rather a concession to his wife, who perhaps suffers from claustrophobia."

Exactly how Holmes deduced these last declarations merely from the approaching man's person I was never to know, for when this fellow spied us standing outside his shoppe's door, he became the very soul of the merry proprietor, calling over as he approached in a bouncing stride:

"How now, gentlemen, is it the case that you find yourselves out of tobacco so early in the morning, and do not wish to face the day smoke-less?"

He gave a little laugh at his own wit, and came near, his smile bright and jolly as he pulled a ring of keys from his pocket.

"Indeed, my most excellent fellow," Holmes replied, "I am but a visitor in your fair city and have a preference for a variety of tobacco which I am given to believe you carry?"

The man unbolted the door and pushed it wide before stepping back so that we, his first customers of this bright and early morning, could enter before him.

"I doubt that not, sir," he replied with his rolling East Anglican accent, "for I have made it a point of honour to carry a great variety of man's noblest plant, as you shall see if you look around you."

He did not lie, for along the walls of his broad and airy establishment were many shelves, all well-made of oak, and deeply varnished, telling of the money that had been invested in such a shoppe. I judged there must have been a hundred types of tobacco, more than was carried by plenty of noteworthy London stores I had visited, and I wondered whether he was the father or the son the sign outside spoke of.

"And what sort of tobacco is it that tickles your fancy this morning, sir?" he asked, once he had placed his coat upon a stand at the far end of the room, behind the counter.

"I seek a fine Kentucky broadleaf," said Holmes, "cultivated in the Bluegrass region, and most ideal for a relaxing smoke."

"Ah, yes, indeed, my good man," answered the proprietor, pleased to hear of the request, "you were not misinformed, for I have just such a high-quality variety which I import through a brokerage in Paris, Kentucky, in the Bluegrass hills of that corner of ever-sprawling America. Each plant is carefully nurtured throughout its growth under the warm, even rainfall of that state, which permeates the limestone below the rich southern soil, fed by a degree of sunlight so perfect, the result has never failed to please even the palate of the most refined connoisseur such as yourself!"

Holmes nodded, seeming satisfied, and ordered a quantity of the prized commodity, and paid the rather steep price asked for it, then opened the tin and sniffed deeply, before giving what I felt was an honest sigh of approval.

"It is a masterpiece of cultivation!" he declared at last, making the proprietor break out with a wide grin.

"I am pleased that you find it so, sir," the man stated, appearing happy indeed.

"And now," began Holmes, "I think there is one other matter with which you might be able to help me today."

"Indeed?" said the man affably and with no small curiosity. "If I can, sir, I certainly shall."

"My friend here and I are newly up from London,

arriving just yesterday, and were told much about you and this fine city, by an acquaintance of ours, who is the only soul known to us in the entirety of Norwich. He, too, smokes excellent Kentucky tobacco, and was in fact the very individual who suggested that were we ever here, we should call upon you."

"I am grateful the gentleman thought me worthy of such a recommendation," said the man, humbly. "I do strive to please all my customers, and leave them with a favourable impression."

"Seeing as he is a customer of yours," Holmes continued, "we thought you might know him and could direct us his way. We, I must admit, have lost track of him in the time he has been here, and would be most interested in paying him a call while we are here in Norwich, which I dare say would be a very great surprise to him, indeed."

I alone caught the ironic humour in that last remark.

"That does sound like it would pleasant," the man agreed with a nod. "What is your local acquaintance's name?"

"Ah, better still, let me describe him," said Holmes dancing around the name, as he knew it was likely Turner called himself something different. He gave a detailed description, the one provided by Ada, and before he was done, the tobacconist was nodding forcefully, his polite smile even brighter.

"I know just the fellow!" he confirmed. "You are surely referring to Mr. Herrington, of Tanner Alley, just off King Street here, not four blocks up. A fine chap he is, Mr. Herrington, and an excellent customer. Why the stories he tells me of his life, young though he is, I declare, sirs, they do so dazzle, being about America and—"

But having gotten what he came for, Holmes did not invest further time in listening, and instead strode quickly toward the door, not thinking upon his rudeness, leaving me to call over apologetically to the bewildered tobacconist:

"We thank you, sir, but as you see, my friend is in quite a

rush to see our acquaintance, he…"

As I did not know how to finish, I, too, hurried out of the shoppe, feeling awkward at the way we'd repaid the man's geniality with brusqueness.

"Tanner Alley, just off King Street!" Holmes cried. "So near to our quarry these past two hours! Hurry, Watson, keep up, there is not a moment to be lost when Turner might learn of matters at any instant through one of many means."

And hurry I did, but drew no closer to my onrushing friend than half a block, his Ulster trailing him in his extreme haste. He located Tanner Alley, and dashed onto it, and as I turned a corner, I saw him halt before a door to a residential structure through which a businessman of advancing years was exiting. Pushing into the door before the other man could close it, and eliciting an outcry of disapproval from the fellow, Holmes burst into the building, and I heard him stomping up the stairs, and only just caught the door in my own hands before it was shut.

"Beg pardon!" I called to the older gentleman as I passed him with much rudeness, but did not wait to hear his reply as I likewise sped up the stairs, my side aching but my tiredness momentarily dispelled by my urgency and excitement, for surely we had closed-in upon Turner at last.

There was a great crashing sound ahead of me, and I mastered the final set of stairs in time to see Holmes shoving through a doorway that marked the left-hand flat on this, the fifth and highest floor of the building.

Had he truly shouldered his way in? I marveled.

Seconds later I too was in inside the flat, aware we had broken and entered into a private dwelling, but trusting Holmes must have had his reasons, as indeed he had, for he cried out to me, even as he was making his dash toward an open window above the street some sixty feet below:

"The instincts of this man are keen, Watson, for somehow he was tipped to our coming, and I heard him making his flight out this window, and toward the rooftop!"

"And so you shoved through his door!" I confirmed.

Holmes hefted his way out the window and onto a metal fire-stairway bolted in place there, and I lost sight of him as he vanished like quicksilver up the clanging steps, I close on his heels, my breath coming rather hard, but was only in time to see the swirl of his coat tails as he took to the roof, eyes now on his target.

Across the roof itself, Turner was fleeing, Holmes directly after him, until his quarry leaped atop the yard-wide ledge which encircled the building, and dropped down from its farther side, Holmes doing exactly the same. I ran across as well, stepping up onto the ledge and lowering myself onto a second metal staircase affixed to the building's distant side, and followed the pursuit I spied underway several yards below, proceeding down this staircase just as previously it had been run up the other.

Turner was now mid-way down this second set of fire-stairs, Holmes hot on his heels, one landing behind, and yet his next action startled me greatly, for instead of re-entering the building through a window, as might be expected, Turner leapt flat-footed up onto the metal railing at the staircase's outer edge, barely an inch wide, landing with precision, and there he stood perfectly balanced still thirty feet above the alleyway.

At once, Holmes stopped and stood in place, staring expressionlessly at the other man, two arm's length between them. As for me, I felt my heart freeze, for I saw that in his desperation, this Turner intended to make a leap toward the far side of the alley, where one floor down a sort of balcony lay jutting from an adjoining building at least ten feet away.

It was clearly too far for one to leap.

Turner paused balanced on the rail under his feet, and Holmes for his part drew no closer to him from where he stood on the stairwell itself, his footing much more sound.

When Turner shifted so he was facing his purser, to my surprise I saw it was a vast smile that he wore on his young and handsome face, quite suntanned and with an easy charm in his every aspect.

"How's that for a lucky leap up onto this railing?" he asked, genially.

"It is the best I have yet seen," replied Holmes.

"I think I know who you are," Turner said in a conversational tone, his accent partly that of America, partially that of his native England, a strange but not displeasing mixture of the two dialects, representing the best of each. "You are, I think, that Mr. Sherlock Holmes, of London, the detective I have read so much about of late since coming back over here, whose adventures I have enjoyed so thoroughly."

"I am the same," Holmes confirmed, and I thought what a strange conversation this was, one man balanced like a tightrope walker on a narrow handrail still a dozen or more yards above the alleyway below, the other standing a little a distance off, seemingly content to stay there and speak a moment.

"I thought so," said Turner, "because you fit the description. When I happened to see you coming down King Street, all quick and sneaky, while I was fixing to fry up some bacon for my breakfast, I got a flash as to why you were here, and lit out, like you see. But not quite fast enough, it looks like."

"That is why you fled," Holmes inquired, "because you happened to see me? You were not tipped off?"

"Who would tip me off?" Turner asked. "I keep my associates at arm's length. Not sure how you found me, and somehow I doubt you're going to tell."

"It was through your tobacco ash back at the Four Keys Inn, in Cottersfield," Holmes replied, causing Turner to raise an eyebrow.

"Well that doesn't explain much," he laughed.

"Perhaps you'll have time to read my monograph on the subject while you are languishing in a well-deserved prison cell," said Holmes.

"I wouldn't take odds on my ending up in any prison," Turner said with a boast that somehow still ended up sounding friendly enough in his cockiness. "I always keep a few extra cards up my sleeve."

"You are not as skilled an opponent as you think yourself to be," Holmes told him levelly. "If you had not by chance spied my approach, I should have had you in the flat."

"Yeah," Turner agreed, "I just caught a break there, but that's the way I am, lady luck's with me as a rule. The stories I could tell about my luck would fill a magazine in themselves. I escaped a furious mother bear once out in Colorado. Another time I talked some Cheyenne out of taking me prisoner. Had the wife of the mayor of Kansas City fall in love with me just from my smile. And I once won a carriage off a riverboat gambler down near Natchez while playing with his own crooked deck. Sure, I'm a rogue, but my fortune is made in the stars. My, oh, my, I am living quite a life."

He paused his boastful musings and said:

"Guess you know my name, don't you?"

"You are Turner," confirmed Holmes, "late of America, originally a wanderer of our own island here, in the company of your father, an engineer, whose travels took him across the nation."

"That'd be me," Turner answered, and to my utmost shock, I saw him, still balanced on the handrail with a jaunty air, remove a cigarette from a gold case in his pocket, and set about smoking."

"Kentucky tobacco, I perceive," Holmes stated.

"Only the best. Got a taste for it over there, you see," Turner confirmed.

"Then I think I shall join you in partaking," Holmes stated, dipping into his own pocket. After a moment he had rolled out a cigarette, and in a truly bizarre spectacle, smoked along with the man from where he stood.

"Now you'll be spoiled," Turner laughed, "and never want to go back to plain old tobacco anymore!"

He was an exceedingly self-confident young man, I thought, and yet I despaired of anyone maintaining footing on such a small surface for long. A fall from the height would surely be fatal.

"Why don't you step down from there?" I urged.

He looked at me and a grin soon occupied his face.

"And you'd be Dr. John Watson," he said, "writer of those stories about Holmes." He gestured at me with his cigarette and said, "Pleased I am to make your acquaintance."

"I wish I could say the same," I replied.

To this he only chuckled, showing no shame, no fear, no hurry. Such a friendly if audacious sort he seemed, entirely out of keeping with the brooding villain I had expected. He was, I felt, a taker of risks, as Holmes had said, but I was not prepared to find such a daredevil as this.

"You took the Morley boy," Holmes said simply, as if discussing the weather.

"That I did," Turner confirmed. "couldn't see any other way around it."

"You make light, sir, of a vile misdeed," I charged.

"Well," Turner said ruminatively, "history is full of ambitious men and those that get shoved aside in their pursuit of what they want. I'm no exception to the type."

I recalled how smitten he had rendered the maid Ada back at the Morley household, and began to understand how such a man might hold great appeal to women, yet also realized such a man as he would see women as there for his own use, to be bent to his will as pawns in his machinations. Oh, he was a scoundrel, I knew, but an exciting one to know, I doubted not.

There were not yet many out upon the street, not at this early hour, but from the all-but deserted alley below I heard a woman gasp and looked down to see her pointing upward, one hand over her mouth, in shock.

Turner waved down at her with a grin, and as he did, I noted his balance on the railing did not alter. Seeing my noting this, he said:

"When you've climbed as many mountains as I did across the ocean, you learn how to keep a solid footing. Don't be worrying about me there, Doctor, I am not going to accidentally fall."

Accidentally, I noted.

Holmes, who had made no effort to approach Turner, now said:

"You know, of course, however pleasant it may be for you to show off your skills as you have a smoke with me, I must bring this matter through to its necessary conclusion, however it is fated to unfold."

I did not detect regret in his words, but there was something like a grim truth in his statement.

"That seems the situation," Turner agreed. "You caught me flatfooted this morning, and the shame is mine. Another hour and I'd have heard about you on the case, and lit out for America and not been back for years, and then under a new identity, whole new ball game, as they say, but you got the jump on me."

He tossed his half-smoked cigarette toward the alley and watched it fall to the cobbles.

"What now?" I asked, though I was unsure as to whom I addressed.

"Yeah," said Turner, "that's the big question, isn't it, Doc?"

"It is," agreed Holmes, "and the choice I leave to you. Submit to me, or gamble upon a highly uncertain outcome."

"Step down!" I urged, sensing the matter racing now toward a conclusion I knew could go very wrong. "Let us take you to the police. You'll be given fair treatment."

Turner laughed. "You have to admit, 'fair treatment' doesn't favour me much."

He looked across the alley at the distant balcony a floor below on the other building and noted:

"I make it a ten foot leap, and a story drop after that to reach the other side."

"Which even then shall not be a conclusion to the chase, but only its continuation," Holmes doggedly promised, tossing the remains of his own cigarette down into the alley.

"And even if you make it, you may be too injured to flee far on foot," I told him. "Medically, I can say you are more likely to shatter bones in landing on the balcony than to walk away unscathed."

I swallowed at the thought and added:

"In my estimation, it's probable you shall miss your mark and plunge to your death."

Turner did not reply for a moment, but stayed poised on his perch, his body ramrod straight, almost like some Greek statue of a proud warrior-youth.

"Yeah," he said, sounding more the American at that moment, "that seems the situation, doesn't it?"

I felt some relief to hear him agree, but lost the comfort when he added:

"But as Mr. Sherlock Holmes could tell you, I've always been a gambler."

I watched with horror so profound that an involuntary shout left my lungs, as with those words, Turner leapt outward from a flat-footed pose, flinging himself through the air, arms reaching, sailing like an arrow in human form.

Holmes looked on impassively, and said:

"Unwise."

Yet what happened next was unexpected and amazing, for Turner cleared the distance and reached the far-off balcony, though as he landed with a roll, his trailing foot clipped the railing there, and he fell violently forward, his impact audible even from where we stood.

There was a pause which seemed interminable as I stood riveted and staring, til finally Turner rose, his breathing hard, the life or death thrill heavily upon him, and he grinned back at us with a carefree audacity, and gave a wave as he yanked open the doorway there and disappeared, but not before I noted he was limply badly.

"Holmes," I called, as my friend broke into a run down the fire-stairs, "I think he has broken a foot in his landing."

"I mark the same!" Holmes noted.

"He will not move quickly now!"

And so this proved true, for we had no sooner reached the cobbles of the alleyway and turned the corner to the fore of the building opposite, when we saw Turner sitting there on the outside stairs, lighting another cigarette, one leg outstretched, calmly waiting.

When we appeared, he raised his hands, palms upward in a self-deprecating gesture and announced without obvious rancor:

"Took a bad landing, as you saw, and find I can't walk much beyond a limp, so no sense in trying to run off from the likes of you, Mr. Holmes. I'd have made it, though if I hadn't gotten busted up just then."

To me he added:

"I think something shattered good and hard in my foot, Doc. You mind taking a look?"

He flipped a coin to me for my services, which without thinking I caught in mid-air, then tossed it back to him.

Turner laughed and to Holmes he announced:

"Your prisoner now, sir."

"Indeed you are," Holmes agreed, "as I promised."

As I had given my oath to heal where I could, I did take it upon myself to kneel and lift the roguish criminal's swollen foot gently into my hands. I saw at once from the angle that he had incurred a bad break, and told him so, yet despite my inner condemnation of the crimes this darkly charming man had authored, I told him:

"That was the most courageous and foolhardy leap I have ever seen. I never would have imagined it could be made."

Turned basked in this praise, though I read much pain in his eyes.

"Funny what desperation will drive a fellow to do, isn't it, Doc?" he asked me.

"You hit upon the story of the ghost and shaped it to your plans," I said.

"I did," Turner agreed. "Worked well, too, up to the point your friend there got called in. Yesterday morning that would have been, I reckon?"

"Almost from the first," Holmes told him, as a small crowd gathered around the scene, and I knew it was only a matter of time until a constable appeared to see what was the cause of the conglomeration.

"And the gypsies? Your confederates?" Holmes inquired.

"Old friends from my boyhood, those. Always did like their sort. Useful, because they know a lot more about what's going on than most people would credit, since they travel and see everything while they do."

"Utterly true," Holmes agreed. "I have often used them, myself. But they failed to penetrate my disguise before it was too late, and I retrieved the boy from their clutches, and saw all your associates, them and the house-maid you left so smitten, in irons before sundown."

"*All* my associates, you say?" Turner replied with a mysterious grin.

"A not unexpected boast, but you know no others remain at large," Holmes told him.

Odd, I thought, how my friend seemed to bear Turner less ill will than was usual in his apprehensions of the guilty. Was it possible he admired the quality of daring that was so clearly within him? My thoughts, though went backward and came to rest upon another matter.

"Mr. Turner," I asked, as I finished binding his foot with a makeshift bandage, "what made you seize upon the legend of the ghost instead of abducting the boy through other means?"

He looked at me with a degree of evaluation that seemed almost probing, then with a small smile answered:

"You saw her, too, out in the yew alley."

Holmes looked sharply at me, and though I wished I could say otherwise, and stand with my friend's confident belief that the supernatural did not inhabitant his reality of purest logic, I nodded.

Turned smiled and confessed:

"Then you might understand, that's why I wanted the estate. I saw the ghost many times as a boy that summer my father and I were there, and after a while it got so she didn't vanish as soon as she appeared, just stayed there floating near me in the dark, beautiful and serene and shy, and being the age I was, I fell in love with her. It was the most profound experience of my life. They got it wrong, you see, in saying there is only the ghost of a scoundrel from the Middle Ages, because if there is one like that, I never saw him, no, just that beautiful and lonely lady I've spent every day of my entire life thinking of, and wanting to see again."

Holmes frowned then, a deep, grave, and final judgment on Turner and his account, and the supernatural as a whole.

But as for me, I remembered what I had glimpsed for that merest instant the night before as we'd left the estate, and the sense I felt radiating out from the apparition, if indeed apparition it had been, was much as Turner had said, so despite myself I understood how the experience could have had so deep an impact on a boy of just the right age to feel such things, and how such a memory might continue on, even in the man Turner became.

Poignant and tragic, I judged it all.

My thoughts were interrupted when Turner called:

"The police at last."

He gazed past Holmes and me, beyond even the gathering crowd, where a blue-uniformed constable was approaching with an uncertain expression on his whiskered face.

"Now," Turner said, almost with amusement, "we'll see how my luck holds in court, for a good lawyer, gentlemen, can work true wonders. Might be I walk free after all this yet."

"Not after my testimony," Holmes boasted back.

"Then it'll be a contest between us," Turner replied.

He released a hearty laugh, tinged with pain, and nodded a goodbye to us both, as the constable elbowed through the crowd, and reached us with an inquisitive stare.

*****

After giving our statements at the police station, and leaving Turner in their custody to roll the dice on the expertise of lawyers, Holmes and I were soon at Norwich-Victoria Station, to catch a London-bound train.

"Watson, I have had more than enough of pristine East Anglia," my friend said, "and look forward to nothing so much as a return to the familiar grime of London."

Tired as I had been throughout the night, I found that sleep was elude me on our two hours' journey back to the south, my thoughts returning to what I believed I had seen in the yew alley, and Turner's claims concerning his experiences with it. And then there was young Barry Morley's words on the subject as well, his assertion that he was seeing the ghost even as his abduction unfolded. So what *was* the truth...?

Thus I sat in the compartment with Holmes, more wide awake than I wished to be as verdant fens, brimming with herds of spotted dairy cows, sped by, and across from me the masterful detective smoked contentedly, returning from the elevated energies the case had brought to him.

I knew the slumber I needed was to prove in short supply when I returned home to 221B Baker Street, as I had a patient to see in the afternoon, and a pleasant obligation I had to fulfill that evening, escorting Miss Mary Morstan, toward whom I had come to harbor deep feelings, out to dinner.

It was as I brought to mind the woman who would become my first wife, that I finally put my thoughts into words, and broached a subject which had lingered in my head throughout this case, indeed ever since the morning of the attempt on my friend's life.

"Holmes," I began, "it is true a woman nearly took your

life earlier this month, but I believe your self-anger over having failed to foresee her intentions has hardened your heart toward all women in general. Yet I remind you in Suffolk, a young woman likewise *saved* you when the gypsy matriarch would surely have stabbed you through the back. Does not one deed in some fashion nullify the other, and ease your sentiments, at least that much more?"

Holmes inhaled from his pipe and let the smoke linger long in his lungs, before he answered:

"Women have their natures, Watson, and it does not do for me to disregard this truth. Yet I confess, for me to hate the fairer sex for doing what comes naturally to them is likewise a shortcoming on my part, and a disservice to women as a whole."

"So you have softened the harsh regard you seemed to evince after the incident at Baker Street?"

"No, Watson," Holmes said carefully, "rather I have come to recognize a valuable truth arising from recent matters."

"Which is?" I demanded.

"That a woman," he said leaning toward me, utter seriousness in his every word, "is every bit as dangerous as a man, and both warrant the same caution."

I stared at him a moment, then turned away, and looked again out the train window.

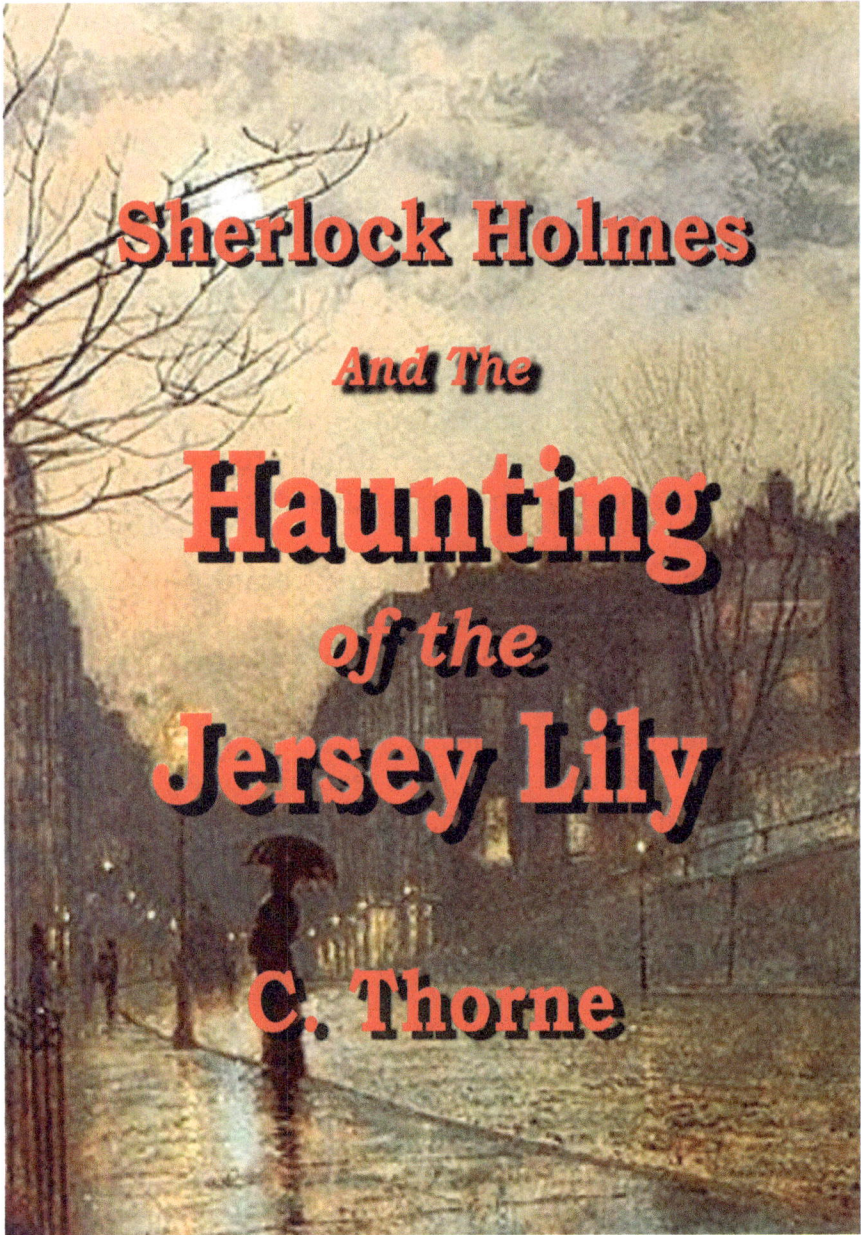

Sherlock Holmes

And The

Haunting

of the

Jersey Lily

C. Thorne

THE HAUNTING OF THE JERSEY LILY

What an irony it is that what would turn out to be among my friend Sherlock Holmes' oddest cases began with a seaside holiday.

Holmes had just been most successful in resolving a matter of blackmail in favour of a client, Mr. Harrison Montgomery, a Canadian gentleman who sat on the board of a major trans-Atlantic shipping concern headquartered in Liverpool, and in a show of gratitude, Montgomery offered Holmes full-use of his country home, which occupied a spot on the north shore of Cornwall, a place of great rocky sea cliffs battered by roaring waves, surrounded by splendid moors adorned with early-summer wildflowers: sheer Heaven compared to the pressures of summer in London.

Holmes, true to character, had been on the verge of declining the beneficence, when in a rare instance of an excess of boldness on my part, I spoke before him and thanked the client on his behalf, telling him Mr. Holmes would be amply happy to take up his generous offer, pleasing the grateful Mr. Montgomery no end.

The look on my friend's face at that moment amuses me still to recall, a mixture of incredulity, drollery, and incipient outrage that someone else would dare put words in the mouth of one so august as the world's foremost consulting detective. Though he'd said nothing, merely allowed a small smile as I shook the client's hand and accepted a key to the house on a decorative iron ring, I could tell he fully intended to be stubborn about the matter.

When we were outside the building where the great shipping company's offices were located, Liverpool's ubiquitous scents of sea and factory smoke swirling around us, Holmes turned to me, still wearing the same mingled expression he'd had inside, but I was truly in rare form, and before he could speak I waded in.

"Have you ever taken a holiday in your entire career, Holmes?" I demanded.

"I once went to Lake Como, and it bored me to distraction."

"Perhaps it was merely a case of going to the wrong location," I challenged.

"My work sustains me, Watson, and save for my sessions with the violin, I have no need for any of that multitude of mundane digressions other men find pleasing."

"Ah, but I think you do, my friend, for never have I known of any fellow whose constitution was not improved by a fortnight on the coast. Think of how a brief pause might sharpen your brain cells to the hone of a rapier. I pity the criminal classes with such a keen mind rested and launched in ready pursuit."

"My mind is already kept at sufficient sharpness," he said, ruffled, "but for your concern I do thank you."

With that he stepped into a waiting cab, and I after

him, where I continued: "As a doctor I can tell you, there is a salubrious effect in fresh air and the wholesome sounds of the sea at night, while in the daylight one sees the wild birds in the sky, the seals basking on the beach, and even, I've no doubt, herds of wild ponies living out on the untrammeled Cornish moors."

"It sounds utterly dreadful, Watson! No, I am surrounded by all I need back in the clutter and clatter of London, and have no wish for this."

"Then do it for Norah, Holmes," I pressed, playing my trump card.

"For Norah?" he repeated, betraying a rare instance of puzzlement.

"Why, yes, my wife would adore a trip to the coast, and since Montgomery's house is ample enough for both of us and you as well, I would take it you'd not be troubled if we accompanied you."

I saw the well-oiled gears of his mind grind at this until he finally allowed, "Watson, if that's the nature of the matter, please, by all means take dear Norah on holiday to this client's house with my consent and blessing, *dictum factum*."

"I thank you, Holmes, though therein lies a slight problem. I would have to reveal to my wife how I came to be in possession of a fortnight's use of such a splendid cottage, and if she were to hear that you were bestowing onto her and myself lodgings intended for you, why I know her forceful nature, and she simply would refuse to go. It must be you along or nothing in Norah's eyes, and I do hate to think of her deprived this chance...."

Holmes snorted. "The ways of women, Watson, are ever so troublesome."

"Norah would love this rare opportunity to get out of London and see the southwest, a region to which I do not think she has ever traveled, Holmes. The life of a doctor's wife is not always an easy one, so will you not allow her to have this brief moment of enjoyment?"

I knew Holmes held Norah in a high regard nearly rivaling his opinion of his ever-patient landlady, Mrs. Hudson, and saw the processes of thought turning inside the powerful mind that lay behind his high, pale brow.

Finally he exhaled almost with consternation and allowed: "I suppose country air might be agreeable, and I could take the time away from Baker Street to compose a monograph I have had in mind, but which the interminable parade of clients has permitted me little time upon which to work. It shall be a splendid piece concerning, if you can encompass it, the classification and identification of thirty-two common types of glues and pastes."

"Doubtless a fascinating read," I said drily, though I knew Holmes' exercises in scholarship were useful works consulted by police across the world.

At last he declared: "Very well, Watson, you may inform your wife that the house is available and that I have invited the two of you to accompany me for the fortnight, as my honoured guests."

"Capital, Holmes!" I very nearly cheered, for it had been a busy month, indeed, in my life, both professionally and in my times in Holmes' kinetic company. "I shall inform Norah as soon as we return to London, and may we then, depart, say, in two mornings hence?"

Sighing, as if it were some terrible burden he'd undertaken, Holmes said, "If we must, Watson, then we must...."

*****

The Cornish coast was expectedly beautiful, and the promised lodgings more of a vast house than what the word 'cottage' might conjure up. We were not far from the picturesque landscape known as the Bedruthan Steps, which Norah and I were soon to discover and cherish amid our day-long walks together, a picnic basket in one hand, my wife's arm hooked about the other. For his part, though, Holmes stayed monastically inside the downstairs solar, meticulously penning his monograph, peering outside only in the late evenings, and then merely to stare broodingly at the horizon, puff out his pale cheeks and with a heartfelt sigh of boredom, go back inside, clearing mourning for Baker Street while enduring for Norah's sake this self-imposed exile.

Sitting outside on the grass just after twilight on the sixth evening of our stay, my wife turned to me with an observation in mind.

"He's being quite stoical at heart, isn't he, John?" she said to me facetiously, as from out on the lawn she watched Holmes pace across the solar, pen in hand, thoughts about the identifying characteristics of pastes doubtless pressing into his impenetrable mindscape.

"He certainly is at that, my dear," I agreed, "and we should take it as a sign of the affection he clearly feels for us under that indemonstrable exterior."

Norah smiled at the thought, and looked beautiful, and we were at that moment under the star-rise two very happy people.

A moment or two later Sherlock Holmes emerged from the house, and seeing his martyr-like poses upon the sea-cliffs in the blue hour which comes before the night gave the two of us a gentle chuckle of fondness for our complex friend.

"Ah, just look at him now, John," she said, "standing amid a near-paradise, but he is the very image of a tortured soul."

"The poor fellow," I added.

Yet what neither Norah, nor I, nor even Holmes could know at that moment of light contentment was that this was to be the last restful night we'd enjoy on our holiday, and that the morning would bring with it tidings of an event which was occurring not ten miles away....at nearly that very instant.

*****

Our seventh morning in Cornwall broke beautifully, with an orange sunrise over the wild moors fit to dazzle the senses. We'd sat down to a breakfast of fried kippers straight from the sea, the discussion centering on what Norah and I intended to do that day, she always one for itineraries, and Holmes, while thoroughly pleasant toward us, sat, I perceived, brooding over some matter concerning his monograph.

It was just as we were finishing up the meal that we heard a knock on the front door, a rare disturbance in this isolated spot, and a moment later, the maid, a local woman of middle-years called Mrs. Dowy Bennath, came to the door. In her thick Cornish accent she announced: "'Tis a let-ter, ser, hand-delivered fur Mr. Holmes. The woman who brought it is saying she is to wait for a d'rect r'ply."

While I admit my own thoughts were of annoyance that even in so lonely and perfectly isolated a place Holmes' reputation had followed him, my friend's reaction was completely the opposite, and dismissing any lethargy he'd displayed a moment before, he veritably sprang from his chair and seized the envelope held in Mrs. Bennath's fingertips, startling her with his zeal.

Ripping open the seal, Holmes pored over the contents and I saw an expression of something like fierce delight take hold of his face.

"Ah, at last!" he cried. "I was positively starving for a matter, *any* matter, to alleviate this tedium, and now it looks to be a promising summons indeed which has come!"

He tossed the letter onto the table, where Norah beat me to it, lifting it to read, and then a little gasp left her lips. "My goodness!" she exclaimed. "Why, Holmes, do you know who this writer *is*?"

"Of course," he said, shortly, "a potential client who possesses the sound wisdom to seek my incomparable services."

"But the identity!" Norah pressed, leaving my curiosity

now at an almost fevered pitch. "Surely you know who this lady is?"

"Mrs. Edward Langtry," Holmes stated, as he stood before us, once again the very image of energy embodied and unbound.

"Yes," said Norah, "but Mrs. Edward Langtry is none other than the famed *Lillie* Langtry, the Jersey Lily of stage and society!"

Dear me! I thought, though Holmes remained unmoved by the revelation.

"I am aware of the lady's identity, my dear Norah," he said, though with a gentleness not matching the sharpness he had been known to cast toward me when I challenged his knowledge. "It is in my professional interests to know all who are deemed significant in the eyes of society, as one never knows when such information may prove vital."

"But, Holmes," I called over, "you must admit, this is remarkable! Such a client, and in these distant parts? What is she doing out here?" I wondered aloud. "The most celebrated woman in the nation, save the Queen herself, here, in the wilds of Cornwall!"

"She is staying at a seaside house called *Klihen Tegow*, or 'Beautiful Height' gifted to her by an admirer, Mr. Thomas Shale, an industrialist from Manchester. She has retreated here *sans entourage* for several weeks over the last few summers."

Norah and I gazed incredulously at one another, stunned Holmes would have such knowledge in his mind, ready for retrieval. He noted our expressions and said, "I maintain a storehouse of information archived in memory concerning any locale where I happen to be. It might interest you to note I know who occupies *all* of the significant houses roundabout, and some of their histories as well."

I shook my head and Norah smiled at this. "I wonder sometimes," she said to Holmes, "if you even comprehend how remarkable such matters, apparently so mundane to you, seem to us?"

"I am aware that my knowledge is remarkable," he said carelessly.

And so modest, I thought.

"With so much loaded inside it, it's a wonder your head doesn't explode from off your shoulders," Norah teased.

Holmes stared at her puzzled and asked, "And why should it do that?"

"Oh, nevermind," Norah said. "Mrs. Langtry has asked you to tea this morning," she clarified, shifting the subject while hastily skimming the letter for the second time, "and states that a matter, which she dubs 'odd,' has arisen which compels her to seek outside aid. Having heard that you were staying nearby, she calls it fortuitous that she may ask for you directly."

The letter, which made its way at last to my own hand read simply:

My dear Mr. Sherlock Holmes,

Imagine my delight to have learned that a man of your reputation was staying nearby, and how fortuitous this fact seemed to me when I found myself confronted by my own mystery, a circumstance both terrible and devoid of all shred of logic. I beg of you, whatever your present schedule, please come to tea this morning down the coast at a house called Klihen Tegow, *and hear of my plight. Here I will tell you of a situation that defies the mind and holds no ready explanation, save one which I struggle by the hour to refuse to allow myself to contemplate.*

I am yours in hope,
Mrs. Edward Langtry
Klihen Tegow, *Cornwall*

Holmes found a pen and wrote a one-sentence reply—

Will come. S. Holmes

—which he handed to the maid, Mrs. Bennath, that she might take it to the servant who awaited in the foyer.

He then he paced about for the next several minutes, his placid mood gone, anticipation transforming him from the lethargy of past days into the manic detective I so often knew in London. Finally he snarled and bared his teeth, the expression a strange revelation of the almost bestial energy I had often seen overtake him. He then stated: "No, this will not do! Tea is too distant. I shall go at once!"

With that announcement he strode from the breakfast nook and I heard him rush upstairs to his room to prepare for departure.

"John," Norah said playfully, "we both know you can't let him go alone."

Yes, I desired to accompany Holmes, but this was a holiday I'd planned to spend with my wife, so despite my gratitude at her understanding, I protested, "Dear, you had planned us a day down on the beach, gathering shells and sea glass to take home again."

She laughed and said, "Oh, John, do you think I cannot see where your thoughts roam? I would not be such a taskmistress as to keep you from the side of your friend, so go, with my heartiest blessings! It will give me time to catch up on writing to friends, leaving them all jealous as I tell of our splendid holiday. We shall see the beach together another day."

I ask, could any man possess a more understanding wife? Springing to my feet, I kissed her cheek and hurried upstairs to grab my walking stick and lightest jacket in case it proved a windy day. Holmes was just exiting from his room, prepared for the little journey up to *Klihen Tegow*, and was out the door. I emerged glad to find Mrs. Bennath had sent the stable boy to prepare the gig and took the reins as Holmes settled in beside me. With one final wave goodbye to Norah in the doorway, we were off at a steady clip along the coast road, toward the celebrated lady who might soon prove my able friend's newest client.

We arrived an hour before we were expected at tea, and the door was opened by the Italian servant woman we'd seen through the window back to our own lodgings, a woman called Dominique, and with a broad and sunny smile she invited us to please step into the morning room while she fetched her mistress.

"Oh, my poor Mrs. Langtry," she told us. "You can little know how welcome you are here, Signore Holmes, Doctor Watson," she said avidly.

The morning room was elegant, if slightly out of date as country houses used only for seasonal visits so often seemed to be, its décor hinting more of the late-'80s than the present, some decade on, but the air was bright and the surroundings pleasant, and it was but a few moments before Mrs. Langtry appeared downstairs amid Dominique's gushing introduction. The famous lady was clad in a plain black dress, mourning her husband, I seemed to remember, and her hair was pulled back into a modest bun above her nape, looking quite simple and yet somehow even in so plain a state, fashionable, as if the mode suited her from long and precise practice. So it was I found the celebrated Mrs. Langtry still very much a beauty, though surely well past forty by now, the leading light of London society and stage in her day, famed across two decades.

She entered the room gracefully and in response to our bows, extended a hand, which Holmes received with the lightest touch of his fingertips, but which I took more cordially.

"I sensed an urgency in your letter, Madam, so came straightaway," he explained, already focused upon anything she might be about to reveal.

"And I am grateful," she replied. "Dominique shall bring us some refreshment, but please, do make yourselves comfortable."

I could see a desire to learn the facts behind the summons grinding at Holmes, who was capable of deep patience when such was called for, yet who felt most social niceties to be little more than a distracting game.

"If you please," he said, "your letter spoke of 'a mystery,

terrible and devoid of logic,'" he quoted from memory, "and I am most anxious to learn what this circumstance is."

Mrs. Langtry, a bold and direct woman, I sensed, still found it necessary to glance downward for the merest instant before she answered: "Gentlemen, are you aware that last October I lost my husband of twenty-three years, Mr. Edward Langtry?"

"I'm afraid I am," I told her, "and may I express my condolences."

"I thank you," she said simply. "But I think you may also be aware that ours had not been a happy marriage, and it was marked by a long separation. Edward and I had not been close for many years."

I nodded with sympathy while Holmes sat immobile, overtaken by concentration.

Here Mrs. Langtry drew a breath and said, "So you can imagine my utter shock, my horror, my state of captive disbelief, when I tell you that last night, just before I took my slumber, I espied my late husband, Edward, standing outside my window, on the lawn beside the woods, staring up at me as I gazed out at the stars."

Her words, softly spoken though they may have been, reverberated in my ears almost as if they'd been a clap of thunder. Beside me in his own chair I saw Holmes shift, and say, "Please explain, Mrs. Langtry. You say you have seen your *deceased* husband outside your window?"

"Yes," she said, eyes cast downward, keenly aware, I sensed, at the nature of the thing she stated. "I came down here to get away for a few weeks while the theater where I am performing is undergoing painting and repairs, thinking to clear my mind as I have the past several summers, yet from my bedroom on the second floor I looked out at the sky, as has been my habit in my time here, and down on the lawn...there he stood, a man I cannot possibly mistake, my late husband, and none other. He was standing by the woods, staring straight up at me with what I can only term unbroken menace."

"In a ghostly form?" I inquired, truth be told not knowing precisely what to say. "Ethereal and transparent?"

"No, Doctor Watson," she insisted, "I *saw* Edward as if still a man of flesh and blood, every bit as corporeal and living as you or I are right now, yet I know him to be dead, for I saw him in his casket, attended his funeral, and witnessed his burial, I even..."

Here she produced a paper from a folder which had been left lying on the desk by the sofa, then continued.

"....possess his certificate of death, duly signed by the coroner in the city of Chester, a Dr. George P. Henry, who attended to the body and certified my husband's passing. I am a widow in the eyes of God and man, Church and law, for there can be no doubt of my husband's deceased state, and yet...I tell you, Mr. Holmes, without drama or explanation, that last night he appeared to me."

My mind rushed for some reply, for I saw she looked at us with an urgency that betrayed her own conviction in the account she gave, and under the careful control she maintained on her expression, my senses as a medical man could not help but perceive that her nerves were all but vibrating, so tightly drawn was she by all that had transpired.

This was an incredible claim, yet I knew human history was riddled with tales of the dead returning to visit the living. I also knew that given the popular reports of the nature of the union of Mr. and Mrs. Edward Langtry, a visitation by the spirit of the late gentleman was unlikely to be one inspired by love.

Holmes broke the silence when he said, "What actions did the figure on the lawn undertake, Mrs. Langtry?"

She replied: "My husband gazed steadily at me, unblinking, unmoving for the longest time as I stood riveted to the floor for easily an entire minute, too frightened to scream, horror-struck, reeling with the unreality of what I was beholding, yet witnessing it all the same, and finally he lifted a hand, held it suspended in the air a moment while his eyes stayed locked onto me, and then he...."

"Yes?" Holmes demanded.

"He...*beckoned* to me."

Like the thespian she was, she lifted her arm and imitated the gesture to which she referred, and after a number of seconds crafted a wave in reverse, an unmistakable summons toward itself, and for some reason, under her eerily precise demonstration, I felt a tingle travel the length of my spine.

"And there is also this," said Mrs. Langtry. "The stable boy from the hamlet found it on the kitchen doorstep this morning."

She produced a sheet of paper and held it out to the maidservant, Dominique, who delivered it across the room to Holmes, who took it and seemed to stare at it before reading, seeking clues before content, I surmised. Finally he handed the note off to me and I saw it was brief, and said merely:

You are mine, and always will be, Lillie. There is no escaping, for I will bring you to me, and nevermore shall we be parted.

At these brief, cruel words another frisson passed across me.

Holmes said at last: "Well, the leaving of a note rather rules out one theory I had been entertaining, that of you merely having vividly dreamed the matter, unaware that you slumbered."

At this Mrs. Langtry frowned and said, "I assure you, Mr. Holmes, I was wide awake during the incident last night."

"I no longer doubt that," Holmes answered. "However I bid you tell me, are you satisfied, Madam, that this handwriting resembles that of your late husband?"

"Resembles?" she repeated Holmes' word. "It is *his*." She spoke this in an almost whispered breath.

Holmes retrieved the note from me and again looked at it. "Its composer," he claimed, "was a right-handed man, as I take it your husband was, along with most men?"

"Yes," Mrs. Langtry confirmed.

"I see there are clues here which hint that the writer was educated in his most formative years in a Protestant school, in, I think, Belfast."

The lady shut her eyes and shook her head violently at this news. "As was my husband."

Holmes went on. "Based on certain distinctions in the writing, and from slight indentations in the paper, I think this was not the first version of his handiwork, but rather the product of at least two other draughts composed before this one, done upon paper lying above this sheet. One can see the signs here and here."

With his fingertip he indicated these, then said, "It was done in an ill-lighted space, most certainly at nighttime, yet, curiously, I think not via candlelight."

"No candlelight?" I asked.

"A light source would have resulted in a slant against the shadows it cast. This was written in an unbroken dimness so drear the writer could scarcely see his own words."

As might befit the state of the dead, I thought, despite myself.

Holmes stood and spun to the window and held the paper to the daylight before saying, "Mrs. Langtry, have you in this house any personal item belonging to your late husband? Anything at all which he may have held or touched? It would be of great assistance to me if you had."

"No," she said, without apology in her voice, "Edward has never been here, and I confess I have not relished having reminders of him nearby at hand."

The maidservant nodded as if to unconsciously confirm this, and I thought: *She sees the lady as her truest friend.*

"A pity," said Holmes, "for I should have liked to have dusted this note for fingerprints. I suspect the result might have been rather interesting, and may have placed you at ease in at least one particular."

"That it was not my husband who wrote the note?" Mrs. Langtry asked.

"Precisely," confirmed Holmes, "for if he is dead, *quod erat demonstrandum*, he obviously could not, and the absence of his prints would have shown this. I am, I most readily admit, no believer in ghosts, Madam," Holmes said evenly, neither judgmental nor as if to mollify. "And hold that the scenario on the lawn last night contains another answer which I have yet to define."

I saw the eyes of the Italian maid, Dominique widen, and intuited that clearly she was most assuredly a believer in baleful spirits which walked the realm of the Church Militant.

"I have investigated a number of cases," Holmes explained, "where the preternatural was held to be in evidence, yet never have I found the culprit of any of these misadventures to be other than our fellow mortals, very much in their place in this physical realm, unworthy motivations of malice or greed fueling their errant hearts. And so shall it prove in your case, I have little doubt."

"Pray, sir, do you think so?" Mrs. Langtry breathed, relief and hope vying against the troubling evidence she claimed she had seen.

"Doubtless." With that Holmes added, "I should, nevertheless, care to see the lawn. Might you show me the precise spot where so intimidating a figure stood last night?"

"Oh, yes," said Mrs. Langtry, glad, I think that some action in the matter was stirring at last. She rose and I hurried to rise with her, as politeness demanded, and she said, "If you gentlemen should be so good as to come with me...."

She led us out of the morning room to the foyer, the ever-present and always smiling Dominique faithfully at her heels, and finally took us out the front door before turning and announcing: "It would be more direct to go out through the kitchen, yet I think the approach here may give you a better understanding of the layout of the lawn."

"Quite so," Holmes passively agreed, his face neutral, whatever his thoughts at present.

The lawn to which the celebrated Mrs. Langtry referred

was immaculate and lush, covering about a third of an acre behind the house before giving way to a well-kept woods to the west, which I saw became more of a wild forest after another fifty yards, the undergrowth thick there, and to my eye undisturbed. The county road itself, dusty and little used this time of day, bordered the property to the east, and beyond all of this lay steep cliffs as old as the world, falling sheer to the sea.

Mrs. Langtry halted at a spot behind the house and indicated upward. "That is the room I have occupied since taking my retreat here, the last window at the corner." She then pointed to a spot just inside the tree line and said, "And Edward, that is my late husband, was standing there, precisely."

She moved to take us forward but Holmes held up a hand and said, "Tarry, if you please. The less the area is compromised by human approach, the more revealing my examination shall be."

As he started forward and I behind him, he called, "Madam, has anyone else been on this ground since last night?"

"No," Mrs. Langtry answered, "I have not been outside the house til this moment, as I…was rather upset by what I saw."

"Completely understandable," I assured her, as Holmes reached the indicated place on the lawn, and I paused behind him.

My friend first stared at the spot where the alleged phantom was said to have stood, and moved around in a wide semi-circle, taking care not to approach too near, before crouching and staring still more closely. He then let his eyes trail off into the woods, stood once more, and was silent a moment before he said:

"Our 'ghost,' Madam, had the odd practice of leaving his shoes prints in the soil."

"What does that mean?" Mrs. Langtry asked in return.

"I am no occultist," Holmes answered, "but are ghosts not said to defy gravity itself in feats of *levitation*? When I see a footprint, I generally think of it having been made by a living being, not an apparition from the beyond."

Under his breath, unheard by Mrs. Langtry and Dominique, I heard Holmes mutter: "Which troubles me all the more."

He knelt and pulled a tape measure from his pocket, which he stretched the length of the shoeprints, then seemed satisfied, for he rose and turned back toward the lady across the lawn and asked, "Pray, Mrs. Langtry, do you happen to know what size shoe your late husband wore?"

"Why, yes," she replied, "I often bought him shoes as a gift early on in the years of our marriage. He wore a gentleman's size nine."

At this news Holmes turned thoughtful before he admitted, "The prints upon the lawn show that whoever stood here in the night wore a shoe that was likewise size nine."

The news seemed to jolt Mrs. Langtry, for she opened her mouth slightly and I saw her hand briefly touch her chest. At that moment the maid Dominique hurried from inside the house, where I gather she'd been watching, and took a place at her mistress' side. "*Signora, signora*, be brave at heart. God protects all His children. *Più grande è colui che è in te di colui che è nel mondo.*"

"'Greater is He who is in you than he who is in the world,'" Holmes repeated the noted verse in English. "The First Book of Saint John, I believe, chapter four, verse four."

Mrs. Langtry appeared to take scant comfort in her servant's consolations in either language, for as if speaking from a state of awe bordering on shock she admitted aloud, "I never saw so cruel a smile on any man's lips, as the one Edward wore last night when he glared up at me."

"Oh, my lady, my lady," Dominique gasped, "has he come now, in revenge?"

Revenge? I thought. Had things between the couple truly

been so bad as that?

Mrs. Langtry reeled now at these words, and I left Holmes and went to her side, seeing her at that instant nearly overcome by strong emotions. As a doctor I bade Dominique to bring her a chair, which she swiftly did, then I helped her mistress down onto it. As close as I was to the lady, I saw that though she was stylish and displayed the trappings of an attempt to preserve her illusions, under her copiously-applied face powder and the light cut of her mourning dress, Mrs. Langtry was well beyond the healing vigour of youth.

"Calm yourself," I said in my gentlest tone. "You are completely safe. Mr. Holmes and I are here, and with him you could be in no better hands."

As if in mocking reply, at that instant an errant wind rose and blew through the treetops, hissing almost menacingly, and Mrs. Langtry's eyes went toward the clacking of the branches. It was, I confess, somewhat eerie, though why it was so I would struggle to explain.

I saw her shudder, then she recovered and said, "Thank you, Doctor Watson. I was overcome for a moment but I am otherwise quite well, I promise."

"Then that is good," I told her, stepping back a little distance.

"Signora," Dominique counseled, "excuse me, please, this impertinence, but perhaps we consult the wrong source today. I could go instead to seek Padre Ryan at the chapel, and get his blessing upon the house...."

"No," Mrs. Langtry said simply. "This is what I wish, for I place my full trust in Mr. Sherlock Holmes, of whose powers I have heard so much."

Across from us Holmes was continuing his examination of the ground, seemingly unaware of the little drama that had just unfolded where we three stood together, or of the lady's declaration of her confidence in him. At last he faced us and announced, "The shoes which made these tracks were of a type sold at Harrods, in London, hand-crafted by a master cobbler employed there on the basis of commissions only, a Monsieur Pierre Gilbert, of Lyons. I would recognize his unique handiwork from any decent imprint, and judge these shoes to have been worn no more than half a year."

At this Mrs. Langtry again gasped and then confirmed, "Edward always bought his shoes from Harrods, and had them custom-made to fit the rather unusual dimensions of his feet. He insisted upon it, even in his later penury, when we were estranged, believing a good pair of shoes was a better investment in the long-term than a lesser pair at half the price. He had one made but a few months before his passing."

Holmes looked toward her and continued, "Unusual construction of the foot, you say? The man for whom the shoes were made, I can tell you, had a foot which was high in the arch, and broad at the bottom."

Mrs. Langtry squeezed shut her eyes and declared, "All that matches Edward perfectly. I tell you, it is him...."

Behind her the maid shrieked, "*Per favore, il Cielo ci assista adesso.*"

Mrs. Langtry barely breathed out her reply to the sentiment: "May Heaven help us indeed, dear Dominique."

Yet at those words, as if determined not to entertain their sentiments, Holmes turned sharply away and began to follow the tracks out from the yard and toward the lane which ran a little distance out, and I trotted to catch up with him before making the trek at his heels.

"Note, Watson," he said to me, "how the lady's 'phantom' passed from the yard here, into the tamer trees around the lawn's perimeter, choosing the way of easier footing rather than simply *floating away*.... And now you see, as he reached the rougher ground with its tangles of undergrowth, he used the same half-worn path out that he took in from the direction of the sea cliffs, quite stamping it down. Our fellow is not by any means stout, but lithe, and strong enough to have pushed through the foliage both silently and yet thoroughly. As a consequence he has made our own travel that much simpler."

Holmes took in the sight of the brush and especially a twig dotted with small thorns, at which he stopped and peered before grunting: "Luck is not with us, for I was hoping the intruder might have caught a thread or two from his attire in these brambles for I may well have guessed at his tailor from so much as a scrap."

We continued on until we reached the county lane, at such time all sign of our intruder was lost to the passing of wagons and other pedestrians on the dirt, yet even there Holmes knelt and tried for several moments to find a trace of his prey, checking the ground on the far side of the road for some distance seeking to find an indication of where he left it, but was in all of these efforts unsuccessful.

"I had thought the road little used, but it might as well have been the morning of market day for all the disturbance I see here," he said ruefully, frustration writ upon his features, annoyed to be shut down when a few moments before things had seemed to hold such promise.

He turned and retraced the path through the wild-wood and the tamer inner tree-line to the lawn, where Mrs. Langtry still sat, the maid Dominique behind her.

"Madam!" Holmes said almost sternly, though I think more caught up in the thrill of the case than truly piqued. "I see doubt upon your brow when I'd rather see commonplace worry, for it is much wiser to face the known than imagine the unknowable. We must resist any temptations to endow this person who approached your home in the night with abilities I assure you he simply cannot have."

"Oh, would that I could grasp your confidence, sir," Mrs. Langtry said, shaking her head, her eyes showing fright.

Seeing a woman reduced by her fears, Holmes seemed to feel a moment of that touching compassion of which I knew him fully capable when he chose, for he said with remarkable gentleness:

"I bid and beg you, Mrs. Langtry, do not give way to thoughts born of darkness. There is a logical explanation for this matter, even I've little doubt, a commonplace one, and I intend to uncover it! I tell you it is my conviction based on many years in the field of deduction, that these tracks were made by no phantom, and that whomever stood on this lawn last night, beckoning with such impertinence to the famed Lillie Langtry, was a man no less of flesh and bone than I myself. Even so early in this case I have several working theories, and I intend to do my utmost to apprehend our trespassing imposter this *very* night!"

Dominique gasped and Mrs. Langtry's eyes took on a ray of hope. She said, "You truly think that is possible?"

But Holmes had expended his shallow reservoir of sympathy, it being in most instances unnatural to his character, and all he said was a less reassuring: "We shall see."

He requested permission to smoke, then lit his pipe and said, "I beg you, Madam, hear me, for I do now stress the importance of the instruction I am about to give."

The lady swallowed and nervously gave her agreement. "All right...."

"You *must* go about your regular habits tonight. Make no alterations. You must be seen to dine at your regular hour, to do the things you have done during any given night of your visit here this summer, and to turn-in for the night as you would at any other time. There is singular importance in all of these things."

"Then it shall be so," Mrs. Langtry consented.

"Yet I further caution, you must also stay inside, with locked doors, and bring in no one else, no constables, no private guards hired down from London, not even a trusted male relation to make the house feel more secure. Nothing whatsoever must alter tonight by even the slightest degree if my baited trap is to catch its prey. Is this entirely understood?"

"I admit I had been thinking of having the stable boy from the village sleep over in the barn tonight, and perhaps—"

"No!" Holmes thundered. "*Nothing* must be any different, Mrs. Langtry. That is most keenly significant. If you cannot promise me this, I fear I cannot aid you. Do you promise me all shall remain in a state of stasis, unaltered in any way by this troubling and unwelcome circumstance?"

"Signora," the maid began, "if not to the padre, then perhaps it is to the police that we should go—"

"To the country constabulary?" Holmes barked out a mocking laugh. "Men who enforce the operating hours of public houses, and keep the peace among farmers on market day? You would place your faith in such over me?"

The maid winced before such sudden forcefulness, birthed, I knew, from my friend's longstanding disdain for the police in general, and the rural constabulary in particular, and also from his well-earned confidence in himself. It was still, I thought, an overreaction to her timid suggestion, and it had been as if some tightly-coiled spring had abruptly let loose inside Holmes' barely contained state of innermost excitement, revealing the concealed mania that always hid behind the seemingly controlled exterior he maintained before the unsuspecting world.

"No," said Mrs. Langtry firmly. "We shall do as Mr. Holmes bids, and with courage we shall continue on as if....as if this nightmare of an event were not unfolding."

"Very good!" Holmes cried, his excitement high at what lay ahead. "Then Watson and I will take our leave at this time, but know we shall return at the appropriate hour, and though you shall not perceive that event, I promise you we will be nearby. With luck our patience shall yield the result of the unmasking of our would-be phantom before your mantel clock strikes midnight!"

"May it be so!" Mrs. Langtry cried.

Finding no further need for instruction or conversation and judging the interview at an end, my friend turned and set off back toward the gig which had brought us out to this place, leaving me in the role of diplomat on-hand to augment his lack of social graces.

"Ladies," I said, "I do make apologies for my friend's

lapses in courtesy, for he does not mean them, I assure you, and urge you to feel no more fears, for if Mr. Holmes has promised you results, I am confident we shall have them. His instructions I will leave you to consider, and in the meantime, I bid you both the most pleasant afternoon possible under these trying circumstances."

I bowed, and as I set off after my friend, I heard behind me the maid Dominique begin to recite what I felt certain was a prayer, in her native Italian.

"*Padre Nostro, che sei nei cieli, sia santificato il tuo nome, venga il tuo regno, sia fatta la tua volontá, come in cielo, così in terra....*"

*****

I found Holmes already in the gig, pipe still emitting clouds of the rich Nile tobacco he had been smoking that season in a rare instance of a deviation from his set routine.

"Well," I noted, as I stepped in and took the reins, "I think that went rather well."

"What makes you say so, Watson?" he asked, no irony or teasing in his words.

Taken off guard I answered, "Well, from your confidence, if nothing else, and from my own confidence in you."

"Hmmm," Holmes offered.

"After all," I pressed, "you found where the man had stood and discerned several facts about him that hopefully put the lady's mind to ease that this is no case of the supernatural."

"And did you find nothing troubling about certain striking oddities in this matter, Watson? Nothing whatsoever?"

"Such as the—"

"The lady's insistence," he said, "that the handwriting not only matched that of her late husband, but *was* his."

I thought a moment and said, "An hysterical woman,

already deeply upset could perhaps prove not the most reliable of witnesses."

"Medically speaking, would you say that you found Mrs. Langtry hysterical?"

"No…" I admitted, contradicting myself.

"On the contrary, Watson, to my eyes she appeared to be bearing up with remarkable fortitude to this strange assault upon her domestic life."

"Well, I only meant—"

"And I confess I did find the matter of the shoes most peculiar as well. The same size, though not an uncommon one, but the manufacturer, by Gilbert at Harrods…that is closing the mists of coincidence rather deeply around us."

"Yes," I admitted, "that was strange." Giving in, I asked, "So what do you make of it, Holmes?"

He shrugged and answered, "A lingering suspicion arises, Watson, that Mrs. Langtry does not possess the widowhood she believes she presently holds."

I started at that supposition and demanded, "You think Edward Langtry to somehow still be alive?"

He frowned deeply and took another draw on his pipe, before admitting to me, "That I do not know, but it is one theory, and one which would explain much, unlikely though it is, for what members of your profession often lack in their ability to sustain life, they make up for in their capacity to accurately diagnose death."

"Holmes," I chided, defending my profession.

"In any case," he said, "I will set aside all theories for now and concentrate on the plan at hand, which is the apprehension of whomever it was on the lawn, for I hazard he shall return tonight, as his business with the lady is obviously unfinished, and it is the nature of a criminal to return to the scene of his offense. Once I have him secured, all hypotheses can fall aside and truth be revealed with shining clarity."

As the countryside passed us under the stride of the former client Montgomery's fine thoroughbred, we found ourselves halfway back, and with quite a tale from the morning which I was looking forward to revealing to Norah over dinner. In that vein I said to Holmes, "I am just thankful you were able to somewhat allay Mrs. Langtry's fears as you did."

At this, however, he snorted, and I looked sharply at him. "What is it?" I quizzed.

"The irony of your words, Watson, for the lady would be wrong indeed to put her fears to rest merely because I have said the figure on the lawn shall prove to be no spirit. She would do better to let her worries motivate her to heed to the letter my instructions for tonight."

I let his words roll across my mind, then asked, "You fear, then, that Mrs. Langtry is in actual danger?"

He said at once: "*Deadly* danger."

*****

When we arrived back at the holiday house so generously made open to us by Holmes's grateful client in Liverpool, I found Norah out on the lawn, seated under a tree, so lost in a moment's contemplation that she did not discern our arrival, or even my approach.

"Why, John!" she called out, when finally she apprehended my drawing near her. She rose and reached out to me, confirming once again that in all of a man's life there are few sweeter things than to be welcomed home by a loving wife.

"What were you thinking of just then, sitting under the tree?" I asked her.

"Of, of old times and times yet to come," she answered. "I was completely gone into my senses for a moment, it is so beautiful here and so transporting."

Indeed it was, yet I also thought of the case which was unfolding before us, and how even in so wild a place as Cornwall, as distant from London as the island itself allowed, human malice was yet to be found.

The day passed, and Norah and I dined out on the lawn as the afternoon dulled in the sky, though for his part Holmes ate little, merely walked the perimeter of the property, saying nothing, as lost in his own contemplations as my wife had been earlier.

Having told her that Holmes and I would be going out again at day's end, Norah was prepared, and saw us off in the gig for the trip back to *Klihen Tegow*, where we would, according to Holmes' plan, conceal ourselves against detection until such time as we could rush the intruder, and apprehend him.

All she had wished for, I knew, was a quiet fortnight in the country with me, and yet here once again events of a sordid and perhaps perilous nature had snatched that away. I heaved a rueful sigh, yet also felt boundless gratitude to have a wife with such forbearance.

Holmes and I arrived well before dark at a place where we stopped some distance before the house, and took a circuitous route there, close to the sea cliff and in through the trees, which we used for cover, and had soon concealed ourselves at a location Holmes had apparently chosen that morning, a vantage point that presented an opportunity to take in the entirety of lawn, yet be neither too distant nor too close-by. We could see all, and intervene in scarcely a moment if need be, yet in the dark we would be all but invisible to prying eyes. All that was required of us was to wait....

....And wait we did, I tensely, Holmes with that more relaxed species of patience I often noted in him, which reminded me of a tiger assuming the tones of ambuscade. Several hours passed, the crescent moon made a half-course across the sky, and there, so far removed from the lights and fogs of London, the stars twinkled with an almost mesmeric intensity, brighter here than anyplace I had seen in long ages. Under other circumstances our wait in the country stillness could almost have been a merry adventure, but all was spoiled by my remembrance of what Holmes had told me earlier in the gig:

Deadly danger.

As the night transpired, I found myself looking toward the house a hundred yards away, and saw that it appeared Mrs. Langtry and Dominique had followed Holmes' advice, and kept up their normal routine in every particular—doubtless a trying prescription under the circumstances—for through my spyglass I observed Dominique light the lamps in the parlour, and through the lowest bay window saw her sit and sew, while Mrs. Langtry reclined at an escritoire, composing letters. When the hour reached 10:30, Dominique spoke a moment to Mrs. Langtry, then went upstairs alone, leaving her employer to herself for a time. Knowing the intruder had entered the lawn only after the lady had gone upstairs, I felt surely our wait was nearing its conclusion.

Indeed, but a moment after I'd let that thought entertain me, I felt Holmes give my elbow the slightest nudge, then lean close to whisper in my ear: "We are no longer alone in these woods, Watson."

My heart jumped at this news, and though from my crouching position behind a stand of small yew bushes I scanned the trees all around us and detected nothing, I trusted Holmes' superior senses, which at times almost struck me as containing a keenness that defied all explanation.

I watched as Mrs. Langtry rose from her seat by the little writing desk, then carried her lamp with her as she crossed from the parlour to the foyer and took the stairs to the second floor. Another moment passed and I noted the light had reached the bedroom she'd indicted that morning as her own. The drapes were at first modestly drawn, but after she'd prepared herself for bed, I watched as she went to the window and drew back the thick white drapery there, and stood gazing out into the night, lit from behind by the light of the room. The similarity of her action had no doubt skillfully recreated the circumstances of the precious night, and the intruder was soon drawn to this like a moth to the flame.

Having waited for so long a time for his appearance, it was nonetheless jarring to my nerves to actually see this man come forth from the darkness of the tree line and trod out onto the lawn. Though the figure was dark and its features concealed by shadows, I saw that it was a man of usual height and proportion, clad in an everyday suit coat, his head bare, his hands empty, and with what looked to be complete concentration, he stared up at the window, where Mrs. Langtry, her face caught in an expression which melded terror and horror, stared back down, transfixed by what she saw there.

Holmes stood, and slowly and with great care began to advance from our hiding place and onto the lawn. Whether he would have had the man or not we shall never know, and the fault there is my own, for as I rose at Holmes' heels, my own foot caught the fork of a stray branch which had fallen long ago, and it cracked in two under my weight as I dragged it forward with my step, creating a racket which tore the still night asunder.

Turning to see us, still many yards away, the man on the lawn abruptly fled toward the tree line opposite, his speed quite remarkable to behold.

"Watson, after him!" Holmes cried, and now he too flew forward with that energy at which I never failed to marvel. Once free from my improbable foot-trap, I too set out as swiftly as I could, though far back from Holmes, who rushed into the woods hot on his quarry's heels. Under the trees there was little light, a cloud having covered the tiny moon, and I was forced to slow my rush out of fear of colliding with a tree, yet from beyond I could hear the crashing sounds of Holmes in heated pursuit, and after a moment I emerged out onto the dirt track of the county lane, neither Holmes nor the man who had menaced Mrs. Langtry anywhere to be seen.

I risked a shout, calling out my friend's name, but received no reply, so went onward, running full-tilt across the road onto a wide grassy plateau, my vision still encompassing no more than a few yards to my front.

I had determined to continue this course when I heard a sharp warning from somewhere off to my left. "Watson! Stop!"

I froze and realized only then the reason for Holmes' outcry, for not ten feet beyond me sat the edge of a sea cliff, the precipitous drop one of in excess of sixty feet onto rocks below: the most certain of deaths.

Reeling for an instant at the comprehension of how nearly I had come to losing my life, I turned away and found Holmes approaching me, a look of concern on his face which was replaced an instant later, after seeing I was unharmed, by one of deepest frustration.

"Eluded me!" he cried with a snarl. "The man has escaped my pursuit, Watson! The devil himself could not have been half so clever as this one, plunging like a rabbit into those trees!"

"It was my fault," I began, cognizant of my misstep in the woods.

Holmes waved this away. "It was unavoidable and in keeping with the nature of the surroundings. It could as easily have been my own misfortune to have been standing where you were in the woods."

He gazed at the cliff so near to us and added: "Though he has escaped us for now, I am glad we count no actual losses among this evening's score."

As we began our walk back toward the house a furlong distant from where the chase ended, I demanded, "But, Holmes, how did he manage it? You were nearly onto him at the tree line."

"He knew these parts better than I," Holmes admitted. "And luck was with him tonight."

"Where is he now?"

Holmes pointed behind us in a sweeping gesture. "Out on the sea."

"The sea?" I had pictured him someplace in hiding,

perhaps in an old mineshaft left over from the tin trade, for the Wheal Mary works were nearby, or behind one of the innumerable stands of rocks that jutted up from the ancient Cornish soil, each ample to conceal a man.

"The sea is the key here, Watson," Holmes informed me, "it is his means of ingress and egress onto the property occupied by Mrs. Langtry, and his appearances are made all the easier by the proximity of *Klihen Tegow* to the shoreline. He must have had a small boat concealed in an inlet somewhere nearby, and rowed it to a larger craft out on the waters. He can now sail off to hide for another attempt some other time."

"Surely having realized his behavior is known, he will not try again in the same way?" I pressed.

"That depends on the level of his desperation, and why he seeks his prey."

To hear a lady referred to as "prey" was a disturbing matter, though I did not doubt it was no accident Holmes chose that word.

We reached the house, which was now lighted from within by what looked like every lamp in the place, and upon seeing us, Dominique unbolted the door and stood back in her state of nervousness to admit us inside.

"Mr. Holmes!' Mrs. Langtry cried out. "You saw him, as I did! You know now I was right!"

"I saw," Holmes began, "a figure on the lawn, looking up at you, just as you have told with great accuracy in your description, an intruder trespassing where he had no right to be, his presence illegal, unwelcome, even immoral, but his face was never seen by me. Is it the case that you saw him more closely tonight?"

"Yes," she exclaimed. "Oh, yes, yes, and it was he, I am more certain than ever, it was Edward, my former husband, who should be dead. My husband whom I saw buried before my own eyes!"

Across the room I saw the maid, Dominique, cross herself in the Roman Catholic manner, a gesture my Calvinistic mother always told me was no more helpful a superstition than the gypsy ward against the evil eye, yet that night I understood the comfort it doubtless gave the woman, and envied her more than a little for its solace.

Holmes drew a deep breath and said, "By your leave Watson and I shall stay on the premises tonight, Mrs. Langtry, and linger until dawn. As my client, I owe you every measure which I may take to ensure your safety. I doubt the intruder will return, but if he should be so foolish, it will be to his pity, for we will be here waiting for him. Rest now, and in the morning I shall tell you of our next course of action."

Dominique advanced and took her mistress by the arm, gently leading her toward the foyer, but the celebrated lady turned at the last and asked, "Is there truly anything you can do, Mr. Holmes?"

"There is, my dear lady," he answered, "much I can do. You will be completely safe, and I *shall* penetrate this mystery, you may be sure."

I'd seen it before, the effect his sheer confidence had on clients, and tonight was no exception, for at his words, Mrs. Langtry seemed to revive something in her spirits, and even her posture became straighter. She nodded and managed a smile before saying, "Then I shall continue to place my every trust in you, Mr. Holmes, and take my rest, as you recommend."

She bade us each farewell, and my friend and I found resting-places in the parlour, myself at the ready, though napping slightly through the night, Holmes seated straight as a ramrod, smoking, staring out into the darkness, almost seeming in some mystical fashion to sleep while awake, fortified by his retreat into the kingdom that was his vast and wondrous mind.

*****

At first light Dominique, a most remarkable and dedicated servant, came downstairs and heated water for her mistress, who likewise appeared at breakfast-time to take tea and converse with Holmes on the next course of action.

"Should I flee from this place, or even depart the nation altogether?" Mrs. Langtry demanded. "I can go to America, you see, I have many friends there, or even on to the continent."

"I cannot determine your desires there, Madam," Holmes said politely enough, "but as for my advice, it is to stay here. This place is a known element, and I feel you can be kept safe."

"Are you certain?" she asked, an almost pathetic tone of helpless fear in her voice.

"One can never be certain," Holmes admitted, "merely discern what seems the wisest course of action, and conduct oneself accordingly."

"But," she demanded, "how does one escape a dead man returned for.... For some purpose unknown?"

"Dear lady," Holmes said adamantly, leaning out toward her, "dead men do not return to this world! Nor do they flee into the night, nor leave behind tracks in the ground. Your intruder was as much a living entity as anyone in this room."

"But his face!" Mrs. Langtry persisted. "Why do you doubt me so?

Here Holmes did look thoughtful. "I have not thought it a proper thing to enter the bedroom of a lady, and look down through the window for myself, so I ask you, are you certain you could see the man's features so well in the dark?"

"One does not mistake one's spouse," Mrs. Langtry replied somewhat sternly. "It was him, and I know it."

I thought at that moment of the Langtry's union, and of what I had gleaned from the newspapers, which all told of its unhappy state, Mrs. Langtry's having abandoned her husband to carry on her life both in and on the edges of society, paying him monthly bribes, if rumours held, to stay apart from her. Yes, I could see how it might enter her mind to think the unhappy spirit of a husband so treated might find death a state of unquiet misery. Guilt, I further noted, was apparent on her face with every mention of the man. Yet she was my friend's client, and it was for me to judge no one, only to lend aid as it lay within my capacities to do so.

After a steep silence, Holmes announced, "I shall be returning to London, but before I depart from Cornwall, I shall send a telegram to a most capable man and his equally remarkable wife, and ask them to come stay with you until this matter is resolved—as it soon shall be. They will leave at once upon faithful receipt of my telegram, and arrive before nightfall, and you may put your fears entirely to rest and place yourself in their keeping, for they have never failed me, and I doubt they ever shall."

I knew he described Mr. Paul Olmstead, a retired Sergeant Major in the Royal Marines, and his wife, who was called Ginny, for I had known of their involvement in Holmes' cases in the past. Olmstead was a man of fierce abilities, who had spent twenty-one years battling the enemies of the nation with a courage which had won him many decorations. As for his wife, she was a most capable woman, and with her guarding Mrs. Langtry, I felt the chances good that nearly any assault could be repelled. The two were part of what I knew to be a remarkable network of associates Holmes kept in London, and even beyond. He had among his far-reaching connections, I often felt, a person for every eventuality and circumstance which might ever arise.

"There is one thing more," Holmes added. "I should like for Mrs. Watson, our good doctor's wife, to stay with you as well. This I ask as a favour, for I am conscious of the fact that my investigation, and her husband's role in it, stands to rob that lady of a country holiday I perceive she is enjoying very nicely."

I gaped, for an instant startled, then was impressed by Holmes' generosity and insight into Norah's character.

"I should be delighted and she is most welcome," Mrs. Langtry said graciously. "Have her come whenever she is ready, and Dominique shall prepare her a room."

Another five minutes saw us taking our leave and returning back to the house where Norah awaited. Upon the news that she was to be a guest of so famed a person as Lillie Langtry, Norah covered her mouth for an instant with sheer delight, then embraced me even as she gushed her thanks to Holmes for his thoughtfulness.

"Yes," he said with understatement, "I gathered this arrangement might please you."

It was only much later, long past when the case was behind us, that he would confess to me that his thoughts that day had also been of my wife's safety.

So the morning concluded with Norah packed and en route for her stay with the actress, while Holmes and I went to the depot in the village, where he sent off the promised telegram to the Olmsteads, requesting their services.

As the train started off with a jolt and our trip back to London began, I asked, "So what is the next step in the case, Holmes?"

He did not answer right away, but after a moment spent looking out at the countryside that blurred past us at forty-five miles per hour, he said, "I should have thought that obvious enough, Watson."

"Perhaps to one such as you," I answered, "but I am puzzled as to why we even return to London at all, when the case is so clearly here in Cornwall."

"Watson," he said, "consider for a moment the facts. We know a man is seen on the lawn of a property in the dead of night. We have a client who vows this man is one whom he simply cannot be."

"Her late husband…"

"What does this suggest?"

I thought and said, "That either he is a ghost as she says…."

Holmes scoffed.

"Or—"

"Or an imposter," Holmes finished, "playing the part for

reasons yet unknown."

"Yes," I agreed, "I think those are precisely the facts."

"And then is not the next logical step, Watson, to eliminate at least one of those possibilities from consideration?"

For a moment nothing arrived in my mind, then I felt an unpleasant tingling in my stomach, afraid I knew too well the answer, only to have it confirmed when Holmes said it aloud.

"I mean to have the remains of Mr. Edward Langtry exhumed."

*****

The train encountered few impediments, and we were back at Baker Street by late-afternoon. I went inside and took my rest after a long journey, while Holmes wrote several telegrams, which he sent off in the hands of a boy he'd seen lingering outside the door, one of his "Irregulars" by the unlikely name of Timmy Proud.

After a while, Holmes announced he was heading across to Fleet Street to meet one Martin Tolhobby, Esq. a solicitor, and inquired whether I should like to take the trip with him.

We arrived half an hour later at the third floor chambers of the solicitor's firm, and were soon shown into the office belonging to Mr. Tolhobby, who greeted us warmly and with a certain blank puzzlement, despite having been made aware of our impending visit.

"I know of you very well through the Doctor's stories of your work," Tolhobby rather openly gushed. "But to meet you in the flesh, Mr. Holmes, is, well, a most unexpected honour."

Given the late hour, going on five, I guessed the lawyer had been about to take his leave for the day, so I expressed special appreciation for his waiting on us, though I still was unaware of why Holmes had arranged the meeting at all. I was soon, however, fully enlightened.

"Mr. Tolhobby," Holmes began in his most solicitous and

cordial tone, one I associated at once with his being about to request a favour the one asked may or may not have had any reason to grant, "I am informed you have represented a client, Mr. Edward Langtry, husband of the celebrated Lillie Langtry of society and stage."

Weighing confidentiality for an instant and clearly deciding the connection was public enough to safely merit confirmation, the awed Tolhobby answered, "Yes, I can confirm that is so. Mr. Langtry had for some years entrusted the sanctity of his legal affairs to this firm, and more specifically to my own care. That connection ceased, of course, at his unfortunate passing last autumn in a northern county. He had for some time been….ermm, *unwell* of mind and body, one gathers."

"Quite so," Holmes agreed. "A grave misfortune."

"I intuit, of course," Tolhobby went on, "your visit today concerns some matter relating to the late Mr. Langtry, and will not burden you by reminding you unduly of the confidentiality which binds any solicitor to his client's interests, even a late client, so pray, how is it I might be of service?"

Holmes reached into the pocket of his Ulster and removed the paper given to him in Cornwall by Mrs. Langtry, the infamous note left on her doorstep in the night, which she maintained was composed by her husband's hand.

"What I ask is a very simple thing," Holmes said. "This note was provided to me by Mr. Edward Langtry's widow, Lillie Langtry, whom I represent as my own client, and I wish to compare what is written on this paper, to some sample of Mr. Edward Langtry's handwriting. The document could be anything at all, so long as it allows an example of the gentleman's penmanship, and need not be anything of too sensitive a nature."

Tolhobby considered a moment and decided, "Yes, I believe I could accommodate you in that respect without intruding on my late client's interests. A moment, if you please."

The solicitor rose and exited the room, only to enter a moment later and explain, "I have sent my clerk, Devaney to the firm's archives, for a folder. He is a most efficient fellow, and should require but a moment."

In the intervening time, the lawyer offered us cigars and as we smoked, he regaled me with notes of his favourites among Holmes' cases about which I'd written.

"'The Faceless Dutchman,'" he marveled, "I truly thought I knew how that would come out, yet," he shrugged and his eyes twinkled, "I was surprised."

"Then my skills as an author were not wasted," I said, modesty hiding how his sentiments pleased and flattered me.

About this time the clerk, Devaney returned bearing a thick brown file folder, which he set onto Tolhobby's desk, and with a demi-bow, left the room, proper as any country-house butler.

"Now then," Tolhobby mumbled, "let me find something. Is one sample sufficient, or should you be better served with two or three?"

"If it is copious, one should be enough, thank you," Holmes answered.

Tolhobby gazed at several, reading while his lips moved in time with his eyes, then finally slid a long sheet of foolscap across the desk toward Holmes, who took it into his hands, and leaned close to it, his eyes all but boring into the words inked there. His gaze flashed back and forth from the small note to the lawyer's document, which apparently contained a long passage of several paragraphs on the insuring of a yacht, which Langtry had been required to copy out in his own decidedly thick and sloppy hand.

Holmes' expression darkened but he said nothing until after some moments he carefully returned the paper onto the desk and leaned back in his seat, stating, "Well, I was wrong! I was certain the sample from Cornwall would prove a forgery, albeit a forgery skillful enough to fool the eyes of his widow, though I can now state with certainty that the note left in the dark is no reproduction of Langtry's penmanship, but was, rather, written by the man himself."

"Remarkable!" I exclaimed, awestruck.

Holmes snorted in irritation and declared: "And so the mystery grows murkier!"

"Do you mean," I said, incredulously, "the note in Cornwall was actually *left* by Edward Langtry?"

Holmes clarified: "I have said that Edward Langtry composed the note that was found at *Klihen Tegow*, Watson, and can with certainty say no more."

"Then he is alive? He was there?" I pressed, while the lawyer gazed confusedly from Holmes to me.

"I said only that the note was written by Langtry, and offered no additional speculation," Holmes said dismissively, and volunteered nothing more.

Turning back to the solicitor he said to Tolhobby, "With your permission, sir, may I conduct one further test? I assure you it will in no way damage the document."

"By all means," the lawyer allowed, clearly quite entertained by all that was so unexpectedly transpiring in the confines of his rather undistinguished office.

With that Holmes removed from his Ulster the vial of charcoal I knew he created by burning palm ash, and sprinkled it upon both the lawyer's document and the note from Cornwall, til it was freely dusted about both surfaces. He used a brush to spread it finer still, then tilted the excess back into the vial, and with a puff of breath sent the remainder a-drift in a tiny dark cloud. With a loupe withdrawn from his pocket, Holmes looked down at each of the two papers, and when he raised his head, there was a look of sheer, puzzled fascination betrayed in his piercing eyes.

"A match," he said simply and with amazement. The prints on both papers...are an indisputable match."

"We are seeking a ghost?" I asked, unable to refrain the question, despite myself.

"No, Watson, somehow Edward Langtry lives."

"Impossible...surely," Tolhobby spoke up, intruding into Holmes' and my moment of private amazement. "The gentleman's death was certified by the Crown coroner up in Chester. I have here..." he withdrew a document from the folder, "the certificate of death. The firm sent flowers to his funeral, as we do for all clients. Mr. Edward Langtry is...as certainly as one can say, *deceased*."

"It is true, even the most lackluster doctor is capable of recognizing when death has occurred, Holmes," I said in open defense of my profession. "A dead man is not easily mistaken for anything else."

Here Holmes' gaze turned inward, likely parsing through the facts in a rush and seeking to match them to possibilities. After this he straightened and rose to his feet, taking on his usual cool efficiency, and with a bow he thanked Tolhobby for his aid and courtesies, and departed the room, leaving me to do the same, while the lawyer stood behind his desk looking disappointed.

He called after us, "I do so wonder how it will turn out! You will be so good as to write of this matter one day, I hope, Doctor Watson? And will spell my name right...?"

Stepping out onto Fleet Street in the first bounds of approaching twilight, Holmes walked swiftly toward a cab, and hopped up into it.

"I am still reeling," I admitted to my friend. "You confess yourself expecting to find the note forged, and an imposter behind the action, yet learned it was Edward Langtry who was its author. So what are our thoughts now?"

"As is ever the case, Watson, my thoughts seek to fit the facts."

"But what facts could align with so peculiar a development? A man has, what...skillfully faked his death? And what is his motive? Revenge upon his wife, perhaps, or some gain? And how, then, did he do so? This is no body lost at sea and conveniently never recovered, the death was attested to by a Crown coroner, sworn to duty, and he was witnessed in his casket by a multitude of mourners, who saw him placed within the ground, and properly buried."

"It is a fluid investigation, Watson, one subject to change as counter-facts arrive, and I state little as certain, but at the moment, like you, I have shifted my suspicion to the strange but apparent fact that somehow Mr. Edward Langtry is indeed both alive, and as the speed with which that gentleman fled us last night demonstrates, quite well."

"But again, Holmes, how? How could a coroner and an attending physician be fooled? Not to mention an undertaker!"

Holmes leaned back and thought. "I shall need more clues before I know that, clues the morrow promises to deliver, for I have already sent a telegram off to Inspector Hollister, of the Chester Police, who owes me, shall we say, a rather profound favour. Indeed back in '90 his very career once hung unjustly upon a thread, and I pulled him back from the fire. I dare say being the fine fellow he is, he shall welcome the chance to assist us by getting an exhumation order through a magistrate who may in turn have a sympathetic sentiment toward the Inspector."

"So tomorrow we travel up to Chester?" I asked.

"Before first light, in fact, so my advice is, sleep early and sleep deeply, Watson. Tomorrow the game may be afoot...."

I did go to bed early, being tired after so little sleep the night before, and a long day coming after, but it seemed I had no sooner shut my eyes than Holmes was rapping at the door to my old bedroom at Baker Street, occupied for the night, telling me the appointed hour had come.

"Up, Watson, up! We have answers to obtain, and a casket to uncover. The day promises to be a propitious one for the cause of truth!"

Stumbling out of bed for a wash in water so cold it goose-fleshed me, and then dressing in the dark was a rude start to any day, though my thoughts rapidly turned to what lay ahead, and I was soon in excited spirits, sleep little missed.

We were out the door and in a cab Holmes had somehow arranged to be waiting at five AM, and a third of an hour later were mounting the platform at St. Pancras Station. Settled into our first-class compartment, which Holmes had likewise arranged for us to have to ourselves, I settled in with a copy of the morning *Times*, while Holmes sat with fingers steepled, his mind elsewhere, a hundred possibilities and outcomes probably under consideration in his head.

About an hour into our journey, he broke the silence at last when he asked me, "Watson, did you happen to notice out on the lawn that while he deliberately stood in plain view, Mrs. Langtry's sinister intruder made no effort to enter the house?"

What I remembered then but did not say aloud were my grandmother's tales of ghosts out on the Highlands, who were unable to enter the dwelling places of the living without an invitation.

"Now you mention it, that was a peculiar detail," I admitted. "It might have seemed a more sensible strategy for our fellow to have waited for the ladies to retire and then to have sneaked quietly into the house."

"Yet he did not," Holmes said.

"Have you a theory for why this is?"

"Several might cover the facts, Watson, though one seems to rise above others, this being that Mrs. Langtry herself was not the *object*, but rather the *means*. The intruder did not seek her directly, but rather something it might have been in her power to provide him. Some knowledge, or some object, which he had reason to feel she might have been able to access."

"Edward Langtry seeking one of his own possessions held by his putative widow?" I hazarded.

Holmes tossed up his hands and a sneer tugged at his lip. "Nothing along those lines can yet be known, a fact which I confess supremely annoys me, Watson. But, come, back to your *Times*. We shall be in Chester within an hour."

And so we were, and found ourselves greeted at

Northgate Station by a slightly portly, though agile, man of six feet, who introduced himself as Inspector Clement Hollister. Holmes shook his hand, as did I, resisting the urge to wince at the vice-like quality of his grip, and with booming voice and broad stride the inspector led us courteously enough to a coach belonging to the local police department, driven by a decidedly young-looking constable sporting a rather sad attempt at a mustache.

"Look sharp, Foster!" he thundered at the lad. "These are my guests, up from London, Mr. Sherlock Holmes, and Doctor John Watson! I'll have no reports going back to the capital that any of my officers are less than first-rate!"

"Yes, sir!" young Constable Foster answered smartly, straightening his back in the driver's seat and taking on an almost military bearing, clearly terrified of the Inspector. "Good day, gentlemen!" he cried toward Holmes and me.

"And you, sir," I replied to him.

"Inspector," Holmes plunged in, once the horses had started up, "I came today on blind faith in your ability to obtain the thing I asked, so tell me my trip was not wasted. Have you obtained the necessary order of exhumation for Mr. Edward Langtry?"

"It was not easy on such short notice, or indeed an easy thing at all without the cooperation of the deceased fellow's family," Hollister confessed, "but I knew of a cooperative magistrate, and frankly, mention of your name greased the lock a bit, so, yes, here it is."

He took a court order from his great coat and handed it to Holmes, who regarded it an instant, looked pleased by what he saw, then handed it back with a cry of, "Well done, Inspector!"

"The gentleman lies in Overleigh Cemetery, across town," Hollister informed us. "The headstone itself was only put in last month, by his own family in Belfast rather than his wife, I gather. A story there, no doubt, though we up here in Chester keep ourselves clean of the London scandals, you see. I don't know, nor wish to know, what I don't need to know."

"An excellent philosophy," Holmes complimented.

"Foster!" the Inspector growled at the driver, "Must you manage to hit every loose stone in the blasted road, boy?"

"Most sorry, sir!" the lad squeaked back, the backs of his jutting ears blushing.

We arrived on the grounds of the cemetery, a place I would describe as neither opulent nor poorly tended, and saw from a distance that a crew of three were standing at ready beside a plot that sat just at the foot of a small hillside.

"The diggers work for the cemetery," Hollister informed us, "and know their trade. The grandfather of the tall one in the middle there, Jennings, was a resurrection man hanged by one of my predecessors for his trade, so this line of work might be said to run through his blood."

He chuckled at his own joke before shouting back at Constable Foster in the coach, "Sit up there and wait!" Then called to the men gathered around the grave marked as Langtry's, "All right then, lads let's get to it then."

The man he'd dubbed Jennings tugged his forelock and in a northern accent said to his fellows, "Let's bring 'im up then."

The ground was beset by the sound of picks ripping at the carefully-laid sod, followed by spades pulling out shovels worth of soil that had lain for too brief a time to turn very solid again after the burial which had taken place—or not, I mused—the previous October. The cemetery was shown to be an honest place, because at four feet there was still no sign of the coffin, when I knew a commonplace practice among burial grounds of lighter scruples was to deny the deceased his six feet under, and set the casket down at a mere yard, to save time and expense.

Or...a thought came to me, perhaps there was simply no casket at all.

In the midst of the journey I had almost lost track of the fact that there was evidence that the grave before us now was going to prove an empty one, with no body buried here. I thought of the matching handwriting, when even Holmes had expected a forgery, and I thought of the certainty of the man's widow that she had not once, but twice, out on the lawn recognized the man she'd called husband for nearly a quarter-century. I pondered this and looked on as thrust after thrust of the spades tossed up the earth, and a disquieting certainty took hold of me. They were surely deep down enough now, and there was nothing to be found!

But then a sound rose into the air, as a shovel struck a solid object at a depth of some six feet.

"Aye," said Jennings with a happy voice, "coming to him at last!"

To him this was but a job, and after the labour he and his crew were no doubt ready for a few pints at the corner pub, so his tone was almost merry.

Another few moments of more careful excavation and the entire top of the casket stood revealed. It was somewhat streaked with mud but in a fine state after less than a year below the earth. Its top was rounded rather than flat, and the wood, well-varnished, gleamed darkly in the sunlight, oak, I took it. As a physician I had encountered death many times, on the battlefield and in the sick room. I had seen and participated in dissections, surgeries, autopsies, and yet I admit a certain dark dread coursed through me, and I did not relish the lifting of the coffin lid. I reached for my pocket handkerchief, doubled it lengthwise and put it to my nose, as I saw around me both Holmes and Inspector Hollister do the same.

As for the diggers, they chuckled at our actions, and grinning, Jennings called up, "Now, Inspector?"

With a swallow and a steeling of his soul, the policeman nodded and answered, "Do it."

It will be empty, I thought, for the handwriting proved the man walked alive, even now. It will be empty, of course, I told myself. It will be empty, because....

The handkerchief was insufficient at the odour which

arose with the might of a tidal wave, causing me to take a step back and resist the strong gag reaction that seized hold of me, the Inspector doing the same, though Holmes stood fast, and without expression gazed downward into the grave.

Below us lay revealed a body well into a state of decomposition, the hands skeletal, yet the face, with its hollow eyes and lips peeled back into a dead man's grin, was sufficiently intact for me to recognize the fellow I had seen in several photographs back in Cornwall. In the grave which duly bore his name, undeniably lay the mortal remains of Mr. Edward Langtry.

*****

Darkness lay around us outside the evening train back to London, and darkness described the state inside our first-class compartment as well, my own dismay meeting Holmes' bitter frustration at this shocking backset to a working theory which had seemed so correct in every particular. Had Edward Langtry been alive, however he achieved the feat, that fact would have explained all. Where did the results of the grim exhumation leave us now? An eerie possibility, once dismissed, had returned, unwelcome to my mind. The dead did not rise to act against the living, I accepted this both as a doctor and simply as a man of a modern age, yet there seemed something so disquieting about this sudden reversal of facts that there in the twilight I felt such thoughts creep in at the edges of my mind wanting to be entertained, dismiss them though I might.

Holmes had been left in a state of annoyance and manic self-recrimination, a column of energy with nowhere as yet to go. "I had been so sure, Watson," he admitted ruefully. "The evidence suggested most plainly that the man lived...."

Holmes had even said this to me as we stepped onto the train, but said little for some time thereafter as he sat brooding as well as thinking, doubtless parsing through the facts, trying to perceive where they'd led him to his misstep in calculation. I almost spoke up at one point reminding him the error was not strictly his, but rather the result of his drawing what seemed the most logical conclusion based on what could be known, but I intuited he sought silence and whatever reach toward redemptive validation which could come out of it.

It was as we passed into Buckinghamshire and were still the best part of an hour from St. Pancras Station that Holmes finally broke his flinty silence.

"Our trip was not a waste, Watson," he vowed, sounding clearer and more directed than at the journey's start, "but a vital step in this case, for through it we have eliminated one very strong possibility, leaving the picture clearer, if not yet fully in focus."

"Have you formed a new theory?" I asked, concealing my eagerness under a show of polite concern, for I knew he took it hard in each rare instance when reality refuted his convictions concerning the facts of a case.

He released a long exhalation and said, "Theories have the capacity to be both the most hazardous and most necessary segment of my profession, Watson, but, yes, even having backed the wrong one today, I have another, which I will test once we are back in London. Alas the late hour shall prevent my doing so tonight, but first thing in the morning, I shall visit the destination I have in mind."

"And it is in the city?"

"It is."

"And shall I be going to this place with you?"

"Watson, I should like few things better."

Reassured, I slept well that night once we finally arrived back in London, and upon my taking to it for the second time in as many nights, found my old bed upstairs at Baker Street singularly comforting. It was like a nostalgic travel back through time to when I'd been a younger man, unaware of all that I now knew would lie ahead of me: my wives, my flourishing medical career, and all the many cases it had been my privilege to take part in by the side of Mr. Sherlock Holmes.

*****

I was a very tired man, I fear, for I slept straight through and was only awakened by Holmes' insistent rapping at my bedroom door.

"Come, man, it's nearly eight o' clock!" he chided, amused at my groggy state.

'Eight?" I burst out, shame at my indolence mixing with realization of how drained I truly must have been.

"I let you lie in slumber as long as I could, but really now, Watson, one must rise and greet the morning ere it gives way."

On the table lay the remains of Holmes' breakfast, sent up by Mrs. Hudson, and after taking only those few minutes needed in preparing myself for the day, I bolted down some porridge and bacon, and consumed a cup of tea before taking heed of Holmes standing impatiently by the door, and joining him in tromping down the stairs, finding as I often had over the years something almost child-like in the sheer joyous enthusiasm he showed when hot upon the trail of some mystery.

"A splendid breakfast, my dear Mrs. Hudson!" he called as he passed his landlady on the lowest landing. "As I've no doubt Dr. Watson will join me in proclaiming."

I tipped my hat to her as I went by and said, "Most delicious as always, Mrs. Hudson, and thank you!"

She inclined her head to us with an indulgent smile, long used to the peculiarities of Holmes' many entrances and exits from the premises at all hours, often in states of disguise, or as today boisterous and almost frolicking enthusiasm.

Outside, making our way down Baker Street toward the intersection of Dorset, I demanded, "You certainly seem in better spirits this morning than last night, so may I know where it is we are heading?"

"Have I not mentioned it?" he said, knowing full well he had not.

"Holmes..." I said with light annoyance.

"Clerkenwell, Watson, to the rooms where the late Mr. Langtry passed so much of the last years of his rather brief and unhappy life."

"But he's been dead since October," I countered. "Surely someone else has since taken them over."

"We shall see, though whilst you slept I made inquiries, and learned from one of my invaluable Irregulars, Little Arthur Schillington, that the rooms have not been leased, which, given the part of town, is indeed a peculiarity, and one that further stirs my interests."

"That does seem significant," I agreed.

"And even should they have been, I might yet have learned something from the visit, as I intend to now."

A hansom driven by a shaven-headed Irish lad of about sixteen brought us across town to the street in Clerkenwell where Langtry had resided. The building was chequered brick and respectable enough, though far from the prepossessing domicile one might have expected the spouse of so wealthy a lady as Lilly Langtry to have occupied.

Holmes stepped up to sound the knocker on the door, and we were shortly admitted inside by a maid whose face bore the unfortunate scars of skin lesions which must have tormented her when younger. She showed us down the hall to a first-floor sitting room—all the rented chambers apparently being on the upper floors— where we were ushered into the presence of a woman just short of elderly years, who possessed one of the sternest and most unfriendly faces one might imagine, and from her dismissive reply to the maid's introduction of Holmes and myself, I guessed her to be a Cockney by birth who'd climbed up a bit in the world, and had doubtless contended each step of the way for the gains she'd made, this building certainly being the greatest part of them all.

"Well," the woman said setting down her tea and rubbing a hand down the side of a gray Persian feline which reclined on the overstuffed sofa beside her, as fat as the woman herself was bone thin, "my time ain't never my own, is it? What do you gentlemen want here? To come quick to the point I've no rooms for let, if that's what the matter is."

No rooms? I thought, remembering Holmes had said Langtry's former dwelling place had yet to find a new occupant. Was someone paying for it to sit empty?

"I thank you, Madam," Holmes began, affecting humility and gratitude, "for what I'm certain must be a costly intrusion on your scant time, but I am making inquiries into a one-time tenant here in the building, Mr. Edward Langtry, and thought it possible you might be of assistance to me in this matter."

"I don't make a custom of assisting nobody, no more than I asks for nobody's assistance. As for the rest, do I seem a tattle-tale to you, sir?" This said, she lifted her teacup and took a gurgling sip.

"You do not," Holmes agreed, chastened and docile, allowing her complete control over the situation.

"That's because I ain't," said the landlady. "I keeps to my own business, and so long as I'm paid proper each quarter by them as lives upstairs, I see fit to keep out of affairs that ain't my own."

"Doubtless wise, and it is much to your credit that you do so," Holmes replied, his tone patient, his face beaming a strange species of meek friendliness I knew to be unnatural to his formable nature.

"Now don't you be trying any fancy sentiments on me," the lady said, "I tell you I ain't a gossip."

"Ah, yes," Holmes said, looking to me, "then it is as I remarked as we came up the outside stairs. 'Watson,' I said then, 'this lady shall know nothing at all.' And I find I was right as to your being uninformed. Madam, I still thank you for your time and bid you good day. We shall interrupt you no further."

I saw something shift in the woman's demeanor and her eyes took on a frown before she insisted, "I never said I didn't know nothing, I said I didn't make a habit of telling what I know."

"Oh, it's of no moment, I assure you," said Holmes, as he began to back away, hat in his hand. "I knew coming in that what I sought to know was likely beyond the range of your knowledge."

"Oh, is that what you think?" she told him, haughtily. "Fact is I know a great deal, for don't nothing go on in this place as escapes my eye, I tell you what."

"Truly, you keep as tight a ship as that?" Holmes asked, impressed.

"The tightest in all London!"

"But surely you couldn't be expected to keep aware of everyone your tenants might entertain here. That is simply too much to expect of any landlady, however diligent."

"Don't you be thinking that!" the woman scoffed. "If so much as a city mouse invites a country mouse into his parlour here, I know of it. If the scullery swipes a crust of bread and sticks it in her pocket, you can be sure I'll find out, for my eyes go everywhere." She said this with such confident fierceness that her features reminded me of a bull mastiff in the fighting ring.

"But Mr. Langtry, I gather," Holmes went on, feigning a reticence to accept her claims, "was a private sort, who kept a degree of secrecy in his dealings."

"Him?" the woman laughed disdainfully, her bony figure jostling where she sat, making the Persian cat stare disapprovingly at her. "That man was nothing but a lush, and his bills were paid for not by any honest work, no, but by a lawyer fellow, what represented his wife, the actress what run off on him." Leaning forward she added in a whisper, "The one as was the Prince of Wales' harlot." She gave a knowing nod.

"I see..." Holmes said, as if this information were troubling, and came to him as completely unexpected.

"That man, Langtry, would lay up there for days on end with no company but his gin bottles, being sick half the time.

Fell down the stairs more than once, he did. I had to get the maid to clean his blood off the landing once, from where he hit his head. Wouldn't see a doctor afterward either, the fool, not that I cared much either way. If it weren't for that lawyer coming by each month to bring him money, wouldn't nobody have seen him at all save that brother of his."

From my place by his side I all but felt the spark that blazed to life in Holmes at the revelation present in the landlady's last words, though outwardly he showed no change when he asked, "His brother came often then?"

"Funny thing that," the landlady told him, "never seen the fellow for all the years Langtry was here, and then those last weeks, out of nowhere, like, he comes, showing up regular as rain just before Langtry took ill and left for up north, planning on coming back, he said, but, well, he died, didn't he, up in Liverpool or someplace like that."

She sat up straighter, clearly deciding to go all-in, since Holmes was showing himself duly impressed by her diligent grasp of her tenants and their lives. "Tell you what else," she said, warming to her narrative, "and this is strange and all."

"Yes?" Holmes inquired, demonstrating a degree of interest that balanced between polite concern and nonchalance, though I knew he was hanging on her every word.

"Oddest thing, that brother, the one who only showed up a couple months before the end, he's paying for Langtry's rooms now. Ain't living in them, no how, just keeps up the payments each quarter. And the room, it just sits there empty as a cracked egg."

Oh, I thought, things had definitely deepened indeed!

"A strange situation," Holmes concurred, nodding. "And how often did this brother visit Mr. Edward Langtry?"

"Regular some weeks, irregular others. But I knew it was his brother because, well, I heard them speaking sometimes."

More likely you stood in the hallway and shamelessly listened in, I thought.

"And Langtry addressed him as 'brother'?" Holmes asked her.

"Not so I ever heard, mind you, though the thing is, they looked so exactly alike, I figure they was twins!"

And there it was, I thought, the solution

"If not 'brother,'" Holmes asked the woman, "then what did Mr. Langtry call the man?"

"Why he called him by his name, of course, didn't he? 'Franklin', he said. Mr. Franklin Langtry."

With much due thanks to the landlady for her information, coaxed though it was at first before so much came spilling out, Holmes led me outside, his step light, his eyes shining.

"So we have him!" Holmes cried, almost radiant in his glee. "Watson, we return to Cornwall at once, our journey to begin this same hour."

He stepped into the street and rather vigourously waved down a cabbie, before leaping in and demanding, "Paddington Station, at your quickest!"

"It is so clear now, Watson," he told me in the cab. "A brother... The records into which I inquired show Langtry had three sisters, but no male sibling. A secret brother, yes, it fits so well! A relation unknown to Edward Langtry til the last weeks of his life, a man born outside his father's marriage, raised doubtless in ignorance of his true heritage, who somehow discovered it sometime last year, and sought out the brother he never knew he had, finding him there, in that building we just visited, discovering the sibling he'd doubtless held out such hopes of coming to know was a sad wreck of a person, a drunk, defeated by circumstance, abandoned by his own wife."

"Mrs. Langtry doubtless had reasons, Holmes," I began in defense of the lady, only for Holmes to wave this away.

"I do not judge her, Watson, nor particularly care what passed in the private sphere of their marriage, I tell you only what this natural child of Langtry's father must have thought when he finally made his way to London to find his long-lost brother. How crushing the reality must have been, and all the tales of woe and wrongdoing toward him with which Edward Langtry must surely have filled his newfound brother's ears."

A realization hit me, striking a bolt of fear through my heart. "And how angry he must have felt at Langtry's wife for her part in his brother's reduced state."

"Indeed, I fear so. From the station I shall send my man Olmstead, there at *Klihen Tegow,* a telegram, for we now know the name and nature of the danger I from the beginning sensed Mrs. Langtry faced."

"Pray he keeps all in the house safe!" I cried, thinking of my wife there as well.

"This explains it all, you see, Watson," Holmes told me, "including the fact the note left for Mrs. Langtry in the night was not a forgery, but composed in Langtry's own hand for other reasons at some point in the past. It must be one among many bitter letters he wrote to his wife over the years, but given their arrangement, never sent, for the continuation of his monthly income depended, I have learned, on Langtry never contacting the lady. This Franklin Langtry, the brother —though I doubt Langtry is the name he was allowed to grow up under—must have formed his plan in anger while watching his brother waste away under the effects of drink, and seeing this note and others Langtry composed, realized their potential use at some future date. Blackmail, a threat..."

"But why pose as his own brother's ghost?" I demanded. "That part is the strangest of all."

Holmes threw back his head and laughed. "Oh, Watson, that is the one farcical component of this troublesome case. He never meant to be seen as a ghost, it was only the fanciful mind of an actress, such as Mrs. Langtry is that conceived such an idea given the apparent extreme similarity in their features. Doubtless also he took his brother's clothing and shoes after his death and wore them himself as a comforting reminder of the sibling he barely got to know, for Langtry, as we know from his custom-made shoes, was fond to the end of his days of maintaining a fine wardrobe, and so it was in this attire that he was seen when he appeared on the lawn to demand a secret meeting with the lady, which it was wise of her not to keep."

"Would he have harmed her?" I asked, as the station drew in sight.

"Possibly," Holmes said, "depending on the state of his mind and the depths of his anger. Perhaps he sought some other recompense at the time, money, an admission of cruelty and an atonement for it, but the clue that reveals so much and which frightens me all the more lies in the note he chose to leave for her. Out of many he might have selected, that one spoke of *deep love*."

"Yes," I realized.

"Watson," Holmes said gravely as the hansom drew to a halt, "I have seen far too often in my career how warped love can grow, how dark it may become, how deeply into the realms of less wholesome emotions its roots may sink. Resentment, rage, even hate, may tint the feeling, yet still it retains something of the sweetness of love. I fear this secret brother has, even as he has for some time trailed Mrs. Langtry, angry and bitter on behalf of his brother, fallen in love with the lady, while still demonstrating how un-dispelled his resentment on his brother's behalf remains."

"Then it is terrible!" I said.

"I will send the telegram," Holmes said, handing the fare off to the Irish driver, "you go secure our tickets by the fastest train!"

Oh, Norah, I thought, *what have I done in leaving you there?*

*****

The next hours were doubtless slow to pass, each of us wishing to be in Cornwall already instead of on a train, my thoughts with Norah as well as the client and all those in her house, yet I tell you, as I recall it, the day seems in memory like a blur of suddenness, like some chalk drawing smeared by the wind.

*****

We reached the depot in the town just as night was coming on, and the skies were boiling with thick storm clouds, threatening one of those brooding tempests for which the West Country seems so infamous. Rain began to sheet down on us as we pushed out in the gig kept at the house we ourselves had been occupying on our holiday, the place owned by the erstwhile client, Montgomery. Still even amid the sloshing mud of the county road, which became nearly a quagmire under the thoroughbred's hooves, we reached *Klihen Tegow* before ten, and below the splashing of the deluge, and even a peal of thunder from overhead, we dashed up the walkway.

The door flashed open and Dominique, Mrs. Langtry's faithful maid, said, "Oh, Mr. Holmes, Doctor, you have come too late by only moments!"

The words seared through me, fear hitting like a hammer blow, yet I saw Norah come dashing across the foyer, "Oh, John!" she called. "John! She has left. She has certainly gone to meet the man, the intruder!"

Yet for a moment I could not take in her words, swept up as I was in the sheer gladness of seeing her, and I drew her to me in a grateful embrace, the deepest of my fears dying away in that wonderful instant spent holding my wife against me.

"So he has taken her, then?" Holmes demanded, sounding alarmed but somewhat unsurprised.

"No," Dominique cried mournfully, "somehow he has persuaded her to slip away unseen, and go to him. She excused herself just moments ago and when she did not return after a few minutes, I went to find her, only to see she left this note on her bureau that said she had gone to meet him."

Holmes took the note from her hand, scanned it and found it as Dominique told, then he said hollowly: "A grave mistake."

Somehow within another minute Holmes managed to untangle facts from the confusion by hastily lining everyone up in the parlour, the Olmstead couple, my wife, and Dominique. From them came a tale of the cunning of Franklin Langtry, who, as they'd learned several hours earlier, had made a rather clever move some days previous back in London that involved the theft by deception of Mrs. Langtry's jewels, which she kept in a safe at the famed Pulverden Bank, where, posing as her husband, he had taken everything. Greatly to her distress, Mrs. Langtry had learned of this by a telegram delivered earlier in the evening, then in the final moments of Holmes' absence she had apparently been lured out alone somewhere beyond the house, going out to face the peril of her own free will.

"He must have appeared outside her window, and promised her the jewels," I said quietly.

"Indeed so," Holmes agreed. His face was troubled, yet I also saw some begrudging admiration for his foe. "A master stroke," he ruefully dubbed the man's machinations.

For Franklin Langtry to have taken so bold a gambit, though, left me wondering how deep his rage went, or how high his countering feelings of deranged love, and, if as Holmes feared he was bent on vengeance for his brother, Lillie Langtry were even still alive.

"We are dealing with a clever, bold, and likely unstable man," Holmes declared. "Not to be underestimated!"

"Then what is our next course?" I demanded.

Here Holmes erupted. "The lady chose poorly in disappearing out in such a night, drawn away by Franklin Langtry's latest and most effective summons! I suspect he would have made an appearance outside her window while holding the open jewel box, showing he had it, and luring her out with him. Where she is now...." He shook his head. "But still we must try, and with no further time lost. Olmstead, Watson!" he called, "Out with me, into the night! Let us see what can be found!"

Norah and Dominique we left in the capable hands of Mrs. Olmstead, who was, I noted, armed with several derringers upon her person, a woman regularly employed to guard the well-being of her husband's female clients. Only her own voluntary egress had taken Mrs. Langtry beyond the safety of her watch, I felt sure.

"Can there be any tracks left after this rain?" I asked lugubriously as we pushed through the door but three minutes after entering it.

"There may yet be some sign!' cried Holmes.

The rain continued to come down, not as hard as it had on our drive to *Klihen Tegow*, but still we were soaked inside of a half a minute. Holmes stooped low til he found some meager trace of Mrs. Langtry's passing, which he pointed out with the cry: "It is this way they traveled!"

From there we had several instances of luck, for the woods showed evidence of her and the man's path. On a small thorn bush Holmes even spied a fragment of cloth from Mrs. Langtry's dress, ripped and clinging. At this Holmes abandoned the search for stray clues and shouted, "To the dock below the cliffs! He means to be off with her, though we can hope that in this weather he has had to wait for the storm to pass! Luck may still be with us!"

We three dashed through the woods and across the mud-pit which was the county road, entering the tops of the sea cliffs beyond. Holmes found a trail that led us safely down one of the shallowest among the hillsides, and another moment had us on the rocky beach below, where in the distance, illuminated by bursts of fork-lightning, I spied a sight that at once gave me hope and filled me with trepidation, for there he was, the brother Edward Langtry never til his last days knew he had, Lillie Langtry's dogged and sinister pursuer, visible to our eyes at last, in the flesh, a near doppelganger of the man he was once taken to be.

He was standing with his back to us, at the base of a high

rock that jutted from the beach near the dock, and atop the stone, some thirty feet up, hanging on even in the buffeting of the tempest, was Mrs. Langtry, high above her assailant, clinging to the granite's surface, having climbed there to find even that much safety from the mad-man.

Franklin Langtry stood at the rocks' foot, snarling up at her like a rabid dog, crying out terrible words and accusations, but also, I heard against the roar of the wind, mixing in declarations of affection, protesting his true and abiding love for her, all of it the ranting of a lunatic.

"Why did you run from me, you whore?" he screamed. "Don't you know I will forgive you, even though Edward couldn't? Don't you know that because I love you I will show you the way to be redeemed for all your sins and cruelties inflicted on my poor brother? Do you truly think there is anywhere in the world you can go where I will not follow and find you? Come down and face me, you vile Jezebel, your hour of reckoning has come!"

"Langtry!" Holmes shouted, and I saw the man spin around, caught by surprise as we closed in on him.

"You!" the man roared with loathing at the sight of Holmes. "You are the very devil in my garden!"

He turned from the rock with one final castigation howled out against Mrs. Langtry, crying, "You'll never escape me in the end!"

Then, clutching the jewel case, he sprinted toward the dock, where I saw a small rowboat was lashed, the waves raising it high and dropping it low again, the ocean waters sloshing into it as it rocked like some ghastly mockery of a child's cradle.

"He can't mean to try to take to the sea now!" I thundered. "He'll be killed."

Holmes and the bodyguard, Olmstead, reached the dock, its boards old and weathered and slick underfoot, closing in on their quarry, while I went to the large jutting stone and called, "Mrs. Langtry, hold on, I will climb to you!"

I had meant to do just that, but to my astonishment the lady instead began to come back down, sliding the last part of the way on her hip til she was safely on the beach with me, her achievement of escaping from the height taking but a few seconds, though leaving her hands and arms badly scraped against the surface of the stone.

Seeing my astonishment at her action, Mrs. Langtry, though breathless and soaked by the storm, her once carefully-arranged hair in tangled disarray, explained, "I learned early on in my childhood on Jersey how to climb rocks along the beach, and often did so with my brothers. It seems it is a skill that never goes away."

Amazing woman, I thought.

We looked together to the dock, where Langtry stood holding the rope which had tied the boat in one hand, the jewel case in the other.

"Give it up, Langtry," Holmes said to him. "You are quite defeated. There is no need for the rest of it."

The stalker once thought to be a ghost looked beyond him to Mrs. Langtry and said in a tone of longing, his face rapt, "Oh, my sweet lady!" Then just as suddenly he sneered savagely and shouted, "Faithless harlot!"

"The jewel box, if you please," said Holmes. "Now!"

Looking at him, Langtry snarled instead and stepped down into the pitching rowboat, the black jewel case still clutched to his side, before he tossed it to the floor of the craft and with great speed and apparently some experience, shoved off into the sea before Holmes and Olmstead could reach him. By the time they stood at the dock's edge, he was a too far out for them to grab, and in a number of seconds was rowing out into the darkness of the storm-tossed night, soaring and plunging with the waves, his laughter manic and cruel.

"I have avenged you, Edward!" he cried, his voice half-lost in the howling wind. "I have ruined her finances and left her with barely a penny to her besmirched name! And I shall be back for her! I shall be back!"

In seconds more he was lost to our sight while the angry waves rose and fell.

Watching from the dock, we four, I felt both relief at the client's safety, and shame that wet and cold as I knew she must be, I had no blanket or even a dry overcoat to offer her, or even ointment to apply to her bleeding hands, sliced upon the rock face.

For her part, given the magnitude of her ordeal, Mrs. Langtry seemed composed and thoughtful rather than lost to hysteria. "Will he truly be back?" she asked Holmes at last.

"If the villain returns tonight, I shall have him," Holmes replied, his blood still up. "As it is there will be few places in all of England where he may hide, for by morning I'll have every police force in the country in pursuit with charges of bank robbery, abduction, and even criminal trespass!"

And with that we made our way, soaking wet and wind-buffeted across the rocky Cornish beach, to the hillside and back through the dripping trees of the wood, to the house dubbed *Klihen Tegow*, where I cleaned and bandaged Mrs. Langtry's hands, before Dominique took her upstairs for a warm bath, and a change of dry clothes.

For her part, Norah soon had hot tea at the ready, and found blankets for us to bundle ourselves in as we sat by a fire she had stoked to roaring life.

"I had been so worried for you, John," she told me from a place by my side.

"And I for you, my dear," I answered, taking her warm hand in my own, still chilled by the storm.

When Mrs. Langtry reappeared an hour later, we were all much closer to restored after the events of the night, and Holmes began to relate the full story of the mystery he had unraveled over the course of three hectic and complex days.

The events of the present evening had begun around seven, when a telegram arrived at the door, from London, telling the news, shocking and unwanted, that the Pulverden Bank wished to confirm with Mrs. Langtry that she had five days previously authorized the removal by her husband—not knowing of his passing—of her jewelry stored in the secure vaults there. Pulverden's had tried to reach her that same day at her London address, yet discovering her not at home, had found itself requiring the intervening days to locate her out at *Klihen Tegow.*

I remembered then the emphasis Mrs. Langtry had placed in stressing to Holmes that first morning that she was 'hiding away' here, escaping the city, her whereabouts known to few.

Mrs. Langtry had reacted to the telegram with shock and horror, for she had made no such authorization.

"And this," Holmes explained to us all, "was the flaw in Franklin Langtry's plot, for he expected from that first night on which he appeared on the lawn to find that you, Mrs. Langtry, would already know of your financial loss, and hoped that the knowledge would draw you outside to speak with him concerning the theft, as it ultimately did tonight. His plan was then to abduct you by whatever violent measures might prove necessary."

"Yes, I see," she agreed, with careful poise reacting little to the chilling revelation, though surely inwardly affected by it. "He did not count on me remaining in a state of ignorance as to the matter of the heist itself, nor did he expect I would take him to be a ghost."

"I was sure it was *il fantasma*— his spirit," gasped Dominique, who shook her head with what looked to be embarrassment, or perhaps simple relief.

Holmes continued. "Additionally the note left for you to find in the morning was meant to demonstrate that he was in possession of many sensitive letters and personal effects once belonging to your late husband, which he hoped you might wish kept from public eyes, rendering you still more malleable to his plot. Again, I do not believe he meant for you to think it actually *from* him."

"Such a comedy of errors," Mrs. Langtry noted, ruefully.

"Could I have been a greater fool?"

"Nonsense," I told her, "throughout all of this abysmal matter you conducted yourself bravely."

Holmes added, "You guessed none of this, Madam, for Langtry's plan was unclear from the start, and instead of your worries making you compliant, you sent for me, having learned to you doubtless delight that I was nearby. The rest has unfolded as we know."

"So he was a blackmailer?" I demanded. "That was his ploy all along?"

"It was perhaps his scheme at first," Holmes said, "but I fear in his clandestine following of the lady he...developed rather deeper feelings that lay alongside the terrible rage he at times harboured for her on his brother's behalf. Love, as I have said, is a thing easily twisted into terrible shapes and forms, even into a weapon."

"And the jewelry theft?" I asked. "How does it fit into his twisted schemes?"

"It shows us money was not his primary concern," answered Holmes.

"So it truly was *me*, that he sought above all else?" Mrs. Langtry asked, with a small shudder.

"Yes," Holmes replied solemnly.

"He took many risks," I opined. "For anger, and for love."

"The robbery was, I must admit, a brilliant idea," said Holmes, "and an audacious one, of course, for it could have brought all his hopes crashing down and landed him in gaol on the spot had the bankers known Mr. Edward Langtry was deceased. He took the jewels both as an enticement to dangle before Mrs. Langtry while he laid out his declaration of love, and as a means, I suspect, to fund the new life he hoped to have with her on the other side of the world once his kidnapping was complete, for I believe it will prove the case that Mr. Franklin Langtry was raised in America, likely on the coast."

"So my late husband's father," Mrs. Langtry began, "was so ashamed of having a son out of wedlock that he had the boy and his mother sent away across the ocean?"

"That is my suspicion," Holmes confirmed.

"I wonder how he learned the truth?" Norah asked.

"I find it likeliest this knowledge came via his mother, on her deathbed," Holmes answered, "it having been kept from him for many years owing to an allowance paid by lawyers, which permitted the boy some decent degree of upbringing, and which she was given to understand would continue only as long as she held her child's parentage a secret. She must have felt at the last that telling him of his heritage outweighed all else."

With a bitter smile and an exercise in utter candor, Mrs. Langtry admitted, "No wonder the knowledge that a similar an arrangement was in effect between Edward and I had so drastic an effect on him, he only having just learned of the original agreement that had passed unknown to him all his life in America, and now finding his brother hamstrung by another."

"Doubtless it enraged him to encounter a second instance of such bribery fobbed off on his family,' Holmes agreed, not couching his words.

There came a silence, which I broke by asking, "Can any man survive being out on the water on such a night?"

"I grew up on a Channel island," Mrs. Langtry answered, "and this is as bad a storm as I've seen in many a year. Even a master mariner would not have gone out on such a sea."

There was no mistaking the hint of hopefulness in her voice, and I thought of how the ocean making and end to her assailant would have been a tidy conclusion to things, and provided her with much relief. I could not wholly blame her.

For his part, Holmes walked to the window, where the rain was still falling, and allowed only:

"Thereof time shall tell."

As indeed it did, for two days later the body of Franklin Langtry was found by kelp-gatherers where it had washed upon the shoreline some two miles distant, severely battered upon the rocks. Neither the wreckage of his boat nor the case which contained Mrs. Langtry's jewelry were ever to be recovered, and a fortune in gems now lies forever, I suppose, on the bottom of the sea amid so many lost treasures from other ages.

We were able to finish our Cornish holiday, though something of the quality of escape had been lost by the intrusion of the case, and like Holmes, Norah and I were more than ready for our return to London when the day came.

Mrs. Langtry received a settlement from her bank over its incompetence, which amounted, Holmes informed me, to about ten-percent of the value of the lost jewelry, but which she accepted with equanimity, and pressed on, preferring to stoically put the entire matter behind her.

She was, I judged, a lady of some fortitude, whatever infamy might be said to have chequered her celebrated past.

She professed herself grateful, however, to Holmes, and even to Norah and me for the role we played in the case, and beyond promptly paying my friend's fee, some several weeks in the future, my wife greeted me at the door excited with her news that a courier had hand-delivered tickets for us to be at the Olympic Theater in a fortnight to see the grand opening of Mrs. Langtry's latest play.

"And box seats too, John!" she said with delight.

Holmes, too, reviewed tickets delivered to 221B Baker Street but, as I think surprised no one who knew him, did not attend.

For Norah and me, however, the evening was a complete delight.

ABOUT THE AUTHOR

C. Thorne

C. Thorne is a writer who lives in the United States, and a lifelong fan of Sir Arthur Conan Doyle's stories of the world's most famous fictional detective. He is the author of more than a thousand short stories, and nearly three-dozen books of prose and poetry, with even more tomes beneath his belt through the years as ghostwriter, and contributor to a number of college-level textbooks. The Continuing Chronicles of Sherlock Holmes is his most recent series, and a labor of love. He hopes you enjoy these stories as much as he and illustrator L. Thorne have enjoyed producing them.

BOOKS IN THE SERIES: THE CONTINUING CHRONICLES OF SHERLOCK HOLMES

C. Thorne now presents many exciting, never-before revealed adventures of the greatest detective of all time, Mr. Sherlock Holmes. There are many more to come.
Please peruse them all!

Go to:

The Continuing Chronicles of Sherlock Holmes

Made in United States
Orlando, FL
29 June 2025

62479004R00174